The Littlest Giant

D.J. Wray

ISBN: 979-8-9905625-0-9 (paperback)

Book Cover, Illustrations, and Interior Layout by Melissa Williams Design

Editing by Anna Walker, Eschler Editing

To Diane Smith:
for being a most energetic and supportive cheerleader. Without you, the release of my book would have to have been postponed to a later date … a much later date.

To the illustrious members of The Utah Valley Legends and The Nebo Novelists, my writing group family:
Thank you ALL for your invaluable suggestions and patience as I took you on Li'l Bits's journey.

To my incredible Beta readers:
I bless you all for having the patience and fortitude to read this book from cover-to-cover, and offer your heartfelt critique. I treasure the sacrifice of your time on my behalf.

To Anna Walker, editor at Eschler Editing:
Thank you for completing your edit in such a way that I was able to glean the why's, and wherefore's, from the changes you made. I learned a lot from your thorough critique.

Introduction

The Treaty of San Francisco, more commonly known as the Treaty of Peace with Japan, came into force on April 28, 1952. It was this treaty, not the signing of Japan's surrender announcement on September 2, 1945 (V-J Day) that formally signaled the end of the nightmare that was World War II.

1952—a year of monumental endings . . . and unexpected beginnings.

Chapter 1

Outskirts of Oil City, Louisiana
May, 1952

"Everyday courage has few witnesses. But yours is no less noble because no drum beats for you and no crowds shout your name."

—Robert Louis Stevenson (1850–1894)
Scottish novelist, poet and travel writer

The woman stole through the trees like a phantom. Used to being quiet and remaining unseen, she made her way toward her target. The house furthest away; the one by the water. She'd practiced the route before and could navigate it in the dark, so despite the bulky basket and the bone deep ache in her injured shoulder, she pressed on. Unseen.

Heaven had blessed her this night with cloud cover, so her dark gray dress blended beautifully with the shadows of forested growth. Heart pounding, she couldn't believe she was doing this; it went against all she held dear. But there was no going back now. He had quite literally pushed her too far; *he'd* pushed her to this. May God forgive her.

The woman was adjusting her bundle to even out the pressure on her injured shoulder, when two forms burst from the front door of a home just forty feet away. Her heart nearly leapt out of her throat, and she clutched the basket to her chest, seeking to blend deeper into the shadows of the nearest tree.

"Claudine, my angel." The big, black man's deep voice was pleading, "Didn't I warn ya this wasn't gonna be easy?"

He'd called her "my angel." The woman had never heard those words from her own husband's lips. Nor any other term of endearment, for that matter. Despite the tension on the dimly lit porch, she was intrigued. Fighting her own urgency, she was compelled to remain hidden and see what happened next.

"*Mon chéri.*" The dark-haired, pale beauty reached a gentle finger to trace the giant man's chin. "You did. Warn me, you did."

She sounded tired.

"Then why do ya think about leavin' me and takin' the children?"

The woman could tell the big man's heart was close to breaking. Perhaps because she'd been denied any true compassion, seeing it on display touched her. She hadn't known a man was capable of such caring. In the few words she'd heard exchanged, she gleaned more tenderness from this stranger than she'd had from her own husband in five years.

She had come to realize that courting didn't count. A man would do and say whatever he needed to in order to snare the woman he was trying to catch. And once caught, well, what was the need? In her case, the piece of paper she'd signed, the one called a marriage license, bound her to a man she'd discovered she never knew. One who could make a name for himself on the stage, if he took his acting skills to a professional level.

Perhaps those skills had served him well in the war? Maybe they had even saved his life? The woman had done her best to justify his callousness based on those assumptions, but it was getting harder and harder to do so. He wasn't the only one to have suffered . . . heaven knew what; but did that justify his ceasing to try? His ever-growing dependence on alcohol?

Prior to marriage, to fill the financial gap left by her male family members who'd served, she had worked in a department store and, believe it or not, rose to the rank of manager. Formerly, a position only available to men. She'd thrived and had transformed the housewares department into a top-selling division. No general on a battlefield could have done better. She'd felt useful, productive, and alive. Now? Well, she was still alive. There was something to be said for that.

A voice from the porch brought her back to the present. "I do not wish to go, but go I must. To remain would mean the death of us all. Only by going will you know of what worth we are. Mon guerrier, you must choose your fight."

"Claudine, please. Sweetheart, can ya give me one more chance? There's nothin' I wouldn't do for ya. You know that, right?"

"I know your heart is good." Claudine laid a hand on her husband's chest, then wearily allowed her head to rest atop the hand as she stepped into the big man's embrace.

Whatever the two said beyond that was in a lover's whisper. The woman was tempted to march right up to that porch and let these two strangers know, in no-uncertain-terms, that despite the obvious obstacle and whatever else they were dealing with, what they had together was worth fighting for. Then, the weight of her bundle shifted, and her own battle was remembered.

Leaving the couple to their choices, the woman slipped noiselessly into the shadows of the next tree, and then beyond sight of the still-occupied porch.

Further on, among the few, sparsely spaced houses, she spied her target. A low, neat, tin-roofed structure with shutters, window boxes of herbs, and a porch that jutted right out over the water. The porch and its roof had a hole in it to accommodate an ash tree growing straight up from the murky depths below.

For some reason, she liked that. That he'd made room for the tree to remain as it was instead of cutting it down. It had taken her a long time to find this man, but she was glad she'd made the effort. He would do just fine. She had to pray he would. Time had run out, and she couldn't look for anyone else. But now that the time had come, she wasn't sure she could go through with it.

If only her husband had been more tolerant, more patient, more . . . No, if only *she* had chosen more wisely. She had one little girl that might stand a chance, but this one? The woman peeled back a corner of her blanket-wrapped bundle to peer lovingly at the cherubic, sleeping face within. No, this little one would be eaten alive beneath her husband's constant gaze of criticism and judgement and, she was sure, physical abuse. No, so many noes should have been said before now. Perhaps she'd find the courage to say them in the future, but she couldn't bet her daughter's life on that.

For many reasons, none she could name politely, she had been forced into an unholy position and her heart was breaking. The woman looked at the porch of the house and then at her baby. Her sweet little tow-headed angel, asleep and trusting, would never remember her face. Would never remember the songs sung to her at bedtime. Would never know just how much her mama loved her and wished things didn't have to be this way. Why couldn't the world be a place where everyone got along? Was everything they'd just fought for only for those in Europe?

The hour was late, if she was going to get home before her husband woke from his drunken stupor, she couldn't spare too much time. But she'd made sure there was an extra bottle and her lip quirked at the thought of the powder she'd added to the first. Just a sleeping draft; nothing harmful. She wasn't sure she was capable of going that far . . . not yet, anyway.

Stealing a few last moments with her daughter, the woman moved to the shadow of a large oak near the tin-roofed home and sank to its base. Her little one's eyes lifted at the movement and came alive when they focused on her face. Oh, how she would miss that! She pulled one of the prepared bottles from the small basket she carried and then held it up to the baby's mouth, enjoying the feel of her daughter grasping her finger as she suckled the nipple. Breaking suction, the little girl smiled at her mother as milk dribbled down her chin.

"Now, sweetheart," she cooed to the child as she gently wiped the milk away, "I hope you'll have better table manners for your new papa." She prayed the man would keep her daughter. "I need you to be on your best behavior. You mind your manners, and if you show him the sweet smile you always share with me, I know you'll win his heart." Her lips touched her daughter's forehead, nose, and cheek; then she nuzzled the crook of her baby's neck, making the little girl smile and coo.

When the bottle was finished, she checked her daughter's diaper to make sure she'd remain asleep as long as possible. Holding the sweet form to her chest, she swayed and patted the little back until a series of burps bubbled up. "That's my girl," the woman praised. "Now, it's back to bed for you."

The baby's eyes slowly slid closed. It was the wee hours of early morning, she could delay no longer. Pulling the blanket back up around her daughter's head, the woman sang her favorite song, "Somewhere Over the Rainbow," one last time to ears that would not remember. Standing, she jigged her angel to sleep as silent tears dripped down her face and fell to mingle with the soil at her feet. Perhaps one day, her daughter would sit in this spot and feel something, a pull of some sort, toward a long-forgotten but lovely memory.

With a prayer of deepest love for her now-sleeping angel, the woman planted a final kiss on her daughter's head then laid her in the basket, wishing she had more than these few meager possessions to leave with her. There were two more full bottles, some diapers, a hand-crafted rattle her grandfather had made, and a letter. She had labored over every word to make it just right because it had to convince this man that her daughter was worth keeping. That she wasn't a terrible person for abandoning a baby.

Abandon—what an awful word. She fought hard to remember what she'd written to convince the man, and as she remembered, tried to convince herself.

The woman gathered up the little basket and moved silently toward the house, then laid the precious bundle gently before the door.

"God, oh God, watch over my baby. You gave her to my keepin', and I failed you."

The dam holding back her flood of tears was near to breaking. With a final, "I love you, baby girl," the woman disappeared into the shadows. Her heart, as gloomy as the night sky.

Chapter 2

Remy

"Behold the turtle. He makes progress only when he
sticks his neck out."

*—James Bryant Conant (1893–1978) American
chemist and former president of Harvard University*

Remy yawned and did his best not to open his eyes.
Some part of him knew it wasn't time to wake up
yet, and he wanted to do his level best to honor
that notion. But gall-dern-it, something was hell-bent on stealing into his consciousness. He was equally hell-bent on refusing it entry . . . but try as he may, Remy could not ignore the
something.

"Damnation and hell's bells!" Remy protested as he wrestled with the notion of getting out of his nice, warm bed. He
had stayed up later than usual last night to get a good start on
his new project, so he was a bit ornerier than his usual orneryself.

With a final, strangled gasp of frustration, Remy whipped
back the covers, flung his legs over the side of the bed and
sat there. Staring about his small bedroom, he ran lean, strong
fingers through unruly, sandy-brown curls and dragged the

hand down his face. Muttering every step of the way, Remy stalked into the kitchen to turn the gas on beneath the coffee pot. His hand started for the box of matches, but he stopped mid-reach and cocked his head.

"What the hell?" If he didn't know any better, through the living room window he'd left open to circulate the night air, Remy could swear he'd just heard what sounded like a baby. "George Dollis! You'd best not be playin' with me again, you big ole son of a bitch."

Remy marched to the front door, ready to confront his best friend, and sometimes enemy, when George took it into his head to try and knock off some of Remy's harder edges.

"Remington Alexander Dubois," George would say. "You, my friend, are a diamond in the rough, and all good gems require a certain amount of . . . *polish* to make 'em shine. Think on me as your own personal sandpaper."

Well, the dang blasted man had gone and done it this morning. Remy was in no fit mood for sporting banter, so George would just have to take his sorry self, back to the depths of . . .

Prepared to bluster and blow his usual string of obscenities, Remy nearly tripped over something that had not been on his doorstep last night when he'd gone to bed. No siree—he may be a little absent-minded at times, but he was pretty dang sure that last night, there had been no baby in a basket.

Remy looked from side-to-side, hoping to see a big, black, mischievous face, but he saw nothing of the kind.

"What the hell?" he muttered to himself. Then wondered if he should say that in front of the baby. Shaking his head, Remy told himself to just close the damn door and wake himself up. He thought he'd been awake, but this was all obviously a very bad dream, so there was no way he was actually awake. Then, the basket's contents wiggled and cooed.

A small hand made its way from beneath the coverlet to reach for him. Then, the other small hand appeared, its movement knocking the blanket fully away from a little round face. There, looking up at Remy, were two eyes the color of cornflowers.

Damnation. They would have to be his favorite color of blue.

Little blonde curls wisped about the round face, and two dimples appeared when the face broke into a wide, happy grin. Little legs kicked as little arms pumped up and down. The critter obviously wanted to be out of the basket, but there was no way in hell he was going to touch it. Dragging the basket inside, he did what Southern men do when faced with a deep dilemma: He called his mama.

* * *

Lynne Anne Dubois cuddled the tiny form close to her chest as she bounced and jigged about the room, cooing, "Well, aren't you just the cutest little thing." She tickled the tiny chin as drool seeped from a corner of the child's mouth.

"Remy," Lynne Anne said, turning to her son, "tell me again how this sweet angel came to be here. I wasn't able to understand a decent word ya uttered over the phone, 'cause we won't repeat the words that came before 'help.'" Lynne Anne shook her head in dismay. "My dear boy, how I have tried to make you see the error of your sorry ways when it comes to your limited and rather colorful use of the English language. But I digress. Tell me again."

Remy again stated, in plain language this time, how he'd been roused from sleep only to stumble across the child his mother now held. He had to admit, now that the baby was in the arms of someone, not him, she was a cute little thing. And he did mean "little", because the baby was a dwarf. Her legs were stunted and slightly bowed. Her arms, too were abnormal in size, and her head was a little larger than it should've been. But that smile! The child's smile was something akin to a beacon glare on the darkest night.

"And the letter? Did ya read the letter ya said was left with her? Or are ya allowin' me the pleasure of that little chore as well?" Lynne Anne chided her son pleasantly.

"I, uh . . . actually didn't think to—"

Lynne Anne shook her head and put her hand out. "Hand it over."

Embarrassed, Remy reached into the baby's basket and pulled out the unopened letter.

"If ya expect me to do all the work this mornin', you get to hold this angel while I read. And Lord Almighty, I hope whoever left this child will not be leavin' me wantin' to hunt 'em down."

Remy was reluctant to touch the infant, but afraid of what it was going to say, he wanted to touch that letter even less. *Damnation*, he thought to himself.

His mother must have heard the thought, because she crooked an eyebrow in warning as she handed the little girl over to him.

"'*Dear sir,*'" she began aloud. The shaky handwriting indicated the letter had been written by someone under duress.

"'*I know what you must be thinking of me, and I can't blame you, because I feel the same. Know that if I had any other choice, I'd never leave my precious baby like this. My story doesn't matter. What does is the story I want her to be able to tell when she's grown. I did not leave her to you without knowing a bit about you. One day, when I traveled into the city, I saw you and knew you were the one. Something told my heart that you could raise her up with the loving she deserves. I asked around about you. I know that even though you aren't as small as she is, you know better than anyone some of the things she's going to face as she grows. And I'm not saying that as a judgment, it's just what I saw. You hold yourself as proud as any full-sized man, and the one time I passed close enough to see your eyes, what I saw in them is what made me know you were the one. God led me to you because he heard my heart crying every night. I never gave my little one a name. I think part of me always knew I wouldn't get to be the one to raise her up. So I leave it to you to do the choosing. She was born last July on the nineteenth. All I have to leave with her is this rattle. It isn't much, but my granddad made it. Could you let her know? And if she ever asks, please tell her that her mama did, and always will, love her. I don't want her thinking that she was just given away for no good reason. I . . .'"*

Here, there was a tear where the pencil had pushed right through the paper. Judging from the small stain around the edge, tears must have soaked the letter, making it weak.

"'I'm so sorry. I'm so, so sorry. I hope that you and God will forgive me because heaven knows I may not be able to forgive myself.'"

Lynne Anne held the letter in shaking hands as she silently read it again.

Emotionally numb, Remy could do nothing but stare at the baby in his arms as he felt the weight of responsibility settle about his shoulders. Whoever this woman was, she had chosen him—*him,* of all people. The tenuous flame of compassion that attempted to warm his heart, cooled when it came up against his own feelings of inadequacy and self-doubt.

Looking at the child, he focused on her abnormal limbs. On her slightly over-large head. On all that must have been what his father had focused on the first time the man had held him. Not—normal. A heavy, nasal exhale escaped as he shut his eyes up tight and tried *not* to be his father.

Oh, how he had hated the comparisons to the beauty and perfection of his older sisters. To the athletic ability of the *normal* boys in the neighborhood. To all that his father felt he'd been robbed of by having *him* as an only son. He knew his father had wanted someone to be the 'face' of the family company. What he'd wanted and what he got, were two very different things.

Remy hadn't realized his mother had come to stand right

next to him, until she placed a gentle hand on his arm. The woman always seemed to know what he was thinking, even when he wasn't sure himself.

"Rem—breathe, okay." She smoothed the back of his hair. "You are and have always been stronger than ya know. Do not doubt that strength. Especially not now. I know you think your condition makes you less than other men, but darlin', I've done some research on Fairbank's disease. There's not much out there yet, but what I found says nothin' about you not havin' every opportunity available to others. I also know, or can guess pretty well, you've been prayin' for what you see other twenty-five-year-old men havin' in their lives, and dang, son, the Lord just slapped ya right in the middle of what they've got. Since you haven't seen fit to get out there and find yourself a wife, he brought a family right to your doorstep."

Remy hadn't thought of it that way. Hearing it put in those terms made the flame of compassion that had tried to touch his heart grow just a little brighter. But he wasn't ready to let the cool familiarity of self-doubt be overrun—not just yet.

Lynne Anne continued. "Heaven knows this is nothin' to be taken lightly. I'm not sayin' that it's gonna be easy, but if—and I do mean *if,* you allow yourself to look on this as a blessin', I know with my whole heart, *you* are up to the task." Lynne Anne gently cupped her son's chin and angled his face up to hers. "Moses came to his new mama in a basket. Look on this as a sign. Just as his birth mother had to give him up to save his life, so too, has this child's mother faced the burden of lettin' go. I cannot imagine the pain these women went through in bein' forced to trust their beautiful babies into the hands of God, but the Almighty moves in His own ways and in both cases, I believe the right parents were found."

"Are you sayin' what I *think,* you're sayin'?" Remy blinked hard as he tried to process the abrupt turn his life had taken since he'd awakened just a few hours ago. "You think that I, that I should . . . *can* keep this child?"

"Well, with as busy as I know child services are right now, I can't see 'em wantin' to deal with whatever paperwork a thing like this'll cost 'em. Your daddy's done a fair bit to help 'em out on more than one occasion, let's see how much red-tape we can cut through. Besides, ya have a letter from the mother actually givin' the child to ya. But I can check into it, if ya like?"

Remy looked deep into his mother's honey-colored eyes. Eyes that had never led him wrong. Eyes that now shone with nothing but patience, love and trust. She trusted that he could do this. Did he trust himself?

Chapter 3

And So, It Begins

George stared down at the tiny form that looked as white as snow against his big, black hands. "Well, ain't she somethin'? She's such a li'l bitty thing. Claudine, for ten months old, can ya believe how tiny she is?"

Claudine Dollis tickled the feet of the little girl cupped in her husband's large hands and teased, "My love, in hands other than yours, the child may not seem so small. But yes, petite she is. Though so very adorable. Aren't you, ma petite belle? Yes, you are." Claudine cooed to the baby, who smiled broadly in response.

"Well, she may be a li'l bitty thing, but that smile sure lights up a room, don't it?" George said. "And ya say you're gonna keep her? Good on ya, Rem. Course, you know what this means, don't ya?"

Remy looked up at George, daring him to say what he knew was coming.

"No more shits, damns, or hells. No damnations. No hell's

bells. Remy, we may never hear another word come from your mouth!" George laughed. It was a deep, pleasant sound that did nothing to remove the scowl from Remy's face.

"Ah," George sighed. "I can see it now. Your sainted mama, kneelin' in prayer, askin' that her boy learn how to curb his waggin' tongue, and wham!" The sudden noise startled the child in his hands.

The little thing pursed her lips as if to cry, so Claudine rescued the infant and snuggled her in close, bouncing and lulling her with a French lullaby.

George, cowed by the look Claudine gave him, quietly went on. "A miracle came . . ." Seeing that Remy wasn't in the mood for more teasing, George thought better of what he was going to say, pulled his friend onto the couch and sat down next to him. At this level, his six-foot-five frame was able to more closely match Remy's four-foot-eleven stature.

"I don't mean to make light, I don't, and I'm sorry." George said. "I do want to say that whatever ya need, whenever you need it, I'm here for ya. I can promise this isn't gonna be easy. But I can also promise that nothin', absolutely nothin' else you do will be more worth it. Bein' a daddy . . ." George teared up.

Remy couldn't remember ever seeing George even come close to shedding a tear, so he knew the big man meant every word. And that meant *everything* to him.

Remy laid a hand on his friend's massive forearm, and in the way of men, they finished their conversation with nods and a final slap to one another's backs. Then, each broke out in a wide grin, and gentle laughter bubbled up from George.

"A papa. Remington Alexander Dubois, you're gonna have a little ankle biter all your own. What are you gonna name her?"

"Name?" Remy looked blank. Not a single inspiration struck, so he went with something George had said. "Well, you said it best for now—she's a li'l bitty thing—so 'til another name comes, I think I'll just call her, Li'l Bits."

Both the men looked to where Claudine stood, still swaying with a now-sleeping, newly christened, Li'l Bits in her arms.

* * *

Two months later, Remy was putting the finishing touches on a cake he'd made for Li'l Bits's first birthday party. Just as he moved to the side to get a different view of the confection, the girl crawled out from beneath the table. He stepped on her hand and she screamed in pain. Frightened, Remy reflexively squeezed the pastry bag in his hand and a massive blob of blue icing landed smack atop her blonde head.

A loud "Shit!" escaped Remy's mouth before he could think better of it. He had just given her a bath and would now have to repeat the laborious process. He didn't have time. People would be arriving soon, and he wanted everything to be perfect.

In the moment it took Remy to take a few deep, calming breaths, release the pastry bag from his panicked grip and look back to Li'l Bits, she had reached up and spread the gooey blue icing all through her hair and down her face. Before Remy could stop her, she then jammed the blue fist into her mouth and giggled as she sucked icing from it.

"Damn, but you're quick . . . I mean, darn." Remy really was trying to keep his tongue in check. "Child, it's a good thing your sweet ears are too young to burn from my words. Heaven help us both in another year."

Remy was holding Li'l Bits at arm's length, en route to the bathroom, when he heard a loud knock and a "Hellooo," from the front door.

"Remy, we're here! We came early to . . ." Lynne Anne stopped mid-sentence when her embarrassed and somewhat frazzled son appeared from the short hall holding a blue baby at arm's length.

Janelle and Sienna, Remy's older sisters, had walked in right behind their mother and burst out laughing when they saw their baby brother in his current predicament. On more than one occasion, he had mocked them while they were in the midst of dealing with some poop or pee crisis, a dog running amuck in the house or some other parental dilemma that non-parents so love to make fun of. Payback made their laughter all the more enjoyable and they held nothing back.

"Now, girls," Lynne Anne said calmly as she controlled her twitching lip, "your brother needs your help, not your—" She just couldn't do it. She could not stop the short bark of laughter that leapt into the air. When she realized the sound had come from her, she quickly covered her mouth to suppress what wanted to come next. But it was all so endearing: Her son's look of embarrassed resignation, the handmade cake on the table, the freshly swept floors, Remy's attempts to brighten the drab rooms with wildflowers, and the baby. The very blue child with the bright smile seemed to think it was all quite fun.

She couldn't remember how many prayers she'd said over the years asking the Lord to bless her son with all his tender heart desired. And here he was, experiencing the very thing he had yearned for. Granted, this particular blessing had come wrapped differently than most. But due to some wheel-greasing, and calling in a few favors, she held in her hands the papers to prove that the child was now, indeed, his.

"Son, ya look like you could use some help." With a wave of the hand, Lynne Anne motioned her daughters into action. "Janelle, put our food on the table and start to set things out. Sienna, bring the decorations in from the car and set to work makin' this a fit party for my newest grandbaby. Remy, I'll help ya get that sweet thing all cleaned up, and boy, you look like you could use a moment to yourself. Get on into your room and put your game face on. We're havin' us a party soon."

Within the hour, Remy's small home was near to bursting. His mother and sisters had rearranged the furniture to make more room, and had decorated the kitchen and living room. Unaccustomed to being around so many people at once—it didn't matter that most of them were family—Remy was getting a little claustrophobic. Stepping out onto the porch, which was flanked by citronella candles and mint plants from Orvalee to keep the bugs at bay, he wasn't surprised to find Trinny Jenks already there.

Trinny was a few inches taller than he. She had a lean, lithe figure and long, straight, waist-length black hair. She was timid and didn't speak much, but if you paid attention, you could read what she was thinking in her mocha-brown eyes. Remy attributed her reticent nature to having spent two years in an internment camp during the war. Knowing some of what he did about *those places*, Remy didn't dare think too much about all that Trinny had been through.

"Hey, Trinny. Shoulda known you and I would be the first to make our way out here." Remy smiled, careful not to sit too close to her on the long bench he'd made to span the porch. She didn't like to feel crowded.

Trinny nodded a greeting and offered a slight smile. "The baby is cute. How are you?"

"I'm good. It's all just takin' some gettin' used to, ya know?"

Trinny nodded understanding.

"Mama says it's official now. Even brought the papers. With the letter that came with Li'l Bits, she was able to work things out with child services." He shook his head in amazement. "Don't ask me how, but she did."

Remy buried his face in his hands and sighed. Peeking above his fingers at Trinny, he admitted, "Mama's on cloud nine. I still feel like I'm spittin' dust, it all happened so damn . . . so darn fast. Pardon my language. Apparently, I'm a work in progress."

Trinny's lips curled into a full smile. "You try. Be proud."

"Thanks. You know, I had no real idea what it was like to be a parent. You see people doin' it every day. Some make it look easy. Some even make it look fun. *Ozzie and Harriet* sure don't seem real now. I think *I Love Lucy* comes close to showin' the truth of how crazy life can be. Course, they don't have kids yet, but I can just picture what'll come when they do."

Trinny nodded in agreement.

The sounds of laughter from inside wafted out the door and echoed through the tupelo trees. Remy loved living here. He'd purposely built the porch out over the water so that he could hear the gentle sound of it lapping against the ground beneath where they sat. For a few moments more, he and Trinny enjoyed a companionable silence, just listening to the night sounds.

Then, Amanda and Gus, Janelle's two oldest children, came out.

"Uncle Remy," Amanda said, "Nana says you two are to haul your keisters back on in so we can sing the birthday song. Come on!"

"Yeah," Gus said. "I want cake."

Trinny followed Remy, hovering just inside the door.

Remy took Li'l Bits from his mother and held the birthday girl while everyone sang to them both. After all, in a way, it was his first birthday too. First one as a caregiver, as a responsible adult, as a dad. Part of him wanted to run back to the comfort and security of the boring, uneventful life he had existed in a few short months ago. But, as he looked around the room at the smiling faces, his heart leapt to the bottom of his throat, and he had to choke back an emotion that threatened to sweep him away. Unused to emotions of any sort, let alone strong ones, he wasn't exactly sure what he was feeling, but he liked it.

The song ended, and Remy helped Li'l Bits blow out the candle. When everyone started clapping, Li'l Bits mimicked them enthusiastically, which of course, made them all think she was absolutely brilliant.

As slices of cake were cut and handed out, Remy noticed that Trinny was nowhere to be seen. *It was good of her to even come*, he thought.

"Now, I have to get on home," said Orvalee Benson, Remy's war-widowed neighbor, as she leaned in to give Li'l Bits an affectionate tap on the nose. "You know I'm just a holler away, should ya need anything. I have medicinals for tummy aches, tooth aches and any other aches."

The older woman fell silent as she looked long and hard at the yawning child in Remy's arms. Her French-Creole grandmother had been gifted with the "sight," and Orvalee had inherited the same gift. "Ya know, I have a strong *feeling* this sweet baby was left for all of us. She's gonna be a strong one. You know what I mean?" She looked at Remy, who looked at Li'l Bits, and yes, he did know. He tucked the girl's head beneath his chin and jigged her. Actions like this were coming more easily.

Orvalee left, followed by George, Claudine and their three children. Careful not to disturb the droopy-eyed child, George gave Remy a gentle pat on the back.

"This was great, Rem. Never thought I'd see this house so full of life. I like it. It looks good on ya." George winked and ducked out the door.

Remy's brothers-in-law had driven all the kids over for the party and now left with their respective wives. Janelle and Sienna each stopped to give their brother a mighty hug.

"I know this isn't easy, Rem," Sienna said. "But we are both so proud of you."

"We've been talkin'," Janelle said, "and to help, we'd like to be your babysitters. After all, you do need to work, and your shop is no fit place to try and keep the child safe once she's too big to content herself in the play pen."

Sienna stroked her youngest son's white-blond head as he tugged on her leg. "Li'l Bits has plenty of cousins willin' to tote her along on their adventures, if you're open to that."

"We just wanted to let ya know," added Janelle.

Remy's heart was overwhelmingly full. With a tear glistening at the corner of his eye and a nod of the head, he acknowledged his sister's offer.

His mother was the last to leave. "Don't worry about the mess. I'll be back tomorrow to help set things right." Lynne

Anne softly stroked the soft blonde curls of the now-sleeping child. "How this takes me back. Doesn't seem so long ago that I was holdin' you this way. Strokin' your sweet little head, wonderin' what dreams were makin' you smile."

Just then, Li'l Bits's mouth turned up at the corners and she nestled further into the crook of Remy's neck.

"Treasure these moments, Rem. Some are gonna be outrageous, hilarious, or maybe even dangerous enough to make ya think that you'll never forget 'em, but believe me, you do. I wish I'd written 'em down. Sometimes, you or the girls'll say somethin' and I'll think to myself, 'Where was I when that happened?' 'cause I can't recall it."

Remy seldom broached the topic of his father, but in this moment, with Li'l Bits tucked in his arms, he needed to know. "Mama, did my father ever . . . Did he ever hold me?" Remy stroked Li'l Bits' soft curls. "Did he help get me in bed? Get me a glass of water at night? Did he ever once walk the floor with me when I was sick? Anything?"

Remy knew that if he did not put Li'l Bits to bed right then, he might start blubbering and wake the poor thing up. Motioning his mother to wait a minute, he walked the short hall to the small room he'd cleaned out and painted a very pale shade of pink. Remy gently laid his tired girl on the handmade animal-print sheets his mother had given them, then pulled the crocheted baby afghan from Orvalee, up to her delicate chin. Never had he ever, felt anything like whatever it was that pulsed through him right then. Maybe it was just the feeling of an adult wanting to protect an innocent child, or maybe it was that tenuous flame of compassion settling a little closer to his heart.

His mother had taken a place in the rocking chair near the unlit fireplace. Remy found her, eyes closed, gently rocking to the rhythm of night sounds that filtered in through the open windows. Without opening her eyes, Lynne Anne motioned her son to the chair she'd placed next to her.

Wordlessly, he sat.

She reached over, laid a hand on his arm and released a long, slow sigh. After a minute, she opened her eyes and said, "Son, I hope you'll be able to understand what I'm gonna tell ya. Your daddy, bless his soul, he tries sweet pea. Really, he does. Seein' as how you two have never quite got on, I know you probably don't actually know much about him. So, let me tell you a few things and I need ya to listen. Okay?"

Remy nodded.

"Okay. Your daddy was born dirt poor, and I do mean *dirt* poor. The family was looked on as nothin' more than plain white-trash. The home he was born in, if you could call it a home, was more like a slapped-together shack with a salvaged tin roof that was likely to blow off every time a strong wind decided to tease it. A far cry from the home you're blessed to bring a child to."

Remy looked around his cozy living space with appreciation.

"Now, whether your granny was plumb worn out from havin' kids, not much to eat, and no husband around 'cause he was *workin'*, or just ornery, I don't know, but she was none too pleasant. It was actually a good thing she died not long after you were born because I wouldn't have wanted you to have to know her. It was all I could do to keep a Christian tongue in my mouth when she got to spoutin' off on me. Anyway, as one of the older children, your daddy had to learn young how to care for himself, because there wasn't anyone else to do it for him."

Lynne Anne absentmindedly twisted her wedding ring as she talked. "In 1901, oil was discovered in these parts. Your daddy got himself a job workin' the rigs round here when he was just twelve-years-old. Remy, think on what you were doin' at that age."

Remy remembered reading his favorite books on his own bed, in his *own* room. He thought of the tree outside his second story window and how he'd wished that he dared jump from the sill to its closest branch. Thanksgiving dinner with family. Christmas morning with stockings hanging by the fireplace and plenty of presents beneath a beautifully decorated tree. Definitely not the same experiences his father had had.

"Your daddy worked his *ass* off. And I'm pardoning myself for sayin' that, because there's really no other way to put it. Those workers slaved through twelve-hour shifts every day, seven days a week. They slept in tents. Back then, Oil City had wooden sidewalks, muddy streets and boasted over twenty-five thousand residents. It was the first boom town in the region and it was *wild*. The crews on passenger trains were told to keep the window shades down to protect the women and children from seein' the street fights and murders that happened right out in the open."

Remy tried to process all that his father, at such a young and impressionable age, had witnessed. It had probably been like living through the aftermath of a war. And his father had been alone.

"He was so young, but your father did a man's work. After learnin' the oil business from the ground up, he realized that he didn't want to mess with the oil itself. What he did decide to do was go about *supplyin'* the oil business."

Remy thought of the thriving enterprise his father ran. Of the brand-new warehouse and supply store near the edge of town. The business he'd always felt that he was being *forced* into. He thought of his own modest custom wood-crafting venture and how hard it was to properly market and grow. They were very different businesses, but the basic concept was the same.

"By the time your daddy was twenty-one, he'd birthed a dream, faced rejection, redesigned the dream, had the dream crushed, and then started the whole process over again. We met when he was in one of his slumps. We were at a dance and he was off in the corner, sort of hangin' out all on his own. There was a look in his eyes that made me want to know what was goin' on behind 'em. I was wearin' a new blue dress, so I was feelin' my oats. I walked myself on over to him and asked straight out what he was thinkin'. I wasn't sure if it was me that caught his interest or the fact that I offered a listenin' ear, but we got to talkin' and the rest, as they say, is history. I was nineteen and he was twenty-three when we got married. My parents were not exactly happy I was marryin' a man that came from nothin'. But I knew my heart. And I'm glad to say, my heart was right all along."

Lynne Anne reached out to stroke a thumb along Remy's stubbled jawline. "Now, think on the child that you just put to bed. Are you askin' that she change anything about who she is or where she came from, to suit the dream you had for yourself? Are ya thinkin' you can't love her because she came in a completely unexpected manner? Or are you just takin' her as she is?"

Remy looked at his feet, knowing where his mother was going with this.

Lynne Anne gently cupped her son's chin and forced him to look at her again, but before she could say anything, Remy said, "I know Mama. I know what you're sayin'."

"Then tell me, boy. Tell me what it is I'm sayin'." She had a look of pleading in her eyes.

"You're sayin' that I shouldn't be judgin' the man because I don't really know him. That I should just accept him as he is. I do Mama. I do my best to just let him be. It still don't take away the hurt that he never loved me like he does Sienna and Janelle. That he's never fully accepted me for who, and *how*, I am."

"You listen to me, Remy, and listen good. Give me one example of when your father ever said a mean or unkind word to ya. Has he ever once expressed anger at you not takin' an interest in *his* business? Who was it that helped you get the money for this house *and* your own shop?"

Remy wanted to continue arguing his point but had to stop

and think. True, his father had loaned him the money to get his start, but he'd always assumed it was just his father's way of getting him out from under foot. Of removing him from the sight of those his father did business with, so they wouldn't see that he had a circus freak for a son.

Remy got up and paced about the room, trying to recall the words he was sure he remembered his father throwing at him, all the words that had wounded and scarred him. Why couldn't he remember? He'd lain awake many times ruminating over some hurt or another. A disapproving look; a harrumph or eye roll.

His mother's voice was gentle, almost a whisper. "When seein' it head-on for what it truly is . . . his behavior's not so easy to label, is it? How much of what you've held against your father is just him being him? And how much is simply you—being you? Now that you've begun to open your heart to someone who truly needs and depends on ya, can you perhaps begin to open your heart to another who needs you too? He may not need you in the way you *want* him to. And he may not show his love the way you *want* him to, but that doesn't mean he hasn't cared. Did he hold and rock and coo over ya when you were a baby? No—but he didn't do it for the girls either, because he has no idea how to express himself like that. No one ever rocked and cooed over him either. What he has done for you, is give you the security of a good home. The home he *never* had. The meals and educational opportunities he *never* had. Choices, Rem. He's given you the choices he *never* had."

Remy's protests in his own defense fell silent, as an inkling of understanding seeped through the cracks in the wall he'd built between his father and himself. He pondered his mother's words and thought of Li'l Bits. How he wanted to give her all he felt he'd been denied. How he was able to hold and love her because he had been given the same by his mother. The kind of mother his father never had. And just as Remy had made a promise to himself to be a better dad to his daughter than he felt his father had been to him, he now saw that his father had done the same thing. Same gifts, different wrapping.

"I'll be on my way. When I come back tomorrow, if ya have anything you'd like to talk about, you let me know." Lynne Anne rose from the rocking chair, enveloped Remy in a warm embrace, kissed his forehead and said, "Night, son. You sleep well."

Remy stood on the porch as he watched her go; then, turning back to his house, he looked through the open door at the room that had been crowded with happy, smiling faces as they celebrated a new family member. For the first time, he wondered if maybe his father hadn't come not because he didn't want to participate but because he hadn't felt welcome.

"Well, damn it!" Remy ranted to himself, allowing an unrestrained string of curses to quietly spike the night air. Remy paced the length of the porch, bare feet making no sound as he wore a path across the boards, pondering everything his mother had said.

Thinking of his comment to Trinny about being a work in progress, Remy laced his fingers through the hair at the crown of his head. Hair that was the same light-golden brown as his mothers. Exhaling a breath he hadn't known he was holding, Remy got a hold of himself and went inside. Slipping silently into Li'l Bits's room, he just stood there, watching her breathe. Moonlight highlighted her angel face, and he felt a physical ache in his chest. He rubbed at the pain to make it go away, but it didn't.

He wouldn't realize this for a while, but the kind of pain he was experiencing would only go away once the shell it was cracking had been fully peeled back. Suffering births the strongest souls.

Chapter 4

George
June, 1956

"Sometimes even to live is an act of courage."

—Lucius Annaeus Seneca (4 BC–65 AD)
Roman Philosopher and Statesman

Li'l Bits rode atop George's shoulders as they strolled the water's edge on their way home from what had become a weekend ritual. Li'l Bits loved being up so high. Spreading her arms wide, she tipped her face to the sun. "Uncle George, I love shoulder rides. Makes me feel like I'm flyin'."

George took that as a cue to pick up the pace. Lengthening his already long stride, he began a slow jog, which left Li'l Bits clinging to his ears as she bounced up and down.

"Still feel like you're flyin'?" George teased.

Laughing, Li'l Bits exclaimed, "No, sir—feels like ridin' in the back of Orvalee's old truck."

"That old truck'll definitely set your teeth to rattlin' if you're not strapped down good-'n'-tight," George agreed as he slowed to a stop. "You okay up there? Haven't jiggled a tooth loose from your head have we? I can't be gettin' ya home with missin' teeth. Your pop would skin me alive."

"I still have my teeth," Li'l Bits assured. "But my behind feels like I got caught doin' wrong."

Concerned he might have hurt the girl, George swung Li'l Bits carefully to the ground so he could examine her.

"What you doin' Uncle George? I was just teasin'. Honest." Her eyes twinkled with amusement.

Setting her on his solid knee, George said, "Now, Bits, don't you be teasin' your old uncle like that. One day, I may go and forget to believe ya when you tell me you're really hurt. Then what'll ya do?"

He had meant to tease her back, but Li'l Bits touched his face, seeing something in his eyes he hadn't been able to hide.

"I miss her too Uncle George. When is she comin' back? I miss Jeremy, Beau and Aline. I ain't got no friends with them gone. I do have my cousins, but they're family. So do they count as friends?"

George swallowed hard, not knowing what to say to the too-observant child. Claudine and the children had been gone three months now, and even he had no idea when they'd be back.

When he and Claudine had gotten married in France after the war ended, coming to the States had been all she could talk about. In her mind, the United States had been something akin to a piece of heaven.

George had tried to explain that it was just a place, like any other, filled with people who were learning and making mistakes. His dream had been to stay in Europe and continue working with the military peace-keeping effort.

As big as he was, soldiering had suited him just fine. He'd found the kind of courage that only comes from facing the flames of hell and not turning away or backing down. He'd found beauty in the land and the people that had welcomed him with open arms as he helped liberate them from a living nightmare. And, most powerful of all, he'd found love. He knew Claudine loved him as much as he loved her, and on some level, he knew she'd been right to go back home. But he didn't want to face those truths just now.

"I think on cousins as friends, especially the kin you've got. They're a rowdy bunch but they suit ya just fine." To divert her attention away from the tender topic, George asked, "So Bits, what do ya want for your birthday? It's comin' awfully fast. If you don't plant an idea in my head, I might sprout one of my own. How about I bring ya one of them remote control cars? I saw a nifty new '56 Chevy Hardtop last time I was at the store."

George watched the child puzzle through an answer, quite sure that she was trying to come up with a nice way to shoot down his offer.

Li'l Bits patted his cheek and said, "Um, no thank you Uncle George. But I can get you one for your birthday if ya like." She brightened. "I'm gonna tell Papa that you want one. What number did you say it was?"

"'56—same as the year right now." George smiled.

She moved in close to whisper, "I know ya most likely want a real one. I can't do that, but I'll make sure Papa gets the control one ya want. You can count on me."

"Yes, Bits, I sure can. I can always count on you to watch my back."

"Or ride it!" Li'l Bits jumped up and down. "Put me back up and let's run home."

"Yes, ma'am." George did as ordered, and jogged the rest of the way to Remy's with a giggling little girl telling him to "giddy-up."

* * *

Mont Dollis was waiting on the porch when George got home. Rocking in Claudine's chair, George's father looked like he owned the place. Of course, that's how Mont tried to look everywhere he went—like he owned it.

"'Bout time ya made it home, boy." Mont stopped rocking and leaned toward George's approaching form, looking like a snake about to strike.

George prepared himself.

"Seen ya out with that *white*, midget baby again. When you gonna learn? Folks is laughin' at ya. Laughin' and sayin' you ain't got a lick a sense. You're always hangin' around with the wrong people. It's embarrassin'. You always was an embarrassment. Makes me look bad by association."

George stopped at the bottom stair, not daring to go further lest he put a fist through his father's vile mouth. More than once, Claudine had encouraged him to stand up to his father, but the-laying-on-of-hands may not have been what she meant.

"*Mon Guerrier, his child you are no more. You stand now as the best of men. Were you not, I would not have let you catch me. Here, in Louisiana, you are not a man but a child. A child afraid of his papa. A papa who only finds peace by tormenting you. Do you not see it? Only when you show him you are a child no more will his hold over you be broken.*"

Guerrier—warrior, George never knew why Claudine had chosen that as her pet name for him, but he'd always liked it. Despite the momentary urge to finally do her bidding, George did not feel much like a warrior right now.

Seeing his son's clenched fists, Mont backed off his verbal attack and the silence paid off. George's shoulders eased and his tight fists fell loose. Mont smiled.

"Why are you here Daddy?" George asked curtly.

"You ain't even got it in ya to say hello? Now, that just ain't polite. Especially when I come all the way over here to pay my respects."

"Respects for what?"

"Why, for your loss, of course." Mont rose from the chair and walked to the top of the stairs, momentarily positioning himself so that he could look down on his son. His youngest. The son that should never have defied him by going to fight for a country that had failed them. The son that always had ideas above what he ought. The son that, had he not outgrown Mont by more than six inches, might still be able to be whooped. Of all his children, George was the only one who had ever dared stand up to him, and he didn't like it.

"Loss? What loss, Daddy?"

Step by slow step, Mont descended, stopping on the last stair so he could remain eye to eye with his son. "I see no rug-rats runnin' around, clutterin' up the place. No *woman* hangin' laundry on the line. You're alone now, ain't ya? It's probably better that way. Maybe now you'll come to your senses."

George wanted to protest but heard Claudine in his head, so he took her advice. Without a word, he stepped onto the same stair as his father. Now it was him looking down on the other man and for a split second, he thought he saw Claudine smile from the yard.

Mont didn't like the close proximity of their bodies and moved away, toward the street. "Come to church on Sunday. Spend some time with your *own* family. Lord knows you left us behind when you went off to *fight*." His lip curled into a sneer as he said the word. "Came back a big hero, didn't ya. Yessiree—a hero was in our midst, but did ya bother to come round? Hell no. We wasn't good enough for ya because you had *them*. Well, they're gone now, so maybe you can take pity on your *mama* and come round."

Mont knew where to leave George hanging. The mention of his mother was the sweet-spot Mont had no trouble using to his advantage. With the wave of a single hand, rather like a lordly dismissal, the older man strolled casually up the road.

George watched the retreating form, feeling a sense of relief wash over him.

Claudine's rocking chair was moved to action by a gentle breath of wind, and the sudden urge to cleanse it of any lingering malevolence overcame George. He moved to it and reverently ran large fingers across the hand-carved crest on the back piece. Remy had made this chair as a belated wedding gift for his best friend's bride when they had arrived from France. It was a delicate combination of the initials of their two first names within the protective arch of a fleur-de-lis that lay just above Claudine's head when she sat in it. The chair's beauty had overcome George when Remy had presented it to them. Slumping into it now, George leaned back into the chair as if it were the arms of his beloved.

Remembering the feel of her embrace, George could practically hear the melodic sound of his children as they laughed and ran around the yard. He rocked a little harder, as if the motion could somehow propel him to where his family waited. To where, away from judgment, away from the past, they could be happy.

"Mon Guerrier," he heard Claudine say, *"there can be no future if in the past you always live. Courage is an act performed every day. To face changing another diaper"*—he could hear her slight giggle—*"knowing that will make yet more laundry to wash, takes courage. Working to feed your family takes courage. And our union, I fear, will take yet more courage than either of us can imagine."*

How right she had been. George looked around before swiping at a tear that broke free to slip down his cheek. Had he known the greatest opposition he'd face was not that of the battlefield; not running into fire to save men he didn't know; but to once again face-off with his own father, he *never* would have let Claudine talk him into coming back.

But as much as he wanted to be with his family, the time wasn't right. He wasn't yet the man they needed. He wasn't the man he *wanted* to be.

* * *

Purposely arriving late to avoid sitting with his family, George quietly snuck in the church doors and took a seat at the back. Relieved his father hadn't appeared to notice, George relaxed his large shoulders against the wall and let out a long sigh. He recognized a few faces from when he was a child and silently offered a polite nod to those who glanced his way. As they were in church and supposed to be feasting upon the word of one who lived in non-judgment, George tried not to imagine what thoughts might be running through their heads as they turned away from him. Perhaps recalling whatever tales his father had spread after his last visit.

He spied his mother, head bobbing in spiritual communion as her hand kept a fan waving to counteract the stifling air. Her mostly gray head was still peppered with black, and her Sunday hat was the same one she'd worn for as long as he could remember. It was just a hat. Why couldn't his father buy her a new one?

George, he told himself, *don't go there. We're in church. Think on the Lord.* George bowed his head and prayed to cleanse his heart and mind of ill will toward his father, focusing instead on his mother and the sweet smile that would light her face when she saw him. It had been a while.

When the meeting ended, George let those on the inside of the pew slip past as he waited by the doors for his mother to see him. Meeting in church was a gamble, but he knew his father wouldn't want to be seen behaving poorly in the Lord's house. And, hopefully, not within earshot of said house either. George hoped since he had attended the meeting, the family gathering afterward would go smoothly.

When his mother finished greeting her Sunday friends, she turned to head down the aisle, and there it was: the smile he'd been waiting for. George's heart lifted as he saw her prepare to sprint toward him, but a hard hand clamped onto her upper arm and she winced in pain.

George's jaw clenched at the sight.

His father had seen him, but so had the reverend.

"George!" Reverend Marrs's voice boomed off the white-washed walls. Making his way down the aisle between wooden pews, Reverend Marrs steepled his hands saying, "God's glory be praised, son. It's good to have ya back." With the tact and finesse of a true man of God, the reverend skillfully extricated Mrs. Dollis from the iron grip of her husband, guided the grateful woman to her son, and planted her in his arms as he gave George a hearty pat on the back.

"I hadn't thought to see you." The reverend said kindly. "It's been a few years, but you're always welcome."

Mont came up behind the reverend and wrinkled his nose in annoyance at the last part of the man's statement.

Knowing Mont Dollis as he did, Reverend Marrs said, "The Good Shepherd has seen to the safe return of a valiant member of his flock. I know the war seems a lifetime ago now, but thank ya, George, for all you did over there. I never got the chance to say that. I can't imagine the devils you faced and had to chase down."

"That's mighty kind of you to say, sir." George shook the man's offered hand. "And may I say, my absence from this place is in no way a reflection on you. Just wanted you to know."

Mont rolled his eyes.

"Mrs. Dollis," the reverend turned to her, "you raised this boy right."

Mary Dollis looped an arm through her son's and looked at her baby boy with evident pride. "Thank you. If you don't mind, sir, I'd like to get this boy of mine on home so I can feed him up. He's lookin' a mite scrawny, don't ya think?"

Reverend Marrs let out a mighty laugh. "Miss Mary, if that" —he indicated George—"is your idea of scrawny, may I be so blessed. Maybe I should come on over and you can feed me up too."

Mary Dollis tapped the reverend's arm. "You're more than welcome any time. You know that."

Throughout the exchange, Mont grew impatient with the

attention being lavished on George, and interjected himself between the preacher and his family, propelling Mary toward the door. "Yeah, well, Reverend, we'd best be gettin' on home. See ya next Sunday."

George automatically moved as a buffer between his parents.

"Miss Mary," the reverend called after them, "I will be takin' ya up on that offer. I'll be seein' ya soon. Real soon."

Mary Dollis waved a pleasant goodbye over her shoulder.

* * *

Not ready to go inside, George sat on his porch, thinking over the evening at his parent's. As per *command*, all his siblings and their families had been there. As the youngest of seven children, that meant there were quite a few of them when gathered in one place.

It had been at least a year since they'd last seen him, and his nieces and nephews had obviously not known how to react. Hugs or averted glances? The children watched their parents for cues. Based on his last appearance, heaven only knew what might have been said about him since then. It was that *last time* that had greatly influenced Claudine's decision to finally take the kids to her homeland, where they would no-doubt receive a warmer welcome from her family than they had from his.

George could still hear his father's caustic words. Thank heaven his sweet children had not heard their own grandfather call them "mulatto-tadpoles" or their mother a "frog."

"What'd ya think was gonna happen?" Mont had said, not caring if Claudine heard or not. "You think that kissin' a frog would turn ya into some sort of prince? Wake up, boy. You done nothin' but fall prey to her apple-butter tongue. And frogs do have *long* tongues . . ."

A menacing glare from George had stopped his father from finishing the rest of what would most assuredly have been a very lewd comment.

Some part of George knew that most of his siblings, had it not been for the influence of their father, would have opened their arms to his children, just as his mother tried to do. But over the years, they'd all learned that going against their father never amounted to a hill of beans, so they'd stopped trying.

Why couldn't they see that the man simply kept changing the rules? You could spend all your energy to please the jackass, think you'd made some headway, but nope—somehow, he'd find a way to shoot you down and leave you feeling like it was all *your* fault.

His mother had become lost within the twisted game, and it broke his heart. George got up to pace back and forth across the porch, absentmindedly touching Claudine's rocking chair each time he came close to it.

"*Mon Guerrier,*" Claudine's image whispered from the chair, "*you are no more your father than our sons are you. Each so different. As different as a blue sky is from the hot, yellow sun; the wind from the mountains. All are part of the day. Some add color. Some cast a shadow. Some make you feel; others you, see.*"

George thought on this. He hadn't understood what she'd been saying, but now, he thought he might. Mountains are solid, immoveable, but they add to the landscape in a way nothing else can. In Europe, he'd seen for himself how incredibly beautiful and dangerous, a real mountain can be. Maybe she'd been trying to help him see his father that way. You don't know how high you can climb unless there's something to challenge you.

Lord, but he missed her.

Chapter 5

Trinny

July 8, 1956

"The ultimate measure of a man is not where
he stands in moments of comfort and
convenience, but where he stands at times
of challenge and controversy."

—Martin Luther King Jr. (1929–1968)
American Minister and activist

It was Sunday, so Li'l Bits wasn't at the cousins'. She sat outside by the large oak right next to the house, watching the light chase shadows across the dirt. She didn't know why, but this spot always made her feel loved. Like the tree itself was sharing a portion of its great heart with her. Papa Rem had built their home around it and the ash that had become a lovely part of their front porch. Sometimes, in the evening, she and Papa would sit on the porch bench and listen to the voices of the night as everything settled in to sleep.

Papa said that if you listened "with ears that could hear," like it said in the Bible, that the earth would whisper her secrets to you. So Li'l Bits sat, eyes closed, leaning heavily against her large oak-friend as she opened her ears. She wanted to know how to help her friend Trinny.

With most people, Trinny was quiet. But when she and Trinny were alone together, the woman would smile, talk a bit, and even laugh. Li'l Bits loved Trinny's laugh; it sounded like the song of a bird. But her friend hadn't been laughing much lately, or even smiling. Something was wrong. Li'l Bits knew the grownups wouldn't tell her anything. But she also knew that if anyone could bring back Trinny's smile, it would be her. She didn't know how she knew this; she just did.

So she pondered, watched the shadows change shape as the sun rose higher in the sky and then looked to the water to see if it would tell her anything. When she was on the verge of losing hope that an answer would come, a fish broke the surface of the water, causing ripples to arc out in an ever-growing circle that caught the sunlight within its glistening folds. The undulating glimmer reminded her of a candle's light, and that made her remember that her birthday was just a couple of weeks away.

Yes! That was it. Nothing made people happier than a party. A dress-up party! Afterall, she was turning five and that was a special age. It was halfway to the double-digits. She could hardly wait to be double-digits because Papa said that was when, if she still wanted to, she could learn to help in the shop. If she did a good job, he might even pay her, like a real job.

Li'l Bits jumped up, excited to ask Papa if she could have a dress up party. Running across the porch to the shop, Li'l Bits knocked on the door with the metal knocker that Papa had added so she could get his attention when he was working.

"Bits, what is it?" Remy asked when he opened the shop door, annoyed at the interruption. "I'm puzzling through some plans and could use a bit of quiet to do my thinkin'."

"I'm sorry, Papa."

The enthusiasm drained from her bright face, and Remy suddenly felt bad for the sharp tone in his voice. He'd had

Li'l Bits for four years and he was still a work in progress. With a sigh, Remy knelt down and pulled Li'l Bits in for an apologetic hug. "No, Bits, I'm the one that's sorry. I shouldn't have snapped. I know you'd never interrupt my work unless it was important. You've been a good girl that way. I know it's Sunday and this is usually our time, but if ya can just give me a little longer, I promise, I'll be done soon. Then we can go on our walk."

"Papa, can I say just one thing? I promise, cross my heart"— Li'l Bits crossed her heart to solemnize her words—"that after ya listen, I will *not* bother you until ya decide to come on out."

Her cornflower-blue eyes shone with hope, and of course, Remy gave in. "All right, darlin'." He sat down in the doorway and pulled her onto his lap. "You say your piece."

Li'l Bits explained how she'd noticed that Trinny was sad about something and that she'd come up with a plan to help make their friend smile. As she talked, the light came back to her face and her voice rose to an excited pitch. "I haven't ever seen Uncle George and Orvalee in their war clothes. I hear about the war all the time and really want everyone to dress up in things they wore back then. Do ya think they'd do that?"

"Bits, I'm actually not sure. For some folks, the war still goes on in their heads. Askin' 'em to dress in them clothes might be too much."

Again, the light seeped from her eyes and Remy couldn't stand that. "But I see no harm in simply askin'. After all, they have the right to say no, don't they? Can you give them the right to choose and not get your feelings hurt if they don't wanna do things your way?"

Li'l Bits nodded enthusiastically. "Yes, Papa. I promise not to feel bad. And one more thing, can we make a birthday card to give everyone so they'll come?"

"Do you mean an invitation?"

"Yes. Will you help me color 'em? I know how to write my

own name, so I can put that at the bottom. Will ya help me write the rest?"

"I certainly can, but why all the fuss? We've never done invitations before and everyone always shows up."

"I'm gonna be *five* Papa. That's a whole hand." She splayed the fingers on her right hand as far as they would go to indicate the enormity of the number. "I'm growin' up. I want this party to be nifty. Besides, I think Trinny needs somethin' different right now. Have you seen her eyes? She's sad, Papa. I don't like seein' her sad."

Remy didn't dare admit that he had seen Trinny's eyes. In fact, when she was around, he felt the urge to look into them a little too much. They were the darkest, richest brown he had ever seen. Like freshly tilled soil in springtime. And yes, he too had noticed they lacked their usual luster. As young as she was, it was just like Bits to see someone in need and want to help.

* * *

Li'l Bits knocked and then stepped back so Trinny would be able to see her better when the door opened. She had brushed her hair, was dressed in her Sunday best, and was holding a colorful invitation before her.

A smile touched the corners of Trinny's mouth when she saw Li'l Bits. "Hello, Bits. You look nice." Trinny motioned Li'l Bits through the door.

Li'l Bits stood in the middle of the room, gaping at the art-covered walls. She'd never been in Trinny's house before and was in awe of the photographs, watercolors, and black-and-white ink drawings. An art table was set in front of the big picture window where people usually had a couch, and full book shelves lined the walls. Li'l Bits noticed that beyond these items and the single chair at the art table, there was no other furniture in the room.

"Umm, Trinny, I've come to pay a call, but . . . where do I sit?"

"Come to the kitchen." Trinny walked through an arched doorway and turned to the left. Li'l Bits followed.

The kitchen was the cheeriest room Li'l Bits had ever seen. White cabinets were set off by yellow tiles with a black inset and black trim. The stove, fridge and sink were a buttery yellow. The floor was white linoleum with randomly placed yellow squares, and a white board across the radiator held pots of geraniums that matched the red vinyl kitchen chairs. The table was white with a broad, shiny metal band around it. For as quiet as Trinny was, Li'l Bits had not expected to see such a vibrant room in her house.

"Please, sit." Trinny pulled a stool from beneath the sink so that Li'l Bits could climb up onto a chair all by herself.

"Thank you." To avoid damaging the invitation, Li'l Bits scooted the paper onto the table before she made the climb up to the chair.

"Would you like lemonade?" Trinny asked.

"Yes, please," Li'l Bits said properly, and she remembered another "thank you" when Trinny set the cute, daisy-patterned glass before her. "The yellow lemonade matches the glasses and your whole kitchen," Li'l Bits said admiringly. "How'd you get everything to match?"

"The hardware store and catalogues," Trinny said. "I did the tile and painting. Hired out the rest."

"Oh, Trinny," Li'l Bits exclaimed. "Just think of what you and my papa could do if ya worked together. You could make the most beautiful house in the whole world!"

Trinny looked around the room as if seeing it for the first time and nodded approval. "Your papa does very good work. Thank you for comparing mine to his."

"I saw that different table in the livin' room, with the picture on it. Did you draw that?"

One corner of Trinny's mouth quirked into a half smile. "Yes."

"Did you draw some of the pictures on your walls?"

"Yes." This time, Trinny offered a slight nod of the head with her half smile.

"Will you show me which ones?" Li'l Bits asked eagerly.

"Yes. First, drink your lemonade."

Anxious for a tour, Li'l Bits forgot her invitation and gulped down the drink. Sliding from the vinyl seat was difficult because her skin stuck to it, and weird squeaking sounds came from the seat as she struggled to free herself from its grasp, but she finally managed it. Next time she came, she'd have to wear trousers and see if that made it easier to slip off the chair.

In the front room, Li'l Bits got a better look at all the art. The largest photograph caught her attention. It was of a bunch of young girls—one looked like she could have been Trinny. They were outside some sort of a school. The girl that might be Trinny was holding a small newspaper and wore the slightest of smiles. All the other girls smiled big as wind blew strands of hair in front of their faces. There was a large, dangerous looking barbed wire fence in the distant background. Li'l Bits stepped closer to get a better look. Yep, there were even a couple of soldiers with guns.

Trinny watched Li'l Bits's innocent eyes study the photograph. Saw puzzlement as the child's eyes focused on the fence and just like that, fourteen years melted away. "A man," Trinny said quietly, "Ansel Adams, came to the camps. Took pictures so people wouldn't forget. But they already have."

"Forget what, Trinny?" Li'l Bits asked as she moved on to look at the next photo. It showed the same girl that had been holding the newspaper, only she was now standing with people who looked like they were probably her family outside a ramshackle-looking home. Trinny didn't answer.

"Is that girl you?" Li'l Bits pointed at the almost-smiling girl in both pictures.

"Yes."

"Where were you? What's that paper? Why are there men with guns looking at y'all? And what's already been forgotten?" Li'l Bits peppered Trinny with questions, not seeing that with each one, Trinny's breathing became more labored.

Despite keeping the reminders so visible, Trinny did not like talking about the past. And her sister's calls over the last few weeks concerning the movement she was involved with had only added to Trinny's reserve. Knowing that Li'l Bits meant no harm and could not possibly know about the camps, she thought about how to answer.

"Has your papa or George told you much about the war?"

"I know my papa didn't have to go fight like Uncle George did. Uncle George is a hero," Li'l Bits said proudly. "He ran into the *fires of hell*" —she emphasized the words like her papa had— "to save men from dying. That was so brave."

"Indeed," was all Trinny said.

"And Orvalee, she was a nurse. She saved people too. But she couldn't save her husband when he was shot doctorin' the field."

"*In* the field," Trinny corrected.

"Yeah, *in* the field. And she couldn't save her son when his airplane was shot down. I know we beat a bad man named Hitler." Li'l Bits's brow furrowed as she said in a hushed tone, "That Hitler man, he was mean. He made lots of people cry by takin' away their families. I don't like him."

"Yes," Trinny agreed. "To forcibly separate people from their homes and families is a bad thing. To steal lives, is a bad thing."

Puzzled, Li'l Bits asked, "How do you steal a life, Trinny? Is that like killin'? Papa says that's against the commandments and we only kill an animal if we're gonna eat it."

Now she'd done it. How do you explain to a five-year-old what it means to steal a life? To steal all the hard work from someone's past and all the possibilities from their future? To steal the very soul from a still-living being? Trinny looked at the copy of the Ansel Adams photograph, and remembered.

Despite the wind, it had been hot that day. The day her

article had been featured on the front page of the little school's newspaper. She'd been so proud and could hardly wait to show the paper to her mother, sister and brother. She had written about her father. About the superhero she imagined him to be while he was away fighting.

With the family being part Irish, her father had hoped they would be spared the camps. After they were taken from their home in Salt Lake City, Utah, and sent to the Mayer Assembly Center in Arizona to await processing, Trinny's Irish grandfather and their extended family members wrote letter after letter attesting to her family's good character. But every letter went unheeded. So, her father enlisted to fight for a country that had deemed his family a threat, simply for their heritage.

Heritage? Her mother, Rose Ogawa, had been born in California. Trinny's maternal grandparents had arrived in California during the 1870s and worked as laborers to get their start in the new land. Her paternal grandmother had been born in Hawaii, where she met a young Irishman working in the pineapple fields; his parents had immigrated to the United States during the Great Potato Famine. Trinny had felt as American as anyone she knew . . . until the day her family was forcibly carted off with only what they could carry. Had Grandfather Jenks not stopped by for a visit that day, no one would have known where they'd gone. They would simply have disappeared into the lists that lay beneath other papers on some general's desk.

They'd stolen her soul that day. A soul that, every day since, had struggled to cling to the life her physical body held. She breathed. She ate. She slept. But it was through her art that she lived. Her art, she could do in solitude. Her art, she could control.

"Trinny?" Concerned, Li'l Bits tugged on the blank-faced woman's hand. "Trinny, I'm sorry. Did I say somethin' wrong? Trinny, are you okay?" Tears began to well in Li'l Bits's eyes.

"Trinny!" Li'l Bits gave a mighty tug at limp fingers that slowly stiffened to curve around her small hand.

Trinny blinked, furrowed her brow and blinked again. Her absent stare finally took in her surroundings and the fear-laced visage of her young friend. Feeling absolutely terrible for frightening Li'l Bits like that, Trinny knelt down and embraced the girl who cried on her shoulder.

"Oh, Trinny, I'm sorry for what I said. Honest. Will you still come to my party? You don't even have to dress up like everyone else." Li'l Bits sniffed. "Least ways, I think they will. Papa says they might not want to cause the war was hard." She sniffed again.

Trinny handed her a handkerchief, which Li'l Bits put to good use.

"Li'l Bits," Trinny soothed, "I will come to your party. You've done no wrong. Please don't cry. You've done nothing wrong." Trinny smoothed a tear from beneath the child's eye and gave her another hug. Unused to physical contact, Trinny felt odd touching another person but forced her arms to remain around the child she had frightened.

"Please don't hate me, Trinny. You're one of my best friends. I already lost Jeremy, Beau, Aline and Aunt Claudine. I can't lose you too. Please say you'll come to my party," Li'l Bits begged.

"Bits, it's all right." Trinny smoothed the child's hair as she stroked her back. "We are most definitely still friends."

Li'l Bits snuggled into the embrace, relishing the assurance.

Trinny again looked at the copy of the Ansel Adams photo. At the girl holding the paper, standing among friends. At the girl in the other Adams photo with her family. Then, at the child in her arms. It dawned on her that Li'l Bits considered *her* family. This child had been left on a stranger's doorstep. As far as Trinny knew, the child had never known the loving embrace of a mother. Never had siblings to cuddle up next to in bed on cold nights. She'd never had friends her own age to play with.

Li'l Bits had none of the things Trinny had been blessed with at that age. But this child knew what it was to be loved and had a heart that she held open to the world, and all the good it could bring her. Her young heart hadn't let her down so far.

And a little child shall lead them, Trinny remembered from the Bible. She hadn't placed much faith in that book since the day they were taken to the camp. But maybe, just maybe, the person who wrote those words knew what they were talking about.

"Bits," Trinny said, "let's go look at what you brought."

Like the sun emerging from behind a rain cloud, Li'l Bits's eyes shone with delight. Grabbing Trinny's hand, Li'l Bits merrily led the way back to the sunny kitchen, where her hopes for the best birthday ever lay in the pictures and words she had written.

Chapter 6

Happy 5th Birthday

Saturday, July 21, 1956

"You never change your life until you step
out of your comfort zone."

—*Roy T. Bennett (1918–1988), author*

"**R**emy!" Lynne Anne exclaimed. "I was expecting there'd be a lot more decorating to do, but ya have things well in-hand."

Balloons were tied into bunches and hung from the mantle and high pieces of furniture. A game of pin the tail on the donkey was tacked on the wall to one side of the fireplace. Party hats and streamer-ended horns were set out on a small table by the front door so that Li'l Bits could easily hand one to each guest as they arrived.

In the kitchen, a bright-yellow tablecloth, on loan from Trinny, showed off the cake Remy had made. Five yellow candles were placed in the cake's center. The words "*Happy Birthday Bits*" arced over the top half of it like a rainbow, while the lower half was rimmed with red and blue flowers that spilled down the side to encircle the base. A small bouquet of flowers with a pink ribbon tied around the stems stood in a vase centered on the mantel.

"I must say," Janelle remarked as she carried in an armful of supplies and admired the room, "you're becoming quite the birthday party professional, little brother."

"Yeah," Sienna agreed. "I just might have you do Nathan's next birthday. Anything to save myself the worry over it."

"Agreed," said Janelle. "I think you owe us that much, Remy. All the trouble you raised for us when you were younger."

"Younger as in prior to age twelve?" Sienna asked Janelle. "Or younger as in prior to today?"

Remy was still getting used to his sisters' good-natured banter and stopped himself from protesting their humor. Prior to Li'l Bits coming along, the three siblings hadn't really spent much time together. Upon reflection, that was mostly his fault. In the few short years he'd been a father, Remy had learned more about himself than he knew there was to know. He was doing his best to take the teasing and throw a little back as he could.

"Well, you two bein' *older* ought to know. Older is supposed to be wiser and . . ." Whatever Remy was going to say beyond that was silenced by their mother.

"Come on now, y'all. We are gonna wear our gettin'-along-faces. Let's look as happy as the flowers on the mantle and the cake. And Remy, you know how I love fresh flowers in the house. Those are a nice touch. Daisies, carnations and a rose. What a lovely combination."

Remy couldn't find it in himself to tell his mother that he wasn't the one who had gotten the flowers. Ever since Bits came, every year on her birthday, they'd been left at the edge of the porch. He'd been saving the cards that came with them too. Each one said, "For the birthday girl. All my love." The 'o's were always shaped like hearts. One day, his girl was going to start asking questions, and he had no idea what he would say.

He did know what he would show her; that she was loved. He would make sure she never doubted that.

Lynne Anne watched her children work together to put the finishing touches on the party decorations. Until adopting Li'l Bits, Remy had used every excuse he could not to join in family activities, feeling that he had nothing in common with anyone. But now, he too was a parent and had actually turned to his sisters for child-rearing advice. Janelle had four children and Sienna had two, so there was a fount of information handy whenever he chose to draw from the well.

"Yoo-hoo," Orvalee called from the front porch, then opened the screen door and let herself in. "And where is our sweet birthday girl?"

"Orvalee!" Li'l Bits ran out from the hall to give the woman a hug but stopped dead in her tracks. "Orvalee," Li'l Bits said in awe, "you look like a soldier."

The older woman self-consciously smoothed the fabric of her olive-drab skirt, and touched each of the four large brass buttons on her matching jacket to make sure it was fastened and straight. She hadn't worn her nurse's dress uniform since the day she'd returned from England, accompanying the body of her husband.

"Can I touch your medals?" Li'l Bits asked. "They're so pretty."

"They're not medals, sweetheart." Orvalee crouched down so that Li'l Bits could get a better look at the pins. "Here, on my shoulders, I wear my 2nd lieutenants bar." Orvalee touched the single gold bar. "On each side of my collar is a US pin, for the United States. Here, on each lapel, is the pin showin' that I was a nurse." Orvalee unpinned a gold caduceus with the red capitol N in the center and laid it in Li'l Bits's palm.

"It's got snakes on it. And wings." Li'l Bits closely examined the symbol. "I've never seen a snake with wings. Do they have those in England?"

Orvalee chuckled. "No, sweet thing, they do not. And these

snakes don't have wings either. It's just the way they designed the symbol. Each part means something different."

"What's the big one on your hat? It's about as big as my hand."

Orvalee traded the child the caduceus for the hat, replaced the pin on her lapel, and then pointed to the cap. "This insignia is the regulation coat of arms of the United States. In a way, it's sort of like the family crest that ancient soldiers would wear when they went to battle. The coat of arms lets other people know what family you're fightin' for."

"And you fought for the American family!" Li'l Bits beamed.

"Yes, I did Bits. Both your uncles, George, and I, all fought for the American family." Orvalee teared up at the thought of the innumerable others that fought but hadn't managed to make it back home. Like her husband, Avner, and son, Jonathan. And then she thought of the thousands of others who made it back in body but not in mind, like her Devyn.

Desperate to change the topic, Orvalee commented on the small table that held the hats and horns. "So, Bits, what are these for?"

"Oh! Can't believe I forgot." Li'l Bits handed back Orvalee's hat saying, "Don't put it back on. First, go back outside and knock."

"But child, I'm already planted inside."

"Please, Orvalee. We've got to do it right. Just go on out, knock on the screen and wait for me to answer. Okay."

"All right, don't rattle your cage. I won't be a party pooper. Though, what I'd be a poopin' on, I have no idea." Orvalee went back onto the porch, turned and knocked on the wood edge of the screen door.

Li'l Bits smoothed her new red-and-white-polka-dot dress and, like a proper hostess, opened the door to her first guest.

"Hello, Ms. Benson. Thank you so much for comin' to my party." Li'l Bits took a hat and horn from the side table, and offered them to Orvalee. "Everyone gets one of each. And don't lose your horn, 'cause later, we're gonna *make-some-noise.*"

"Why, thank you, Bits." Orvalee put the hat on at a jaunty angle, held the horn to her mouth, crooked a knee and posed with hand on hip. "How do I look?"

"Not like you." Li'l Bits scrunched her nose in amusement. "You're bein' silly."

"Well, if we can't be silly at a birthday party, when can we? Right. Now, where should I put this?" Orvalee held out the gift she'd brought.

Li'l Bits's eyes lit up. "That goes over by the cake."

Remy caught his daughter's attention by clearing his throat. Nodding at Orvalee's back as she put the gift on the table he mouthed, "What do you say?"

"Thank you!" Li'l Bits blurted.

Orvalee turned to embrace her favorite little neighbor and whispered, "When it comes time to open your presents Bits, I hope you'll like it. I wanted to give you something special this year."

"I'm sure I'll like it." A knock sounded at the door, and Li'l Bits turned to see who it was. George was about to open the screen and walk in when Li'l Bits shouted, "Stop, Uncle George! I'm comin'."

In awe of how different a uniform could make someone look, Li'l Bits ushered him in saying, "Hello, Uncle George. Thank you for comin' to my party. And wow! You sure look different. Just like Orvalee."

George's imposing frame filled the doorway, temporarily blocking the light as he entered. George had not worn his dress uniform but instead had chosen the fatigues that had seen him through many a skirmish. Like Orvalee, had it not been for the sake of Li'l Bits, he would never have put them on again. The knife at his waist had slit men's throats. The canteen had spent too much time empty. The dent in his helmet signified *one* of death's attempts to grasp him, and the scar, hidden by his hair, was a reminder of how he had evaded its cold fingers.

In these very fatigues, he had first seen and fallen in love with Claudine. If he thought hard, he could even recall her scent lingering at his collar. Shaking himself out of thoughts that were no good right now, George made to walk into the room when he was brought to an abrupt halt by Bits putting up her hand.

"No, Uncle George. Wait." Bits's dress bounced with her excitement. "We have to do it right. Take off your helmet." She handed over his party favors.

George donned the offered hat, which looked a bit small on his large head.

"Hmm?" Li'l Bits stepped back quite a few paces so she could make a proper appraisal. "We might need to give you two," she said in all honesty.

George burst out laughing. "Even if you want me to wear three, I'll do whatever ya say." George scooped her up into his big arms and asked, "From this angle, now how do ya think I look?"

Li'l Bits kissed his cheek. "Next to my papa, you're the most handsome man here."

George nearly crushed the child in an embrace that left his heart aching for the feel of his own children. To cover the authenticity of the tear sliding down his cheek, George sniffed and exaggerated a sigh. "Bits, you've gone and melted this soldier's heart. I hope you've got some ice cream to firm it back up again."

"You bet I do! And guess what; it's your favorite. Nea-politan. Ever since you gave it to me the first time, it's my favorite too."

George rubbed his belly as if it were already full of the delicious dessert. Behind him came a ruckus as all the cousins ran across the porch like hound dogs on a scent.

"'Scuse us," they said, edging past the large man and into

the room. Waving presents aloft, they lured Bits away from George and to the kitchen where, wide-eyed, she watched the pile of gifts grow.

"Rem," George said, shaking his friend's hand, "you've done a heck of a job. That girl's on cloud-nine right now. It warms a heart to see."

One look at George told Remy that his friend was thinking of his own children; perhaps wondering what they were doing at that very moment in France. He was most likely picturing the birthday parties he had missed. Part of Remy wanted to lecture his best friend on all the ways he was screwing up his life. The other part kept telling him to shut the hell up and mind his own business. Because damn, he wasn't even sure how to keep his own life from derailing at any given moment. And one of the forces that he was struggling to reconcile with chose just then to step into view.

Alexander Dubois had never been to his son's home. He stood, back to the front door, looking at the ash tree growing right up through both the porch and its roof. He cast an appreciative gaze across the water, taking in the tupelo trees and their mirror images that stretched like rippling giants across the shimmering surface.

Turning, Alexander gazed with appreciation at the long, comfortable-looking bench that spanned the porch's full length. Then, his eyes fell upon his son's shop, on the low metal door knocker and multi-faceted door-knobs that were on both the shop and front door of the house. He gathered that Remy had made them to accommodate his daughter's limited grasp. An inkling of pride at his son's resourcefulness and caring caused a sprig of—was it hope?—to spring up through the infertile soil of their unattended relationship. If Remy could now take note of such a small detail, maybe his son's heart would thaw enough to let him in, too.

When Alexander turned to face the door, Remy saw the look on his father's face change from one of open admiration to hesitant withdrawal. It was a look he knew well. But seeing it this time didn't elicit the usual pain and feelings of failure.

His father had not been drafted because he was more valuable at home than abroad. Remy looked around. Seeing everyone in their uniforms, he realized that despite the hellishness of war, he envied them because they had done what he could not.

Trinny knew what it was to be a prisoner of war. George knew both the pain and victory of being a bonafide hero. Having treated both prisoners of war and their own wounded, and losing her husband and sons to the fight, Orvalee knew better than anyone the pain of loss, and each of his brothers-in-law bore their own battle scars.

Unfettered by the chains of misguided, youthful interpretation, Remy finally saw that it was not "the look" that had caused his feelings of inadequacy, it was the way he had interpreted it. He had compared himself to everyone around him. He'd done this his entire life. None of his family members had ever criticized, talked down to, or belittled him in any way; they hadn't had to. He'd done it for them.

Shame froze him where he stood.

Through the growing crowd, Lynne Anne spied her husband and a smile brightened her face. Michael and Oliver, her sons-in-law, both dressed in their army uniforms, joined Alexander on the porch. Judging by their gestures, the three men appeared to be discussing something that lay out over the water. Then, Michael clapped Alexander on the back while Oliver opened the screen door and herded the older man inside.

Remy stood still, unsure if he should move toward his father or wait to be acknowledged.

Lynne Anne went to Li'l Bits and whispered something in her ear, and a curly blonde head whipped around toward the door. Her eyes grew so large that they captured the light streaming in through the front window.

Li'l Bits ran to her grandfather, who squatted down to embrace her. She hugged him back and began chattering away.

Remy marveled at the warmth in his daughter's eyes as she talked to his father.

He watched, feeling as if he were seeing something on television. He knew that over the years, while Li'l Bits spent time with his sisters, they had taken his daughter to their parent's house with his nieces and nephews. But he'd never actually thought about the fact that his father was there *with* her.

"Oh, and Paw," Li'l Bits pulled out of his arms so she could get him a hat and a horn. "Here, put this on." She handed over a big, gold, sparkly hat. "I saved this one just for you, in case ya came. I'm so glad you did. Papa is gonna be so excited."

Remy heard his daughter's comment and was glad that she was glad, but he . . . hmm. He was still trying to puzzle through how he felt about finally seeing his father standing in his home. A home the man had loaned him the money to buy, and maybe, not for the reasons Remy had always thought. He wiped his sweating palms on his pants.

Both he and his father watched as Li'l Bits grabbed an armful of hats and horns to deliver to her cousins. As the men's eyes followed her, they landed on one another. Neither knew quite what to do. Clenching and unclenching nervous hands, Alexander willed his feet to move toward his son.

Unseen by either her husband or son, hands steepled in prayer, Lynne Anne silently watched.

Step by tentative step, the two men approached one another.

"Son," Alexander said.

"Father." Remy nodded. "Thank you for comin'. I had no . . . It didn't dawn on me that . . . you and Bits were . . . close."

"She's a keeper," Alexander said with a smile as he watched Li'l Bits move through her guests. "Smart as a whip, too. *Loves* askin' questions."

Remy chuckled. "That she does."

Before Remy could think of something else to say, there was a knock at the screen door, and he turned to see Trinny.

His mouth practically dropped open, and his sun-tanned skin seemed to lose all color.

Trinny's long, straight, ebony hair was swept back from her face on one side and secured with a large, enameled comb. She was dressed in a yellow-and-cream silk kimono. Hand-painted cherry blossoms and butterflies adorned the cream-colored areas. Around her slender waist was a big belt of contrasting-colored silk and embroidery that left Remy feeling as though she was a rare blossom in an ethereal garden.

Trinny saw Remy through the screen, smiled hesitantly, and waited for him to invite her in.

Try as he may, Remy could not make his feet move toward the door to open it for her. Alexander followed his son's line of sight, smiled inwardly at the expression on his face and moved to admit the woman, but was cut off at the pass by an exuberant Li'l Bits.

"Trinny! Oh-my-goodness, that's the prettiest dress I've *ever* seen." Li'l Bits reached out to touch it but stopped. Looking up, she asked, "May I please, touch your dress?"

A small smile softened Trinny's face. "Of course."

"It's so soft and smooth," Li'l Bits remarked in awe. She took a portion of the long sleeve and let the fabric slide across her skin. "Someday, I want a dress just like this. Except, I want mine to be blue. I like blue."

Trinny crouched to Li'l Bits's eye level. Tucking a blonde curl behind the girl's ear, Trinny said, "With your eyes, Bits, blue would be a good choice. But I like the dress you have on too. Did you get it for your birthday?" For Trinny, those three sentences were akin to a speech.

Li'l Bits swayed back and forth to make the skirt swoosh. "Yes, I did," she said with pride. "Papa got it for me. I love it cause doin' this"—she made the skirt swoosh again—"makes me feel like a ballerina." Li'l Bits's attention returned to Trinny's kimono. "I've never seen a dress like this before. Where'd you get it?"

Trinny's feet were beginning to tingle from lack of circulation. She wasn't used to wearing the traditional tabi and zori, so she straightened up and moved with Li'l Bits to the couch. Trinny sat and lifted the girl to the spot beside her. "You asked that we dress as we did during the war." Trinny inhaled. There was no help for it. She was going to have to talk—a lot.

"Remember the pictures on my wall?"

Li'l Bits nodded yes.

"I am mostly Japanese. During the war, they, the government built . . . special places for my family and those like us to live. Do you know who the United States fought during the war?"

Li'l Bits had to think for a minute, but she eventually remembered something Uncle George had said. "We fought the Germans, Talions and the *Japanese*." The child's eyes grew wide as she said the last word.

"Italians." Trinny corrected. "So, the government felt that we, Japanese Americans, would be . . . better off living in our own *special places*. They moved us from where we were living to these places. We stayed there until the end of the war. I have no uniform, but I have the traditional dress of my people. This"—Trinny smoothed a hand down the yellow silk—"is a kimono."

"Ki-mo-no," Li'l Bits repeated and smiled.

"This"—Trinny touched the wide swath of embroidered fabric at her waist—"is called an obi. It is similar to a corset. It keeps our posture tall and straight."

Li'l Bits automatically sat taller.

Trinny showed Bits her feet. "These slit-toed socks are called tabi. The straw sandals are zori."

"Those are kind of funny names. I'm just gonna call 'em sandals and socks if that's okay. And this thing"—Li'l Bits gently touched the obi—"is really just a big belt. But I do like the word kimo . . . How do ya say it?"

"Kimono."

"Yeah. Ki-mono. Kimono. I'll remember now."

Trinny almost laughed out loud but managed to keep the outburst pinned behind a wide smile. "You may call them anything you like. And Bits," Trinny stood and pulled a flat, rectangular, wrapped package from behind her obi, "happy birthday."

"Oh, thank you." Li'l Bits was about to go add the new gift to the growing pile, when she suddenly said, "Shoot! I just about forgot." From the dwindling selection of hats and horns, Li'l Bits chose two for Trinny. "Will it ruin your pretty hair if ya put this on?"

Trinny took the offered adornment and snugged it to her head with the elastic chin-strap. Tucking the horn into the top of her obi, she asked, "How is this?"

"Perfect." Li'l Bits surprised Trinny by grabbing her hand and taking her right to Remy, who was doing his best to act like he hadn't been watching the pair throughout their entire exchange.

"Papa, doesn't Trinny look beautiful? She looks just like a flower in the big park across from the library."

"She sure does," Remy agreed before he thought about how that might sound. "I mean, she does look nice. Just like you. You both look nice. But that's what birthdays are for right? Dressin' up, lookin' nice, and havin' fun." He was rambling and couldn't seem to stop.

"Bits." Lynne Anne came to the rescue.

Remy nearly hugged her.

"Sweetheart, I think all your guests have arrived. Don't ya think we should get started?"

Li'l Bits's new dress bounced with her excitement. "Yes, Nana!" she exclaimed. With that, she was off, drawing everyone in her wake.

* * *

Before climbing her step stool into bed, Li'l Bits took inventory of her birthday bounty. From the cousins, she had three board games: Chutes and Ladders, Merry Milkman and Adventures in Disneyland. She'd also gotten a baby doll and a doctor's kit. Trinny had given her a colorful book of rhymes and stories. Papa said they could read a new one every night before bed.

Nana and Paw had given her a red cash register with pretend money to help her learn numbers and counting. From George, she had gotten Silly Putty, a package of birthday cards from the kids and Aunt Claudine in France, and M&M's candy. She shouldn't, because she'd already brushed her teeth, but Li'l Bits snuck a few of the M&M's. "Papa, Uncle George said he first had these during the war. Did you know they were invented for soldiers?"

"I did. Uncle George told me they put the chocolate in this little hard shell so it wouldn't melt so easy before the soldiers could get it. That was pretty smart, don't ya think?" Remy stole a few pieces of the candy and popped them into his mouth.

With a sigh of frustration, Li'l Bits protested the theft and quickly tucked the bag behind her back.

Remy just smiled and picked up Orvalee's gift. "And how do ya like this one?"

Orvalee had given Bits a full-color book on herbs and plants, where to find them, and how to make medicinal poultices and tinctures from them.

Li'l Bits took the book from her papa and held it close to her chest. "Orvalee said, if it's okay with you, she'll take me out plant hunting. She said that I'm smart and a brain like mine shouldn't go to waste. Maybe one day I can be a nurse, like her. Or maybe a doctor, like her dead husband was. I can take my doctor kit along on our plant hunts and use it to tote what we find."

"Dreams are beautiful, sweet thing. But it's best not to get *too* caught up in 'em. You don't wanna lose track of the life you're livin' now, do ya?"

Remy feared his daughter was setting her sights a might

too high. Though he wanted to encourage and support her, as a father, he also wanted to spare her the inevitable pain he knew her future held.

"No Papa. But if I don't dream big, how am *I* ever gonna get where I'm goin'? I'm so small, I suppose I have to dream ten times as much as other people just to make one of 'em come true."

There was nothing Remy could say to that, so he let it be. She would soon be venturing out into a much larger world than she was used to. Until now, he and the others had been able to protect her from the harsh stares, rude comments, and other forms of misery that unthinking, uncaring people can inflict. Intentional or not, even those who turn away instead of offering a smile can lay a cold lash across tender shoulders.

Remy tucked his precious child beneath the covers and smoothed the sunshine-colored curls away from her face. She snuggled Orvalee's baby afghan up under her chin and closed her drooping eyes. Remy let his work-roughened hands paint feather-light caresses from her temple to the back of her head, by combing long fingers through her hair and then stopping to lightly massage the base of her skull.

"Mmm . . . I like that." She opened her mouth in a wide yawn, then sighed contentedly. "Don't stop."

"I won't." Had it been five years since this tiny enchantress had magically appeared on his doorstep? Remy traced a line from the tip of her nose up and around the contour of her face, ending at her jaw.

The corner of her mouth gently curved upward, like an infant lost in sweet dreams.

"Night, Papa. I love you."

Remy's heart squeezed with pleasure at those words. "Good night, my angel. I love you back." He had never spoken truer words.

Chapter 7

Orvalee

Beginning of August, 1957

"It is curious—curious that physical courage should be so common in the world, and moral courage so rare."

—Mark Twain (1835–1910), American writer, humorist, publisher and lecturer

---

"Bits, can ya hand me that pot there? No—not that one, sweet thing," Orvalee pointed to the clay pot on a shelf just above the girl's head.

Looking up, Li'l Bits knew she couldn't reach the right one, so she searched the greenhouse for something to stand on. She quickly discovered an old apple crate, which she dragged over, placed bottom-up, and climbed aboard. Bits stretched her arms as far as she could, and found that with her restricted shoulder rotation, she had to dip to one side to extend her reach. This action got her fingertips close enough that she could ratchet the pot forward. Tongue out in concentration, she coaxed the object forward until enough of it was visible that she could finally tip it into her hand.

Orvalee had turned away without offering any help or suggestions. If Bits was going to make it in this world, the child would have to know how to go beyond perceived limitations to solve problems. As much as she admired Remy and all he had done for the girl, the man was too soft; no doubt wanting to spare his daughter many of the trials he had endured. But personally, she felt the child was being done a disservice.

School was going to start soon, and Li'l Bits would be thrust into a world outside the safe one she had been raised in. With her extra sense, Orvalee *knew* that something, a trial or . . . well, she couldn't name it, but it was coming, and she wanted to help prepare Bits.

Hands submerged in new potting soil, Orvalee kept her back to Li'l Bits and listened. She heard the child emit a grunt of satisfaction as the pot fell into her waiting hands. A second later, Bits's small feet plonked onto the wood planking of the floor.

"I got it." Li'l Bits announced with pride.

"Thank you, Bits. Using that crate was good thinking."

"It's a good thing it was there. I'm not sure how I woulda gotten the pot if it weren't."

"I have no doubt you would've found a way. You're smart."

"You always say that."

"I say it because I mean it," Orvalee said. "You may not have height little one, but you've got what counts. And what you've got'll see you through a whole lot more than you know."

"What do you mean?" Li'l Bits handed her mentor one of the mint plants they were potting, and was then lifted onto the stool next to Orvalee.

Orvalee pinched back some of the growth, cleaned off a few dead leaves, divided the roots and potted the new start as she talked. "You've got a good brain, but you've also got a good heart. Some people just have one or the other, but you've got both. So far, most likely without you even knowing it, you've managed to use 'em as a pair, which is how it should be."

Orvalee poured her specially mixed soil into the pot Li'l

Bits had gotten from the shelf, and then handed Bits a mint start. "Did you see how I did mine?"

Li'l Bits nodded.

"Okay, then you do the same. We'll finish potting the starts, then move on to some tinctures. I'll just keep talkin' as we work. That okay?"

Li'l Bits nodded.

"That's my girl." Orvalee smiled. "Now, where was I?"

"Um, something about my brain, and a pair."

"Right you are, child. As usual. Now, do you understand my meaning when I talk about usin' your thinking parts together to make a job easier? You know what a pair is, right?"

"Well, I know I have a pair of shoes, one for each foot, so that means two. I know my brain can think, but no one ever said anything about hearts bein' able to think too."

"Not many people know that little secret, darlin'. Because most people don't know how to do the heart kind of thinking."

Li'l Bits's eyes grew wide at the thought of being privy to a secret. "If not many people know, then how'd *you* come by the knowin'?"

"Life, child," Orvalee whispered as one corner of her mouth crooked up a fraction. With a deep, centering breath, she continued, "When you're young, inexperienced, full of hope and dreams, the world is a magical place. Every person you meet can be a friend. Every book you open can be Aladdin's cave. And every day brings the promise of learning somethin' new. For some, like you and me, there's a little somethin' extra."

"Like what?" Li'l Bits whispered with anticipation.

"Do you know what faith is, child?"

"You mean like it says in the Bible, 'thy faith hath made thee whole'? Papa reads to me on Sundays. Sometimes we read out on the porch, when the sun is shining on the water through the Spanish moss hangin' on the trees. Papa says that's when you can actually see the spirit of God at work. His spirit's the light behind the moss. That's what makes it look like the curtains of heaven have been pulled back and we can peek in and see the angel's shadows sparklin' on the water. I like that." Li'l Bits sighed contentedly. "The world is a magical place."

"I like that too, and you're right about the magic. When you can see it in the world and in people, that's heart-thinkin'. And heart-thinkin' goes hand-in-hand with faith. That kind of thought is limitless. It lets you know that even though people say bad things, and do bad things, most people aren't bad. Heart-thinkin' opens up your brain-thinkin', so you can actually *think* on more things at one time and in a different way than if you just use your brain. Are you gettin' me? Do you see how having two parts to think with can help make things easier?"

As Li'l Bits thought about an answer, Orvalee cast her eyes around the homemade greenhouse and reverently fingered the hand-made potting table. What seemed a lifetime ago, her husband and sons had built it for her as a place to honor her gift for growing things. Orvalee could just touch soil and know if it was healthy or needed fortifying. Her native Creole grandmother had been the local healer and passed on all she knew to Orvalee. This knowledge had been the catalyst for venturing into the medical world and becoming a nurse.

Her youngest son, Ervyn, had been the one she thought would follow in the family's healing footsteps. But when Devyn, so broken from the war, had died by suicide, Ervyn wasn't able to remain at home and face the loss of nearly his entire family. Her baby boy had converted an old milk truck into a camper, packed up, and headed out to explore the country his father and brothers had died for.

Orvalee wondered if Ervyn ever thought about what his leaving had done to her? With him at home, at least they'd had one another. Now, she had no one. No one except for the sweet child sitting next to her. So eager to learn. So full of life. So very, *very* needed.

"I think so," Li'l Bits finally said. "Do the two thinkin'

parts work together like my feet? Like how I can go faster using both of 'em, than if I tried to get around by just hoppin' on one foot all the time?"

Orvalee marveled at the simple—yet—accurate assessment. "Yes, Bits. Exactly like that." She switched them from the potting station over to her tincture table.

On the table were dozens of pots of peppermint, spearmint, orange mint, and even one called chocolate mint, all ready for harvesting. Li'l Bits's job was to take the small, tender leaves from the tops of the plants and put them in dark-colored jars. There was a chart for Bits to look at so she would know how many leaves of each plant she needed. Then, Orvalee would fill the jars with her home-brewed gin and seal them up so they could sit for six to eight weeks, until the tincture was ready to be strained.

Orvalee had discovered that her own alcoholic brew was more effective than store-bought at extracting the herbs' medicinal properties, thus making them more bioavailable. The tongue and cheeks are full of capillaries that quickly absorb the herbal alcohol.

Everyone in the community had benefited from these tinctures. They worked on stomach aches, anxiety, arthritis pain, and a whole lot of other things. Orvalee even made an insect repellant that worked wonders.

"When you partner with something or someone, you always get more done. Like we're doin' right now." Orvalee cast her forest-green eyes affectionately on the child at her side and swallowed hard. The mother in her vowed to do right by this little angel.

"So, when you learn how to team up your heart and mind, there are *no* limits. The Bible and history are full of stories about people who figured out how to use both of their thinkin' parts. But I have to warn you, it's not easy. No siree, it is not."

The word *history* made Bits think of a book she and George had been reading. "Is it like a quest? Like King Arthur lookin' for the Holy Grail? Uncle George has read me some adventure books. And I've watched Trinny do some of her paintin' and drawing. Sometimes, she stops and gets a strange look on her face, like her mind has gone a long way away. Then, all of the sudden, she's workin' like a mad-woman, and it turns out beautiful."

Surprised, Orvalee said, "Yes, Bits, it is like a quest. Trinny's art is beautiful because when you look at it, you *feel* something. That's called alchemy."

"Al-kimmy," Li'l Bits repeated. "I mean, I guess I've seen it, then, but what's it mean?"

"Alchemy is typically thought of as a process of changing cheap metal into expensive gold, but it is so much more than that. Alchemy is the power of transformation. Which means, it turns one thing into something else or combines things you wouldn't think of puttin' together to make something extraordinary."

Li'l Bits cocked her head to one side, trying to put what Orvalee was saying into a context she could understand.

"It's like you said, Bits. Trinny seems to go someplace else, and then she comes back with inspiration to create a pretty picture. Right?"

Li'l Bits nodded.

"Most likely, Trinny is going deep inside herself to places of remembering or imagination. To places of joy or even pain. On these visits, she's able to feel what she did when those things were actually happening, or how she *wants* to feel in her dreams, and then guess what." Orvalee leaned close to Li'l Bits.

Eyes wide, Li'l Bits stood unmoving, barely breathing, waiting for Orvalee to continue.

"Trinny is able to take those emotions or memories and turn 'em into something you can actually see. That's why her art makes you *feel*." Full of emotion, Orvalee crossed her hands over her chest and said, "She's given us the gift of seein' her own heart *as* it's thinking."

"Wow." The word escaped Li'l Bits as a breath. She closed her eyes and could see Trinny's heart on display in the pictures on her walls. A tear slipped down her smooth cheek. "She's so pretty."

Orvalee stroked the girl's hair. "Yes, child, she most certainly is, as are you."

"You think I'm pretty?" Li'l Bits looked disbelievingly at Orvalee as her hand unconsciously lifted to toy with a curl of hair.

"You, child, have a rare kind of beauty. You may not see it now, but one day when you've traveled some space between 'now' and 'then,' you'll look in the mirror and there it'll be. The next time you see Trinny, George, or even your pa, look in their eyes, just as you're lookin' into mine right now. Those who use both thinkin' parts, well, you can see it in their eyes. One minute they'll be full of laughter, and then you may see nothin' but pain. Sorrow, joy, anger, confusion . . . We're given so many emotions to create with. It's when you only use one of your thinkin' parts that these emotions can end up bein' what kills you."

Orvalee's voice cracked on the last words as she thought of her middle son, Devyn. Dead. By his own hand. He'd gone to war as soon as he was old enough to sign up, anxious to be just as brave as his father and older brother. Sadly, he hadn't been strong enough to handle the coming home part. She'd heard the nightmares; his screams. "Don't make me do it!" had echoed through the night, along with other exclamations of dismay and horror. She had cradled him, soothed him by reinforcing that he'd only done what was necessary to come home.

But despite being told he was fighting the *enemy*, Devyn hadn't been able to relegate those he saw to that category. They'd looked just like him: young, determined and afraid. Killing. Whether friend or foe, watching people die hurt so much. Too much.

Worried by the look on Orvalee's face, Li'l Bits placed a hand on her mentor's arm. "Are you okay?"

"Yes, sweet thing." Orvalee sniffed back a tear. "I am."

Li'l Bits's mouth crinkled and her eyes misted over. "Did an emotion try to paint somethin' sad in your heart?"

"Yes, it did. But I've learned not to let the dark colors cover all the bright, happy ones. I just try to use 'em like shade or a shadow. Something that makes the light better, more interesting."

"I can see that," Li'l Bits said. "It's like sittin' beneath my oak on a hot day. The shade of my tree can take away all the meanness the heat makes me feel."

"Bits, I love you." Orvalee cupped the girl's face in her hands. "And that's why I'm gonna be honest. This is just between us, okay?"

Li'l Bits crossed her heart.

Orvalee's hands fell to her lap, and silence filled the gap between them as she tried to think of how to say what she wanted to. "Sweet thing, some hard times are coming. I can't tell you what they're gonna look like. I can't tell you exactly how hard they'll be. But I can warn you that they *are* coming." Orvalee studied Bits's face to make sure she was paying close attention. "But I *know* that you are strong. I'm tellin' you this because you would want me to let ya know if a tornado was coming, right?"

"Of course," Li'l Bits agreed.

"And why is it good to know when a storm is on its way?"

"So we can make sure to have candles and matches and food."

"That's right. And why do we gather all those things? Does being prepared stop the storm from comin'?"

"No."

"Then why, Bits? Why do we prepare?"

"I suppose because if we're ready, then we have what we

need to make it through whatever the storm decides to hit us with."

"Exactly! See how smart you are. And every time we go through a storm, can we learn a new way to make going through the next one better?"

"Why, sure. That's what Papa says."

"And your papa is so right. You are blessed to have him. We all are. He's a good man and he's been made better by having you. Did you know that?"

Li'l Bits bobbed her head. "Nana Lynne tells me all the time that I am the makin' of her hard-headed son."

Orvalee laughed out loud. "That you are, child. That you are."

Chapter 8

The Walls Come Tumbling Down
September, 1957

"Wake up, Bits." Remy shook his dead-to-the-world daughter a bit harder. "Bits, it's your first day of school. You don't wanna be late, now, do ya?"

Li'l Bits rubbed at her eyes, groggily blinking the sleep away. As what her papa said finally registered, she sat bolt upright, panicking, "Have I missed it? Oh Papa!" she exclaimed as she threw back the covers and jumped to the floor. Bare feet dodged around him and raced to the custom-made wardrobe. Li'l Bits forcefully opened a drawer and got out her best pair of tights and a clean pair of underwear. Nana Lynne said you should never go anyplace special unless you put on clean panties.

"Papa, where's my first-day-of-school dress? I thought I hung it—"

"Now, Bits, don't have a cow." Remy walked to the bedroom door and closed it. "See, you hung it right here on the hook after you pressed it last night."

Carefully laying the dress across the foot of her bed, he said, "While you're gettin' ready, I'll finish breakfast. We can't have you goin' off full of nerves *and* hungry."

"Oh, Papa," Bits said with an exaggerated sigh and an eye roll, "you just don't understand."

Remy turned so that Bits wouldn't see the smirk on his face. More than once, his mother had told him to just wait. One day, he would know all the crap he had put her through. Today, he thought, *will be a day of reckoning.*

Remy drove the seven miles into downtown Oil City a little slower than usual, unable to believe that his baby girl was starting school. He was feeling nervous about letting her go. To reassure himself all would be well, he said, "Okay, Bits, let's go over the plan one more time."

"Papa." Li'l Bits rolled her eyes as she crossed her arms mutinously. "Again? We've gone over it a thousand times already."

"I know. I just wanna be sure you understand what's expected. Plus, your sarcasm has been duly noted. And the eye rolls? Really, Bits. You've been spendin' too much time with your aunts."

"Well, then I guess 'The Plan' will have to change, since 'The Plan' says I'm supposed to meet Jeremy, Claire and Damian at the flagpole in front of the school after the last bell rings. Then, 'The Plan' says I walk with the cousins to Aunt Janelle's house, where I will have a snack and start my homework. 'The Plan' also says that I will not leave Aunt Janelle's *for any reason* until you come pick me up after work."

"You, my little smart-aleck"—Remy gave her a measuring look—"are too cute for words right now."

"Oh Papa." Li'l Bits reddened with pleasure, but then

worry slowly creased the corners of her mouth. "I'm . . ." she licked her lips. "I'm a little scared Papa."

Remy reached over and slid Bits to him across the crinkly, plastic-covered vinyl seat. The pillow he sat on to give him height for driving made him quite a bit taller than Bits, but he nestled her next to his side.

"What's got ya scared?"

"Well, it's just, I've never really been anywhere. The other kids are gonna know more than me. They all probably know each other from growin' up. I only know the cousins, and they won't even be in my class."

"Are you afraid of the learnin' part or just the people part?"

"Mostly the people, I guess. The cousins like school. They're always tellin' me about recess and spelling bees, eating in the big lunch room, and their friends."

"Well, you're a natural at spelling, so that's nothin' to fear. You like to play ball, so recess should work out. You've got a nice peanut butter and blueberry jam sandwich for lunch. Which reminds me, you'd best be careful and use a napkin so jam doesn't get on your pretty dress."

Just then, they pulled into the school parking lot, where Remy was lucky enough to find a spot near the entrance. "I'll walk in with you this morning and help ya find your class. We'll meet the teacher and I can see where your desk is, so when I'm workin', I'll be able to picture right where you're at." He nudged her chin encouragingly.

Li'l Bits took a deep breath. "I can do this," she whispered as she slowly climbed out her papa's side of the car. Remy helped her to the ground, and she nervously smoothed her dress.

"Do I look okay?"

Remy captured her gaze. "You, darlin', are pretty as a picture and smell sweeter than the perfume counter at Penney's." He closed the car door and held out a hand. "Ready?"

Li'l Bits placed her small, trusting hand in his and together, they walked into the unknown.

* * *

Dozens of mothers and children bumped through the school's big main doors all at the same time. Once through the funneled entry point, the crowd fanned out and the classroom was easy to find. They passed the main office and turned right. Li'l Bits's classroom was at the beginning of a long hall that led to the first through third grades. The door to room 118 was decorated with paper flowers, and a plaque above it said "Mrs. Sanders."

Remy went to walk through the colorfully decorated portal but felt a slight tug on the hand that held to Li'l Bits. He stopped and looked down, his eyes asking a silent question: *Do you want to go in?*

Li'l Bits stiffened her spine and trusted that her papa would never lead her into danger. If he was okay to walk in, then she was too. She nodded.

One entire side of the room was taken up by a series of large chalkboards set flush with each other so they looked like a single charcoal expanse. The alphabet, both uppercase and lowercase letters, were written along the top of the boards. Each set of letters was accompanied by a picture of a corresponding object. The wrought-iron based desks were set in three neat rows of seven. Their polished-wood writing surfaces and seats shone in the light that filtered through windows opposite the giant chalkboard. At the front of the room, the teacher's desk sat on a raised platform. To the side of the desk stood a stout, middleish-aged, salt-and-pepper haired woman with a friendly, but potentially stern, face.

There were already a few other children in the room with their parents, taking the lay-of-the-land. Remy noticed a boy and a girl staring, wide-eyed at Li'l Bits while their mothers chatted. His daughter smiled at them. They turned away, so Li'l Bits feigned disinterest. Another girl brightened when she saw Li'l Bits and walked right over.

"Hello," said the bright-green-eyed, brown-pigtailed child. The girl stuck out her hand and waited for Li'l Bits to shake it.

With a gentle hand to the back, Remy prodded his daughter.

Cue taken, Li'l Bits extended her hand and returned the greeting. "Hello."

"I'm Jesslyn Dilbreth. What's your name?"

"Li'l Bits Dubois."

Jesslyn looked dubious.

This response from a child outside their family grouping discomforted Remy. He realized that by not giving his daughter a normal name, he just may have condemned her to a life of teasing. Honestly, they were all so used to calling her Li'l Bits, he hadn't thought about it when filling out the official adoption papers, or even when filling out the school registration form.

"Li'l Bits?" Jesslyn repeated. "Is that a nickname or your real name?"

Embarrassed, Bits said, "I don't really know what a nickname is. So I guess it's just my name."

Remy's adrenaline surged, and little girl or not, he was prepared to defend his daughter against any laughter or ridicule.

Jesslyn contemplated the name and finally said, "You know, I sorta like it. I'm named for my grannies, Carolyn and Jesse. Sometimes at home, they just call me Jezzy. Jezzy's a different name, don't ya think? Like Li'l Bits is different. Were you named for someone?"

Li'l Bits looked at Remy for guidance.

"No, darlin', she was not," Remy said kindly. "When she came, my girl here, was such a bitty thing, my best friend sort of named her by somethin' he said. Since then, none of us ever thought to question it. It just seemed to fit."

With complete candor, Jesslyn stepped back to give Li'l Bits an appraising look. "Yep, I can see that."

With the first introduction out of the way, both Remy and Li'l Bits felt a wave of relief.

"Would you like to see where my desk is?" Jesslyn asked. "See"—she pointed to the desk next to them—"each desk has a name card on it. I can read my name. If you can read too, we could find your desk." Her green eyes went bright. "Maybe we'll be next to each other. That would be fun."

Li'l Bits looked at all the desks. "I don't see name cards on 'em."

Jesslyn looked from the desks to Bits. "Oh, I'm sorry. I didn't . . . the cards are taped on the top. You know what, I'll help you find yours."

"May I Papa?"

With a nod, Remy sent her off.

Jesslyn towed Li'l Bits to her own desk, where she proceeded to show her new friend how to lift the wooden top, revealing the space to keep paper, pencils and books. To the girls' mutual delight, they discovered their desks were right next to each other.

Remy watched the two girls and his heart surged joyfully. His daughter had a friend. Then, his papa-bear ears perked to the sound of snickering. He turned to see that two boys had joined the boy and girl that had been in the room when they entered. One was a pretty tall kid that he didn't particularly like the look of. The four of them huddled together and cast surreptitious glances toward Li'l Bits and Jesslyn. His heart sank, remembering the same glances that had been cast his way when he was in primary school. And he'd thought he had it bad.

He was on the verge of grabbing his daughter to beat a hasty retreat, but an excited Li'l Bits ran to him and tugged at his hand. "Come on Papa. I want to show you my desk. I can even climb up all by myself."

Her excitement bubbled over, and Remy relaxed a bit, allowing himself to be dragged to where Li'l Bits proudly pointed out her very own desk. She also showed him how she and Jesslyn had discovered that part of the pattern in the wrought-iron base could be used as a toe-hold to climb up as she held to the back of the seat.

"And Papa," Bits whispered, pulling him close, "it's a good

thing my desk isn't in the middle row, like Jesslyn's. 'Cause I can climb up on the outside so no one'll see my underpants."

Remy hadn't even considered this being a problem. Boy, there were sure a lot of new things they were both going to have to adjust to.

With sheer delight, Li'l Bits stood on the seat and lifted the desk lid, pointing out her very own pencils, crayons and paper.

"Papa"—she again motioned him close—"do you think you could talk to the teacher about . . ." Oh, how she wished that she could just sit like everyone else and not have her feet fall asleep because the seat was cutting into the back of her calves. She would need a box or stool to prop her feet on, but at least she was tall enough through the torso not to need a phone book or two to sit on. "About, you know." She lifted a leg and pointed to her foot.

Remy got it. "Will do, sunshine. Now, come on." He lifted her from the seat and set her down. "The three of us should go on up and meet your teacher."

Jesslyn and Bits held hands as they walked forward to wait in line to meet the teacher.

The room was beginning to fill with parents and children. Mrs. Sanders was doing her best to greet each grouping personally. While he and the girls waited, Remy scanned the room, noting who was looking where. The four children he'd seen snickering behind their hands seemed to be the only ones who had noticed Bits. Everyone else was busy looking to see where their desks were, perusing the books in the reading nook or being introduced to the teacher.

A pretty girl with red curls bobbed through the classroom door and over to Jesslyn, pulling up short when she saw Li'l Bits. "Oh, hello," she said in a clipped tone.

Remy couldn't tell if the girl was being rude, or had just been taken by surprise at the sight of his daughter.

"Amy Jo!" Jesslyn squealed with delight. "I'm so glad we're gonna be in the same class. And this is our new friend." Jesslyn indicated a now-quiet Li'l Bits. "Bits, this is my best friend, Amy Jo Nolan. We've lived right next to each other our *whole* lives. Her daddy works in my daddy's bank."

Amy Jo didn't look glad to be informed they would now be a trio, but to her credit, she extended a hand of greeting, which a tentative Li'l Bits accepted, thus assuring Jesslyn's happy acceptance that all was well.

"Jess, where's your mama? My ma wants to talk to her." Directing Jesslyn's attention away from the new girl, Amy Jo gestured across the room.

"Oh, she isn't here. She had to run to a meeting, so just dropped me off."

"Well, that's a shame." Amy Jo stuck out a pouty lip. "My mother *really* wanted to see her. Would you come say hello for her? You know how much my ma loves you."

"'Scuse me, Bits," Jesslyn said. "I'll be right back."

"Yeah, sure," was all Li'l Bits got out before Jesslyn was spirited away.

"My, my," clucked Remy. "Two friends and school hasn't even started yet. I'd say you're doin' right well."

"Am I?" With Jesslyn gone, Li'l Bits moved closer to Remy's leg, suddenly feeling very small and alone. "I'm not so sure Amy Jo likes me. She looked at me funny."

Remy crouched down to his daughter's eye level. "Most likely, she'll just need to get a feel for ya. She's known Jesslyn her whole life and just barely met you." Remy hoped his words were true.

The line to talk to Mrs. Sanders inched forward.

"As soon as we meet the teacher, I've got to go. Okay?"

"Okay." As much as Li'l Bits wanted to go back home, she also wanted to be brave, make new friends and learn. Orvalee was always telling her how smart she was, and Li'l Bits didn't want to let her friend down. Smart people learned as much as they could, and a lot of the learning they did was "outside the known," as Orvalee would say.

As she and Remy moved forward, Li'l Bits took in the room the best she could without asking her papa to lift her up. This place was most definitely outside the realm of all she was familiar with.

Standing among the crowd, Li'l Bits was suddenly assailed by a foul stench. She couldn't tell exactly who had let loose, but being well below everyone else's butt-height, she often fell victim to silent, odoriferous attacks.

She scrunched her nose and tried not to gag, noticing that a few other people were also having trouble breathing. At least she wasn't suffering alone. But she *was* positive she had inhaled the greatest portion of the noxious fumes, thus saving everyone else the full brunt of the assault. Oh, to be outside.

It was finally their turn. Up close, Mrs. Sanders had grey-blue eyes that almost matched the grey in her hair. Her ample bosom swayed unsteadily as she stepped down from the dais that raised her desk, supposing this to be more conducive to a proper greeting for one so small.

"Well, hello, my diminutive friend. May I take it that you are *Bits* Dubois?" She said the name as if testing the sound of it. "An unusual name for an unusual girl. I'm quite positive that you will make a *splendid* addition to our class dynamic."

Remy thought that at some point in her past, Mrs. Sanders must have hankered to be on the stage, because she had an over-blown manner that would have suited playing to an audience. "Ma'am." He extended his hand.

In contrast to her strong voice, Mrs. Sanders's handshake was delicate; she daintily pinched Remy's hand and sort of jiggled it, almost like she was tinkling a bell. "And you *are?*"

"Remy"—he decided the nickname was surely too informal for this woman and quickly went on—"ington Alexander Dubois, Li'l Bits's father."

"Ooh, Remington *Alexander* Dubois. Might your father be *the* Alexander Dubois of A & D Oil Supplies?"

Li'l Bits brightened at the mention of her grandfather.

Anxious to contribute, she jumped in. "Yes, ma'am. That's my paw."

"Lovely!" Mrs. Sanders's hand covered her mouth, impressed. "To have the children and grandchildren of our societal paragons *ensconced* in my class is a responsibility I do not take lightly." Her finger wagged at the side of her head like an exclamation point.

The way this woman spoke, Remy wasn't sure the young ones would be able to understand a single thing she said. He hoped she knew how to tone it down, or the kids would be catching some Zs when her back was turned.

Introductions out of the way, Remy escorted Li'l Bits back to her desk. "Okay, sweetie, I've gotta be goin' along. Tuck your lunch box inside your desk, and I'll see you about five o'clock. Okie dokie?"

"Okie dokie, Papa." Li'l Bits offered up the best smile she could muster, hoping it would be enough to bolster her sagging courage.

"That's my girl," Remy said with honest pride. "I'm so excited to hear all about your day when I come get you. So be sure to have lots to tell me."

"I will, Papa."

At the classroom door, Remy cast a final glance over his shoulder and was grateful to see Jesslyn moving toward her own desk. Amy Jo was seated at the back of the third row, nowhere near his girl. For some reason, that made him feel better. With a silent prayer, Remy walked out.

* * *

It was October, and so far, all had gone well for Li'l Bits at school. "The Plan" had been observed and was serving them well. Bits was enjoying homework and her new friend Jesslyn Dilbreth.

Once, Jesslyn had been given permission to walk to Aunt Janelle's with Bits and the cousins after school, where they had milk and cookies while Bits and Jesslyn worked on an art project. Mrs. Sanders had given each student a small bag of dry macaroni and rice in various colors, with the instructions to glue the pieces to a sheet of paper in any pattern they liked.

Jesslyn made something that looked like the face of a clown she had seen in a circus last summer. Li'l Bits had never seen a circus clown, and thought the picture was actually a little scary. But she would *never* say that to Jesslyn because she didn't want to hurt her feelings.

Li'l Bits tried to recreate the look of Spanish moss hanging from the trees in front of her house.

Jesslyn leaned in for a closer look. "What's your picture, Bits?"

"This is the moss that hangs like curtains from the tupelos in front of my house. Our porch goes right out over the water. I love seein' 'em every day."

"I don't know that I've ever seen curtains quite like that. The only water I spend much time around is the water in our swimmin' pool."

"Well, I've never seen a swimmin' pool, except on the television. Jack Benny jumped into one, not knowin' that it was empty 'cause people were cleaning it." Li'l Bits started laughing as she remembered the episode. "And he"—she chuckled again—"he landed right smack in a bucket. The only water in that whole dang pool was in the bucket he landed in. Butt first! There he was, stranded like a crawfish in a net, callin' to the pool cleaners to get him on out. That still makes me laugh. I hope you've got more water in your pool than that."

Jesslyn laughed because Li'l Bits was laughing. "Well, I should hope we do. Can you see me doin' a cannonball into a bucket? That's like trying to throw a bowling ball into a bottle."

"If you were Bugs Bunny, you could do it. That crazy rabbit can do anything."

"I like how he can hang above his hole and do a swan dive right into it." Jesslyn stood on her chair, then did her best Bugs

Bunny impersonation as she jumped off the chair and onto the floor.

"Drat!" she said.

"What's wrong?" Li'l Bits asked.

"No hole." Jesslyn shrugged comically.

Li'l Bits laughed.

The rest of that afternoon sped by. That had been one of Li'l Bits's favorite days.

Today, well . . . October fifteenth would not be remembered so fondly.

When Li'l Bits walked into class, there was no Jesslyn. Mrs. Sanders spotted her from the teacher's desk and said, "I'm sorry, Bits, but Jesslyn's mama called the school to say that the poor mite was laid low due to a bad head cold and wouldn't be here for at least a couple of days. She specified that I make sure you know."

Li'l Bits wasn't sure why, but she moved to her desk carrying not only a heart heavy with worry over her friend's health, but a cloud of dread as well. Climbing to her seat, she looked around the room. Without Jesslyn around, the faces she'd seen for over a month now all seemed like strangers.

Ellie June did offer a friendly wave, but everyone else pretty much ignored her. Everyone, that was, except Rudy Galbraith, or *Moody* Rudy, as everyone called him . . . behind his back. Rudy was a good head taller than anyone else in the class and at least a year older, too. Li'l Bits was sure the boy must have been held back because he seemed to be dumb as a post. She didn't mean to pass judgment on another, because that wasn't kind, but plain truth is hard to ignore.

Rudy had dark, brooding eyes; scraggly, mud-colored hair that constantly fell in front of his face, and a perpetual scowl tightened his fair complexion. Li'l Bits doubted that even a stocking full of candy on Christmas morning could remove that scowl.

He sat in the middle of the second row, right behind Jesslyn, and without her there between them, Li'l Bits could feel his cold eyes boring into her.

"Who can tell me the answer to the equation written on the board?" Mrs. Sanders's voice boomed. Li'l Bits raised her hand.

"Five plus seven is twelve, ma'am."

"Quite right, my dear. Such a bright child," Mrs. Sanders praised.

Li'l Bits smiled. She would have raised her hand to answer the next question too, but something stopped her. Like being in a rowboat at night and knowing the gators were somewhere out there, watching, hoping you'd fall in the water, she could feel Rudy's eyes on her. Those cold, lifeless, glassy eyes that were more frightening than any gator's could ever hope to be.

The recess bell rang, and Li'l Bits was the last student out of her seat. Bile rested at the base of her throat, threatening to choke her. She had a bad feeling and did *not* want to go outside. She walked up to Mrs. Sanders's desk.

"Mrs. Sanders, ma'am, may I stay in from recess and help clean the chalkboards or sweep the floors . . . anything?"

"Thank you for the offer, but children need their physical ministrations to keep in the pink of health. And besides, *you* can hardly reach the sections of the board that need dusting, now, can you? Run along and go hop scotch or whatever it is you do to enjoy the great outdoors. I shall be here when you return. Scootch off." Mrs. Sanders made a shooing motion.

Li'l Bits left the classroom and walked down the hall, her feet as heavy as her heart had been at the news of Jesslyn's illness. They simply did not want to take her outside. Li'l Bits peered through the big doors. Until today, she hadn't realized that Jesslyn had been like a shield.

Li'l Bits summoned every ounce of courage she possessed and walked outside with a smile pasted to her face. Amy Jo spotted her and gave a small smile, but then she focused on tossing the lagger in her hand. It landed on number five, and

Amy Jo airily bet the girls around her that she could finish the hop-scotch game without stepping on a single line.

Ellie June saw Li'l Bits and smiled but did not beckon her over. Severely shy, Ellie June turned back to her solo game of jacks, and Li'l Bits took a place beneath her favorite red maple, trying to shake the dread that had plagued her all morning. She closed her eyes and listened to the sounds of the other kids playing, imagining that she had just kicked a ball and was being cheered around the bases.

"Here ya are, *freak*."

Tingles prickled up and down her spine. Li'l Bits did not need to open her eyes to know who had just spoken.

"You must have been *really* bad in heaven to have God cut your legs off like that," Rudy said. "My pa says that freaks like you have been cursed. What've you done to be lookin' like you do?" Rudy towered over her menacingly.

Li'l Bits summoned the courage to say, "I haven't done any-thing bad. My nana says . . ."

"Your *nana*? Your high and mighty *rich* nana. She tell you things like you're important? Like she *loves* you. She don't love you. I hate to break it to you, little miss sunshine, but you're a charity case! That's all you are."

Li'l Bits cried out, "I'm no charity case!" She actually had no idea what a charity case was, but if Rudy Galbraith was calling her one, then she knew for darn sure he was wrong.

Her outburst drew the attention of the children closest to them, who stopped what they were doing to watch the con-frontation.

Rudy scoffed. "You're too ugly to be anything else. Look atcha." Rudy moved in close enough to flick the tuft of her sleeve.

Li'l Bits backed a few steps away from the tree, toward the other kids, hoping maybe someone would come stand by her, like Jesslyn would have. "I'm not ugly. No one but *you* has ever said that."

Rudy leaned against the tree. From his casual manner, an observer would never know the tongue-lashing he was dishing out. "I'll clue ya. They've said it. Just not to your face. Or maybe they have, and you just can't hear em' from *all* the way down there."

"What's your problem?" Li'l Bits spouted back at him.

A tension-filled hush fell over the slowly growing crowd of onlookers as Rudy cast a discomposing gaze over Li'l Bits. He might be able to have more fun with her than he thought. The more riled up he got her, the more she would cry when he was finished with her. He thought of how his father would keep pushing at his mother, and then, when she finally broke and started to cry, his father would always take him aside and point out how weak women were. Weakness was to be disdained. Weak people were sissies.

"What'd you say?"

"I asked what your problem is. I've done nothin' to you." Li'l Bits's small chest rose and fell with every quickened breath, but she held her ground.

"It don't matter what you have or haven't done. You're *here*, ain't ya? That's enough. Li'l miss high and mighty. Think you're so smart, answerin' all the questions in class. Your rich friend ain't here to stand for you, now, is she?"

Li'l Bits said, "I don't know what you're talkin' about. And why do you keep goin' on about money? What's that got to do with the price of corn?"

Rudy took a step closer.

Li'l Bits took a step back.

"That's just it, ain't it? The *price* of corn. Your nana and grandpa can *afford* to dress you up. Make you look like you ain't a monkey in a circus."

Rudy turned to a couple of his onlooking chums and nodded. At this signal, the two boys laughed. One said, "Yeah, how much does it cost to dress you up?"

"Prob'ly not much," said the other, "seein' as how they don't need much material to make her costumes."

Rudy laughed at that. "Good one."

The onslaught of verbal abuse continued, and Li'l Bits did her absolute best not to cry. She kept trying to back away so she could escape into the safety of the school. But the gathered crowd had grown too thick to part easily, especially for one as small as she was.

Why was no one saying anything to defend her? Rudy had bullied each of them and Li'l Bits knew they hadn't liked it any more than she did. In fact, she remembered Jesslyn standing up to him on behalf of a few of the timid onlookers. Were they paying it forward? No—they remained quiet, afraid, lurking at the periphery of the crowd. If those he had picked on would just stand together, maybe they could give Moody Rudy back a little of his own.

But Rudy, buoyed by his two compadres and the fact that no one else was brave enough to step in, began to feel his oats.

With a little shove to her shoulder, Rudy tested the very little girl who hadn't yet cried. She was tougher than he'd given her credit for. But he could change that.

"Stop that!" Bits yelled at him. "You've got no right to touch me." Her voice quavered slightly as she backed into Ellie June, who retreated, creating space for Li'l Bits to gain a modicum of distance between herself and her tormentor. Li'l Bits looked up at Ellie June with gratitude. A nearly imperceptible smile curved the corner of the girl's mouth.

Rudy closed the gap and shoved Li'l Bits again. This time, Ellie June purposely stepped back into those behind her, silently hoping, in the only way she knew how, to gain an ally that would help her part the crowd so Li'l Bits could make a break for it.

This ally came in the form of Amy Jo, who moved to Ellie June's side and took her by the hand. Step by step, as they backed up, the two girls widened the gap of onlookers.

Locked in his battle of wills with Li'l Bits, Rudy hadn't noticed that a small hole was opening in the wall of do-nothings. Now, the only obstacle between Li'l Bits and escape was the clasped hands of her would-be liberators.

Rudy was beginning to lose his temper with this little blonde-headed . . . rabbit. *Yeah, she ain't nothin' more than a rabbit. Why isn't she screamin' like one?* He could see that Bits's eyes were red, ripe with unshed tears. Her breathing was rapid. Her retorts came out in shaky syllables. But she hadn't caved. She would. By damn, she would.

With Rudy's next menacing advance, Ellie June and Amy Jo broke the seal of their hands, allowing Bits through to open ground.

Feeling nothing but air against her back, Li'l Bits looked up. Two sets of nervous eyes encouraged her. *Run!* they seemed to shout.

Li'l Bits did just that. Mustering all the strength her quaking legs could provide, she turned tail, ran, and prayed.

Having been so focused on his quarry, Moody Rudy was taken by surprise and muttered a quiet curse. "Oh, no, you don't!"

Rudy glowered at the two girls who had enabled the escape and gave them each a mighty shove of frustration. Amy Jo fell hard on her bum and cried out in pain. Ellie June stumbled but managed to remain upright as she clung to the sleeve of one of the do-nothings.

With muttered curses, Rudy made a quick search of the ground and found exactly what he wanted: an irregular, palm-sized rock. With a single toss in the air, like he was flipping a coin, Rudy assessed its weight. His lips quirked into a sly smile.

Despite all her effort, Li'l Bits's uneven, side-to-side gait hadn't covered much ground. Rudy could easily have overtaken her, but where was the challenge in that? *This* would be more fun. To ensure that Amy Jo and Ellie June wouldn't interfere again, Rudy gave them his most menacing glare. He knew he didn't have to worry about the do-nothings.

Rudy focused on the small back of the girl who hadn't cried. "Run little rabbit," he whispered.

Rudy counted to ten and did just as his father had taught him when throwing a ball through the old tire hanging in their backyard. Giving it all he had, Rudy drew back his arm, took aim and fired.

In slow motion, as though waiting to see if the hometown baseball hero's hit would clear the back fence, mouths in the group of onlookers gaped open.

All eyes followed the projectile.

Two high-pitched screams echoed through the disappearing space between the hunter's weapon and his prey.

Like a painted tin duck in a five-and-dime shooting gallery, Li'l Bits went down.

Chapter 9

Be Still

Their search had been fruitless, and now Janelle and Sienna were in a panic. Remy was due to pick up Li'l Bits soon, and their niece was nowhere to be found. Their children said they had waited by the flagpole after school, and when she didn't show up, they had looked everywhere for their cousin. Some of Li'l Bits's classmates had mentioned a kerfuffle on the playground, but no one knew where Bits had gone after that because the recess bell had rung and they'd all high-tailed it back to class.

"We have to," Janelle said to Sienna.

Sienna blew out a pained breath. "I know. But I really, really don't want to."

"Sienna, school got out hours ago. She hasn't been to the Dip-n-Scoop. She hasn't been seen at the art gallery. We've looked at all her favorite places. And besides, you know as well as I do there's no way she'd just up and go off on her own."

"No, you're right. I just can't stand thinkin' of the look on his face when he hears. He trusted us with his precious baby, and . . ." Sienna covered her face with her hands, unable to keep the tears at bay.

Janelle laid a comforting arm across her younger sister's spasming shoulders, but a cold needle of dread stabbed at her own heart at the thought of her brother's potential reaction. Remy treasured his child above all else.

"I'm the oldest. I'll do it." Janelle rubbed a soothing palm up and down her sister's back.

Sienna's tearful sobs had rendered her speechless.

Sucking in a deep, fortifying breath, Janelle picked up the phone and dialed her mother's number. They would definitely need her with them when Remy arrived. No one could reason with Remy like their mother.

That call was like the starting gunshot at a race. After hanging up with Janelle, Lynne Anne immediately called her husband at work, who then ran out to the warehouse to grab George Dollis; the best foreman he had ever employed.

"George!" Alexander Dubois called.

George was busy guiding a forklift driver who was positioning some rig pipes at the top of the storage scaffolding, and didn't hear his boss's desperate cry.

Sans hard hat, Alexander ignored the very safety protocol he had drafted, and ran straight toward George. Arms waving like a maniac, he called out again, "George! George Dollis!"

It was the maniacal gestures that finally caught George's attention. George had never seen Mr. Dubois so out of sorts; it was alarming. With the final placement of the pipe's assured, George turned his attention to the boss.

"Sir, what's the—"

"George." Hands on knees, Alexander Dubois doubled over to catch his breath. "You have to come, now. Li'l Bits,

Remy . . ." The rest was related between puffing breaths as the older man led George to the company parking lot, where Mr. Dubois pulled everything out of his truck's glove box before finding the parish map he was looking for. The two men mapped a grid to cover areas that his wife had informed him still needed to be searched.

George would take the section that included roads heading south-west out of town, towards Remy's house, while Mr. Dubois would canvas a widening arc in the neighborhoods between the school and his daughters' homes. He would knock on each and every door if it came to that.

* * *

Unaware of the mayhem surrounding her little extended family, Trinny Jenks was taking a leisurely stroll as she walked her bicycle through Hughes Park. (A handle bar in one hand, an ice cream cone in the other.) Well, it wasn't so much a park as it was a triangular oasis that filled an irregular space at an inter-section about half a mile from the elementary school.

Licking her peppermint-chocolate ice cream cone, Trinny stopped and read the plaque dedicated to Howard Hughes Senior: "In 1908, this great man convinced the government to locate a post office in the then-named Ananias. He is also the one responsible for having the city's name changed to Oil City."

Trinny wondered if the park's triangular shape had been intended to act as a spearhead of growth in this direction? If so, the design had failed, and now this city gem got little use. That's why she liked it so much.

She pushed her bicycle over to a pretty green, wrought-iron bench that conformed nicely to her tired back. Enjoying the seasonable weather, Trinny savored the double cone from the Dip-n-Scoop. She didn't often treat herself, but today she deserved it. She had *finally* scored a cover at The Ladies' Home Companion. Though she was the best artist that magazine had, her work was constantly overlooked. Trinny knew the oversight had absolutely nothing to do with her talent and every-thing to do with her race. The war had tainted people's perceptions toward the Japanese.

Respected art professionals had said she was ". . . extremely talented, with a gift for depth and perception. Capturing a world of emotion in the stillness of a single moment." Those very words had been written on her last assignment for The Famous Artists School by none other than Norman Rockwell. The man *himself* had actually critiqued her work. The three hundred and fifty dollar tuition for the correspondence school was the best money she had ever spent.

Oh, how she wished she could meet Mr. Rockwell in person. But to know that her work had been judged purely on merit and received such praise, well, it made her feel as though she were floating on a cloud. And now a cover!

Lost in happy thoughts of future successes and what subject matter they would depict, Trinny's senses perked to an unseen . . . something. *What was that?* Head up and alert, like a hunting dog on point, Trinny scanned the small park.

At the north end of the V-shaped walk was a woman with a pram. Nothing out of sorts there. A couple of children rode by on their bicycles, teasing one another. Again, nothing of note. Maybe she was just being overly sensitive and thinking that because all was going so well, there must be an accompanying tragedy to dampen her joy. Yeah, that must be it.

Shake it off, she thought to herself. *Enjoy your big moment and just . . .*

There it was again. Giving the small oasis another perusal, her artist's eye took in all the details. This time, she saw a dog nosing at something in a nook at the base of two enormous landscaping boulders.

"It's probably just smelling a squirrel," she said to herself.

Drawn forward, Trinny got up from the bench, feeling rather than seeing that she was needed. Had the dog hurt its paw? Maybe it's stuck, or maybe . . . Trinny's musing dissolved into a terrified scream when saw what the dog was investigating.

"Bits!" Ice cream dropped, bike abandoned, Trinny sprinted toward the dog, frightening it enough that it ran away, tail between its legs.

"No, no, no!" Trinny wailed as she collapsed beside Li'l Bits's still form. The child was on her side, back to the rocks, hair spilling across her face. Gently tucking golden blonde curls behind a small ear, Trinny whispered, "Bits. Sweet girl. It's Trinny. I'm here."

Li'l Bits lifted her chin and opened tear-swollen eyes, then let them slide shut again.

The most pathetic whimper Trinny had ever heard bled out of Li'l Bits.

Trinny gave the child a quick visual once-over but could see nothing physically wrong. She reached beneath the tiny form to try and hoist her up, but when she touched Li'l Bits's back, the child let out a loud, pained groan. Frightened, Trinny pulled back.

"Sweet heart, what's . . ." Then she saw the blood on her hand.

"Oh, dear Lord." Trinny cupped her clean hand beneath Li'l Bits's neck as she wiped the bloodied hand off on her skirt. "Bits, I need you to open your eyes and keep them open. Bits, can you hear me?"

The child nodded and opened her eyes.

"I need to move you so that I can look at your back, okay."

Li'l Bits whimpered but nodded.

It was difficult to tell exactly what sort of wound it was. A few leaves and some clumps of grass were stuck to the dress in a still-damp, but darkening, spot of blood. Trinny delicately pried at an edge of ripped fabric for a better look, but Li'l Bits arched away from her touch with a sharp intake of breath.

"It's okay. I'll leave it for now. We need to get you home." Wishing she had driven her car instead of riding her bike to work, Trinny puzzled through how she was going to transport the child. Scanning the park, she couldn't see a pay phone anywhere. She supposed she could bike back to the Dip-n-Scoop and ask to use their phone to call for help, but right now she couldn't remember a single number, and besides, there was no way she was going to leave Bits alone, unprotected, on the ground.

"Bits, can you sit up? Would you be able to sit on the seat of my bicycle and hang on to me while I ride us home?"

Li'l Bits weakly shook her head no. "I had to stop here, 'cause when I was tryin' to walk home, it hurt too much to stand up. It's kinda hard to breathe."

Trinny looked from her bike to the child, trying to envision a new plan. "If I have you lay on my back, can you hang on? I'll lean forward as much as I can."

Numb with misery, Li'l Bits said, "I'll try."

"That's all I can ask. If that doesn't work, we'll pray."

Trinny rescued her bicycle and propped it right next to Li'l Bits. "You'll have to help me. I can't lift you to my back without hurting you. Can you climb up?"

"I think so."

Trinny helped Li'l Bits stand, then crouched as low as she could go, her stomach practically touching the ground. She felt Li'l Bits center her weight, and two small arms slowly made their way to her neck. The stifled moans that came as the child moved her arms nearly broke Trinny's heart. What on earth had happened?

Feeling like she was in an egg-and-spoon-race, Trinny carefully rose to a half-bent position. Mounting her bike posed some difficulty and once astride, she had to make sure that as she rode in this bent position, her skirt wouldn't get caught in the chain.

Li'l Bits whimpered, but dutifully maintained her grip on Trinny's neck.

"Sorry, sweet heart. I'm trying."

"I know," came the weak reply. "Thank you."

As battered as she was, Li'l Bits was still the sweetest child.

Trinny pedaled as quickly as she could in her awkward position. But after a few miles, her thighs began to burn to what felt like the point of spontaneous combustion, and she feared that the kink in her back could never be removed. Breath by panting breath, she prayed for the Herculean strength to continue pressing her feet against the pedals. At this point, a snail may have been able to catch up to them, but at least they were moving.

* * *

George—was—frantic. Dismal thoughts paraded through his mind, torturing him as he searched, and prayed that none of the bleak scenarios he was coming up with were true.

"Please, Lord, help me find that baby." Over and over, the words unconsciously crawled up from his panicked heart and across his lips, only to be absorbed by the otherwise silent void of the car. It was nearing six p.m. As per Lynne Anne's instructions, he and Mr. Dubois had agreed to meet back at Remy's by seven if they hadn't found Li'l Bits by then.

The concern he was feeling over how Remy would handle the news of a missing daughter, was compounded by the loss of his own children. It had been a year and a half since Claudine had taken them back to France. George hadn't yet mustered the gumption to pluck himself out his own despair and rejoin them; and for the life of him, he couldn't understand why.

He loved nothing more than his family. He thought of nothing more. He yearned for nothing more.

"*Mon Guerrier,*" Claudine had said. "*You must remember the man your heart leads you to be. Until together the child and the man can stand, you will forever remain at odds with yourself.*"

He never really understood what she had meant, but he was beginning to. The longer he spent time in the place of his youth, the younger he was becoming. More unsure. More vulnerable to the fears of the child he had been. More prone to re-acting to his father instead of trusting his own thoughts and judgment. The man's constant snide and whittling comments were turning him into a simpering puddle of juvenile angst.

Until Claudine left, George hadn't realized how much of a stabilizing force she had been. The only thing that had kept him sane had been Li'l Bits. That blessed child had a spirit large enough to match his own mammoth physique. And right now, the thought of something bad happening to her, was giving rise to an old sense he hadn't felt since the war. And to be honest, despite the fear this reawakening caused, it made him feel . . . alive.

Reign it in, George. Reign it in. You can handle this.

George pulled over and double-checked the parish map that Mr. Dubois had given him. Retracing the routes he'd already searched and re-searched, he noticed a road he hadn't seen before. No one used it much because it headed out of Oil City via Hughes Park. As it was an out-of-the-way little place, he'd only been there a few times. But come to think of it, it wasn't that far from the elementary school. What if?

George swung the car around and headed for the park, repeating his now-unconscious mantra: "Please, Lord, help me find that baby."

With long strides, he was able to cover Hughes Park in a matter of minutes, calling, "Bits! Li'l Bits, are ya here? It's me, George."

Nothing.

The few people that were enjoying the park looked at him quizzically as he peered beneath bushes, behind rocks, and any-where else that a small child could hide herself. Receiving no response to his calls, he sprinted back to the car and headed for Remy's. If he couldn't find her along the way, then he'd just have to wait and see what else they wanted him to do.

With a heart pounding so forcefully that he'd swear it was

actually ruffling his shirt, George scanned both sides of the road and opened himself to whatever wisdom Claudine might dispense if she were here. Imagining his wife in the passenger's seat eased his thrumming pulse, and he was better able to focus on the road.

"What the . . .?" George's question hung in the air. From a distance, what had looked like a large blob of floating fabric, coalesced into a sight that almost stopped his breathing altogether.

A hunched and beleaguered Trinny was balancing a small, still form on her back. Not wanting to honk and frighten Trinny into losing her balance, George pulled off to the side of the road far enough ahead that she would be able to see him and come to a safe stop.

Getting out of the car, George called, "Trinny!"

The woman's head lifted enough that she was able to peel her focus from the road and register that the help she'd been silently praying for had finally come.

Coasting to a stop, she cried in relief, "Oh, George. Thank heaven. Can you take Bits? Be careful with her back. She's injured."

In a voice palpable with concern, George asked, "What happened?"

Trinny's labored breath sawed in and out of her lungs as she tried to catch it. Her thighs burned, and were shaking so badly that she almost couldn't stand still long enough for George to remove Li'l Bits. The feeling of removing her feet from the pedals reminded her of the day she and her family had walked out of the internment camp.

"Trinny, what happened?" George asked again as he cradled the whimpering child to his broad shoulder.

"I don't know, George. I found her as she is, at the base of some rocks in Hughes Park. I couldn't examine her closely without hurting her and there was no pay phone close, so all I could think of was to get her home."

Trying to lift her leg over the bike to dismount, Trinny almost fell over but managed to catch herself. She felt like a wet piece of fabric: completely wrung out.

"Bits," George said soothingly to the child, "I'm gonna lay you on the seat, okay? We'll have ya home and safe in no time."

Li'l Bits nodded. "Okay. I'm so tired from hangin' on to Trinny."

She found the most comfortable position was to face the back of the seat so that nothing touched her wound.

George grabbed a blanket he kept in a box in the trunk for family picnics, a habit he had thankfully decided not to break, and used it to pad the girl's stomach so that she could slump over it. With little effort, he put Trinny's bike in the trunk and tied the lid down while Trinny hobbled to the passenger side and climbed in, grateful for the respite. Rubbing her palms up and down her burning thighs, she tried to calm their twitching. She would need a very long soak in a hot bath.

George finally climbed behind the wheel and kept his desire to peel out and burn rubber under control. Li'l Bits had obviously had enough jostling for one day, and one look at poor Trinny told George that the last thing she needed right now was more questions. So he let her slouch into the seat and close her eyes.

They quickly covered the few remaining miles to Remy's.

Trailed by a still-wobbly Trinny, George gently carried Li'l Bits into the house, where Lynne Anne and Orvalee had been anxiously awaiting word from any of the searchers.

Orvalee had come prepared with her medical bag, hoping against hope that it wouldn't be needed. Seeing Bits cradled against George's chest and the torn, bloodied fabric between the child's shoulder blades, Orvalee's back straightened and her military training automatically kicked in.

"Lynne Anne, gather Bits's blankets into a small mound on her bed. George, when that's done, drape Bits on her tummy over the mound. Trinny, I need ya to bring a basin of warm water, some soap and a clean rag to Bits's room."

Orvalee followed Lynne Anne and George, cautioning, "Don't jostle her too much as you put her down."

"I know," George snapped peevishly, then apologized. "Sorry, Orvalee, I'm a bit done in."

"Lynne Anne, can you scootch that little chair on over here? I'll need it for a makeshift table."

Trinny walked slowly into the room, trying not to slosh water over the side of the metal wash basin. "Is this too much, Orvalee? And I just grabbed the bar of soap by the kitchen sink. Will that do?"

"The water and soap are just fine, thank you. And George, no worries. I've snapped a nose or two off in my time."

With their tasks done, they all stepped back to give Orvalee room to work. She soaked the frayed, blood-stained fabric around Li'l Bits's wound until it came away with no resistance. Li'l Bits started breathing heavily and tears leaked from her eyes.

Lynne Anne knelt by the bed to soothe her granddaughter. "Darlin', you are bein' so brave, and I'm very proud of you right now. You know that Orvalee would never in a hundred years do anything to hurt you, right?"

Li'l Bits nodded and sniffed.

Without a word, Trinny grabbed some toilet paper, leaned in, and gently smoothed the tissue along the half-moon curve beneath Li'l Bits's eyes.

Li'l Bits looked at her appreciatively.

Lynne Anne gave Trinny's hand a quick squeeze of gratitude, then turned back to Bits. "You good now, baby girl?"

Li'l Bits nodded.

"All right then. I need you to hold real still. Pretend we're playin' hide-n-seek and you don't wanna to be found, okay."

"Okay. I'll try."

With the fabric no longer stuck to the skin, Orvalee ripped

the dress so she could get a good look at the wound. The gash was deep enough that she could see the subcutaneous layers, but she didn't want to say so out loud for fear of alarming Bits.

Trinny reached out to grip George's arm for support when she saw what looked to her, like a gaping hole in the middle of Li'l Bits's back. With a silent intake of breath, she averted her gaze until she composed herself enough to watch what Orvalee was doing.

George automatically placed a protective arm around Trinny's shoulders and drew her close, as much to comfort her as to help calm the *something* that had begun to reawaken in him. Though he'd seen worse, much worse during the war, he too was in a fight for self-control. Anger can be a great stimulator. Just the spark one needs to come alive. However, the trick is knowing how to apply the patience needed that will transform a wave of anger into one that can be surfed, rather than one that crushes and drowns.

The child could never have done anything to warrant, well, whatever *this* was. George clenched and released his jaw as he did his best to surf the wave.

Orvalee clucked to herself. Removing the fabric had agitated the wound, and it was bleeding again. She doused a large square of gauze with a skunky-smelling liquid and pressed it to the wound, applying steady pressure until the bleeding abated.

Lynne Anne held her granddaughter's small hand as Li'l Bits sucked in a hard breath, trying not to arch away from Orvalee's touch.

Feeling helpless, Trinny and George could only act as silent sentinels, protecting the healing angels as they attended to the child.

"Li'l Bits, I'm gonna be honest with you," Orvalee said. "You need a few stitches, and—"There was a collective gasp of dismay from the adults.

Orvalee harrumphed at the unrestrained sound. "Now, come on, y'all. This news is *not* the end of the world." To Li'l

Bits, she said, "Bits, you're gonna be able to look on this scar as a battle wound. It'll be proof to the world of how brave you are. But I do need to tell you that in order to do the stitches, I need to give you a shot. One that'll numb ya enough so you don't feel what I'm doing, okay?"

Li'l Bits had never had a shot before, so she wasn't sure how afraid to be.

George piped in. "Just a shot? Well, that ain't so bad, is it, Trinny?"

Taking her cue, Trinny added, "No. No, it's not. I've had plenty of shots."

"Why, it just feels like a li'l ole' bee sting," George assured. "Bits, you've been stung before."

Li'l Bits bravely nodded acceptance of that fact, but also remembered that she had not enjoyed the experience.

Outside, George heard multiple sets of tires decimate the gravel drive as they came to a skidding halt. He knew Remy would be in one of those cars, and hot under the collar. Nothing can make you crazier than fear over your child.

Quickly releasing Trinny, he moved to intercept Remy, who would without doubt, be too overwrought to be of any help in the current situation. Li'l Bits needed *calm* support right now, not a blubbering father. After the stitches were in place, he'd let Remy into the room.

Meeting Remy at the front door, George used his massive frame as a cork, stopping all flow through the narrow opening.

"Where is she?!" Remy shouted as he attempted to force a gap in the wall of flesh before him. "George! Get the *hell* out of my way."

When George didn't move, Remy yelled past him into the house, "Bits! Sweet Bits, Papa's comin'." Then, to George, "Move your sorry ass, or I'll—"

"Remy," George said, sternly but calmly, "Orvalee is with her. As are your mother and Trinny. Now, Bits has been—"

"Then I should be too!" Remy had only one volume right now: hysteric.

"Listen, man," George started to say when, in pure frustration, Remy kicked him in the shin. Hard.

With a glint in his eye, George muttered, "All righty, then."

Quick as a bolt of lightning, George scooped Remy up, carried him to the edge of the porch and tossed him out into the water. The adrenaline rush he'd felt at finding Trinny and Li'l Bits hadn't fully abated, so Remy flew a good bit farther than George had intended.

The act of physical exertion released something in George and with a giant intake of breath, he immediately felt better.

Mr. Dubois, Janelle, and Sienna had watched the interaction with bemused enjoyment.

As his son swam toward the shore near where the cars were parked, Alexander carefully approached George, fairly certain that he would not end up in the water.

"If I may, George, why'd ya throw my son into the water?"

"He needed to cool off," was all George said. His intent gaze was focused on Remy, who was dragging himself onto dry land.

Like a dog drying himself after a refreshing dip, Remy shook his longish brown curls. Only, Remy had not emerged feeling refreshed. The spark of light behind his amber eyes shone like a single candle in the darkness, all the more piercing for its solo glare.

Like a small but menacing bear, Remy came at George again. "You big, ole, sorry-assed son of a bitch!"

"Rem, I'm tryin' to tell you somethin' here." George held up a forestalling hand of warning.

"Shit, man. You've gone and lost the right to tell me anyth—" With a loud splash, Remy ended up back in the water. He spluttered to the surface and fixed George with a withering gaze.

A barely perceptible curve crooked one corner of George's

mouth. The fear that had been building since the news of Bits's disappearance, and then the anger at discovering that she had been injured, found release through this unexpected, but highly pleasant, exercise.

Ablaze with curiosity over her niece's welfare and the reason for the circus act taking place before them, Janelle moved to her father's side and hesitantly said, "George."

"Yep," he answered, without taking his eyes off Remy.

"Um, is everything okay?"

"Yep."

Janelle cast an inquisitive glance at her father, who nodded for her to continue.

"George, would it be too much to ask that ya let me inside?"

"Nope."

"Uh, okay, then. I'll just scootch on by." Janelle flattened herself as much as she could to squeak past the tree trunk of a man, who moved just half a step forward for her.

"They're in Li'l Bits's room. Knock soft. Orvalee needs to focus right now."

"Okie dokie." Janelle tried to sound casual, but the cryptic remark left her even more curious. Behind her back, she motioned Sienna to follow through the small gap George had opened up.

To Mr. Dubois, George said, "Ya wanna go in too?"

"Thank you, but no. I think I'd like to stay right here."

"Suit yourself."

It took Remy a little longer to make it back to the porch this time. Seeing that his sisters had been allowed entry, did nothing to improve his mood. "George," he said between clenched teeth. "I have no idea why you're bein' such a jackass right now."

"Ha!" George spat. "It ain't me that's bein' an ass."

Remy looked to his father for support.

Content to be a spectator, the man simply shook his head, held his hands up in surrender and backed away.

"Now, Rem, we've gone best two out of three. Care to shoot for three out of five?" George resolutely folded his arms across his solid chest.

Looking like a nearly drowned cat, Remy dripped as he paced the length of the porch from one end to the other, trying to calm down.

A ripple of shared understanding passed between George and his employer, tethering both tongues as they waited to see what Remy would do next.

Remy seemed to feel the weight of their stares. At the end of the porch near his shop door, he finally stopped pacing and, shoulders stooped, leaned heavily against the wood wall. Completely wrung out, Remy knew that he'd lost. Between the fear that had gripped him when he'd gone to pick up Li'l Bits, only to be told no one knew where she was, and then the conflagration of rage that overtook him when George refused him entry to his own home, he was on the verge of an emotional collapse.

Resignedly, Remy turned, pulled himself up to his full four feet eleven inches, and walked woodenly toward his silent watchers. Embarrassment and shame wrote themselves plainly across his face. He hadn't sworn like that since Bits had come to him. The fact he'd done so in front of his family made the backslide all the worse.

Remy's mind corkscrewed through all that he wanted to say, but in the end, nothing came out of his mouth. Then, to his great surprise, his father stepped forward and wrapped him in the warmest, most loving embrace of his life. Father to father, they finally stood on a level plane.

George drew in a long, shivering breath of relief, and just like that, the tension was over.

Wiping at his watering eyes, Remy pulled away from his father to face his friend. "Uh, George. Well . . . yeah. Sorry about that."

George moved away from his post at the door and sat on

the bench, motioning Remy to take a seat too. "You ready to give a listen now?"

"I suppose I am." Remy sighed as he sat next to his friend.

George told both men all that had happened: about everything Trinny had related and the need for stitches. At this, Remy's back stiffened, but George assured him that Orvalee had things well in hand. Remy had returned at a crucial time for her ministrations, and that's why he hadn't been allowed to bluster like a storm cloud into the house.

George said, "By now, I think it's safe to assume that Orvalee'll have Bits all patched up. But Remy, your child needs to see you calm, okay?"

"Yes, she does." Remy looked down at himself and laughed. "I may need to change my clothes before I see her."

Alexander Dubois stepped forward and picked something moist and glistening out of his son's hair. "I'd add a bath to that list as well, son."

All three men laughed. After the earlier tension, it felt good.

Remy laughed a little too heartily. A laugh that morphed into a silent cry. "I had no idea," he said whimpering. "No idea that you could feel *so* much all at one time." He wiped a cleansing hand across his face to remove all trace of his momentary outburst.

"This whole parenting thing sure takes ya for a ride." Remy leaned on his knees. His entire posture sagged with the sort of fatigue that only comes with the rise and fall of an extreme surge of adrenaline.

The hand of comfort that George laid on Remy's back was warm, and felt good on the water-cooled skin beneath his shirt.

"Son," Alexander said. "I wish I could tell you this was as bad as it's gonna get, but that'd be a lie."

Head still hanging low, Remy said, "I might could use a lie right about now. I'd even forgive an embellishment involving pixie dust and fairy magic."

George laughed and said, "If we're goin' down that road,

I've got some grade-A unicorn poop I'll contribute to make a beanstalk grow."

Alexander Dubois wanted to add something to the fairy-tale-themed humor, but nursery rhymes and fantasy had always been his wife's domain, so he kept quiet.

"Rem," George said with a gentle slap to the back, "are you ready to go see your girl?"

Remy forced his weary neck to pull his head up, straightened his back, and then allowed his eyes to focus on the two men with him. His best friend and his father. The two of them had been through things like this before and survived to live another day. They were men who loved their families in their own fierce way. Men he was just beginning to understand.

With a nod, Remy rose, wrung the remaining water from his shirt tails, smoothed a hand through his disheveled hair and placidly led the way into the house.

Chapter 10

The Great Teacher

October, 1957

"The bravest are surely those who have the clearest
vision of what is before them, glory and danger alike,
and yet notwithstanding go out to meet it."

—*Thucydides (460 BC–395 BC), Greek historian*

---

*I*t was bedtime. Remy was settled, legs outstretched, against Li'l Bits's headboard while his daughter, who was grateful to finally have him all to herself, lay carefully snuggled against his chest. Not that she didn't love everyone that had been there for her, but by the end of the day, it had all been just a little too much.

Her back ached. Her head ached. Her heart ached.

Why?

Why had Rudy hurt her like that?

Mean words were one thing. If he'd just stuck to using his wicked tongue, she could have taken that. Even as young as she was, she understood herself enough to know that what others said didn't matter.

Uncle George and Aunt Claudine had once told her that

most people said mean things because in some way, they were hurting or sick inside. Later, Orvalee had helped her understand a little more by explaining that when someone has a high fever, it can make them delirious—make them so they can't control or don't even know what comes out of their mouths. Sick people just need time and maybe a good healer to help them get better.

Li'l Bits wondered if Rudy was suffering from some kind of sickness. What could make a person she barely knew come after her like that? And then, not satisfied with nearly pushing her to tears in front of everyone; not satisfied knowing all the other kids were absolutely terrified of him, he had physically hurt her. Considering their difference in size, he could have broken her leg with that rock. If it had hit her in the back of the head, he probably could have killed her.

"Papa." Li'l Bits's voice was muffled by the folds of Remy's shirt.

After being allowed to see his daughter and make sure she was all right, Remy had bathed and changed clothes. He was grateful that George had kept him from charging into the house like a wild bull, knowing he would have scared Bits even more than she had been, and *that* would have been a terrible regret.

"Yes, sweetheart."

"I hurt." A tear gently made its way down her cheek. "I hurt in ways I don't understand, and my heart feels close to breakin'."

Remy twined his fingers gently through her hair as he massaged her scalp, then moved to the base of her neck. Index finger and thumb applied light pressure in a circular motion. "How does this feel?"

"Feels nice. Don't stop, but don't go too far down."

"No, sweetheart, I won't. Orvalee explained real well what I need to do to take care of your back. So no worries there. With a little rubbin' and some rest, your head'll feel brand new in the morning. But you're gonna have to help me understand the sort of care your heart needs. Does it need a good talk?

Your favorite ice cream? We could see if there's a good late movie on the television and pop some corn."

As tempting as the options were, Li'l Bits did not want to move. "I think a talk might help the most."

"Okay, you lead the way. Whatever you want to know or talk about, I'll do my best to answer." Remy kept his fingers moving along the base of her neck and the top of her shoulders.

"I've been thinkin' about what kind of sickness Rudy must have to make him do what he did. Not just to me today; he's mean to everybody. No one likes him, but no one stands up to him either, except Jesslyn. She's done it before. I wish she'd have been at school today."

Li'l Bits was at war with herself. Part of her felt that in a way, what had happened was Jesslyn's fault. If her friend hadn't missed school, Rudy would never have hit her with that stupid rock. But another part of her knew that kind of thinking was just plain silly and really selfish. She didn't like feeling selfish and thinking bad things about her best friend.

Then the thought struck that maybe this was sort of how Rudy felt. Were his bad thoughts also coming because he hurt so much? Was Rudy in some kind of pain? Is that what was causing him to be so mean?

"Papa, can bein' hurt make you feel things or do stuff, like, well, things you don't normally do?"

"It sure can, darlin'." Remy unconsciously ceased massaging his daughter's neck as he thought more about the question. His own earlier pain had caused him to lash out in a way he thought he'd overcome. He'd actually kicked his best friend. George had been more than right; Remy had acted like an ass.

"I'm gonna admit something, sweetheart, and I hope you won't think less of me. Before I came in to see you tonight, your Uncle George and I had an . . . altercation out on the front porch."

"What's an al-ter-cation?" Li'l Bits asked without moving her head.

"It's when you have a noisy argument or disagreement with someone, usually in public, which can be embarrassing."

"Oh."

"Well, your hard-headed papa thoroughly embarrassed himself tonight."

"What happened?" Li'l Bits felt like she was being told a fairy tale, only this time, the people she knew took the place of the fanciful characters her papa usually made up.

"When I got to your aunt's house and was told that you were nowhere to be found, well, let's just say I went a bit crazy. Fear of not knowin' where you were jumbled itself with anger at my sisters for not keeping you safe. I was so mad, it made my heart hurt. When I was out lookin' for you, I was thinkin' all sorts of uncharitable thoughts about my loved ones. Thoughts that now make me sad because really, my sisters had nothing to do with what happened."

Li'l Bits gently nodded in agreement. "No, they didn't."

"Once I calmed down, I knew that too. But at the time, my heart hurt too bad to think straight. Even though everyone that possibly could was out lookin' for ya, I was mad at every single one of 'em. And you don't have to tell me that was plain silly, because I am well aware of that now."

A strong snort of self-derision rocked Remy's chest so abruptly that it jostled Li'l Bits, who winced at the movement. "Oh, baby girl, I'm so sorry." Remy began massaging her neck and shoulders again apologetically.

"That's okay."

"You are the best, most wonderful daughter a man could hope to have, sweetheart. And I guess that's why I went loco at the thought of something bad happening to you. When I got home and your ever-lovin' uncle wouldn't let me through my own door, well, rather than listen to what he had to say, all I could think about was gettin' to ya. And there was that moun-tain of a man, stoppin' up my door like a cork in a bottle, so, I kicked him in the shin as hard as I could."

Li'l Bits exhaled an audible gasp of surprise. "You did! What'd he do?"

"Well, he picked me up and tossed me right into the water, like a beanbag into a cornhole game."

Li'l Bits lifted her head in surprise. Though the movement caused her back to stretch and pull against the stitches, she just had to look into her papa's eyes to make sure he was telling the truth.

Seeing her incredulity, Remy swore an oath, "Cross my heart and hope to die if I'm lyin'. That's exactly what he did."

"Then what did you do?"

"Well, to my eternal shame, I said some things I shouldn't have and tried my hand at gettin' past him again."

"Did you make it this time?"

"No, darlin'. I did not. I ended up back in the water. By this time, I think Uncle George had worked a bit of his own fear out by using me as a hay bale, and we all—your paw, uncle and I—were able to state our piece. After that, I was finally allowed to see you."

Despite the jolt of pain it caused, Li'l Bits couldn't stop herself from laughing at the picture her papa had just painted.

"Oh, Papa, don't make me laugh. It hurts."

"I'm sorry, sweetheart." Remy rubbed above and below the stitches to relax her laughing muscles. "But I'm glad you're seein' the good side of what happened and not thinkin' bad of me. Now, I'm not real sure what sort of pain, if any, Rudy has goin' on in his life, but to answer your question, yes—bein' hurt and feelin' angry can make you do all sorts of things a body might not normally do."

Li'l Bits thought about this. "Papa, I think I'm ready to go to sleep now."

"You sure? Has talkin' helped the hurt in your heart? Because we can keep going if you want to. We can even get that ice cream."

"No, thank you. My heart's not pounding as hard. Now, all

I feel is tired." As if to make the point, her mouth gaped open in a giant yawn, one that made Remy yawn as well.

"See what you did. Now you've got me doin' it too," Remy teased as he eased her from his chest and onto the egg-shaped pile of blankets. "How's that? Feel okay? Do you need another pain pill?"

"No. I'm not feeling too much right now. Thank you for the story, Papa. It really helped."

Remy smoothed hair back from her face as he bent to give her a goodnight kiss on the forehead and carefully cover her with a blanket. "I'm so glad, sweetheart. And I'm glad you know the truth of it, 'cause I have a feeling that your uncle is not gonna let me live that one down any time soon. Now, if he gets to tellin' you *his* version of what happened, you feel free to set him straight since you've already heard it from the horse's mouth."

Li'l Bits gave him a tired smile. "I will, Papa." And with that, she closed her eyes and was fast asleep.

* * *

Due to the position of her wound and the amount of strain the area would have to bear, Li'l Bits's stitches required a good nine days before they were ready to be removed. And in between frequent visits from friends and family, Li'l Bits had a fair amount of alone time to ponder what had happened. Doing her best to draw on everything she'd been taught about right and wrong, forgiveness, and turning the other cheek, Bits struggled to put things in perspective.

During her visits, Orvalee had plied the child's back with salves and herbs to help the bruises heal and to ease the pain. Each time she'd had to look at the wound, Orvalee wished she'd sensed more when she'd had the feeling that a trial of some sort was coming for the child. She could never have imagined anything like this.

She and Li'l Bits had been able to have some very good

conversations while Remy was busy in the shop. Conversations that continued to help Bits reassemble her jumbled puzzle of feelings.

"Child, do you remember when we were in my greenhouse talking about heart and mind thinkin'?"

"About how you can go farther and faster usin' two parts than if you just use one alone?"

"Yes, child, that's right. I'd like to know what your *mind* thinks about the boy who did this. And how you now feel about your friend who wasn't at school that day. I remember you mentioning that you were tryin' not to be mad at her too."

Li'l Bits twisted her mouth from side to side as she thought. "My mind really, really wants to hate Rudy, and his friends too. They're nothin' but littler rocks to his stone."

Curious, Orvalee asked, "What do you mean by that?"

"Well, yesterday, Papa made a place for me to sit outside under my oak. He laid a blanket on the ground and padded me with pillows. He left the door to the shop open so he could hear if I called out for anything. But I didn't." She smiled proudly.

Then, Li'l Bits seemed to go inside herself as she spoke. "I just sat there, feelin' so many things all at once that it began to hurt my insides. I did my best to ask nature to help calm me down, like Papa taught me, and then I saw the rocks. Big ones, little ones, round ones, flat ones. All different colors. Different . . . They're all *different*, but they're all rocks. Some would be easy as pie to pick up, even for me; others'd be a chore. I kicked a few different sized ones into the water and they each made a splash. You could see the ripples from the big ones better than the smaller ones, but they *all* made a ripple."

Li'l Bits remained focused on that inner place of remembering. "I don't know who Rudy's friends were, and they may not have thrown a rock at me, but I can still hear what they said. I still see the ugliness on their faces as they laughed at me. I even think that if they hadn't been so willing to follow Rudy, like puppies on a leash, he might not have been brave enough to throw that rock."

Li'l Bits's eyes shone with emotion and she sucked on a corner of her upper lip. "A stone is a stone. Little or not, when one is tossed at ya, you feel it."

"Have you been able to look at these boys and do any heart thinking yet?" Orvalee asked softly.

Li'l Bits released a short burst of breath. "Yes."

When Bits said nothing further, Orvalee prompted, "And is it okay for me to ask what that part of you thinks?"

"I don't really want to listen to that part just yet, 'cause it's telling me somethin' I don't want to hear." Li'l Bits folded her arms solidly across her chest, readying herself for the adult reproof she knew was coming.

Orvalee smiled at the girl's honesty and reached out a loving hand to gently pat her small, quavering shoulder.

"I think," Orvalee said slowly, "that that's okay . . . for now. But child, don't let the dark colors paint over all your bright, happy ones. Do you remember how we can use the darkness?"

Li'l Bits relaxed when the expected lecture on forgiveness didn't come, and was able to remember their conversation from before, about the sad thoughts that had covered Orvalee like a heavy blanket. "We can use our dark thoughts to paint shadows that hide a secret place to put treasure. Or make a shady spot right in the middle of a sunny patch."

Orvalee bobbed her head with pleasure. "That's right child. You are so right. See, you're a smart girl. You'll know when you're strong enough to let go of hatin' those boys. Now, how do you feel about your friend?"

At the mention of Jesslyn, Li'l Bits's cheeks flushed with embarrassment. "I should never, never, ever have thought anything mean about Jesslyn. Amy Jo called and told her about everything. Oh, Orvalee." Li'l Bits seemed more emotionally overcome now than she had been when talking about the abusive boys.

"When Jesslyn called me, her poor voice was so gravelly. Sort of like Paw's, when he tries to sing. She sounded all croaky and her voice quit on some of her words, but she told me how sorry she was about what happened. Just listening to her made me feel bad, and I knew there was no way she could have been to school that day. I shoulda been the one takin' care of her, and I told her so. Papa says that when she's recuperted, we can go for a visit."

"Do you mean, *recuperated*?"

"Does that mean when someone is over feelin' poorly?"

"Yes, darlin'."

"Well, then yes." Li'l Bits had a thought that put the light back in her eyes. "Hey, Orvalee, could I take her some of your throat brew? It works a wonder, and I want her to have the best."

"Yes, child, you're more than welcome to a bottle of it. I'll bring one over when I come tomorrow."

"Could we put a bow on it? That way it would be more like a present and not so much like medicine."

"I think a bright yellow bow would look just fine against the brown glass bottle."

With that happy color planted to help overcome the dark ones, Orvalee left the child to ruminate over what picture to color on the card she wanted to make to go with the present.

Uncle George had come over every day after work with either a treat or a small bunch of flowers to brighten her bedside table. With the first small bouquet he'd brought, George said, "I swear on my life, Bits, this bunch here called my name. When I saw 'em, they said, 'George, take us to that beautiful girl on Old Fork Road.'"

Her uncle had said this in a falsetto voice, because that's how he thought flowers would sound and Li'l Bits had liked it. So, from then on, he did voices for all the treats he brought.

Flower voices were falsetto. Chocolates said things in a smooth, deep voice. Penny candy sounded like high-pitched piglets and cookies sounded like chipmunks.

Every evening, Li'l Bits looked forward to her uncle's visits.

Uncharacteristically, Trinny had come every day to play a game with Bits, who discovered that her friend was actually pretty competitive. They would laugh together over the games, though Trinny didn't offer casual conversation nearly as much as George or Orvalee. But remembering how interested Li'l Bits had been in the art on her walls, each time she came, Trinny brought a small sketch she'd done. It was never anything elaborate or fancy, but was always beautiful in its simplicity.

One in particular had Li'l Bits staring at it for hours, trying to trace what looked like a single ink line that Trinny had used to depict the outline of a Parisian Street. Flower-bedecked pots lined the walk to a café with a broad, striped awning over the door. A low, wrought-iron fence surrounded an outdoor eating area that was complete with tables and cloths. Across the street was a dress shop sporting a large carved lintel bearing cherubs and flowery vines. A dressed mannequin was on display in its large front window.

Those first two were the most identifiable buildings. From there, the street and all that lay beyond became a twining jungle of black lines that drew the viewer's imagination to wander after the child chasing a balloon at the end of the road.

Li'l Bits knew that she would keep this picture forever. She pressed it between the pages of her large atlas to keep it from being bent or torn and decided she would ask her Papa if he would make a frame for it.

Li'l Bits thought about her conversation with Orvalee, about how you could see Trinny's heart through her work. Tracing a reverent finger along the ink lines that drew her eyes off into the distance, it struck her again just how beautiful Trinny was.

Chapter 11

A New Day

"We must embrace pain and burn it as
fuel for our journey."

*—Kenji Miyazawa (1896–1933), Japanese novelist,
poet of children's literature, agricultural
science teacher, and cellist*

It had been two weeks and Bits was ready to go back to school, at least physically.

Remy coaxed his groggy child awake. "Bits, come on, my girl. Today's the day."

When she had first started school, he'd been anxious and unsure about how things would go for her. Today, he knew things would be different. Much different.

He had already been to the school for a little "chat" with the principal, Mr. Judson. Mrs. Sanders and Rudy's parents had also attended. Mr. Judson had been at a complete loss as to how a thing like this could have happened at *his* school. Upon hearing the extent of the damage done to Li'l Bits and the need for stitches, they were all horror-struck.

"Mrs. Sanders!" Mr. Judson had demanded. "How could

you not have reported that a child went missing from your class after recess?"

An abashed Mrs. Sanders said, "Oh, I don't know. The children returned from recess acting like little angels. So quiet and attentive. A teacher's dream, they were. The child"—she couldn't bring herself to say Li'l Bits's name—"had been reticent about even wanting to go out to play. I thought perhaps she was simply pouting in a corner somewhere over my having propelled her out the door. But honestly, what child doesn't love to be outdoors and run to their little heart's content? Oh, I suppose I didn't want to upset the apple cart, so to speak."

Dissatisfied with the instructor's response, Mr. Judson firmly stated, "We *will* discuss new protocol later, Mrs. Sanders. As for Rudy, he will be suspended from school for a month! His academic performance is not to fall slack, so he will be given assignments to complete at home. He will also be required to report to the school each day *after* hours, where I will *personally* escort him on garbage cleanup duty for *all* the playground areas."

At the pronouncement of the penalties, Mrs. Galbraith wrung her slender, bloodless hands tightly as she solemnly nodded. Without meeting anyone's gaze, in a thin voice, she said, "Thank you, Mr. Dubois, for not involving the police, and allowing us to work things out privately."

Mr. Galbraith shifted his beefy form, and Remy saw Mrs. Galbraith wince as she tucked her shoulder in, as if preparing for a blow. The big man did not look happy. Judging by his demeanor, Remy would bet the man's displeasure was not so much due to the fact that Li'l Bits had been hurt but rather that his son had been caught.

"I'll make sure my boy don't *ever* do anythin' like this again," the burly man had assured.

Remy had taken a good look at the man. He had the physique of a boxer gone to seed. Remy would have bet that in his younger days, he'd done a bit of bare-knuckle fighting. Those hands could still crush a man, or a boy. Quickly sizing up the potential situation in the Galbraith household, Remy decided to include a caveat.

"I would like to add," Remy said clearly enough that Mr. Galbraith could not mistake his meaning, "I want *no more* violence done to these children, by anyone. Should I hear of any bruises being reported, any minor cuts, black eyes, or even limping, I will have to call on the police to do a thorough investigation. Maybe even bring in child welfare services to find out just where and when these things are happening. After all, we must make things safe for *our* children and the others at the school, *mustn't we*." He'd said the last words pointedly, looking up at Mr. Galbraith.

The big man had flexed and released his hands, pumping them like a bellows breathing life into a fire. Through gritted teeth, he'd responded, "Yes, we sure *must*."

Remy had graced them all with a beatific smile, knowing it must've been killing this ape of man not to be able to put him in his place.

Thus, assured of a new beginning, Remy was excited for Li'l Bits today. She, however, was not wholly in support of her forced return to school.

"Come on, now, sweetheart. You know I talked with your principal, and Rudy is payin' a price for his actions. He won't be to school for a while yet, but Jesslyn is right as rain and gonna be there. Remember how she said your present healed her up? And you got those nice cards from the other two girls in your class. What are their names?"

"Amy Jo and Ellie June."

"That's right. I believe that in them, you have made two new bosom friends. But you have to let 'em into your heart, sweet thing. Can you do that?"

Li'l Bits remembered how the girls had helped by watching her back. In their own way, they had been just as brave as Jesslyn and done what they could to help her escape. They may not have *said* anything in her defense, but they had *acted* when no one else would.

"Yes Papa. I know my heart can love them."

Still careful with her, Remy lifted Li'l Bits from the bed, sat on its edge and set her on his knee. "Sweetheart, I'm gonna share something with you, something that's taken me quite a while to learn. The heart is a muscle. A big, beautiful muscle that does so much more than just keep the blood movin' through our bodies. And just like arms or legs get bigger when you exercise 'em, I believe your heart gets bigger the more you use it."

Dubious, Li'l Bits said, "Like, as big as Uncle George's arms? He exercises them all the time and they're *huge*. Is that why his chest is so big, so his heart'l fit?"

"No—I'm not talkin' about *that* kind of bigger. The size I mean is more of a, a . . . Maybe magical is a good word to use? Magic can make big things fit in small spaces, like how Cinderella's fairy godmother made a coach large enough to carry a person out of nothin' more than a pumpkin. The original size isn't what matters. What matters is what you can make out of it."

"Hmm—" Li'l Bits chewed on her thumbnail. "I think I getcha."

"Maybe Rudy hasn't had much practice usin' his heart because he hasn't been shown how to do it. So it's still small and not filled with much. But then you have Jesslyn, who uses her heart all the time. You can tell by the way she watches out for others and stands up for 'em."

Li'l Bits definitely understood this point.

"Well, it's taken me quite a while, but I finally understand some things my mama has been tryin' to explain to me for years. The more we use our hearts as we care for others, the more they can hold. They're not limited to enough love for one person, or even just your own family. People who use their hearts can end up lovin' just about everyone they meet. Now, I don't ever tell him this 'cause I don't want it goin' to his head, but your Uncle George is one of the most love-filled people I know. If he weren't, he would never have run through fire to save people he didn't even know during the war."

"I know that. About Uncle George, I mean. I think that's why he's so sad sometimes. You can see it in his eyes. He misses Aunt Claudine and the kids *so* much, 'cause he loves 'em *so* much. I don't know why they just can't be together. I mean, it's simple, isn't it? If you love someone, you should be with 'em."

"From your mouth, sweetheart, to the ears of all adults. May that someday be true. Love is the greatest gift we have, and sometimes adults lose sight of what's truly important. That's why we have children like you, my little button-nosed angel." Remy playfully pretended to capture Li'l Bits's nose, and she made sure to grab it back and put it in place.

"I love you, Papa."

"I love you too, sweet thing. Thank you for teaching me as much as you do."

Li'l Bits wriggled anxiously, so Remy set her down. She promptly ran to her closet to get dressed.

"Why the sudden hurry? Just a minute ago you were draggin' your heels."

"Well, now I want to get to school so that I can start openin' my heart to Ellie June and Amy Jo. And who knows, Papa, the more I use my heart on 'em, *maybe* I'll make even more new friends. I like havin' friends."

Remy could do nothing but stare in amazement at his child. Magic truly did exist. Were it not so, such an expansive heart could never exist in such a small frame.

As he was shooed from the room so Li'l Bits could bustle about in peace, not for the first time, Remy thought of her mother. He had memorized the letter she'd left with Bits. It, along with the rattle, was tucked away in a safe place. He had even kept the bottles the woman had so conscientiously left for him.

She'd said that her story didn't matter. "*What does, is the story I want her to be able to tell when she's grown."* The words swam before him in the form of remembrances. The blue frosting he'd accidentally spilled on Li'l Bits's head just before her first birthday party. Quietly sitting at night on the porch bench as they listened to the water lap at the ground beneath them. Her wide eyes taking in all he did when he had her out in the shop with him. Their Sunday after-church rambles. The same bunch of daisies, carnations and a single rose that appeared every year on Bits's birthday.

What story would this child he had claimed be able to tell when she was grown? In her tales, he knew there would be times when she would think of him as the villain; parents often fill that role. But on the whole, he hoped that she would picture him as a knight. A companion, constant and true, maintaining a place at her side.

And the woman who had borne her? Who had been forced, by means he knew nothing of, to make an unholy choice; a choice he thanked God she had made. She was the fairy godmother in their story. The one who granted wishes. The one who made dreams come true. The one who had chosen *him.*

Chapter 12

Growing Pains

March, 1958

"Confront the dark parts of yourself, and work
to banish them with illumination and forgiveness.
Your willingness to wrestle with your demons
will cause your angels to sing."

—*August Wilson (1945–2005), American playwright*

George awoke with a start, drenched in sweat. His chest heaved as though he'd just run a marathon. Reflexively reaching to Claudine's side of the bed, he nearly collapsed into sobs when he remembered that she wasn't there. Hadn't been for two years now.

What was he doing?

Ever since she left, the dreams had been getting worse, more vivid, and coming all too often. He hadn't known they could be so bad. Hadn't known what a buffer she had been against the pain of remembering, because she'd always just *been* there.

Being back home and living near his family, his father, to be precise, had reawakened memories he thought he'd buried in Europe, next to the bodies of his buddies.

His father's hostile words were landing with no more softness than the bombs he'd faced during the war. They cut no less than the bullets he'd dodged, and hurt even more than the bullets he hadn't.

His buffer, his angel, was gone and he wanted, no—he *needed* her back.

He swiped a hand down his sweat-soaked face then wiped it dry on the bedspread.

He had to move.

If he could move, maybe his limbs wouldn't feel like the shattered remains of the building he left behind in the dream. The building filled with screams of terror and the stomach-turning stench of burning flesh.

George threw back the covers and got up to pace about the bedroom like a caged animal. Sucking in huge gulps of air, he tried to breathe deep and slow his still-pounding heart. But the room was too small.

Ranging about the house, he made a circuit of the living room, kitchen, even the bathroom, ending up in his sons' room. His wonderful, incredible sons. Two years older now, how tall were they in comparison to him? You could only get so much from letters and photos.

Jeremy would be thirteen on his next birthday, and had always been big for his age. Beau, his bright-eyed Beau, would turn eleven next month. When Aline came along, just after they had moved to Louisiana in 1950, she had been an answer to prayer. He had wanted a sweet angel girl. One that could wrap him around her little finger, like her mama had. At seven years old, he wondered if she was growing to look more like Claudine. He hoped so.

"Oh, God," he moaned into his hands, "please, help me."

Church would have to wait for today; he was in no fit state to be there. Right now, he needed to run. Dressing quickly, George bounded out the front door, down the steps and down the road. Leaving behind the dream and painful thoughts, he pushed his body until it protested with every jarring step he took.

Still, he ran—until he couldn't.

George collapsed into a huge, weeping heap in an unfamiliar field. Hot air sawed in and out of his lungs as they struggled to move oxygen to his starving limbs and brain. His nose ran as freely as his eyes, but he didn't care. Curled in on himself, George wept until there were no more tears. No thoughts, save one.

He pulled himself up onto hands and knees, and the pain in his heart escaped in a prayer. "Lord, it's me," he panted. "George. George Lorenzo Dollis." He gracelessly wiped his nose on his shirtsleeve.

"I'm real sorry about that, Lord. I should probably have more manners when talkin' to ya." He raised up onto his knees and cast his gaze heavenward, taking in the golden yellow light of the morning sun. He had collapsed near a lemon verbena plant, and its invigorating scent drew him to break off a few leaves and crush them between his fingers. Holding his hands to his face he inhaled deeply. The natural stimulant helped chase away the last remnants of the dream.

Between the plant and the gentle morning breeze that cooled the air for his burning lungs, both his breathing and heart rate were able to resume a normal rhythm. In silence, George allowed himself the space to simply *feel* a prayer. Without realizing it, his voice joined in.

"Lord, I know I haven't been talking to ya much lately and I'm sorry, because if there was ever a time I was in need, it's now. I don't know what to do. Claudine and my kids deserve the best and I ain't been at my best in . . . I don't know how long. She tried to tell me, but I couldn't see." He wiped his nose again, with the other sleeve this time.

"I used to read the Bible and not understand how those people could be so blind to all the good you'd blessed 'em with. I used to shake my head and call 'em fools, thinkin' they deserved every plague you sent. But I was the one who was blind, and now I've gone and brought on a set of my own plagues."

George managed to pull his heavy form to a standing position, wobbling a little as blood rushed to his head. When he was steady, he started walking back the direction he'd come, talking as he went. "I told her. I told her it wouldn't be good to come here. Why couldn't she have wanted to go anywhere but here? Family, that's why," he answered himself.

"She lost so much during the war. So many did. Communities and families were ripped apart at the seams. Everything gone in a puff of caustic smoke. Family . . ." George stroked the thick stubble on his chin, thinking that Claudine wouldn't like the fact he hadn't shaved in nearly a week.

Family meant everything to her. He hadn't known what that could mean for him until meeting back up with her after September 2, when the Japs had surrendered. Thinking of Trinny, he respectfully amended the militarily conditioned thought to include the full word, Japanese. She was no more a 'Jap' than he was a 'Nigger'. Let those who didn't know who they were surrender to those words. Titles and stereotypes have no place in the heart of someone who knows who they are.

Wait, had he just answered his own question?

"Knows who they are?" he mused aloud. "Knows—who—they—are. Yeah—I don't know who I am anymore."

Before signing up to serve overseas, he had been Mont's son. The youngest one. The *big* one. He had joined the army as a naïve twenty-one-year-old. As the baby of seven siblings and the favored target of his father, he'd thought he'd known what fear was; he'd been wrong. There's nothing like literally being thrown into fire to bring someone up to scratch. But despite the hellishness of war, or maybe because of it, George had grown into himself over there.

His size and strength had proved quite handy when it came to pulling vehicles out of foot-deep mud, clearing roads through terrain where roads were not meant to go, hoisting injured men onto his back, and pulling more than one person at a time out of an inferno. He still had no idea how he'd made it out of that damnable building with nothing more than a burned calf and forearm. Of course, the bullet he'd taken in the lower back on his fourth trip out of the blaze had put a stop to that. They'd been suckered into that place and thank heaven Taylor Johnson had been there to pull *him* to safety when he'd been the one in need.

"Thank you, Lord. I haven't thought on Taylor in a dog's age. I'll have to remedy that."

George began to get his bearings and realized that he'd run a lot farther than he thought he could. Sure, ten years ago, he could have run this distance without much effort, but now, he was old. At least, he felt old.

His mind wandered back to family. Claudine, his own babies, his mother, and his father. He had no idea how a man could choose to marry one of the *best* women on God's green earth and then do nothing but take her for granted.

In addition to the plague of indifference his father had heaped upon his mother, the man had then added the burden of birthing and protecting seven children, while said man did nothing but whine and complain about how hard *his* life was. Why wasn't *he* given respect in his own home? Why was *he* always passed over for a promotion at work? Why was there never what *he* wanted on the supper table?

Why, why, why!

"Why, old man?" George found himself yelling. "Because you're a sorry-ass excuse for a human being. Because you're cantankerous and as sour as unripe grapes. Because ..." George continued to tick off a list of his father's failings, grumblings, and abuses.

It felt good. To finally say things out loud felt oh so good.

George spied a comfortable-looking downed tree and decided to take a load off. He grabbed a cane-length stick and used it to jab and dig at the earth by his feet as he continued the tirade against his father. With each invective, the force behind his jab increased, and the hole at his feet grew wider and deeper until all of a sudden, he felt done. The vitriol was gone.

Between the running, crying, and vocalization, like the sky after a storm, he finally felt clear.

George looked at the stick in his hands and thought of those his father had used on him. Holding it at each end, he cracked it against his shin, breaking it in half. He then broke those pieces in half, and so on until there was nothing left but kindling. He dropped the pieces in the hole he'd made and covered them over with the loose soil. Pounding hard to seal them in their earthen tomb made George feel even better.

Standing, he stretched, twisting this way and that as his back released a series of satisfying pops. The walk home was pleasant, peaceful. But something niggled at him and he couldn't figure out what. By the time he reached his front door, he was still drawing a blank.

Refreshing himself with a cool glass of water, George sat in his favorite easy chair and reached for the TV guide, accidentally knocking the Bible beneath it to the floor.

He chuckled. "All right, Lord. I get your meaning."

Doing as he had always done when he had nothing particular in mind to read, George held the book between his hands and simply let it fall open. Proverbs. He liked Proverbs. He was immediately drawn to a verse that was already marked. Chapter 26, verse 20: "Where no wood is, there the fire goeth out: so where there is no tale-bearer, the strife ceaseth."

He read and re-read the verse until the missing piece of his cathartic exercise revealed itself, and he knew what needed to be done. The same thing Claudine had been encouraging him to do all along: confront his father.

And now, he felt man enough to do it.

Chapter 13

It's About Time

George stood outside his parents' home listening to the raucous noises coming from inside. Some of the younger children were arguing over something, while others were laughing. Adult voices could be heard bouncing between disciplining the kids and trying to hold a conversation.

His twelve-year-old nephew, Ralph, tore out the front door, knocking the paint-peeled screen door askew on its ancient hinges. Close on Ralph's heels were the ten-year-old twins, Leah and Lucy. Seeing their uncle standing there, all three kids stopped short. The girls' momentum carried them into Ralph's back.

Eyes wide, mouths gaping open, none of them spoke.

With an easy, relaxed smile, George tried to put them at ease by saying, "Afternoon, Ralph. Leah, Lucy, I hope you're not lettin' this young man get away with any mischief."

Ralph simply bobbed his head in greeting.

In unison, the girls said, "No, sir."

"Is everyone here today?" George asked.

The children bobbed an affirmative.

"Well, for better or worse, I guess that's how it's supposed to be."

Two more children tried to come bounding out but were slowed by the non-compliant, off-kilter screen door. Five-year-old Jefferson came alight when he saw his Uncle George and ran straight toward him.

George bent down and scooped the child into a hug. "Well, hello, little man. How are you this fine Sunday evenin'?"

"I'm fine. But are you posta to be here?" Leaning in close so that only his uncle could hear, Jefferson whispered, "Paps said that if you was stupid enough to show your face round here, well, he was gonna show you what's what. They don't think I hear 'em talkin', but I do. I hear everything."

"I'm sure you do." Setting Jefferson down, George smiled and ruffled the boy's hair affectionately. "And I guess I am just stupid enough to come round one more time."

"Do ya think you're gonna get it? Reverend Marrs is over. Paps ain't in the best mood," Jefferson warned.

"Is he ever in a good mood?"

Jefferson thought on this, then said matter-of-factly, "Nope."

"Then I guess now's as a good a time as any to show my face." To all the children, George said, "It might be the last time ya see me, so, well, I guess I just want to let you know, I love you. Love all of ya. If I don't get the chance to say that to the others, you let 'em know for me. Okay?"

All five children bobbed their heads as the tension left their shoulders. Jefferson took his uncle by the fingers and drew him closer to the porch, where George was able to scoop all the children into a crushing hug. George hoped it would not be for the last time.

The moment of truth had come.

Content with his choice, he would now discover where the rest of his family stood.

Ruth, the sister just older than George, came out to the porch, saying, "You kids get back on in—" She ran smack into the immovable screen door and caught the curse that wanted to come out, amending it to, "Dagnabit! This old thing needs a good—" Her eyes landed on George. A brief smile lit her face, then was extinguished by a look of fear as she cast a quick glance back inside.

Sidling past the obstinate screen door, Ruth practically tiptoed toward George. "What are you doin' here?" she whispered.

"I'm here to see you." George smiled affectionately.

Ruth's face softened, revealing the beautiful woman George had always thought she was. It was remarkable how a creased brow, tense jaw and pursed lips could alter one's face. Relaxed, she was a flower. Tensed up, a thistle.

"Paps isn't in—"

"The best mood," George finished for her. "Yeah, our little man Jefferson already warned me. But honestly, Ruth, that's not surprising."

Her eyes grew sad. "No. No, it isn't. But God Almighty, George, every time you come, it's like purposely pokin' a bear. It's fun for a minute, 'til the beast wakes up. Then, all hell breaks loose, and there ain't no cover to be found."

With a look of resignation, George admitted, "Yes, I know. And *that* is why I've come. To put an end to it."

"End it?" Ruth looked nervously back into the house, knowing she was taking too long. Shooing all the children inside, she admonished them to mind their p's and q's and *not* mention their uncle was here, then turned back to George. "What you talkin' about?"

"To be honest, I know what I want to say." His shoulders rose and fell with a heavy sigh. "But I have no idea what's actually gonna happen. So, my advice would be to step back, hold your peace, and if need be, when the shrapnel starts flyin'—run."

At the panicked look on his sister's face, George said soothingly, "Let no worries darken that pretty face of yours. I'm a big boy. He can't hurt me any more than he's already done. And hopefully, he won't be botherin' the rest of you anymore, either. Least ways, not on my account. Beyond that, it's up to y'all."

Ruth looked skeptical.

George quietly shooed her. "Head on back in. Daddy'll be wonderin' what's kept ya. Don't let on you've seen me. I'll wait a spell before knocking so no one'll think you kept mum or have taken a side."

"Be careful, George," Ruth said. With a quick hug, she disappeared through the door.

George strolled back down the lane, regathering his wits. He hadn't planned on running into anyone before confronting his father, so had been thrown off his stride. Knowing that Reverend Marrs had come to call and would witness whatever happened did nothing to calm the butterflies in his stomach. In fact, they seemed to be migrating up around his heart. Rubbing at his chest to break up their little colony, George again thought of the scripture that had glued his puzzle pieces together.

Both he and his father had been fuel for each other's fires ever since he could remember. The time had come to remove the woodpile and stop telling tales on one another. Maybe it was good that his entire family would witness what he had to say. This way they'd know the truth of it, and not have to rely on whatever version his father chose in the retelling. God must have guided both him and the reverend to act on the same day.

George took a deep breath and loosened his neck. All he could do was let go of his part in the drama. If his siblings and mother chose to keep allowing themselves to be pawns in his father's warped game, well, that was on them. He would have to content himself with the knowledge he had done his best.

And then?

Then, he would go get his family.

George again approached the door to his father's home. The home he had been born in. The home he had grown up in. A home that he may never see again. Gently lifting the ancient screen door so that he could swing it fully out of the way, he told himself to shake off the shackles.

George stepped up to the door and gave it a solid *thump*.

You could have knocked his mother over with a feather when she opened the door and saw him standing there.

"Hello, mama." George said warmly. "Sorry I missed church this mornin'. Had a lot on my mind."

He could see anxiety written on her face as he bent down to give her a very warm, very long embrace. Despite the numerous pairs of eyes boring into her back, Mary Dollis sank into her son's arms, breathing in the scent of lemon verbena that still clung to him.

"Evening, y'all. Hope you've had a pleasant Sunday." Feeling as out of place as a priest in a brothel, he cast a meaningful glance at each of his siblings.

Miriam was the oldest. At just forty-four, it pained George to see how ancient she looked. Sadly, she had married to get away from the house, going about it so quickly that she failed to see she'd landed in the same boat as their mother.

Rachael was next in line and the shame of her father. Another girl. Mont just couldn't get over the disappointment.

Henry was third born and his father's pride and joy. Sadly, he had been so coddled by their father that he'd turned out just like the man. But George tried to understand that in a way, that wasn't Henry's fault. His brother had been pigeon-holed, just like he had. Like all of them had. No matter the name they bore, their father had labeled them all: Disappointment, Weakling, Golden Child, Rebel. And once labeled, as far as that man was concerned, the designation would be on their toe tag as well.

Charles and then David had come, adding frosting to their father's male ego-filled cake and redeeming their mother. Three *boys* in a row. Mont would have been content to stop having children there, but Mary had to go and get herself pregnant with yet another girl. George's best friend, Ruth.

Taking after their mother, Ruth was one of the sweetest people he knew, and she'd managed to do better in the husband department than Miriam or Rachael. Thank heaven for that. But Ruth tended to take on more of the family drama than she should. Especially on *his* behalf. Hopefully, that would end today.

By the time *he* had been born, his father was so over having children that despite being a boy, George had been seen as nothing but a pest. And the more he grew, the nastier his father had gotten toward him. The last time his father had tried to whoop him was the day George had finally had enough and fought back. At that time, he was neither taller nor heavier than his father, but he was angrier, and that was all he had needed to be.

Though Mont would never admit it, that was the day he'd become frightened of his baby boy.

A boy of fifteen who should not have had the power to overcome him.

But George had.

A boy whose eyes should not have been so filled with pure hatred that they flamed.

But George's had.

A boy who, from that day forward, had become very cognizant of just how powerful anger can make you. And had been equally cognizant of how much he did not want to lose control like that again. Because that would make him just like his father.

"George." Reverend Marrs rose and crossed the room, arms outstretched in greeting. "Wonderful to see you again. Wonderful."

George extended one hand, keeping his other arm around his mother's shoulders. "A pleasure seein' you too, sir."

With a broad gesture, Reverend Marrs took in the room, saying, "A family come together is a family strengthened." Turning back to George, he said, "I was beginnin' to wonder if you were gonna make it this evening."

George gave him a blank look.

"Why, haven't you come to join in the family blessing?"

George looked embarrassed. He had no idea what the reverend was talking about.

Apparently, Mont Dollis hadn't been inclined to invite his youngest son.

Despite that oversight, the reverend amiably drew George into the room, saying, "Not to worry, Brother George. This year, I've set a personal goal to gather with each family group on an individual basis. In this way, I can offer a blessin' specific to your family's needs and wants. With as fast as our congregation is takin' the Lord's admonishment to multiply and replenish the earth, why, this is my attempt to keep up." The reverend gave George a wide, pleasant smile.

"Well, sir, when a flock has a shepherd as able as you, they can't help but be filled with the spirit of renewal and replenishment."

Reverend Marrs let out a hearty laugh that lifted the spirit of the room.

Mary Dollis looked at the faces of her children, delighting at the change that had come over most of them. Even her grandchildren seemed more relaxed with George in the room.

But then, there was Mont.

Her husband had not wanted George to come, and if looks could kill, her baby boy would have been reduced to a pile of ash and left to blow away in the wind.

Mary stepped in closer to her son's side and his arm tightened around her shoulder. She was surprised to feel his arm quiver, and she knew that George could see the hatred coming from his father. She didn't understand it, but the older her husband got, the more discontent he became. Her poor son had become the symbol of all that her husband felt had gone wrong in his world.

Reverend Marrs said, "Well, George, come on in. Sit. We've just been discussin' the Good Book and how it can be used to answer our questions. Your brother David was kindly relatin' an example of something that happened a few weeks ago. Brother David, would you care to continue?"

David cast a surreptitious glance at his father, who had not taken his eyes off George. "Uh . . . Reverend, I'm sorry to say that I, uh, forgot where I . . . I forgot what I was sayin'."

"That's quite understandable, Brother David," Reverend Marrs reassured him, wishing he could assure himself of what to do next. Mr. Dollis had this family so tightly wound, he'd bet the Christmas sermon that you couldn't squeeze a quarter between the butt cheeks of anyone in this room right now.

"Sir, if I may?" George stepped away from his mother. "I have a story to relate that goes right along with what y'all were talking about, and it happened this very morning."

"Praise be, Brother George. Please, share." Reverend Marrs stepped toward Mary Dollis to take George's place at her side.

"Well . . ." George focused on the pair of hard, unkind eyes that bored into him, and smiled. Remembering that strength can almost feel like fear, he drew comfort from what he was about to do and pressed on.

"This morning, I . . . wrestled with some demons, wantin' to understand how and why they held me captive." George wiped a sweating palm on his pants as he gave Ruth a perfunctory glance. With a nearly imperceptible nod of the head, she encouraged him on.

"I went outside, where I found myself in a place I hadn't been. Sometimes, I think that's how it goes. We have to travel to the unfamiliar in order to find what's been right beneath our nose."

Mont exhaled a short snort of disgust and folded his arms securely across his chest, but otherwise remained silent.

"Sometimes, our answers come on the blessing of a breeze. And other times, it's like our very soul has to be stripped from the flesh to be cleansed before God can put the answers in an uncluttered place they'll be seen. That strippin' process, well, it's none too pleasant."

Reverend Marrs raised a hand to heaven in a silent amen.

Ruth got up and walked over to stand beside her mother, where she was taken beneath the woman's wing in a gesture of comfort.

Knowing that now was the time to bare all to his family, George stood before them, not as the youngest, not as a target, but as a man. A full-grown adult and a father in his own right. A man who had seen things they could never imagine. Things he was grateful they would never understand.

"I'm not ashamed to say that I cried. Like a baby. I cried for missin' my wife and children. I cried for the fact I'd let 'em go. Cried for all the wrongs I've done, mistakes I've made, and things left unsaid." George inhaled a steadying breath and leveled an unwavering gaze upon his father.

Ruth's two children, Abe and Catherine, moved to stand beside their mother, and she stroked both of their heads. It was like those in the cramped room were beginning to sense lines being drawn in the sand. As George continued speaking, everyone shifted to a different seat, quietly stood next to someone, or, like Ruth and her children, actually stepped across the line.

"See, I've learned that it's the things we leave unsaid that actually hurt the most because they eat us from the inside out. Excuses become the common denominator of failure, and like leprosy, the excuses gnaw and twist within us 'til we can't think straight no more. Can't see ourselves outside of 'em. My maker and I, we had us a good communion today. And through Proverbs, chapter 26, verse 20, I was shown what I need to do to let go of the past and move on forward. Cause lookin' back never does a body good."

Reverend Marrs vocalized his amen this time, adding, "Brother George, would you mind if I repeat your scripture? So that everyone'll know where your heart is comin' from in what you say next?"

"No, sir. I wouldn't mind at all."

The reverend stepped toward the center of the room like he was approaching a pulpit. "Proverbs, one of my personal favorite books." He bestowed his "preacher" smile on their small gathering. "Twenty-six, verse twenty says, 'Where no wood is, *there* the fire goeth out.' Children," he addressed the young ones, "do you know what that means?"

Elenore, Charles's daughter, tentatively raised her hand.

"Yes, sweetheart?" The reverend said kindly.

"Well, a fire has to have wood to burn. Where there's no wood, there can't be no fire."

"True enough. Thank you, Elenore. Now, children, how can words be like wood?"

George appreciated how well Reverend Marrs seemed to be setting the stage for him, and some of his earlier apprehension melted away. The man had a good sense of how to use his gifts.

The children, who had gathered in a sort of circle at the reverend's feet, looked at one another, poking and shrugging, as if daring their cousin or sibling to speak first. Having done her part, Elenore remained silent.

Mont had now crossed his legs and had one foot bouncing up and down like an old shock absorber on a stretch of bad road, but the reverend ignored him and pressed on. "How many here have been the recipient of harsh, mean, or inappropriate words?"

Every adult nodded their head, some doing so as they covertly looked at their patriarch.

"Words can be like matches to the kindling of our emotions," the preacher continued. "And *who* is in charge of our *emotions?*"

Again, no one else answered, so George did. "We are, sir. We're the *only* ones who have that responsibility."

If Mont had rolled his eyes any harder, his head would have whipped right off his own neck.

"And a *great* responsibility it is, Brother George." The reverend gently patted a hand over his heart and shook his head as though he were physically feeling the weight of that responsibility.

"The second part of the scripture says, 'so where there is no tale-bearer, the strife ceaseth.' What is a tale-bearer?"

In an uncharacteristically bold voice, Mary Dollis said, "Someone who tells stories on another person. A gossip."

"Right you are, Miss Mary. And when there is no one to tell or spread a story, what happens?" The reverend was beginning to feel the words now. Like he did at church, he paced back and forth before the family gathering, unable to contain the spirit burning within him. "My friends, I'll tell you what happens: nothing. Ab-so-lute-ly nothing. Like removin' the wood from an *unholy* fire, when there is no one to keep a story goin', the story *ends*. Now, in some cases, can it be good to keep a story going?"

George noticed more than one head bob in silent agreement.

The reverend noticed as well and was encouraged. "My brothers and sisters, I tell you that when the story is good, when a story brings joy to the hearts and minds of those listenin', then *yes*, by all means, *keep* that story goin'. *Spread* the good news. Can I get an amen?"

Caught up in his fervor, some of the adults began rocking forward in agreement.

Not Mont. Like a bull facing a red cape, he puffed out a huge exhale through flared nostrils.

Moved by a force outside herself, without giving her

husband a single glance, Miriam stood and joined her mother and sister at the front of the room. Clasping hands, the women and Ruth's two children formed a half-moon behind George. He could practically feel their energy and support. This was more than he could ever have hoped for.

The reverend continued, "But when the news is not of good report or praiseworthy, when the story becomes harmful to the one it's about or to those who are leaning their ears to listen, should we keep *that* story goin'?"

Forgetting their parents, some of the children voiced a unified, "No, sir."

"Right you are, my beautiful children." Reverend Marrs patted a hand over his heart. "Can it take courage to *end* a story? To *end* gossip? To bring an *end* to an unholy narrative?" He intoned each *end* forcefully, like a gunshot, firing the word at the gathering.

Whether or not they knew what they were saying, the children all said, "Yes!"

"And why is that, my children? Why can ending something be so difficult?"

The young ones had no answer, but Mary Dollis did. In a small but steady voice, she said, "Because it means change. Not doing somethin' simply because that's how it's been done before. Clearin' your own path, well . . ." She looked long and hard at her husband, long enough that those in the room began to wonder if she would finish what she'd started to say. Sick and tired of being beaten down by the father of her children, here and now, in the company of her loved ones, fueled by the reverend's spiritual fire, Mary decided that it was time she too made a stand.

Her next word was an unintelligible squeak, so she cleared her throat. "Just because you've walked one way to the wood-pile your whole life don't mean that's the only fuel for the hearth. And I say *hearth* because a fire should bring warmth, comfort, and cheer to a home. Not burn the damn thing down."

Astonished, everyone, including Mont, stared in blank amazement at their matriarch, a woman who had never uttered a swear word in her life.

Reverend Marrs beamed with pride at his parishioner. Sensing it was time to step aside and let this family get to whatever cleansing was about to take place, he offered a silent prayer that the Lord would use peace to guide whatever happened here.

George appreciated how well the stage had been set and could see why the reverend had been guided to them this evening; he was the omen of a good outcome. Whatever words flowed through him, George knew they would be received because his family had been primed to hear them. He could see it in the way they looked. Many of them *needed* to hear what he was going to say.

In a silence more potent than sound, George stood at the center of the room, rotating as he connected with each and every pair of eyes. Some were questioning, some looked calm, a few were wide open and expectant. Finally, his gaze met his father's. The once-powerful glare that had withered him into submission, into causing him to admit wrong-doing whether guilty or not, now landed on him with impotent malice.

George felt as though he were standing within a circle of protective flame. He was on fire; alight with something that at once felt foreign, yet familiar.

Closing his eyes, he remembered running into the flames of a burning building. Remembered hearing a voice guide him through the smoke and haze to where injured or unconscious men lay. One by one, he had gathered them up as if they weighed nothing and carried or dragged them out, sometimes two at a time. Then, listening to the voice, he'd run back and do it again, and again, and again.

That voice had kept him safe. He had trusted it then, and he knew he could trust it now.

Tears of gratitude leaked from the corners of his eyes as he opened them, and gazed upon his father, even though he knew the man would see the tears as a sign of weakness. In fact, he could practically sense his father's anticipation at seeing his *baby* boy wither.

But never again.

"Daddy, I don't know or understand why you are the way you are. Frankly, I don't want to know. I used to, though. I used to want to know what it was I'd done to make you hate me so much. To make you whoop me more than any of the others. To make you look on me as no better than scum on the bottom of your boot. But you know what? I realize now that my wantin' to know only strengthened the power you had over me."

Standing within his protective ring, George didn't flinch or move a muscle when his father shifted in his chair as though he were going to rise. When his father didn't get up, George continued. "Daddy, I'm no longer gonna molly-coddle you while you sift through and continually re-pack your baggage. In fact, you seem to have more baggage now that you're older than you did when we were all young'uns at home, needin' to be fed and clothed. It seems *that* would have been the time to be more stressed. But no, you just keep adding bag upon barrel 'til you're so weighed down, not even the angels'll have enough strength to pick you up; that is, *if* they come to pick you up."

At this, Mont jumped out of the easy chair so forcefully that the backs of his legs scooted the large piece of furniture back a few inches.

Some of the children flinched. Tucking their heads into their shoulders like little turtles, they ducked away from their grandfather.

All the adults tensed, eyes glued on the two combatants.

George half expected the man to launch himself across the space between them and start pummeling him right there. But in front of the reverend, his father managed to reign in the destructive urge that was so plainly written across his face.

Henry moved in to stand behind his father. George didn't

know whether this action was in support or restraint, but either way, one more person had crossed a line.

"Now, I don't say that in judgment that you aren't fit for heaven," George went on. "I say that because I honestly don't think you'd even recognize a heavenly angel if one were to stand right in front of ya. God's already sent quite a few of 'em to surround you, and you've done nothin' but beat 'em back. One by one, you've scorned, scoffed and belittled the best things you have in life, Mama being chief among 'em."

Mary Dollis had tears dripping down her cheeks.

Ruth had gathered her precious children even closer, and her sweet husband had moved to her side. That made George smile.

With a sneer, Mont reviled his son. "What do you know about anything? You've never had to work hard for anything. You know nothin' about my life, what I've been through, had to fight *against*. Everything's always been so *easy* for you."

"Hmm," George adopted a look of puzzled concern. "So, you're saying that all those beatings were to, what, toughen me up? They were for *my* good? Not because you, in any way, lost your temper? Hmm?"

George turned to face his siblings. "Now, I don't know about y'all, but I do recall Granddad Dollis. I remember sittin' on his knee as he read to me, tellin' me what a gift words were. How blessed we were to be born in this time because we had so many more opportunities than his own parents, or even he had."

"My father," Mont spat contemptuously, "was a weak-minded dreamer. Full of all the *good* that was gonna come from 'new times' of prosperity for us. Fool."

"Your father," George countered forcefully, "was a beautiful man full of hope and the knowledge that he had more control of his own destiny than our people had had in a *long* time."

"Hope?" Mont scoffed. "Dreams, more like. Well, dreams

don't get ya a better house. Dreams don't get ya a better car. Dreams don't wipe the judgment out of a white man's eyes. Damn, boy, you're just as bad as he was."

Ah, now George was finally beginning to understand.

By subjugating *him*, his father had actually been lashing out at his own dad. A man who had seen the world as a good and happy place when all Mont had wanted to do was wallow in the sad. Granddad Dollis had done his best to encourage his son out of his despairing funks, prodding him to go to school and get an education, pointing out all the advantages there were, if Mont would just reach out to grab them. Apparently, Mont hadn't seen these things as helpful. He hadn't seen what he was doing to himself by choosing to resent absolutely everything.

George replayed some of the scenes he had witnessed as a child, and they now made sense. The sorrow and disappointed resignation in his granddad's eyes when he had looked at his son.

"You know what?" George said in all honesty, "That's the greatest compliment you could *ever* have paid me. In fact, that's the only one you've ever given me, so I'm just gonna take that and count it as payment for a lifetime. I would rather be a dreamer than a self-involved pessimist like you."

Arms outstretched, Mont wanted to leap at George and put a fist in the boy's smart-ass mouth, but when his mountain of a son didn't so much as flinch at his tentative advance, the man thought better of it.

Everyone in the room seemed to be holding their breath as they watched in frozen silence. Right down to the youngest children, not even a sigh stirred the contentious air.

"You wanna know why people look on you with judgment? And believe me Daddy, it ain't only white men. People look on you that way 'cause you seem to come at 'em like you're itchin' for a fight without even knowin' 'em. You growl, sneer, and menace your way through life 'cause for some reason, you seem to think the world *owes* you somethin'. Well, it don't. It don't owe any of us anything other than the same chance anyone else has got, and *that*, Daddy, we get to make for ourselves. We *get* to decide what direction we want our lives to go. We *get* to gather the tools we'll need to take that road. And then, you know what? We get to *try*. Try Daddy. We get. To. Try. And the tryin' may not always work out. And sure, we may fall flat on our asses. And yes, it's *not* easy to get back up. But, if you don't get back up, you'll never know what *might* come next."

Without realizing he'd vocalized it, Reverend Marrs added, "Amen." He looked apologetically at George, who gave him a little smile. The reverend pursed his lips together and encouraged George with a nod.

This time, George directed his comments to everyone in the room. "I'll say this again: I'm done. No more molly-coddling. No more walkin' on eggshells. No more wondering when this man"—he pointed right at his father—"is gonna blow his top and explode all over the unsuspecting and the innocent."

George's gaze followed his finger. "I feel sorry for you, old man. Sorrier than you'll ever know. But right now, I also feel better than I have in a long time, 'cause when I leave here, I am making plans to go get my family. My lovely, intelligent, kind-hearted wife; my brave, gentle, hopeful sons; and my sweet little pixie daughter, who, I am proud to say, has me wrapped around her little finger. And you know what? I'm perfectly okay with that. And I know that my boss, who is a hardworkin', fair-minded man, is gonna work with me to make this happen. And you know how I know this, Daddy? Because I look on this man as a friend and he knows that he can count me as one too. And I don't see being friends with those that are different as any sort of weakness. Hell, they've been a family to me when I needed one the most."

George could tell that his father wanted to offer some cutting remark but was having difficulty coming up with one. The old man's fists were clenching and unclenching so fast, it was as if he thought by doing so, he could force the right words to his mouth. Though his face remained angled toward George, Mont's eyes darted furtively around the room trying to capture someone with his gaze, as if hoping they might speak up for him.

No one did. Not even Henry.

The moment his father's eyes met his again, George saw something shatter, but he did not look away. Rather, he continued staring so intently that finally, the old man couldn't take it anymore and had to turn his head.

He was broken.

It was a triumph. One George probably should have reveled in, but couldn't.

Slowly and deliberately, he turned his back on his father. To everyone else, he said, "When I get back, I *will* be bringin' my wife and children. Y'all can come on over if you like, anytime you like, and you'll be more than welcome. We, however, as long as Daddy's alive, will never step foot in this house again. And let me make this plain: There will be absolutely *no* derogatory names directed toward me or mine. 'Cause I promise you, from the moment I walk away from this house, I cleanse myself of any one of ya that can't accept, if not love, my family. They mean more to me than anything in this world, and I'll *put down* the next one of ya that can't accept that. Say what you will here, or in your own homes, but in my presence or theirs, just *one* unkind word'll earn my wrath, and I will *not* hold back."

Charles looked at Henry. His older brother's jaw looked to be clenched so tight, his teeth could be rendered a fine powder in a matter of minutes. In that, he was the carbon copy of their father. On occasion, the two of them had joined their father in making a few ribald comments directed toward their sister-in-law. At the time, he hadn't wanted to seem weak in front of the other two, but one look at George let him know who the weak ones really were. If George knew what had been said, the three of them would be dead.

"Reverend." George faced the smiling man. "God is my

witness this day, as are you. I've said my piece. I'm gathering all the wood that's been left here and totin' it on home with me. I also pledge that I'll not voice an unkind word toward any in this room. I don't envy the task I leave here for you, but I know you're the man for the job."

George reached for his mother and drew her into a warm embrace. Kissing the top of her graying head, he whispered, "I love you Mama. And I thank you for always, always lovin' me. If you ever feel the need, you have a home with me and mine."

The teary-eyed woman nodded against the arm that held her close and sniffed into his shirt. "I love you, my boy." She reached up to cup his cheek. "My gentle giant."

George then embraced Ruth and nuzzled the top of her head. "Sweet, beautiful Ruthy, you're such a rose when you smile. Keep smiling for me, will ya?"

She nodded and hugged him tight to her. "You just let me know whenever it is you get back, and I'll be right over with a welcome-home dinner."

"You know how I love your strawberry pie."

"Then that's what I'll bring for dessert."

"You got it." To his brother-in-law, George said, "Treasure this woman. She deserves it."

"That she does," Ruth's husband said as he drew her in close, kissing her cheek.

Ruth beamed.

Those that had gathered on his side of the line followed George out onto the porch, where he hugged and doted on each one of them.

Reverend Marrs was all smiles as he watched the interactions.

Like a deposed monarch, Mont fell back into his chair and gripped the armrest so forcefully, the fabric almost seemed to cry out in pain. As if watching through a tunnel that got longer the more he walked, he leveled a hostile glare at those out on the porch.

Despite Mont's emotional furor, the mood in the room around him reanimated. Like the inhabitants of Sleeping Beauty's castle, once true love's kiss had been bestowed and the dark spell of an unnatural sleep was lifted, they were alive again. Children began to stir. Some of the family went out to join George and the others, while everyone else talked among themselves as if nothing had happened.

The old man in the large easy chair almost seemed extraneous now.

Save one son that stood behind him, no one gave him a second look.

Chapter 14

New Beginnings
Saturday, July 19, 1958

"Oh my gosh, I'm so excited!" Li'l Bits seemed to bounce off the walls like a bullet ricocheting in a tunnel. "Happy birthday to me, happy birthday to me ..." she sang giddily as she surveyed the room. Inspired by her annual birthday bouquet of carnations, daisies and a rose, Li'l Bits had chosen a flowery, garden party theme for her seventh birthday.

For a week, Trinny had come over to help cut out and string paper flowers together as garlands. A long strand festooned the large arch between the kitchen and the living room. Another was draped over the fireplace, and a third framed the front door. Trinny had even taught Bits how to fold and cut colored paper to make little flowers that the two happy crafters had turned into boutonnieres for the men and boys, and small wrist corsages for the women and girls. These were each carefully laid on the small table by the front door, ready to be given to the guests as they arrived. Remy already had his paper-flower boutonniere pinned to the lapel of his Sunday jacket.

In her new blue-and-white-striped dress, Li'l Bits felt like a flower herself. The dress had three-quarter sleeves trimmed with lace and a tiny blue bow. A sash tied in the back, and she even had an extra slip to make her dress poof out like a flower's petals.

"Oh Papa." She sighed happily as she gazed about the room. "Isn't it all just lovely? It's like livin' in my own garden."

Remy smiled. "I'm glad it turned out how you wanted it to. You and Trinny worked awfully hard to make it look this good. We're lucky to have her as a friend."

"Trinny is the best, most wonderful friend, and she knows so much about all the art stuff. I know you like her art as much as I do, Papa, 'cause I see how you look at her pictures in my room."

Remy just about choked on what he was about to say and had to clear his throat by giving his chest a good thumping. His little one saw far too much for his liking.

"Uh, yes, sweetheart, I certainly do appreciate Trinny's talent. Now, everyone'll be coming soon, and I want to give ya my gift first, so you can wear it at the party."

Li'l Bits bounced with anticipation. "Ooh, what is it? What is it?"

"You go climb onto the sofa and then close your eyes. I'll go get it."

Li'l Bits used her stool to hop up onto the sofa and settled her flower-petal dress daintily around her. Closing her eyes, she called, "Ready Papa."

She heard her father approach, then stop just short of being right in front of her.

"All right, baby girl. Go on and open your eyes."

Li'l Bits laughed out loud when she saw her papa, hand

poised on his outthrust hip, with a small, shiny, white purse dangling from his cocked wrist.

"I see you got yourself somethin' new to wear to my party, but what'd ya get for me?" she teased.

"Ha, ha." Remy smiled as he slid the patent-leather child's handbag from his wrist and held it out toward his still-snickering daughter.

"Oh, so it's for me?" she said with exaggerated surprise. "But it went so well with your suit. Are ya sure you don't wanna keep it? I know Uncle George would *love* to see ya with it." The poor girl just could not keep her giggles under control and toppled over sideways as she slapped the cushion merrily.

Remy rolled his eyes. "Come on, now, quit your caterwaulin' and take a gander inside, because what's in there is your big present, little miss."

Trying to compose herself, Li'l Bits hauled up to a sitting position and wiped her eyes with the back of her hand. The purse swayed as it dangled from the tip of Remy's outstretched finger. That almost made her laugh again, because it seemed to her that even the little handbag thought it was funny.

Li'l Bits took the purse and gave it a good look. "Ooh, I really like the daisy by the pinchy thing. That's cute." The clasp was new and stiff, so Li'l Bits had to give the "pinchy thing" a solid tweak to get it to pop open. A spicy floral aroma wafted out. She reached in and pulled out a small perfume box.

"Oh, Papa, my first scent," Li'l Bits said reverently. "Most pre-sh, pre-sh-us," she sounded out as she read the label. "Is that word *precious?*"

Remy sat beside her. "Right you are, sweetheart! I looked and looked through all the bottles at the Penney's perfume counter. This one just came out this year and when I found it, I knew it was the right one for my girl. 'Most Precious' is the perfect name. And the way it smells both spicy and flowery at the same time reminds me of you, my little snapdragon." Remy tickled near the back of her armpit.

Li'l Bits squirmed. "Stop, you'll make me drop it!"

"Why don't ya open the box and take it on out. We can dab some behind your pretty ears and on your wrists."

Li'l Bits gently tugged the lid open and tipped its content into her hand. The tapered, cut-glass bottle held amber liquid that shone like golden honey when she held it up to the light. Savoring every moment of feeling like a grown-up, Li'l Bits twisted out the arrowhead-shaped stopper and let her nose hover over the magic elixir. She inhaled deeply and passed the bottle from beneath her nose to her papa's.

"Doesn't it smell *divine*?"

Divine? Remy looked askance at his daughter. He must be letting her watch too much television.

Li'l Bits delicately dabbed the perfume behind her ears, on the back of her neck, on the front of her neck, and on her wrists, and when it looked like she was going for the back of her knees, Remy said, "Hold on, there, sweetheart, don't be goin' hog wild with that. It's your first time wearin' scent, and you don't wanna overdo."

"But Papa, I'm seven years old now, and I want to smell like a lady."

Remy gently took the bottle from her, put the stopper back in and slid it into the box. "You, darlin' girl, smell sweet enough as it is. Let's save some for another day. You don't want to use up the whole bottle in one go."

Li'l Bits scoffed. "Really, I'm not *that* silly. I just . . ." She closed her eyes and held her wrist to her nose. "I just really like it."

"So, I did good? Got the right one?"

Li'l Bits gave Remy a big hug. "You did good. And I like the purse, too." She couldn't help but add, "That is, if *you* don't want to keep it." She covered her mouth and giggled again.

Remy grabbed Bits up, tickled her, and then danced her around the room.

"Well, now," came a deep voice from the doorway. "Is this

a private dance, or can anyone claim a waltz with the birthday girl?"

"Uncle George!" Bits shouted excitedly. Remy set her down and she ran to her uncle, who scooped her up. "Uncle George, smell me." Li'l Bits thrust her neck into his face, giving him no choice but to inhale a deep whiff of the scent that hovered around her like a cloud.

"Whoa, now, that's not the herb-and-soil scent I'm used to from you. What'd you do? Get into some of Orvalee's concoctions?"

Unimpressed with her uncle's obvious lack of intellect, Li'l Bits pinched her lips together in disapproval.

"No, sir," she said defensively. "You know I'd never do that without permission. What do you think I am? An animal?"

Both George and Remy pursed their lips together, stifling their reactions. As George's face was front and center, he had to work harder to maintain his composure. "I am most sorry, Miss Bits. I know you are a lady and would never do anything like that."

"Well, I should *hope* not. Jiminy Cricket." She exhaled the oath. "Please put me down, Uncle George, and I'll show you."

She retrieved her new purse and opened it to reveal the perfume box. "See, I got a new purse to match my gloves, and it even has a little daisy right here."

"That it does. Makes it go right along with all your pretty flower decorations," George said approvingly.

"And *here* is my new scent." Bits took the beautiful bottle out of the box again. "It's called 'Most Precious.' Papa says 'cause it's just like me. And smell." Li'l Bits uncorked the stopper and shoved the bottle beneath her uncle's nose. "It smells *divine* too."

George jerked back slightly to avoid having the bottle thrust up his nostril. "Divine?" He cast an inquiring glance at Remy.

"I think she saw some commercial on the television about perfume. Her vocabulary is certainly expanding as of late."

"Ah, television'll do that, all right," George agreed.

Oblivious to the men, Li'l Bits went right on. "I'm gonna wear some to school every day when we go back."

"Now, hold up, there," Remy said. "Perfume is only for Sundays, birthdays, or other special occasions. It's *not* for every day."

Perturbed with this unexpected restriction, Li'l Bits was about to protest but George was able to help her see reason. "Bits, I know you love the smell right now 'cause it's new and you're not used to it. But if you wear it every day, a point'll come when you won't be able to smell it at all. Sort of like when someone works in a flower shop. They get to a point where they can't smell a one of them flowers. A daisy'll smell the same as a rose."

"Hmm . . ." Li'l Bits did not like this thought. "You mean, even when they're not in the shop, they can't smell the flowers?"

George's lips twisted first to one side of his face and then the other as he thought of how to explain what he meant. "I know that when I was in France, I *loved* all the new smells. The different kinds of flowers they had, different foods and spices; I swear, even the sunshine had a different smell over there." He didn't mention that all the lovely scents were often over-ridden by the acrid dust from crumbling buildings, smoldering fires, and the like; he let that image go. "What I'm tryin' to say is that always bein' around the smells that I'd once been able to pick out and enjoy made it so I didn't even notice 'em after a while. I wouldn't want your fancy perfume to be like that for you."

Li'l Bits nodded agreement. "No, me neither. I always want to be able to enjoy its *divine essence*."

Again, George and Remy looked at one another in question. First divine and now essence? That one had to have come from Orvalee.

Li'l Bits carefully put the cut-glass bottle back in the box, then placed both the purse and perfume on the table by her cake, where it would be safe. With a quick intake of breath, she said, "Maybe I can make it last and wear it when I get out of high school? I can wear it just at every birthday, when school ends each year, and—"

In the middle of planning how to make the precious liquid last for the rest of her life, all thoughts of conservation fled when her birthday guests began to arrive.

The cousins came in all at once. Amanda, Gus, Claire, Damian, Andy and Jeremy, were dressed in their Sunday finery, eager to see what a garden party was all about. Damian, Andy, and Jeremy didn't seem too thrilled at having to wear Sunday duds on a non-church day, but the massive, florally decorated cake in the center of the kitchen table, immediately assuaged their misgivings. Bits always had the best cakes.

"Uncle Rem." Claire tugged on his arm. "Mama says to say that she and Nana'll be in in just a minute."

Before Remy could thank his niece, Bits shouted, "Hold on, y'all need to get your flowers on. Papa, can you help me get everyone decorated?"

Remy snickered. "Sure thing. You tie the corsages onto Amanda, Claire, and your aunts. George can help me pin the boutonnieres on the menfolk."

George wasn't sure how nimble his large fingers would be with the small pins, so he opted to just hand out his share of the flowers, letting each man do his own. Remy followed suit.

"And that's why I keep you around," Remy said to George.

"Why's that?"

"Because, like Tom Sawyer, you always see the easiest way to get things done."

George nodded approvingly. "I can live with that."

A polite knock at the screen door went unheeded by the raucous group inside. The knock came again, louder this time, and then a "Hello!"

Remy turned to see Amy Jo, Jesslyn, and Ellie June waiting to be allowed entry.

"Well, come on in, you three." He waved them in. "Why stand on ceremony?"

But the girls primly waited for Remy to open the screen door for them and then entered like the three most proper young ladies he had ever encountered. Dressed to the nines, from white gloves to polished shoes, they held themselves like flower girls walking down an aisle.

"Hello, Mr. Dubois, Mr. Dollis," Jesslyn said in her best "company" voice. "Thank you so much for inviting us."

Ellie June held out the gift she'd brought. "Sir, where would you like us to put these?"

The lovely little ladies had obviously been coached on how to behave at a garden party. So, in like manner, Remy fanned an inviting arm toward the crowd gathered in the kitchen. "Y'all may put your gifts on the table, by the cake. Bits is there with her cousins. I believe you're all acquainted. I know she'll be *absolutely delighted* to see you."

As the three girls walked daintily toward the kitchen, Remy sidled up to George, saying, "I do believe they have been put on their honor to mind their p's and q's at this little soiree. Usually when they come over, they're like wild animals runnin' around the house, both inside and out. I think maybe because I'm not as strict as their own parents are, they take full advantage of the freedom they get here."

"A bit of freedom never hurt a child," George said. "If they get in trouble, let 'em fall. They'll soon figure things out. A *little* guidance can go a long way. Kids are smart that way."

"George, I'm learnin' a person can drive themselves crazy if they try to parent a child to death," Remy said honestly. "They sure come with their own personalities. If I were to try and educate all the curiosity outa my girl, we'd be doin' nothin' but buttin' heads. I can teach her manners. I can teach her respect. I can encourage patience and moderation. But I'll tell you, there are some lessons that only life is gonna be able to knock into that child. And I'm content to sit back and let life do its job."

"My mama says that some of her happiest moments have come by watchin' her children get their comeuppance by havin' one just like 'em."

Remy looked at George. "My mama says the exact same thing."

They both looked long and hard at the chattering children.

"Well, then," George said slowly, "I suppose there must be truth in what they say. Our mothers are not stupid women."

"No, they are not," Remy agreed.

Chapter 15

A Twist of Fate

"Wisdom is nothing more than healed pain."

—*R. Edward Lee (1807–1870),*
Military Strategist and General

When everyone else finally arrived, the party moved into full swing. Li'l Bits had planned a memory game wherein competitors matched the picture of a flower to its name; the pictures had been drawn by Trinny.

Orvalee had supplied the essence of as many flowers as she could distill. The essences had then been added to a bit of sugarless frosting, and through either smell or taste, competitors had to guess as many correct flower-frostings as they could. Some really smelled like the actual flower and were easy to guess, while others required a great deal of imagination.

"Mmm, yum," Uncle Michael sighed happily. "This rose frosting is my new favorite. I like this game!"

Everyone seemed to enjoy this particular activity, especially the boys, who, behind the adults' backs, created a game of their own called "Smear your opponent as thoroughly as possible while avoiding the Sunday duds." To increase their target potential, the boys slipped off their suit-coats and rolled up their sleeves to expose more skin.

The party-goers also had to unscramble mixed-up flower names. Whoever did it the fastest was the winner and got a package of licorice. Uncle Oliver emerged victorious and was thrilled, because soft, red licorice was his all-time favorite treat.

Despite their prim entrance, Amy Jo, Jesslyn and Ellie June became just as competitive as the boys. As the party wound to a close and Jesslyn's mother came to pick up the girls, Ellie June leaned down to give Bits a huge hug. "Oh, my goodness, Bits, I've never, in all my life, had so much fun. Thank you for invitin' me." She hesitated before adding, "Before we became friends, before *that* day, you know, I never belonged. This is the first party I've been invited to." Joy was written all over her face.

Li'l Bits squeezed Ellie June's hand and smiled up at her. "We will *always*, always be friends. And you can come to *every* birthday party I have."

"Thank you, Bits. Thank you." Ellie June went out to get in Mrs. Dilbreth's car.

"Bits," Jesslyn said, "you always make things so much fun. This was super."

"It sure was," Amy Jo agreed. "And I'd like to come to your next one too, if that's okay."

Li'l Bits beamed at the compliment. "I want all three of ya to come next year and every year, 'til we're all grown up."

"Yeah," the other two agreed in unison.

"We're gonna be friends forever and ever," Jesslyn said. They heard a horn honk, and the girls darted outside, where they caught Mrs. Dilbreth's mind-your-manners look. The two girls slowed immediately and walked placidly the rest of the way to the vehicle. Faces beaming, they daintily climbed in to join Ellie June.

"Oh, my girl." Alexander swung his granddaughter up into an embrace. "I cannot believe how fast you are growin'. Seems like yesterday you were toddlin' around, wearin' everyone's shoes and hidin' things in the toes of 'em."

Lynn Anne had come up to join the embrace. "Oh my, yes! I remember we'd all have to check our shoes after you left from a visit. Alex, do you remember the time I found a half-eaten piece of cheese in my shoe?" She chuckled.

Embarrassed, Li'l Bits complained, "That *couldn't* have been me. I didn't do things like that."

"I beg to differ," her grandfather teased. "You most certainly did. And not only did your nana find cheese in her shoe, but I found part of a bologna sandwich in mine. I can tell you, bologna squishes like none other when forced to the toe of a shoe, and it does not clean out easily."

"Eww." Li'l Bits scrunched her nose. "That's disgusting. I'm too big to do that now."

"Thank heaven for that, child," Lynn Anne agreed. "We sure love you, darlin'. And your sweet friends have helped make this a wonderful party." To her husband, she said, "I think I'm gonna have to speak to Orvalee about an idea I have for her flower essences."

Alexander put Li'l Bits down. "It's gettin' late, and old people like me and your nana need to be gettin' on home to bed. We need our beauty sleep."

"Speak for yourself, Alexander Dubois. I, for one, am not gettin' old. Like a fine wine, I am simply agin' and becomin' more valuable."

"Tastier too." Her husband winked.

Lynn Anne blushed and slapped his arm. "Come on, you. I'll show you how *tasty* I can be."

Her grandparents left, laughing and holding hands. Li'l Bits wondered if she'd act that silly when she grew up. Then, she looked up at her papa and thought about how she caught him looking at Trinny sometimes. He sort of had the same look that her grandparents just did. Li'l Bits started thinking about a lot of things that had been happening since the day she'd been struck by that rock.

In the midst of her musings, George sat on the chair nearest her. "Penny for your thoughts."

Bits slowly turned to face him. "Uncle George."

"Yes, sweet pea," George said over the din of voices in the kitchen.

"Can I ask you somethin'?"

"Sure thing. Come on up here." George lifted her to his lap.

The two of them sat deep in conversation as Janelle and Sienna were rounding up their wayward broods. "Si, go on out to the porch and holler at the little devils that escaped. Tell 'em they'd best get themselves to the cars. And grab our husbands and Remy from the shop. Whatever Rem's latest project is can be admired later, I'm sure."

With her sister dispatched, Janelle asked, "Ladies, I'm sorry, but would you mind if I leave the rest of the cleanup in your capable hands? These kids are near to drivin' me mad, and I do not want to lose it in front of y'all. I know you call me the 'cucumber queen' 'cause I'm always so cool under pressure"— she gave a self-deprecating nod of the head—"but tonight, I might show my true colors if I stay."

Orvalee whipped a dish towel in her direction. "You go on and shoo. Trinny and I can manage just fine. And just a little advice from someone older and wiser: to help regain your cool, I suggest you find a way to make your man see that a good foot rub after the kids go to bed would go a long way."

"Ooh, that does sound a treat," Janelle said. "It's been, well, longer than I care to remember since Michael has doted on me like that. Orvalee, I will pass your wisdom along to Sienna. May we forever bask in its light."

"Y'all should be so lucky!" Orvalee crowed.

"Ladies, thanks a million. As ever, your company has been a treat. Nighty night." Janelle didn't want to interrupt her niece's conversation with George, so, with a few kids in tow, she simply placed a quick kiss on the girl's cheek and wrangled her brood out the door.

Trinny, dish towel in hand, finally said, "The party went well, I think."

"That it did," Orvalee agreed. "And I do believe your decorations were a huge hit. Did you see the way the girls kept protectin' their cute corsages? I think you created something they'll treasure as a keepsake for quite a while."

The two women were just finishing up the dishes when Remy came in and offered to help.

"Just like a man," Orvalee said to Trinny. "Offerin' help when the chore is just about done."

"Typical," Trinny agreed, smiling shyly at Remy.

"Well, hold on, there," Remy said. "I still see that the tablecloth needs washin', floor definitely needs to be swept, decorations still need to be taken down . . ." Sighing, he looked around the rooms. "Card table put away, rug vacuumed . . ."

"Wait," Trinny cut in, surprising the others. "We never said *which* job was nearly finished."

"Trinny Jenks!" Orvalee was genuinely stunned that her young friend had joined in the jesting this way. For just a second, Trinny looked abashed; then, Orvalee added, "Good on you. It's nice to see I am *finally* rubbin' off on ya."

"Oh no," Remy moaned. "Et tu, Brute?"

With a slight flush of pleasure lighting her cheeks, Trinny said, "*Oui, moi aussi.*"

"Do my ears deceive me?" George came in holding Li'l Bits. "Or am I hearin' *langue de ange?*"

A tentative smile turned the corners of Trinny's mouth into a graceful, upward arc. She'd learned French in the camp from an old woman who spoke the language fluently. That little bit of something, far from her personal reality, had helped save her sanity. She only ever heard Claudine speak English, so forgot that George had learned French while serving overseas. The tentative smile blossomed into a rare, full smile as she said, "The language of angels is never out of place."

"*Non ce n'est pas*," Orvalee joined in, then translated for Remy, "No, it's not." Having come from the French Creoles of southern Louisiana, French was practically Orvalee's native tongue.

"I have just been one-upped in a big way," Remy complained forlornly.

"As long as it's done in French, I don't see how you can complain one little bit." George smiled broadly. "And Trinny, know it or not, you have provided the best possible opening for me to impart a little news."

With a single look, Remy wordlessly questioned his friend.

With a single nod, George answered Remy's silent question, then said aloud, "Would y'all mind takin' a seat?"

Everyone pulled a chair around the kitchen table. Remy took Li'l Bits from George and sat her on his lap. Knowing that what was coming might be a shock to her, he was prepared to wrap her in comforting arms.

Bits asked, "Is your news a surprise for my birthday? 'Cause you don't have to give me anything else. I love my Little Lulu doll and the Play-Doh."

"Well, Bits, birthdays are for bein' happy, right?" George asked.

"Yes. And like I said, I'm happy, real happy, about my *whole* day."

"Then I sure hope that what I have to say will make you as happy as it is gonna make me."

There was something in the tone of his voice, in the way he was looking at all of them, that made Bits unsure if she wanted to hear what he was going to say.

"Y'all know it's been a while since Claudine and the kids went away."

Beneath the table, Trinny and Orvalee reached for one

another. Clasping hands, they hoped their prayers for George were finally coming true.

"Lord, how I've missed 'em. Well, thanks to a lot of patience from those I love, present company included, I have *finally* found my heart and the courage to go claim it. So, next week, I will be flyin' to France to pick up the pieces that broke away nearly two and a half years ago."

Trinny and Orvalee exhaled in unison. Pure pleasure lit their faces. With her heart overflowing, tears of gratitude leaked from Orvalee's eyes as she reached across the table to clasp George's big hand. "Oh, my dear friend, we are so very happy for you. Man is meant to be a joy-filled creation, and this'll bring joy not just to you, but to all of us. I've sorely missed your sweet wife."

Still uncomfortable expressing too much emotion, Trinny managed to keep her own tears of joy at bay, but they were there none-the-less.

Li'l Bits made a sort of squeaking sound as she tried to make words come out her mouth. "Next week you say? Next week?" Today was Saturday, so *next week* was just the day after tomorrow. Li'l Bits performed facial gymnastics as she tried to make sense of what her uncle had just said. "Next. Week." was the only thing she seemed capable of saying.

George reached across the table to cover one of her small hands with his fingers. "Bits, I'm going to bring my family home."

"But they're all the way across the ocean, in *France*."

"That they are. And that's why I'll be gettin' on a plane to go there."

"So, how long does it take? What day are you goin'? Will ya be back by next Sunday?"

"No, sweet thing. I will not be back by Sunday. I'm actually not quite sure when we'll be comin' home." George tenderly squeezed her little hand. "See, while I'm there, I want my children to be able to show me all the places they've come to love.

I want to meet their cousins and share in their family fun. I've missed so much of their growin', and that growth has been in a whole new place than the one I knew when I was there. There are parts of me that need to spend time healing, as I see for myself that . . . some of what lingers in my mind, isn't still the same as I remember it."

All Li'l Bits seemed to grasp was the fact that her beloved uncle, a man who had been around as long as she could remember, a man who had seen her through thick and thin, was not going to be there anymore. Her corn-flower blue eyes grew larger than ever as they filled to the brim with glistening tears. Tears she could not hold back.

Crying, she wiggled free of her father's grasp and went to her uncle, whose big arms enveloped her. Li'l Bits sobbed inconsolably. George scooped her up and held her tight. Standing, he walked into the living room and jigged her against his body, like he had his own children when they were babies.

Bits drew in spasmodic gulps of breath that moved her small frame almost convulsively against his chest. They had all expected that when the time came for George to leave it would be hard for Bits, but no one had anticipated just *how* hard.

Remy was heartbroken. Seeing his baby girl in such a state, left him feeling absolutely helpless. He wordlessly turned to Trinny and Orvalee, as if to ask, "What can I do?"

"Time," Orvalee said. "It'll just take time."

"I remember when they took us to the camp. The first one." Trinny seemed to be speaking from some distance inside herself.

Remy and Orvalee exchanged glances. Neither of them had ever heard Trinny mention anything of her time in the internment camp.

"Everything I knew was stripped away. Friends—gone. School—gone. Extended family—gone. Home—*gone.* But I still had my mother, brother and sister. They became my anchor. They grounded me." As if suddenly aware she'd spoken out loud, Trinny blinked away tears, mustered a weak smile, and focused on George and Li'l Bits in the other room. "Bits has been through a lot lately. As long as she has us to anchor her, she will be fine. Plus, she has your family, Remy. And her three cute friends. All will be well."

In all the time that Remy and Orvalee had known Trinny, this was the most personal information she had ever shared. Orvalee was near to bursting with emotion and couldn't help herself. Pouncing on Trinny, she leaned in and gave the surprised young woman the warmest one-armed mama bear hug she could.

"Thank you for that. Thank you for openin' up to us. Come here, you." Throwing her arm open wide to Remy, Orvalee stood, drawing Trinny up along with her.

With some hesitation, Remy drew close and put an arm around Orvalee's waist. Tentatively, he reached for Trinny, wondering how she would handle so much emotion and physical touch in one day. When she didn't draw away from his outstretched arm, he ventured the rest of the way and gently draped it around her waist.

George strode over, joining himself and Bits to the group. What a mismatched, but loving, bunch they were.

Chapter 16

A Little Nudge

"Don't be afraid of your fears. They're not there to scare you. They're there to let you know that something is worth it."

—C. JoyBell C., author, poet, and philosopher

"**D**id Bits settle in okay?" George asked, when Remy came out to join him on the porch. George sat near the ash, legs dangling over the edge. He motioned for Remy to join him. "I saw Orvalee and Trinny home safe. They were still worried about Bits."

"I eventually got her rememberin' all the fun and friends. We talked about gratitude and what that means. Then, I wound you into the equation and how we needed to be grateful that you were finally gonna be able to be with your family again. She felt like she should remember Claudine and the kids better, but honestly, even with all the letter writin', and photographs they send, she just about forgot that you belong to someone other than her."

"That child has meant the world to me these past two years. Just havin' her around gave me somethin' other than my sorry self to focus on. Honestly, Rem, I don't know . . ." George's head sagged. "I don't know if I'd've made it through . . ."

"I know." Remy nudged his friend with his shoulder, not even rocking the solid form. "I know exactly what you mean. My girl, she's got a bit of magic in her, doesn't she? Her big, wide, blue eyes make it hard to focus on any storm you got ragin' in your heart, 'cause when she looks atcha, all you see are blue skies and seagulls. Her little voice is like what I imagine the waves lappin' at the seashore are like, deliverin' all sorts of treasures from the deep. She makes ya see things in a new way."

The men sat in communal silence, gazing into the night sky as their minds wandered the maze of stars. From the depths of the darkness, crickets harmonized, each an instrument in a symphony of repose. The men's breathing slowed. Their chests rose and fell in harmony with the song.

Remy whispered, "Blessed is the light that shines through your eyes. Blessed are the stars that light the night skies."

Roused from his inner wanderings, George asked, "Hmm? What'd you say?"

"Oh, nothin'. Just somethin' that comes to mind sometimes when I sit out here with Bits. I swear, her eyes get so big lookin' up at the sky that I can see the stars reflected in 'em. It's like she's soakin' up the whole universe. Takin' it all in. It's hard to explain."

"You don't have to. Anyone who's spent a lick o' time with that child'll know what you're talkin' about." George drew in a quick, deep breath, then slowly exhaled. "Rem, I'll be leaving soon, and heaven knows I'm gonna miss y'all, but there is somethin' I'd like to say to you before I go."

Steeling himself for the possible news that George had decided he and his family might just remain in France, or that George had decided they'd be moving away when they got back, Remy did his best to sound casual. "You know you can tell me anything, George. What is it?"

"Rem, I . . . I think you should . . . Well, I think you should muster the courage and ask Trinny out on a date."

Discomposed, Remy remained silent. He hadn't had the slightest inkling that anyone suspected his feelings for Trinny.

"Rem, I know you heard me, and you heard right. I can see it in your eyes, the way they follow her around a room. The way they linger on her back when she's not lookin'. The way they shine with pleasure when she smiles at somethin' you say. You're far from inscrutable, my friend."

Having heard the suggestion aloud, Remy's imagination tapestried the walls of his mind with vivid images. He and Trinny holding hands in the park. He and Trinny laughing with Bits as they push her on the swings. He and Trinny, alone on the couch after tucking Bits in bed, watching the late show. Her head on a pillow in his lap as he gently strokes the silken black strands of her hair. Magical tapestries so real, they wove themselves into the very fabric of his senses.

George continued. "I know this, Rem, 'cause I did the same with Claudine. And I know how scared you are to put yourself out in the open. Like a chicken hemmed in by a skunk, you think the whole situation will explode into a big mess of torn flesh and stink. But Rem, I don't think it will. Honestly. I've been watchin' her too, and I think she carries a bit of a torch for you, and has for a while."

Hearing this, Remy's heart beat with quiet pleasure. The rainbow colors of his imagination shimmered like oil on water. Then, the nasty specter of doubt creeped in and stomped its big, ugly foot right in the middle of his rainbow puddle.

"Man, you've lost your damn mind. Your missin' Claudine has made you see cupids where there are none. I'm sure that no arrow of love for me has pierced any part of Trinny Jenks."

"Well, now, I don't recall using the word *love*, but if that's the one that comes to your mind, then I'm for sure thinkin' a first date would be in order."

Remy scratched his head in consternation. "Why are you

sayin' . . .? What can you be thinkin' . . .?" He blew an exasperated breath and combed a hand through his hair. "What on earth possessed you to say *that*?"

"Rem, I'm finally going *toward* the love of my life. I had it all along but didn't know enough about myself to truly appreciate it until it was gone. Now, I'm tryin' not to say that I wasted my time being sorry for myself, 'cause had I not had all this time on my own, I'd never have gotten the courage to face my demon. But I can tell you with a light heart that a few months back, I did just that."

"Your father?" was all Remy said.

"My father." George gave a satisfied nod. "I'm sorry I didn't tell ya, Rem, but I did it. I finally did it. All those things Claudine said, one day, they made sense. I won't go into the whole of it, but I feel confident sayin' that when we come back, things'll be different, because *I'm* different. Claudine always saw the man in me. And I'm proud to say that I finally see him too, and I like him."

George shifted his large frame so he could look right down at Remy.

"Rem, I see the man you *are*. The incredible man you've become since findin' Bits on your doorstep. You didn't have to keep her, but you did. And you've become so much more than you were before. Nothin' grows you like havin' children. They stretch your heart and your patience."

"That they do!"

"But think on today, Rem. Think on all the other birthday parties, family get-togethers, school field trips, and the like that had you not opened yourself to that child, you'd've missed out on."

Remy nodded. "That I would've."

"Now, I know we'd've still been friends. But I don't think we'd be the same *kind* of friends we are now. You know what I mean?"

"I think I do. We're both fathers who've faced down the

shadows we lived under. And even though those shadows are quite different, the journey hasn't been easy."

"No, it hasn't. But well worth it, I'd say. Wouldn't you?"

"Yes, I would." Remy stood, facing George head on. "I hope you'll take my meanin' when I say this: George Lorenzo Dollis, it has been my pleasure and deep honor to know you. And I hope that in the years to come, I am blessed with even more time to deepen a friendship that comes along once in a lifetime." Remy reached out to shake George's hand.

The big man's lip quivered with restrained emotion. Standing to tower over his diminutive friend, George shook the outstretched hand. "Remington Alexander Dubois, I look forward to that as well." Then, with an impish smile and an eyebrow raise, George added, "To the deepening of our understandin' of one another, through the to-do lists, and complaining about all our *wives* demand of us."

Had Remy been drinking anything, it would have been spewed all over George. "Wives?" Remy croaked.

"Wives." George smirked. "While I'm gone, you, my friend are gonna woo and win the fair Trinny."

Remy swallowed hard. "I don't understand why you . . . What made you bring this up?"

"Rem, know it or not, that magical child of yours has seen through your guise as well."

"What on earth are you talkin' about?"

"Trinny."

You could have stuck a white-hot poker up his butt, and Remy still would not have had the wit nor will to move. He stood slack-jawed, his ink-dark eyelashes fluttering wildly and his sweat-slicked skin glowing in the moonlight that reflected off the water.

"You heard me. Bits knows you have feelings for Trinny. She's not exactly sure what they are, but with somethin' she saw tonight between your parents, I think she's beginning to put two and two together. That's what we were talkin' about when you came in from the shop."

"Bits . . ." Remy struggled to find the right words. "My Bits has talked to you . . . about me and *Trinny*?" His voice shot up an octave on the last word.

Looking like he might pass out, or maybe fling himself off the porch into the water, Remy wobbled on his feet. George carefully guided the light-headed man down onto the bench.

"Sit yourself down and breathe." George wanted to laugh but settled for a quiet grunt of satisfaction as he, too, sat down.

"Even Bits has noticed the way Trinny has begun to open up. Years ago, you could barely coax two words outa that woman, but now . . . Just think back to the kitchen this evenin'. Rem, you put your arm around her waist. She not only let you touch her but allowed herself to be part of a group hug. A *group* hug. I'd say that's pretty amazing. And so I say, why stop now? While she's still open, you keep at her. Don't let her retreat back into that shell she's lived in for so long."

"But I don't wanna push her too hard, or too fast."

"Rem, buck up, man. It's time to step over the startin' line. At this point, you've got nothin' to lose by at least giving it a shot. The gettin' of most things in life is far more rewarding when ya have to break a few eggs in the process. Up 'til now, you've been sittin' on the sidelines, just hopin' the ball would be thrown right atcha. Well, in a way, it has, so start chasin' it, my friend, or someone else is gonna pick it up."

Remy considered what George was saying, his face twisted up in thought. After a moment of silence, George tried again.

"Okay, let me ask this, and if the answer's no, I'll back off and let well enough alone: Do you have feelings for Trinny? I'm not sayin' you have to know exactly what they are right now."

Remy looked down at his own hands, watching his fingers twist and twine together, resembling what his insides felt like. It had thrilled him in a way he could not have imagined when he'd been able to touch Trinny tonight. Other than a simple business handshake, he'd never touched a woman before. Well, he'd hugged his mother and sisters, but they didn't count.

"Rem, come on, now. I need to hear you say it. Yes or no. Do you care for Trinny?"

Defeated, Remy looked pitifully into his friend's dark eyes. "Heaven help me, George, I do. Damn it—I care so much, sometimes it makes my stomach hurt. Since Bits was laid up, Trinny's been over so much. It's been the happiest, hardest few months I've had."

"I know, my friend." George placed a heavy arm around Remy's shoulders and gave him a brusque, jigging hug. "I know. You've sorta done things wrong-way-round, what with gettin' a child before a wife. But, you know, if Trinny's the one you want, I honestly think that's the only way it coulda happened with her. She's been too long in that shell of . . . whatever it is that's had her locked up. But having Bits to care for has done somethin' no amount of psychological mumbo jumbo could have. And danged if that doesn't apply to me too."

"Me three," Remy agreed. "Seven years, George; *seven* years never passed so fast before that child came. I see now that before, I was just livin' day to day. If you could call what I was doin' any kind of proper livin'."

Full of nervous energy, Remy got up and paced as he looked out over the moonlight-kissed water. "George, there are times I've laughed so hard with that child, I thought my stomach muscles would seize up and stop me breathin' altogether. And then, there've been times I cried myself to sleep over not knowin' how to help calm the hurt I saw in her eyes." Remy suddenly stood still, just staring into the depths of a memory.

George rose to stand beside his friend in silent support.

Remy sniffed and quickly swiped at a few stray tears that dared escape. "You know, I thought I had it bad growin' up. I was always the smallest, slowest, last picked for sports, the butt of a joke. They say hindsight's a great teacher, and I've tried to let it be that for me, but sometimes, I feel like it's beatin' a stick over my sorry head for ever feelin' bad about myself." Remy took a deep breath. "Sometimes Bits has come home, and I can see it. She doesn't say anything, but I can see it. You know what I mean?"

"Yes, I know what you mean."

Remy's lower lip quivered as he asked, "Why do people do it? Do you think they actually know what it is? The lash they lay across your back when they say the things they do?"

"I like to think they don't. I like to think they feel like they're just bein' funny. And for the most part, I can make myself believe that, so it don't bother me too much. And for those who do mean it, for those who are just down-right nasty, well, I've learned that a man my size doesn't need to *say* a whole lot when a look'll do. And to his credit, my father, God bless him, prepared me how to hold my temper with a bully."

Remy looked up at George. "I'm sorry for what you went through at the hands of your father. And I'm sorry for thinkin' that mine was as bad, when all he wanted to do was be my pa."

Feeling that the conversation had become too maudlin, George attempted to put it back on track. "But thankfully, we've overcome our child-selves and become men. Good men. Rem, as hard as it's been, I'm not sure what I'd change for fear of not bein' right where I am. Claudine and the kids are so excited I'm comin'. You shoulda heard 'em on the phone when I called to finalize my travel plans. Beau has a whole list of places he wants me to see. And Jeremy, I think he's grateful to be handin' the man-of-the-house reigns back to me. I should never have put that load on him, and I'm gonna tell him so. Aline was so excited, she just cried. I can tell she's gonna keep me so close, we'll be like two peas in a pod."

"I'm so happy for you, George. Claudine's the best of women to put up with the likes of you."

A short bark of laughter escaped George. "That she is. I couldn't ask for better. And Rem, back to what brought us out here tonight, Trinny's a good woman too."

"Yes, that she is."

"So, what are you gonna do about it?"

Remy let out a heavy sigh. "George, how do you go about . . . courtin'?"

"Well, I'm glad you finally asked."

Remy and George talked into the night about the art of wooing a woman. Both men were yawning by the time the conversation wound to a close.

Standing to stretch his back, George said, "Now, Rem, I expect full reports while I'm away. Trinny may not be one for movies, but I want to hear about any walks in the park, art exhibits you attend, the works."

"Just how long are you gonna be gone? That sounds like a lot."

"Nothin' you can't manage. I have faith. And be sure to know that if I get no reports from you, I *will* be askin' Bits when I write to her."

"Wha . . . You wouldn't ask her anything like that, would you?"

George chuckled mischievously. "What do you think?"

"Damn, man, you would."

Chapter 17

Baby Steps
Late August, 1958

"Life shrinks or expands in
proportion to one's courage."

*—Anais Nin (1903–1977),
American author and essayist*

---

nlike last year, Li'l Bits could hardly wait for school to start. This year, she would be walking into class with three solid, tried-and-true friends.

She looked forward to lunch time.

She looked forward to recess.

She even looked forward to homework, because sometimes she'd get to do it at the cousins', while waiting for her papa to come. Plus, her aunt always had milk and cookies waiting for them after school. And for special projects, she'd get to go to a friend's house, or they would come to hers.

Yep, in no time at all, she'd be walking down the hallowed halls of learning into a new class with a new teacher and new friends. Keeping that last thought front and center motivated

Li'l Bits. For someone who, so far, had been surrounded mainly by loving and protective adults, Bits was discovering that she rather liked the chatter and chaos of other children. It gave her something to focus on, something to puzzle through. Her little mind was always in a whir, and for her, the surrounding bustle was fuel for thought.

After the rock incident with Rudy Galbraith last year, everyone at school had begun to see her differently. Like she was a real person. Not some come-to-life doll they were being made to play with.

Oddly, it was the severity of the injury that had softened their view of her. Dolls may cry, but they don't bleed or need stitches. Though she couldn't see it, the scar in the middle of her back was one of her most prized possessions. Like her Uncle George's war medals, the scar meant she'd been brave.

It had been a little over a month since her uncle had headed to France, and oh, how she missed him. Just last week, she'd received a beautiful card signed not only by George but by Claudine and the kids too. They'd each written a short postscript of greeting. Aunt Claudine had drawn a small heart next to her name and said that she was excited to see how much Bits had grown when they got back.

The card was taped to Bits's dresser mirror, and she loved looking at the gilt angels connected via ribbons and bows, that surrounded an oval containing two cherubic children. '*A Toi Mon Amie*' was printed beneath the oval. Trinny told her it meant "to you, my friend." On the inside, the card said, '*j'envoie protection et amour*.' That meant "I send protection and love."

Before school started, Li'l Bits wanted to have Trinny help her write something back in French. As she decided what that something would be, Bits had asked Trinny how to say several things and loved listening to the fluid, melodic response. One day, she wanted to speak French too. Then, she and everyone else could tell secrets about her papa right in front of him, and he'd never know what they were saying.

Li'l Bits thought back to the conversation she'd had with her uncle before he left. She hadn't known what to make of how she felt when she saw Papa look at Trinny. The look on his face made her happy because she could tell that he was happy. But there was something deep in his eyes that connected with Trinny in a very different way than when he looked at her.

Somehow, Bits knew that both looks meant love, but different loves. Uncle George had helped her understand that difference, and said that if she mentioned what they had spoken about to a very special someone, that someone might be able to help. So this year, she knew what she was going to ask Santa for. She wanted a mother.

* * *

"Hello, Bits." It was a fine Saturday afternoon, and Trinny had come over at Li'l Bits's request to help with a letter to Uncle George. Trinny sat at the kitchen table next to her protégé, who was already poised atop the raised-chair her papa had made for her. "Okay, I've written up the things you wanted to say in your letter. All you need to do is copy what I wrote."

"Your handwriting is so pretty, Trinny. Do you think maybe one day mine'll be as nice?"

"Well, this is good practice. Making yourself slow down to think about what you're writing will help you form the letters more clearly."

"Is that how you learned to write so well?"

"Yes. The woman in the camp who taught me French, told me the same thing."

"Well," Li'l Bits said brightly, "if it worked for you, it can work for me too."

Trinny cast a sideways glance at the little blonde bundle of energy and absentmindedly reached out to stroke her hair, but

177

still not sure of herself, or how to express emotion, she diverted her hand by taking up a pencil.

"Let's get started, okay?"

"Ready when you are." Bits paused to look up at her friend. "Trinny, I wish you could be my teacher all the time."

With humor in her eyes, Trinny said, "Well, thank you. But with all the projects we've worked on, and all the mistakes you've so graciously pointed out that I've made, I can't believe you would want me to continue as your teacher in anything."

Bits smiled to herself, knowing that whether Trinny was a good teacher or not, she would do her best to keep Trinny coming over as much as possible. Uncle George had said that while he was gone, that would be her job. And through letters, he would keep working on her papa.

Li'l Bits liked having such a special job. A secret one. Why, Uncle George had practically given her permission to lie. Well, not actually *lie*, but tell little *white* lies . . . to help Santa, of course. The two of them were going to do their best to make his job easier this year.

The afternoon sped by, and soon, it was five o'clock. Li'l Bits had written a nice greeting inside the card her papa had gotten for her to send.

"Geesh." She put down the pencil and shook out her hand. "I feel like I've been writin' for forever."

Looking at the clock, Trinny said, "Well, *forever* might be an overstatement, but you have worked hard. And don't forget, we did stop to have milk and cookies, and to sit on the porch, and to play your Disney game, and—"

Li'l Bits held up a hand. "You can stop now. You make it sound like all we did was play, when *look*!" She held the card front and center before Trinny. "Hellooo, I worked hard."

Trying not to laugh out loud, Trinny said, "Yes, you did. And I guess that Saturdays *are* meant for mixing fun in with whatever else we do."

"See, you are a good teacher. You're already learnin'."

"Is that the sign of a good teacher? One that learns from her pupil?"

"Pew-pull? That sounds like somethin' I'd scrape off the bottom of my shoe after walkin' to Orvalee's through the Kramer's back pasture."

At that, Trinny couldn't help but laugh. It was then that Remy walked in, covered in sawdust and wood shavings he hadn't quite brushed off after turning some table legs on the lathe. A thin coating of dust clung to his eyebrows and five-o'-clock shadow, and it looked like a whole field of dandelion fluff had been blown right into his hair. The overall layer of dust left him looking akin to something that, indeed, might need to be scraped from the bottom of one's shoe. His appearance set off a round of laughter between Bits and Trinny that left him wondering at their sanity.

"O-kay," he said hesitantly. "Y'all all right?"

Having released the floodgate, Trinny was finding it difficult to reign herself in. It was disconcerting, yet strangely liberating.

Remy was quite used to his daughter laughing at him and thought nothing of it. But he was rather affected by the sight of Trinny in such a state. Her usually smooth, pristine brow was creased with laugh lines, and her keen eyes twinkled with uncommon merriment. Her laughter sounded like a happy bluebird had taken up residence right in his kitchen. He liked it.

To cover the swell of emotion that wanted to carry him to her side, Remy playfully stalked toward Bits, threatening to empty the contents of his hair onto her own.

"Don't you dare Papa!" Bits hurriedly climbed down from her high-stool and darted away, evading his grasp. "Papa, if you touch me, I'll have to take a bath and waste part of my Saturday."

He lumbered after her, making raspy dust-monster noises as he muttered threats of endless baths, no popcorn for movie night, and other unthinkable penalties. Bits again scampered out of his grasp, and using Trinny as a human shield, stayed on the side of her chair, opposite her papa.

The jocular atmosphere had been infectious, but when face-to-face with the discomposure of two adults who were currently unwilling to give credence to their own feelings, the playful tide quickly ebbed away.

"I'm sorry, ladies," Remy said as he walked to the kitchen sink to wash off. "I shoulda thought to make myself more presentable before walkin' in on ya. What were y'all laughin' at, other than me?"

"Trinny called me a *pew*pull," Li'l Bits said, emphasizing the first syllable, "and I said that sounded like somethin' that would get stuck to the bottom of my shoe."

Remy stopped washing his hands and arms, and stared at Bits. "Called you a what?"

"*Pew*-pull."

Trinny was sucking on her bottom lip, even biting it a little to stop herself from laughing. Releasing her lip to answer made a sound that caught Remy's attention, one that made his blood pulse faster.

"Bits said she thought I was a good teacher because I was learning from *her*. I asked if learning from a pupil is the sign of a good teacher. It all sort of fell apart from there."

"Oh, *pupil*," was all Remy said before returning his attention to washing up. He really wanted to watch Trinny's lips make that sound again. Internally, he shook himself. "Hey, it's gettin' on to supper time. What do ya say we three put a casserole in the oven and give you two a break by goin' for a walk? When the food's done, we can break out the TV trays and eat in the livin' room while we watch *People Are Funny* or *Perry Mason*."

"Oh, I wouldn't want to intrude on your mealtime together." Trinny made to collect her things from the table and leave, but Bits put a quick stop to that.

"Oh yes, please, please, Trinny. I mean Perry Mason is good

and all, but he's no Ellery Queen. Ellery Queen is my favorite. But he was on last night, so I guess Perry'll have to do."

Being a mystery aficionado, Bits had made the comment in all sincerity, and Trinny couldn't help but melt right into the child's grasp. But not wanting to seem too eager, she put up some resistance.

"If I stay longer, you two might get tired of having me around."

"What *are you* talkin' about?"

The force of Bits's reply made Remy want to stuff the dish towel he was drying his hands with into his mouth to stifle a reply. His daughter might have a better handle on this whole keeping-Trinny-around thing than he did. And suddenly, something George had said the night they talked made sense.

George said that if he, Remy, wanted a woman like Trinny, then maybe having a child first was the best way to get her. He could see that now. Trinny would feel more inclined to bend to the will of a headstrong, blonde dynamo, than she would to a five-foot-nothing craftsman.

"Land's sakes, Trinny. The things you say. Us not wantin' you around?" Bits snorted. "That's like sayin' no one likes ice cream." She sighed. She knew she was probably getting a little more wound up than was necessary, but these two were near to driving her crazy. How was she supposed to do her secret job when they kept making it so hard?

Li'l Bits muttered to herself as she cleared her things from the table. All Trinny and Remy could do was look at each other over her, smile and remain silent. Bits seemed to have become oblivious to them and went right on muttering.

"I swear, you two are like children sometimes. Maybe I should just take you over my knee. Course, then, you'd crush me, so that wouldn't work."

Verbally processing how to deal with her recalcitrant adults, she kept on. "I could get a switch . . . nope, can't reach. I won't go to school . . . no, then I'll miss my friends. I could just go to my room for the rest of the night . . . ugh, nope, then I'll be hungry." Stymied, Li'l Bits turned to her papa and said, "You know what, this whole discipline thing is harder than it sounds. How do you get grown-ups to stop talkin' nonsense?"

Trinny was doing her best to bite down a giggle by sucking on her lip again, and Remy almost forgot to pay attention to his daughter. His cute, adorable, loveably outraged daughter.

Doing his best to be seen taking the question seriously, Remy walked to the table and sat near Bits. "Well, now, sweetheart, I'm sure that neither Trinny or I meant to cause you such consternation. Right, Trinny?"

Trinny nodded in agreement.

"If Trinny agrees to stay for supper, will that help smooth things over? We can get back on track with that walk I mentioned, and I've got the casserole your nana brought over yesterday. It's in the fridge, just waitin' to be popped in the oven."

Trinny enjoyed watching Remy and Bits together. They were such a natural pair. Remy had changed so much since the adoption. And until that fateful day when she'd found Bits injured in Hughes Park, she hadn't realized just how much she not only valued the pair but treasured them as well. And by the way Remy had phrased the proposed remedy to Bits's soured mood, she knew there was no way she could decline the invitation. But that was okay; she didn't want to.

Li'l Bits took a cleansing breath, as if preparing herself to reason with wayward children. Looking up at Trinny, she calmly said, "Trinny, can you see your way clear to stayin' for supper? It's not like you live miles and miles away. Since you'll be goin' home after dark, Papa can drive you so the bogeyman'll lose his chance atcha."

Trinny nodded. "Yes Bits. I can agree to that."

"Right. Now Papa, you go get that casserole in the oven while Trinny and I get our shoes on. Oh, and you really might want to brush your hair. It's standin' out around your head like a firework on the Fourth of July."

Behind the child's back, Trinny's shoulders lurched as a hand shot up to cover her mouth. Her face went red with the effort of stifling the laugh, and she suddenly found the floor very interesting as she looked for her shoes.

"Well?" Li'l Bits said to her blank-faced papa. "What are ya waitin' for? Chop-chop." She clapped hard, twice.

Bemusedly, Remy shook his head and went to preheat the oven and spruce up.

"I swear," Bits said, more to herself than Trinny, "the casserole isn't gonna cook itself." Trinny almost lost it again. She hadn't felt this inclined to laugh in . . . well, she wasn't sure how long. Bits was certainly worked up this evening, and Trinny was getting quite a glimpse of the girl's headstrong nature. Not that she hadn't known about it before; she just couldn't remember ever seeing Bits act quite like *this*. Usually, talking to Bits was like talking to a mini adult. Her mind was lively and insightful. Often, her innocent questions necessitated slowing down to give them due consideration.

Tonight, however, Bits seemed more determined than usual to have her own way. Trinny knew there must be an underlying reason for the behavior, but she'd leave that to Remy to ferret out. For now, she would simply do her best to be amiable and open to enjoying an evening with two people, she was finding it very difficult to keep her walls up against.

Chapter 18

Confessions

Saturday, November 29, 1958

"Every man has his own courage, and is betrayed because he seeks in himself the courage of other persons."

—Ralph Waldo Emerson (1803–1882),
American poet and essayist

To prepare themselves for all they'd be doing today, Trinny enjoyed a moment of peace in Orvalee's cozy kitchen with a steaming cup of one of Orvalee's special herbal tea blends. Unlike her own bright, cheery, yellow-and-white kitchen, Orvalee's was done in earth tones. The home had been built in the 1890's and remodeled when Orvalee and her husband purchased it from the original owner.

Brick floors had been installed. These would hold up to the wear and tear of her three active sons, and all the dirt dragged in from the herb and vegetable gardens. Orvalee had fallen in love with the ornate, heavy metal stove that had been original to the home and kept it, sure that in its day, it had been at the height of fashion. It had four oven spaces, six burners on the lower cook surface, and three burners on top of the triple-stacked ovens. Those were a bit of a reach, even for her five-foot-six frame. But when her boys had been little, she'd used those upper hot plates a lot because they could never accidentally be reached.

On the next wall over, her husband had created an alcove filled with built-in cupboards that surrounded the newer oven. They had replaced the original icebox but kept the massive farm sink. She'd bathed all her baby boys in that sink, even a dog or two. The walls were a jewel tone emerald green, and the cupboards were a creamy milk color.

Trinny liked this kitchen; it *felt* like Orvalee. A mix of old and new. Soft, yet solid. And quiet. With no men-folk rummaging through the fridge or cupboards, it was just quiet, like her own kitchen. But Trinny was beginning to think that a little more fuss and noise might be nice.

"This tea is delicious, Orvalee. You should package and sell it."

"Others have said the same. Maybe I will." Orvalee sat at the table with Trinny and took a sip from her own cup. "It is a nice start to the day, isn't it?"

"And what a day it's going to be."

"Oh my, yes." Orvalee sighed happily at the thought. "Our second Thanksgiving dinner in three days. I'm so happy that George and Claudine are back and get to share this with us. And I can't believe how big the children have grown. Why, Jeremy is taller than I am."

"Well, Beau is taller than me."

"How was Thanksgiving with your family in Utah? Were your brother and sister able to be there too?"

Trinny released a heavy sigh. "Yes, they were."

Orvalee could see there was a whole lot more to the story than the three-word reply suggested. "Do you mind my askin' if it went okay? You don't seem like you had the best time."

"It was . . . interesting. My brother and sister have each

gravitated to their own . . . extremes." Trinny paused, and Orvalee waited, knowing this was her friend's way.

"My brother has been in California a while now and found Anna. They got married and are now expecting their first child. My mom and dad are so excited to finally be grandparents."

Orvalee could relate to that. Oh, how she wanted to be a granny.

"My brother is working in Hollywood and has dreams of one day being in a movie as something other than 'waiter number two.' He does anything and everything. Assistant to the assistant script supervisor. Office boy. Anything he thinks will get him one rung higher on the ladder. It's a fanciful world, but it seems to make him and his wife happy. Conversely, my sister has been entertaining more *radical* ideas."

"Radical? I'm not sure I follow."

"There are many who are upset over how those of Japanese descent were treated during the war." Trinny took a fortifying sip of tea. "Louelle is working with others to force the government to 'recognize' us. See us. Remember us. You know, when the war was over, most didn't even have their own homes to go back to, especially those in California. The blacks who migrated from the south to take advantage of defense industry jobs had taken over the homes."

Trinny looked long and hard at Orvalee, who sat, as patient as a statue, waiting for her to continue. Trinny knew she didn't have to, but this time, she did. "You know, there were photographers for the war relocation authority there to take pictures of us as we were forced to leave our homes, shops, farms . . . I remember them. Men with large, single-lensed eyes where faces should have been. Eyes single to the glory of a cover story: 'Page one! See how President Roosevelt is protecting *us* from the enemy within.' Orvalee, I was fifteen, Louelle eighteen and, Tomi was thirteen. What threat were we? We were citizens. My parents were citizens. They were *born* here. That should have meant something. Shouldn't it?"

Orvalee heard the pleading in Trinny's voice and moved to stand behind her, enveloping her friend in a loving embrace. "Yes. Yes it should have, and I'm so sorry." A tear dripped from her face onto Trinny's dark hair, where it glided down the silken strands and was lost. "I'm sorry for bringin' up the past. Sometimes that's a place we don't want to go and yet can't help thinkin' about *all* the time."

Trinny turned, extended a hand, pulled Orvalee back down onto her own chair and said, "I know you have your own hell. I still have my family, whereas you . . ." Seeing the pain in her friend's eyes, Trinny couldn't say it.

"Whereas I lost all but one. I hear from Ervyn. He hasn't stopped long in one place yet. I'm hopeful he'll find somewhere that feels like home. Then, since he seems to have no desire to return here, I can go visit him. I just hope he can find himself."

Trinny took out a handkerchief and blew her nose. "What a fine pair we make. We're supposed to be preparing for a Thanksgiving feast and here we are, crying over spilled milk."

"Honey, when the darn jug is emptied over your head, I think a bit of a sulk is in order. And that's why we have each other—a second family to help ease the pain, to lend a listenin' ear or a shoulder of comfort. And, my friend, you are a comfort." Orvalee took both of Trinny's hands in hers. "You're like the daughter I never had, and I hope you know how much I love you."

Trinny's nose began to run, and her eyes filled with large, glistening tears of gratitude. Trinny blew her nose again and looked at her handkerchief.

"I think I'm going to need another one of these. I don't know why, but for the past while, I haven't been able to keep my emotions under control."

"I know, honey, and it's a wonderful thing."

"How can being an emotional wreck be wonderful?" Trinny dabbed at her eyes.

"Because it means you're feelin'! Happy, sad, confused,

angry; Trinny, they're just emotions, not rabid dogs. Feelin' 'em won't kill ya, but it might just bring you the life you've been wantin'."

"I'm not sure I follow."

"Oh, child, I think you follow just fine. You're just afraid of lookin' around the bend in the road. The one with a family waitin' for ya. The one with a blonde child and a caring man who loves you with all his heart."

Trinny blinked and stared.

"Loves me? What do you mean, loves me?"

"Now, don't tell me you haven't seen the way Remy looks atcha. Haven't seen the respect he treats you with. Why, the light of love practically hangs over the man like a halo these days. And when he sees you with Bits, how the two of you are together, my dear, I don't think God himself could look on another with more love than that."

Orvalee's words made the hollow part around Trinny's heart feel warm, like honey melting into a slice of hot, fresh bread. As she thought, she unconsciously sucked on the corner of her lip. Her dark, mocha eyes fixed on Orvalee with a question, one she hesitated to ask, but desperately wanted answered.

Trinny drew in a long breath through her nose, then let it slowly escape through bowed lips. She scratched the back of her neck, then her nose, cheek, and forehead. In fact, every part of her seemed to be a mass of nervous, itching-energy. She rose from her chair and paced for a minute, then stopped to look at Orvalee, who remained irritatingly calm.

Orvalee smiled. "Trinny Jenks, you heard me. He may not woo you like they do in the movies, with flowers and walks in the park. He's not a flowery man. But you two have been spendin' more time in one another's company, and he trusts you with the thing he values above all else: Bits. The question now is, do you love him back? Or are the feelings you've got for the man tied to Bits first—and him second? 'Cause if that's the case, my advice would be to walk away now, before he says anything that can come back to haunt him. He's a good man with a good heart. Don't break it."

Trinny stared out the kitchen window, seeing outside herself. Watching her "alone" self, gravitate toward the warmth of the unlikely duo like a moth to a flame. Her feelings had developed so slowly over the years, that she hadn't realized what they were becoming until, with a convulsive swallow, she saw them plain as day. She did love Remy. Trinny raised and then lowered her shoulders with the revelation. She'd known she loved Bits; everyone did. But Remy . . . Yeah. She did.

Oh, holy cow, she was in love!

With her face a naked display of pure emotion, Trinny turned to her friend. "Oh, Orvalee . . ." was all she could say.

"Well, now we're cookin' with grease!" Orvalee slapped the table triumphantly as she went to Trinny. "I knew it! Oh, sweet thing, I knew it." Orvalee threw her arms around the young woman, who, eyes wide with the realization of what all this could mean, simply stood there and allowed the embrace.

Orvalee practically buzzed with excitement over the revelation. She had yet to release Trinny, so they both jigged as Orvalee bounced up and down, praising the Lord.

"This is gonna be the best, most wonderful Thanksgiving ever!"

"Orvalee!" Trinny exclaimed. "You can't tell anyone. Not yet. I'm not ready yet. I . . . Why, I just realized it myself. I need time to . . . adjust. To think. To . . ."

"To what, sweet thing? Over-think it? Don't burn the toast." Orvalee turned Trinny to face her and cupped her cheeks in her hands. "This is love. Just love. You're in the *first* phase, the bloomin' phase. That's all. I'm not sayin' that now you know it, y'all have to run out and hitch your carts together. Though I am lookin' forward to that."

Trinny was glad someone was excited. She was petrified.

"Oh, child. Love isn't a fixed point on the horizon that once you lay eyes on it, ya *have* to move toward it and only it. Love is a vehicle. It's like . . . well, like a clown car in a way, if that makes sense. It starts out sorta small, but can carry a lot of laughter and fun. Then, the more you cram in it, the more that can spill out when ya open the door. And then, when you can't seem to shove one more person in, all of a sudden, the middle crinkles open like an accordion, and lo and behold, it's doubled in size. You gettin' any of this?"

Hoping she'd followed Orvalee's line of logic, Trinny nodded. "I think so."

"Come on. Let's get to work on the food, and we can talk as we go. And don't worry about me. I won't spill the beans to anyone 'til you're ready to talk to Remy first." Orvalee gently chucked Trinny on the chin. "But I do think that'd better be done sooner than later. Don't let your feet get colder than a well digger's butt in January."

"A well digger's . . .?" Trinny just shook her head. "Oh, Orvalee."

"I know; it's rather poetic, isn't it?"

"Poetic? Questionable. Visual? Definitely."

"As long as I got my point across, that's all that matters. Now, come on, let's get cookin'."

By the appointed two o'clock dinner time, Orvalee and Trinny had peeled, cooked, and mashed enough potatoes to feed an army; made Orvalee's famous cranberry sauce with candied orange peels; baked parmesan buttermilk biscuits; and made green bean casserole with pecan chips. It took a couple of trips to load everything in the car and secure it for the short drive to Remy's, but they got it all there on time.

As Trinny and Orvalee pulled into Remy's driveway, Li'l Bits heard the gravel crunch beneath the tires and ran out to greet them. Dressed to the Nines, Li'l Bits had her blonde curls held back with a new, cranberry-colored ribbon around her head. Face aglow, she called, "Orvalee, Trinny! It's about time y'all got here. What can I help carry in? Uncle George, Claudine, and the kids are already here. Oh my goodness, your car smells *divine*. What can I carry?"

"Now, hold on there, sweet Bits." Orvalee said getting out of the car. "Inhale, okay?"

Bits was full of energy, but she did her best to obey. Remembering what her papa had said about holiday manners, she stood ram-rod straight and politely held out her hands, waiting for them to be filled.

"That's my girl." Orvalee bent down and gave her an affectionate squeeze, then handed her a covered basket filled with the aromatic parmesan biscuits.

Li'l Bits inhaled a deep breath of satisfaction. "Oh my goodness. I'm startin' my dinner with one of these. They smell *divine*." She walked in the house, sorely tempted to sneak one.

Orvalee shook her head. "Divine?"

"I know," Trinny said, smiling. "I thought she'd be over it by now, but ever since her birthday, everything smells, looks, or tastes *divine*. And *essence* somehow works its way into her descriptions as well. We think she got that one from you." They both laughed as they loaded up and started for the house.

Before the women made it to the porch, Jeremy and Beau came out to help.

"Oh, thank you, boys," Orvalee said. "The big pot of potatoes is on a towel on the backseat. Careful as you get 'em out. The hot pads are right next to the pot. Make sure to use 'em. I don't want you gettin' burned."

"Yes'm," the boys said in unison.

Inside, Remy's living room was decorated with paper pumpkins Li'l Bits had taped to the walls, using a chair to get them as high as she could. The big front window had been painted with a huge pumpkin still attached to a vine that twisted into the words *Happy Thanksgiving*.

"Trinny, I'll bet we can thank you for that lovely window creation," Orvalee praised. "It's absolutely gorgeous."

"Thank you."

Orvalee heard the blush in Trinny's voice.

"While Bits cut out and colored her pumpkins, I painted the window."

Orvalee moved in close so only Trinny could hear. "Mm-hmm. Now, just think on all the other things you can work on together once you set that man's heart at ease." Orvalee gave a nearly imperceptible nod toward Remy, who was in the kitchen taking orders from Claudine.

The kitchen table had been angled lengthwise through the archway into the living room so the additional leaf could be added. A card table had been set up at the end in the living room to comfortably accommodate the nine diners.

As soon as Orvalee set the casserole on the kitchen counter, she hugged Claudine. "Sweet woman. Have I told you how good it is to have you back?"

Pleased, Claudine cooed in her thicker-than-ever accent, "Of course you have mon amie. You have said it when at my house, when I first returned. You have said it when you kindly invited us to share in this dinner. And now, you have said it again."

She beamed, grateful that these good people held nothing against her for leaving George and taking the children. She knew how beloved George was to them, and she'd been a little worried that when she came back (for she hadn't doubted her husband would come for them), these people might despise her for her actions. Thankfully, they had not. It was indeed good to be home.

In the moment Orvalee captured Claudine's attention, Remy used the opportunity to escape and move toward Trinny. "The food looks and smells incredible. Y'all did an amazing job."

"Thank you." Embarrassed, Trinny lowered her gaze, then said, "But we can't take credit for the entire meal. Your turkey looks like it belongs in a Norman Rockwell painting. And Bits did a wonderful job cutting the vegetables for the relish tray."

"She sure had fun. Said she felt big standin' on the chair next to me as we put everything together this mornin'. Thursday's Thanksgiving with my family was a lot of fun, but I think my girl's been more excited about today. And thank you for comin' over and decoratin' the house with her; she absolutely loved it. She's so proud of those pumpkins. And last night, she made me go stand on the porch with her so we could see how the living room light lit up your window-pumpkin from behind. It really is beautiful seein' it that way."

Trinny appreciated that Remy was always so open with compliments for the things she did. She never thought they were much of anything, but Remy had a way of making her feel like she'd scaled the highest mountain to help them.

The Thanksgiving spread included Claudine's French version of stuffing, the enormous turkey and relish tray, George's cornbread and deviled eggs, all that Orvalee and Trinny had made, plus pie. Eager to help welcome George and his family back, Lynne Anne had sent over pumpkin, apple, and pecan pies.

Never had a group of people eaten with so much gusto and enjoyed such pleasant conversation. Eager to hear all about France and what everyone had done over there, Li'l Bits peppered the Dollis clan with question after question.

A couple of times, Remy had to remind her not to talk with food in her mouth. "Bits," he whispered, "please remember your manners. Wash a bit o' that food down with your Grapette and give people a chance to answer before you fire off another question."

Embarrassed that she'd had to be reminded—again, Li'l Bits took a swallow of the soda pop—a holiday treat—and did her best to slow down.

By the end of the evening, everyone had eaten until they were undoing buttons and loosening belts. Then, some played charades and a fun Thanksgiving match game, while others plastered themselves to any surface they could lie on, dozing in a blissful, food-induced coma. Then pie had been consumed in quantities no one thought possible since everyone but George already felt they were on the verge of throwing up. All in all, it was a *perfect* Thanksgiving dinner.

Chapter 19

Orvalee

Friday, April 3, 1959

"Success is not final; failure is not fatal: it is the
courage to continue that counts."

—Winston S. Churchill (1874–1965),
United Kingdom Prime Minister

Working in the greenhouse usually soothed Orvalee in a way nothing else could. Today, she was supposed to be putting together some skin irritation salves for the Alberts, who ran a roadside "pharmacy" of sorts. The Alberts were naturalists who promoted their homegrown fare as "Nature's Pharmacy." Each fruit or vegetable they sold came with a little card detailing potential medicinal uses. But there were some things they didn't like to take the time to make, such as many of the things Orvalee delighted in. In the years they'd done business together, the arrangement had worked to their mutual financial benefit.

Today, though, Orvalee could not keep her mind on the task at hand. There was an uneasiness in the air. An unease that had her ruminating on the months since the neighborhood

Thanksgiving feast. That had been such a wonderful day. She had loved the conversation with Trinny and was overjoyed to see how her young friend was blossoming.

Over the years, one painstaking petal at a time, Orvalee had watched Trinny begin to open to life. To feeling safe. To allowing friendships, and, at last, to love. Love was such a beautiful thing, full of layers, each with a life all its own. The budding phase that Trinny and Remy were in was especially fun to watch. Glances filled with anticipation. Flushed cheeks. Hidden touches beneath a table or behind the backs of others. Secret touches that made lovers feel alive and restless to move on to their next phase.

Just like a bouquet of flowers, the different types of love could be bound together into a thing of beauty. The thought reminded Orvalee of an ancient history class she'd taken in college. She'd been enthralled with how the Ancient Greeks had denoted each type of love.

Orvalee saw her friends experiencing "Ludus," the flirtatious love found in the beginning of a relationship. "Eros," or romantic love, may come next, if they could each overcome their innate shyness. She smiled, remembering how it had been for her and her beloved Avner.

Avner Benson was destined to become the hometown football hero in both high school and college, and had been the most handsome young man in New Iberia. His long, sun-bleached, sandy-brown hair swept back from his forehead like a lush, feathery crown. His eyes were the dark green of an emerald, and his chiseled jaw and high cheekbones would have left Michelangelo in awe. Orvalee sighed, remembering.

She had been tall for a girl, a little too lean for her own liking, and bookish. Where Avner's eyes had glistened like a jewel, hers were the deep green of new forest growth. But she'd always had long, thick, dark-brown hair, almost black, which, as they courted, Avner had loved to unpin and run his fingers through.

She'd had to make sure her hair was put back up before going home after an evening with Avner. He'd gotten pretty good at helping her restyle it, and the process had made them both feel a little naughty. Oh, how she missed him.

Her hands began to shake, and she had to abandon the salve-making. Sinking into a high-backed wicker chair that commanded a sun-filled corner of the greenhouse, Orvalee thought about "Pragma:" enduring love. A unique love that matures over the years and everlastingly bonds a couple. You do not "fall" into this kind of love; you "stand" in it. This love is purposeful and keeps you by the side of your chosen indefinitely, bound together through mutual desire. Indefinitely—a blessing when your chosen lives a long life with you. A curse when they do not.

"Oh, Avner, I feel so old. So *very* old." She leaned her forehead against a hand and stared blankly at nothing in particular. "I'll be sixty this year, my love. Sixty." Saying it aloud almost hurt physically. She couldn't be that old; her grandmother was . . . Actually, her grandmother was dead.

"Dead Avner, Gran is dead. Just like you. Just like Jonathan. Just like Devyn. Just like . . ." Giant tears sprang to her eyes, and before she could stop them, they spilled down her face and onto the wood floor, making tiny, crater-like shapes on its dirt-dusted surface.

"Sometimes, it feels like even Ervyn has followed y'all to heaven. He writes when he's in one place long enough to find pen and paper. Sometimes, he even sends a photograph. I got one a month or so back. He was by some redwoods out in California. Said he'd always wanted to see 'em. Now he has. Checked that off his bucket list. Avner, that poor boy is so preoccupied with the fear of death that even though he's out there doin' what he *thinks* is livin', I'm not really sure he is. Seems to me like he's just chasin' the end of a rainbow. Somethin' he can see but'll never find."

Sinking back into the cushion of the chair, Orvalee dried her eyes on her work apron and absently turned to gaze outside. "Do you remember the July picnic at Spanish Lake? The one the town had to welcome our overseas soldier boys back home? I was so grateful they hadn't lowered the draft age to eighteen until the war was practically over, so you never got called up. After seein' Buddy Bustermenter with his lower left leg gone, and Joe Cotton. Joshin' Joe, they used to call him. Well, he wasn't so jovial at that picnic. Though I remember you tryin' to wheedle him out of his funk. And even though I was only sixteen to your nineteen, I think that's the moment I truly lost my heart to you and vowed that one day, I'd get you to notice me."

The sky outside had darkened, and Orvalee thought it matched her mood perfectly. "When you went off to the university in Sewanee, I thought my heart would just about break. I thought you'd meet up with some woman that was everything I wasn't, and I'd never get my chance with ya. But when you came back for that picnic, even more handsome than I remembered, and you smiled at me at the pie table, oh, I thought my knees would fail and I'd embarrass myself by starin' up atcha from the ground."

Orvalee slowly levered herself out of the chair and shuffled around the greenhouse as she pinched back a plant here, watered another one there.

"I feel old, Avner. Ervyn's almost thirty-three. Can you believe our baby boy is that old? Then there's George; he's thirty-nine. Remy and Trinny are just thirty-two. I could be a mother to 'em all. I could be a grandmother." She felt the weight of a world that was lost to her and sighed.

"I *should* be a grandmother. I should have dozens of sweet babies clutterin' the ground around my feet. I should be shooin' 'em outa this place and havin' to guard all my bottled stock. I should have a hoard of cookies hidden in the pantry that the kids think they're sneakin' into. Bless 'em. They'd wear such smiles of triumph as they ran out to the garden to eat 'em in secret. I'd've loved that. Seein' 'em skedaddle fast as their little legs could carry 'em."

She snatched the bottom of her apron and pulled it up to cover her face, hoping to blot out the despairing thoughts. Her muffled voice cried out, "Oh, Avner, can I keep on like this? Sometimes, I get so tired, I . . ." She dared not say it, but she'd thought about it many times.

When she'd found Devyn, her sweet-hearted, gentle-spirited middle son, with the gun in his hand and . . . and what should have looked like *his* face but didn't. The sight of it was worse than anything she'd seen as a nurse in the war because he was *hers*. Now, all her remembrances of his chubby-cheeked child face were marred by what she'd seen.

"Why? Why did he have to do it behind the shed? On this very property? Why couldn't he have gone someplace else? Someplace where I . . . I never would've had to be the one to find him."

The apron fell from her face, and she steadied herself against a raised planter. "Oh, Avner, I do thank God it *was* me who found him and not Ervyn. That sight would've done him in for sure." Closing her eyes against the image that still haunted not only her dreams but also, in times like this, her whole being, she did recall one thing, the only thing that had brought her any solace at the time. And, perhaps, the single thing that had stopped her from following her men-folk to the other side when Ervyn had up and gone. In her dead son's open left eye, the one that had been left intact, she'd seen . . . the only word that came to mind was *peace*. She'd focused on that good eye. The eye through which she saw the joy of release. Of no more pain. Of no more remembering things young men should never be made to witness in the first place.

"My sweet boy. Is he with you, Avner? Have the two of you found Jonathan? Have ya gone fishin'? I'll bet the water there is clear as crystal and glimmers with rainbow light. When you're out on a boat, does it sing to you, like you said the waters here did? I remember you sayin' that listening to the water was the real reason you loved to take the boys fishin'. My love, I hope the water there sings you sweet songs and that in the melody, you hear *my* voice whisperin' how much I love and miss you. 'Cause I do, you know! I still love you somethin' fierce, and I'm doin' my level best to keep on livin'."

With a heaviness born of seemingly endless years of loneliness, Orvalee lowered herself to the floor of the greenhouse. Kneeling in supplication, she clasped her trembling hands to her chest and cried out, "Avner, please, please send Ervyn home. Send my baby boy a sign. Something to let him know I need him, if only for a while. Please, even if only for a *little* while, I'd take that. I long to see his smile again, it reminds me of you. To see *life* behind it. To hear his laugh echo through this house, like when he was a boy. I miss my boy. If it's not too selfish a thing to ask, I'd *really* like to have him back. Maybe you, and Devyn, and Jonathan could put a good word in with God for me, 'cause even I know it'll take some sort of miracle to bring that boy home."

Completely spent, Orvalee sank all the way to the ground. Curled in on herself like a cat on a hearth, she let the tears fall as her prayer for comfort stirred the air. "Please, Lord, send me a sign. I need to know I can do this. I need to know I am strong enough to keep—on—doin' this. I'm so tired. Tired . . ."

"Orva-lee-ee! You in here?" sang out a little voice.

Orvalee's head snapped to attention. She rose to her hands and knees, pulled herself up using the same sturdy planter that had been her altar, and saw two corn-flower blue eyes, bright with exercise. Eyes that quickly dulled when they caught a glimpse of her own dirty, puffy, tearstained face.

"Orvalee," Bits said tentatively, "you okay?"

Making a quick pass over her face with the apron, Orvalee tried to make her voice sound as cheery as Bits's had been. "Why, hello there, sweet thing. Course I'm alright. I was just . . ." Orvalee glanced quickly about, trying to come up with an excuse for her appearance, and saw her unfilled salve jars. Pointing to them, she said, "I was just workin' with some rascally plant that left a film on my fingers that stung my eyes when I touched 'em. You know, like how when you cut onions, they make you cry."

Li'l Bits didn't look at the salve jars. She just said, "Mm-hmm."

Unnerved at having been caught mid-cry, Orvalee asked, "What are you doin' here, baby girl? I don't recall us having a time set to work on anything."

"We didn't. I just *felt* like comin' over to say hello."

Orvalee noticed the sky beyond Bits had changed even more. With a fixed stare, she walked slowly forward asking, "Does your papa know you're here, child?"

Li'l Bits hesitated, not answering.

Orvalee's tone became insistent. "Child, does your papa know where you are?"

"Well," Bits said sheepishly, "not exactly."

"What do you mean, exactly?"

"Well, Uncle George came over for lunch, and he and Papa got to talkin' out in the shop. Well, I had nothin' to say, so I told 'em I was gonna walk around a bit. And, here I am. Jesslyn and the girls are all busy with their families today. The cousins are all on vacation, and spring break can be boring when it's just me."

Orvalee took another look at the sky. Something didn't feel right. "You can stay a few minutes, but I think I ought to walk you home shortly."

"Oh, no. Can't I stay and help work on the salves? I promise I won't touch my eyes."

"What? Oh, yeah. Eyes. Um," Orvalee sniffed the air. "Was the walk over okay?"

"Yeah. Pretty much the same as always." Li'l Bits pushed her tall stool over to the workstation and used the step stool to climb up. "Except for the birds."

"Birds? Bits, what were the birds doing?"

Swiveling toward Orvalee, Bits said, "Oh, they were goin' crazy at Miss Banes's bird feeder. There were, like, a *hundred* of 'em flappin' around tryin' to get to the food. I've never seen that many all at once. Maybe they were havin' a party. That would be fun if birds had a party. Don't ya think?"

Without answering, Orvalee walked outside and looked up to where a flock of ducks was flying low. A couple of the neighbor's dogs were barking. Invisible needles of cold dread prickled up her spine.

"Bits!" Orvalee turned back to the greenhouse, calling out, "I think we should get you back home—now."

"Oh, Orvalee, I just got here. I don't want to go home. Papa's busy and I've got nothing to do there. You know I'm a good helper. Can't I help with the salves?"

"Sweet thing, let's go to the house. I need to make a couple of calls, one to your papa so he'll know where you are."

"But he's in the shop with Uncle George."

"Don't you worry; I have the shop number too." Orvalee secured the greenhouse and hastened them both through the back porch door. Just as they got inside, the first chunks of hail began to fall. Grateful for her brick home and sturdy roof, Orvalee dialed Remy.

Chapter 20

A Great Storm

Remy could barely hear the telephone over the din of hailstones that had begun to pummel the metal roof of his shop.

"Hello!" he shouted into the receiver. "What? I can barely hear you."

As Remy tried to figure out who he was talking to, George went to the door and looked out over the water, not liking what he saw.

"Bits? No, she's in the house." He had realized the caller was Orvalee. "Wait, what? No, that's not possible. She said she was just walkin' around the house." Remy didn't want to believe that, in light of what was raining down upon them, his daughter was not safe inside *his* home. "Hey, George, run into the house and make sure Bits is there, will ya?"

Back into the phone, he hollered that George had just gone to check on Bits. "What do you mean he won't find her there?

Of course . . . What?" Remy swung toward the shop door just as George skidded into view, shaking his head no. "Shit!" Remy yelled as he slammed a fist against the wall. "No, not you Orvalee. I know you . . . What? No, I'll be right over to pick her up . . . the hell you say; I will too."

If it were possible, the metal roof began to thunder even louder, and Remy could no longer hear a word Orvalee said. He hung up and darted out the shop door past George, thankful he had covered the entire porch between his shop and the house. Though it was a little quieter in the house because of the insulation between the ceiling and the metal roof, it still sounded like he was standing in the middle of an active train yard.

George had followed him in, and just stood, staring out through the open doorway, watching hailstones beat the water into a churning froth.

Remy dialed Orvalee's number.

"Hey, it's me. I'm in the house now. I know you think Bits should stay there, but I can . . . No, I . . . Now, you're soundin' like my mama . . . Of course I know you're a mother, I just . . . Orvalee, I meant no disrespect, but I'm her father, and I . . . Of course I don't want to die. I'm not gonna get killed comin' to get her. It's just a little ole storm . . . You don't mean that! . . . Okay! Fine!" Remy slammed the receiver into the cradle and muttered, "Have it your own damn way."

"The woman's gone off her rocker, George. She's as windy as a sack full of farts. Thinks this storm is a tornado and I should just leave Bits with her to ride it out. That's ridiculous. I can't leave Bits there. She'll be afraid and need me to keep her calm. I usually make cocoa to get us through a storm. We read books, and I tickle her back. I . . ."

"Rem, look." George pointed. "I think Orvalee is right."

Remy stalked to the door and looked to where George pointed while George took up the receiver and dialed his own home, wishing that instead of coming here on his lunch break to talk to Remy, he'd have gone home.

"Honey." George cupped the phone close. "You gonna be all right? You've never been through a storm like this. I could come—"

Claudine told him pretty much the same thing Orvalee had said to Remy. Jeremy and Beau could take care of her and Aline. He tried to convince her otherwise, but as the words left his mouth, he knew they weren't true.

He asked for Jeremy and then instructed his eldest son how to secure the windows, telling him to keep everyone as close to the center of the house as possible. "Maybe get the mattresses and make a fort for everyone against the far wall of your bedroom. The main thing is to keep 'em all calm. Can you do that, son?"

"Yes, sir." Jeremy's voice quavered only slightly as he tried to assure his father that he was capable of being the man of the house. "I'll hold down the fort 'til you're able to get here. And Pa?"

"Yeah?"

Jeremy cleared his throat nervously. "I love you."

It took all the strength he had not to drop the phone and run home, but George managed to say, "I love you too, son. And I . . ." George pinched the bridge of his nose to hold back some pesky tears that were threatening to break free. "I . . . wish I could . . ." Damn the tears already.

"I know Pop. I'll take care of 'em. Just be safe and get home when you can."

Dejected and heart sore, George hung up and went to stand by Remy. The two of them just stood there, looking out over the water at an eerily green sky. Thick, dark clouds pressed low toward the earth, a shamrock glaze seeping through the gray seams like grass-colored vomit. This was bad. Really bad.

George's voice was a lifeless monotone. "I'm not sure it'll actually touch down here. But it's not gonna be pretty. Well"—

he sighed heavily—"we'd best latch the shutters. It's a good thing you have sturdy shutter dogs, or this wind would twist 'em like the ties on store-bought bread. You got a board or somethin' sturdy we can use as a shield against the hail?"

Remy felt as beaten as the water.

"Come on." He sighed wearily. "I've got plenty of scrap board in the shop that'll do." The two silent men set about securing the doors and windows. With that done, they dodged back inside, where all they could do was wait.

"You think Orvalee and Bits'll be okay? I mean, I know the woman's house is strong and all, but . . ."

George's weighty hand settled on Remy's quaking shoulder, and the warmth of it spread through Remy like hot coffee on a cold morning.

"They'll be fine," George assured. "Just fine. This isn't Orvalee's first rodeo, and besides, she's a nurse and more than qualified to take care of—"

Remy's eyes shot open, alight with animalistic fear. "Oh, George, you don't think Bits'll need a nurse do ya?"

"Now, come on, Rem. You know darn well that's *not* what I meant."

Remy couldn't seem to stand still, so he paced nervously about the living room. Back and forth, up and down, back and forth, up and down.

"Rem, you're gonna wear a path in the rug if you don't stop that. Want some coffee?"

Blowing a hard breath, Remy tried to gather himself together by pretending that Bits was in her room and he had to set a good example for her. "Sure, I guess so."

While George got a pot going on the stove, Remy turned on the radio, then went to stare out the front window, grateful that both the pitch of the roof and the ash in the middle of the porch were deflecting a great deal of the wind's growing force. Maybe because of the tree, Remy hadn't thought to put shutters on the front window, and morbid curiosity now made him glad he hadn't.

Mesmerized by the trees' frenetic dance, he watched. Bend, dip, sway, crack! Branch, by weak branch, the trees were being thinned. Thank heaven he had a sturdy metal roof.

For some reason, he was drawn to reach out and place a hand on the piece of glass in front of him. Cool to the touch, it moved and seemed to breathe like a living thing beneath his palm. Closing his eyes, he could feel the window bow and arch with each unseen gust of wind that slapped against it.

It was funny, but the glass reminded him of Bits. Compared to the world around it, the clear membrane was as thin as Bits was small. But it could let in the light of day to warm and illuminate the cozy living room or keep unwanted things out. It could be broken with the simple force of a closed fist, or, like now, shield him from the raging force of a storm. Bits, his Li'l Bits . . . Unheeded tears leaked from the corners of his eyes, and he sniffed. *How is she so strong?*

"Rem."

No response.

"Rem!"

George's voice penetrated his mental sojourn. Hand still on the window, Remy swiveled his head toward George.

"Yeah."

"It'd probably be best if you moved away now. Come on over to the table and sit. Coffee's almost ready."

Remy was reluctant to remove himself from the unexpectedly tangible connection to his daughter, but with a final caress of the cool, smooth surface, he obeyed.

The task of doing nothing was arduous. Oblivious to the drone of the radio, each man sat lost in his own thoughts while the clock ticked away the seconds, the minutes, the helpless nothingness.

Remy finally said, "I didn't expect it to be so hard."

"What?" George looked blank.

"Waiting."

"Yeah, waiting. Had my fill of it overseas. Thought I was done with that sort of . . ." George tried to think of how to put it. "Sometimes, waitin' was like bein' on fire. Adrenaline pumped, but we had to *wait* to burst through a door, knowin' a glimpse of hell might be on the other side. Had to wait out storms while rain water filled our boots and soaked us clean through. Once, when we came upon a field of bombed-out tanks, we had to check inside 'em to make sure none of the enemy were hidin' there."

Remy saw George's Adam's apple make a quick trip up and down as the big man choked something back. Grateful he had no idea what George was seeing in his mind's eye, Remy sat quietly, until his friend continued.

"Well, let's just say that when I opened the lid of one of those big ole tin cans, the stench of cooked flesh burst out so strong, I had me a good long wait before I could check another one. As bad as the smell was, what it looked like on the inside was even worse." George shook his head, as if to clear it. "Sorry. Didn't mean to . . . Well, just sorry."

"No, that's fine. Sorta lets me know things *could* be a lot worse. Right? I mean, the storm, well, that's not as bad as . . . as what you've been through, right?" Remy spoke in hopeful tones.

The storm—Remy could not call it a tornado—was nowhere near as bad as war. In war, there were bombs, guns, an enemy you could blame for the loss of life and destruction. Storms were just natural things filled with wind, rain, and lightning. The force pummeling his roof thundered even louder, as if to say, "Would you like me to show you just how bad *I* can be?"

And then, all of a sudden, the cacophony of hailstones ceased, and the two men were momentarily lost within a silence so loud, it was almost worse than being pummeled by the heavens. After a second, they could actually hear themselves think, which may not have been a good thing, because now they could hear the radio.

"We're continuing to update our warnings for severe weather in the cities of Belcher, Mooringsport, Vivian, Shreveport, Ida . . ." The man named town after town. "High winds and hail continue to wreak havoc as city police from surrounding areas have already reported uprooted trees and toppled power poles, leaving live electrical lines strewn across the wet ground. Authorities are advising all residents of Caddo, DeSoto, Sabine . . ." Again, parish after parish was named, as well as a few counties in Texas.

Without realizing he said it aloud, Remy wondered, "Sweet Lord, just how big is this storm?"

The announcer continued. "Already, there are reports of several large structures having been destroyed by high winds. A Bossier Parish spokesperson, has reported that six homes off Butler Hill Road have been damaged, and downed trees cover Wynnesca Road, east of Benton."

"Rem, you okay?" George could see that Remy wasn't doing so well. His friend's face was pallid and he looked like he wanted to hurl. Then, the announcer said something that turned Remy to stone.

"This just in, it looks as though the tornado *has* touched down and is headed directly for Oil City."

"Trinny." The word escaped as barely a whisper. Nothing more than the imagined sound of an exhale. "My family."

"Trinny's fine; your family's fine. Your sisters are on vacation outta state somewhere, so they and their families will all be fine. This time of day, Trinny'll be safe and sound in her office . . . in . . ." Then, George understood. Trinny worked in downtown Oil City.

"George, I've had to abandon Bits, but at least I know where she's at. I know she's close by, and what I see goin' on out my window, she sees too. But Trinny? My parents? I know it's almost ten miles away, but the man said 'tornado.' George, the man said it, a tornado!"

As much to soothe himself as Remy, George said, "I'm sure they're fine. Trinny's probably more than safe in her brick office. The walls of that building have withstood a fair sight more than what we've got goin' on right now."

"But a tornado? I'll just call Trinny and my folks to make sure they're okay. Yeah, I'll call. Trinny will answer and let me know I've just got a board up my butt." Remy breathed out a frenzied little hysterical laugh as he picked up the receiver to dial her work number.

His eyes grew wide, and his face went ashen.

Wordlessly, Remy held the receiver out to George, who couldn't understand what Remy wanted him to do.

"What?"

With an insistent thrust of his hand, Remy again indicated the receiver. George went to him, took the thing from his friend's hand, and put it to his ear. Nothing. No dial tone. No busy signal. No static. Just nothing. What was to have been their lifeline to family members, was silent. Their isolation was now complete.

For some reason, George continued to hold the receiver against his ear, thinking that maybe if he held it there long enough, it would give him the catch of sound he needed to restart his heart.

A clash of thunder split the air outside, and a simultaneous bolt of lightning illuminated the house's interior as though every light socket held a hundred-watt bulb. For an eerie twenty-seven ticks of the clock's second hand, they heard nothing, and then the wind came, beating against the house like a lunatic at an asylum door.

Chapter 21

Trinny

"True bravery is shown by performing without
witness what one might be capable of doing
before all the world."

—*François de la Rochefoucauld (1613–1680),
French author*

rinny had been thinking about taking her lunch to
Hughe's Park, but one look outside and she knew that
would not be happening today. Standing at the large
front window of *The Ladies' Home Companion's* lobby, Trinny
watched some poor woman across the street struggle to keep
her hat on, her dress down and her packages from blowing out
of her arms. The winds had kicked up unexpectedly. She hoped
the woman's car was close by.

The sky had a sickly, greenish hue that made her think of
chewed, cow cud, and the clouds looked like they were heavy
enough that if they fell to earth, they would crush everything
below them. A shiver ran the length of her spine, and she wished
that she'd driven to work instead of riding her bike. She had the
sudden, overwhelming feeling that she wanted to go home. To
be anywhere but *here*.

Paper debris swept down the road like tumbleweeds, clotting against anything in their path. The ever-increasing wind forced the trees into a primal dance. Branches arched and swayed fitfully as they tried to buffer the winds and protect the trunk from the storm's growing attack.

Trinny didn't know how long she stood there, mesmerized, but her artist's eye saw the mad swaying as a plea, a call for help. The poor trees had to witness the human's ability to seek shelter and hide from what they were forced to remain in the open and endure. Rooted as they were, this was their Alamo. Live or die; they could do nothing else.

Then, she heard a woman over the loudspeaker say, "Please remain calm. We have just received word that some severe weather is headin' our way."

No kidding, thought Trinny.

The voice on the loudspeaker continued, "Please, y'all, head to the break room as soon as possible. And if ya happen to pass a bathroom along the way, could ya poke your head in and make sure that anyone who may not have heard this message gets it? Thank you. Again, please remain calm."

The way the woman was trying to make the message sound like everyday news irritated Trinny. And her overdone emphasis on "please remain calm" was more frightening than the view beyond the great window. Then, whoever was manning the sound system put the microphone next to the radio so the actual storm warning could be heard.

"The United States Weather Bureau in Vivian has just been informed that there are indications a pattern of thunderstorms currently heading through northern Louisiana are potentially more severe than anticipated. Residents of the following parishes, please seek shelter immediately: Caddo, Bossier, DeSoto, North Sabine, Red River, Bienville, Webster. Winds in these areas have already reached an excess of one hundred miles per hour. Do not attempt to drive. Some power lines are down. Trees have blocked roads. Stay away from windows. Gather in a basement if possible. This is a caution from the Severe Storm Warning Broadcast System. Updates to follow."

Incredulous, Trinny mumbled, "They're just telling us this now? One look out the window and I could have told you . . ." Trinny stared blankly as the words "stay away from windows" finally registered. Realizing that she was smack-dab in front of the largest window she knew of, Trinny began to back toward safety, but her feet wouldn't turn her away from the dangerous view. *Why am I not moving?*

Because to her, what she saw was beautiful.

Watching this ravenous wind was what she imagined it would be like to witness a lion stalk its prey. A lion would bat at the legs of a fleeing animal to throw it off balance, like the winds were batting at tree limbs. Then, it would launch itself onto the neck of its prey and bite down, cracking the spine. With a convulsive jerk, the once proud animal would drop to the ground.

The beastly wind did the same to its prey. Lashing and lashing, it whipped unceasingly at all in its path, until she saw, with a loud, explosive *pop*, the spine of a large red maple in the park across the road snap right in two. Down it went. The limbs of its corpse rocked and swayed as the untamable force continued its onslaught.

Backing up, Trinny managed to put enough distance between herself and the portal into the wild outer world, that she'd nearly reached the hallway leading into the belly of the building. But when a blast of the unseen beast's breath caused the glass before her to bow and quiver, she finally managed to pull her gaze away. Turning, Trinny was just about to make her way down the familiar hall when a snap, pop, and sizzle caused her to once more turn and face the terror outside.

A shower of sparks rained past the front of the building as thickly as if she were standing behind a waterfall. Something told her to run. Just as she went to sprint down the hall, the lights went out and she was left in near-total darkness. The only light came from the waterfall of electrical sparks outside.

Hands on the wall for guidance, Trinny felt like she was pushed forward by an unseen hand just as the power pole that had borne the blown-out transformer suddenly splintered and crashed through the giant front window.

Feeling the cold wind rake her back, Trinny forgot all about the storm's beauty and ran. First left. Second right. Past the proofing room, copy room . . . she heard something.

Still feeling the specter of fear deep in her gut, she did not want to stop, but she skidded to a halt anyway. Heart pounding like a freight train, she strained to hear what had pulled her up short. Her instinct for self-preservation told her to keep going. It whispered that whatever she'd heard must be nothing more than the building crying in the face of the storm. But the hand that had pushed her forward, saving her, now beckoned her to go back.

Bending over, hands on knees, Trinny tried to slow her breathing to avoid passing out. In this stillness of time, when all about her seemed to be moving in slow motion despite the howling terror outside, she heard it again. A faint, pitiful "Please, help me."

With this plea, her own fright was forgotten. Trinny's ears perked to where she thought the sound had come from, and she moved cautiously toward it. With no electricity, the hallway was so dark she could barely see her own hand.

"Hello," Trinny called into the gloom. "Is anyone there?"

"Oh, help! Please help!" came a desperate voice.

Trinny felt for the handle of the door closest to her and twisted the knob. Nothing but an abandoned office was on the other side. She called again and heard a slight thud just behind her on the other side of the broad hall.

Unnervingly aware of the sound of her own steps on the linoleum floor, Trinny moved toward the pained voice.

"Is someone still there? Please, I'm trapped."

Trinny found the doorknob and twisted. This time, she was rewarded with an exhaled, "Oh, thank God."

"Who's there?" Trinny whispered. Why she was whispering, she didn't know, but somehow, it seemed appropriate.

"Trinny Jenks? Is that you? It's me, Dorothea Evers. I'm trapped here on the floor."

Trinny moved cautiously so as not to step on the downed woman. "Dorothea, what happened?" When her foot connected with something that said, "Ouch!" Trinny hurriedly apologized. "I'm sorry Dorothea. I'm so sorry." Trinny bent down and felt a hand poking out from its prison.

Making the connection, Dorothea grabbed at Trinny like a drowning person who'd been thrown a life preserver and whimpered, "Oh, Trinny, God bless you for findin' me."

"What on earth happened?"

The room wasn't very large. It had been an old supply room, but when the magazine had acquired a brand-new Xerox 914, the space had been turned into the photocopy room and stocked with all sorts of paper and supplies.

Trinny crouched low. As her eyes adjusted to the gloom, she was finally able to make out that Dorothea had been trapped next to the giant copy machine by a large, heavy supply shelf that had somehow fallen over. Thank heaven the massive Xerox had stopped the shelf from actually crushing the older woman.

A widow in her late fifties, Dorothea was neither grossly overweight nor thin. She was nestled somewhere in the comfortably plump range, and Trinny could tell that a simple rescue was not going to be easy, given the size of the small room and all the debris.

"Here," Trinny said as she cleared all the paper, ink and toner cartridges off of the poor woman. "I may need to pull on your legs to get you out from beneath the shelf far enough so that you can stand up."

"No, wait," Dorothea said. "I have a broken right leg. That's how I ended up in this blasted mess. I was makin' these here copies and had my crutches propped against the wall right there when a freakishly loud noise scared the bejeebers outta me. I jumped, lost my balance, and grabbed at what I could to keep from topplin' over. Well, as you can see, that did *not* work out."

Since they didn't work in the same department, Trinny didn't see Dorothea often, and in the gloom hadn't noticed the large cast that covered the woman's leg from mid-calf to just above the knee.

"Okay, then, what's the best way to get you up and out of here?"

Dorothea thought for a minute. "I guess I could sorta scootch myself round so my back is to ya. Then maybe, you could get me under the arms and pull me on out. But I have to warn ya, I think I broke my left arm when I tried to stop myself from fallin'. It hurts like the dickens. Just like my leg did when I broke it. Funny thing though, I think havin' the pain to focus on is keepin' me more calm than I would be otherwise."

"We can thank heaven for small blessings then," Trinny said. "Is there anything I can do to help you twist around?"

"I'm not sure. Let me see if I can do this." With a grunt of determination, Dorothea used her good arm to push against the shelf as she tried to turn herself around. But she bumped her left arm on a box of ink cartridges that had fallen between her and the Xerox and let out a cry of pain.

"Are you all right?"

Trinny heard a few hard, heavy exhalations, and then Dorothea said, "No worse than before. But I don't think I can do this."

"If I just tug gently on your left leg, do you think you could use your right arm to help lever yourself out from beneath the shelf?" Something hit the building with a loud clap, and even in the confines of the small room, Trinny felt the vibration of it rock her to the core.

"Oh, Lordy," Dorothea whimpered. "I'm sorry, Trinny.

If it weren't for me, you'd be safe with the others right now. I heard the announcement to go to the break room but was already on the darn floor. If you were there, you'd have food and water to get ya through whatever the heck this is gonna end up bein'."

Managing to keep notes of panic out of her own voice, Trinny said reassuringly, "No, Dorothea, I'm right where I should be. No one should go through a storm like this alone. In fact," she said brightly, "this little room may actually be a fantastic sanctuary."

Trinny removed the ink box Dorothea had hit her arm on and tried to lighten the mood. "Here, just scoot a bit closer to the copy machine, and I'll climb in on this side. That way, maybe the machine can protect your injured arm, just in case I grab at you for support." The two women settled in for however long it would take this storm to blow itself out. Then, Trinny remembered the lunch bag she'd dropped on the hall floor when she'd come to a skidding halt.

"Hold on; I'll be right back."

"Trinny! Where the heck do ya think you're goin'?"

"I dropped my lunch out in the hall. I'm just going to get it. That way, like you said, we'll have something to see us through."

Despite having to grope around in the dark for the treasured bag, Trinny was back in a flash and again settled in next to Dorothea.

"Here," Trinny said. "If you can sort of angle your legs toward me, I'll cross mine over yours and that way, we'll be completely covered by the shelf. Just in case."

Dorothea allowed Trinny to help angle her legs, cast and all, so they could both be as comfortable as possible, then took Trinny's steady hand in her own shaking one. In a quavering voice, Dorothea said, "Trinny, I was prayin' that someone would come find me. Since my husband died and my kids all sprouted wings and flew away, I thought I'd become quite the independent woman. I live on my own, shop alone, and even go to the picture shows by myself. But if I'd've had to go through this alone . . ." Dorothea's voice quavered, and Trinny could sense the tears that wanted to fall.

Giving the woman's hand a firm, reassuring squeeze, Trinny said, "We're never alone Dorothea. I . . ."

For so long, Trinny had allowed herself to be lost, trapped with the ever-present memories of the internment camp. Of the isolation. Of the fear. When she was almost sixteen, not long after they'd been sent from the Mayer assembly camp in Arizona to the Jerome camp in Arkansas, Trinny had found herself hiding in a place very much like the one she was in now.

None of them had been at the camp for long, and everyone was still getting used to all the restrictions and rules. Trinny didn't think that any of the internees, all being American citizens, were truly prepared for how they were now unreasonably feared.

Just a few weeks after her family had arrived, an older couple that Trinny was getting to know, Mr. and Mrs. Korematsu, had been out for an evening stroll. She had seen them and waved, then continued on her way when she heard gunshots pierce the air behind her. Dropping to the ground, heart racing, Trinny covered her head in fear. When the shots ceased, she managed to pull her face out of the dirt and look behind her.

The poor older couple stood frozen in each other's grasp. Not knowing what they had done, in a shaky voice, Mr. Korematsu called out his question to a nearby guard. Trinny could still hear the guard's gruff response; "Get. Away. From the fence."

Mr. Korematsu placed a protective arm around his wife, and the two elderly people obeyed the command. Trinny gauged the distance between the Korematsus and the fence to be roughly forty to fifty feet. Was that too close? While the guards were focused on the retreating pair, Trinny slunk back to her quarters. Willing herself to remain unseen, she couldn't help but wonder over what she considered to be a rash reaction to an innocent mistake. To open fire on someone, let alone an elderly couple, for simply wandering too close to the barbed wire fence? How had she gotten here? What had they done to warrant being forced into a place like this?

That incident had been a wakeup call for all of them.

So, on the day that twenty-one-year-old Fred Kanegawa, who had been pre-law at Berkeley before being taken, was fired upon and killed for coming too close to the perimeter while playing a game of catch, Trinny had run into her tiny, shared bedroom, pulled the straw-stuffed mattress from the bed, and tented it against the wall. Dragging in every blanket and pillow she could lay her hands on, she'd made a deep nest and burrowed in to hide. If she never left, she would never accidentally wander where she wasn't supposed to and they wouldn't shoot her too.

A gust of wind rocked the building so strongly that the two women felt it vibrate through the floor beneath them. Whatever Trinny had been about to say died on her tongue. Silence gripped the duo as they sat listening, anticipating, praying.

Outside, they could not see the white funnel cloud coloring itself from the ground up with earth as it sped toward their hiding place. Thick, dark, mushroom-shaped clouds anchored the funnel as its undulating base seemed to dance randomly across the vulnerable ground, delighting in destruction.

The women could not see rain drops being hurled against buildings and cars with such force, that having one hit you would be akin to being struck by a bullet.

They could not see the knives and forks that had been sucked out of homes and restaurants, flung with forceful abandon and embedded into tree trunks, signs, and buildings.

They could not see the swirling skirt of dirty, debris-filled, ravenous air that billowed out from the quickly darkening funnel. It was black-brown at the base, where its hunger was slowly being sated, and the mushroom head discharged furious arcs of lightning that reached down to scorch the harried earth.

No, they could not see these things. But when the full force of the demonic cloud formation passed directly over them, they felt it—all of it.

Dorothea and Trinny attached themselves to one another like strips of Velcro.

The walls around them groaned painfully, and they could feel the one they were leaning against begin to sway. The air around them filled with the most horrendous sucking sound they could ever have imagined, and their ears popped. The next thing they knew, frigid air swirled into their hiding space, choking them with dust and cold. And then, just as suddenly as the air had seemed to drown them with debris, it began to vacuum its deposits right back out, taking their breath with it.

The hair of both women was pulled loose and swirled upward, twisting and twining with the vortex. Papers slapped against them, like frantic moths seeking escape from the heat of a growing flame. The women were gasping, feeling like they were going to be sucked so thin they would fold in on themselves, when all of a sudden, it was like the vacuum turned off and everything went still. Not a calm, peaceful silence, but an eerie, heart-pounding, hold-on-to-your-hat silence.

Trinny dared to peer out from beneath the heavy shelving unit. Where a ceiling and two upper stories *should* have been, she saw the smooth insides of swirling clouds. Mini twisters broke free from the clouds, hissing as they detached from the main wall to dissipate like mist. Lightning zig-zagged along the funnel's interior, creating a bluish light that enabled her to see everything clearly. The cavernous interior seemed to be about a hundred feet across and a mile high. There was a strong, gassy smell that made her want to hold her breath. Then, the rear wall of the funnel passed over them and she ducked back under cover.

Trinny heard a rumbling like a freight train speeding overhead, accompanied by things beyond her sight crumbling and crashing to the ground. And then, everything went still. This time, the stillness was absolute, like death.

Had they died?

Mirroring one another, each woman placed a hand over her heart to make sure it was still beating.

Praise be! They were.

Chapter 22

A New Day

"Pain nourishes courage. You can't be brave if you've
only had wonderful things happen to you."

—*Mary Tyler Moore (1936–2017),
American actress, producer, and social advocate*

"**...A**nd that's when I saw it touch down. I swear, in all my life, I ain't ever seen the twin of it."

Remy re-tuned the car radio through a bit of static, then heard, "Thank you, Mr. Roland Deeds, for your harrowing firsthand account. This is NLBC reporter Cabe Bramwell with an update on the EF4 tornado that cut a heavy swath after touching down just south of Vivian."

Remy had to slow down to avoid a large tree branch that had fallen across the road. Mustering patience he was in rather short supply of, he deftly maneuvered the car around the obstacle and then picked up speed again.

Cabe Bramwell continued his report. "Due to the many interruptions in both television and radio communications this close upon the heels of the storm, local broadcast systems have done what they can to combine resources. That is why those used to seeing me on the television news are instead hearing me via radio. The winds of this afternoon's storm reached an incredible one hundred and seventy miles per hour as it ripped roofs off buildings. Hundreds of homes have been damaged beyond repair. Hundreds and hundreds of trees litter the ground or lay across homes and cars like Lincoln Logs."

Now that was a visual Remy didn't appreciate running a loop through his already frazzled brain.

"As more information on the damage to property and loss of life becomes available, you can rest assured that we will all do our best to keep you informed with accurate updates. Our thoughts and prayers go out to one and all at this time. Outside the heart of Oil City, where the most severe damage was done—"

Remy immediately switched off the broadcast. Gripping the steering wheel tightly, he focused on simply reaching Orvalee's to make sure that she and Bits were alright. One step at a time. Right now, he just couldn't listen to anything that mentioned Oil City.

Once he was assured that all was well with his daughter, he would meet up with George, who was currently racing home to check on his own family. From George's house, they would go to Mother Dollis's place and then work their way into the harder-hit areas, to check on friends and neighbors.

Pulling to a hurried stop in front of Orvalee's, Remy saw that though a couple of trees were down, there was no apparent damage to the sturdy brick house. But judging by the tiles he saw littering the ground, the roof would need some attention. Remy ran to the door, pounded furiously, and then, without waiting for a reply, pushed it open and started through the house, calling, "Bits! Orvalee! Where are you? Bits! Orva—"

"Here Papa! We're in here," said a small, excited voice.

"In the bathroom, Rem."

Remy reached the bathroom off the kitchen just as the door swung open, and out popped the most beautiful sight he had ever seen: his daughter. Blonde curls bobbed as she flung herself at him. Remy fell to his knees and held her tight, whispering into her hair, "Thank the Lord you're all right. Thank the Lord. I was so worried. I shoulda been with you. I shoulda known you'd left. I . . ."

He stroked her hair and reveled in the solid feel of her in his arms. Then he held her at arm's length so he could make sure that she was truly all in one piece. He probed each limb for injury and then turned her around to inspect her back.

After another rotation, they were face-to-face again and Remy simply stared at his angel. Li'l Bits smoothed her small hands across his cheeks, where she captured the tears that began to leak from his eyes. "It's okay. I'm okay," she said softly.

Wordlessly, Remy pulled her to him and wept all the worry out of his soul.

As Orvalee shimmied through the narrow space between Remy and Bits and the door to the kitchen, she graced each of their heads with a beatific touch, thinking that God was indeed good to bring these two safely back together. She would give them a few moments alone by going out back to inspect the greenhouse.

Her beloved sanctuary was a mess. Panes of broken glass littered the ground where debris had been hurled through, tumbling the innards like clothes in a dryer. Her wicker chair had been blown against the back wall. Its cane webbing was torn and frayed. Sorting through the broken pots on the ground, she was relieved to see that most of the tender plants could be saved and repotted. Sadly, not many of her salves and ointments were going to be salvageable.

With a deep, soul-weary sigh, Orvalee did what she did best when faced with tragedy: She focused on what it would take to set things right. Finding her broom beneath one of the workbenches, she got to work.

A few minutes later, Remy and Bits emerged from the house to help.

"Oh, Orvalee." Bits sounded heartbroken. "Your beautiful greenhouse is all torn up."

Turning, Orvalee saw tears spring to the child's eyes. That sweet girl had not shed a single tear through the whole of their ordeal as they sheltered in the bathroom. Tucked in the bathtub beneath a mattress, they had been able to pretend whatever scenario came to mind. They had been cave explorers hunting for secret pirate treasure; they had searched for an ancient city swallowed by a tropical jungle; they'd ridden the rails out west in search of gold or silver. There had been no end to what Bits had come up with to go look for.

The winds had howled and pounded at the house, hail had pummeled the walls, and mighty flashes of lightning had cracked and zipped along the sky as if tearing it in two, but it was the small, simple sight of broken glass, pots and plants that affected this child the most.

Orvalee said soothingly, "It's okay, sweet thing; nothing broke that can't be replaced. We're all safe and sound, and that's what matters most, right?"

Li'l Bits nodded. "Is there a broom I can use? Or somethin' I can do to help? I really wanna help."

"Orvalee," Remy interjected, "after all that's happened, I don't want to seem like I'm leavin' ya to yourself, but could I ask that Bits stay with you a while longer?"

Bits whirled on him. "Where you goin'!"

"Sweet heart, now that I know you're both safe, Uncle George and I need to make sure that everyone else is okay too. Some people may not have someone close by to check on 'em like we do. It's our duty to see to them as well."

Resignedly, Li'l Bits nodded again. "Yes, Papa. I know. You go help Uncle George. I'll stay with Orvalee. She needs lots of help right now too."

"That I do," Orvalee agreed. "And thank you, Bits. You sayin' that means a lot. To speed the process, maybe we can come up with new pretend games that go right along with the ones we played during the storm. How does that sound?"

Bits brightened. "That could be fun."

"Orvalee . . ." Remy started to say, but he didn't know how to thank her for all she had done. He wanted to say, "Thank you for taking care of my daughter. Thank you for being there when I could not. Thank you, for *everything*."

"I know," she said. "You go on, now. Bits and I have everything under control here."

With an appreciative nod, Remy just said, "All right," and turned to go.

Chapter 23

Assurances

On the short drive to George's house, Remy was able to get himself under control. Having made sure of Bits's safety, he now felt free to turn his attention to everyone else. Unsure how many, if any, vehicles would be able to make it into the city once they got closer, Remy left his car at George's and climbed in the back of his friend's A & D work truck with Jeremy and Beau.

Now that the worst was over, Claudine felt comfortable sending the boys to help at their grandmother's.

"Remy!" Claudine called, happy to see him. "All is well with Orvalee and Bits, no?"

Thankful that he could pass on good news, Remy said, "It sure is, thanks for asking. Though Orvalee's greenhouse is gonna need a fair bit of TLC. The framework is still sound, but there was a lot of broken glass and damage to her plants and stock."

"Oh, *mon dieu*. When Aline and I finish a few things here, we will go to help. Bits is there still, yes?"

"Yep. Orvalee said she could stay as long as I have to be away."

"*Bon*. It will be good for her and Aline to be together right now."

"I sure appreciate y'all offering to help. I get the feelin' that despite everything bein' sunny-side-up, for the most part, Orvalee could really use a friend right now. An adult friend."

"Ah, yes, as could I. Like hens in a coop, we will cluck as we work."

George had been gathering rope, saws, a wheelbarrow, and anything else he could think of that might be needed. With the final addition of a few jugs of water and a bag of sandwiches Claudine had put together, George slammed the tailgate closed. Before climbing behind the wheel of the truck, he paused to plant a big kiss on his wife's surprised mouth, right in front of everyone.

"You terrible man," Claudine scolded with a smile, as she slapped at his chest. "We are in public. What will people think?"

Still holding on to her, George took a gander in all directions and, short of his own sons and Remy, saw no one.

"There's no one here to be embarrassed in front of." He winked at his sons and Remy. "And those that are here are bein' given a free lesson in how to treat the woman they love. You don't want to be deprivin' these young, single gentlemen of a lesson like that, now, do ya?"

Claudine blushed to the tips of her ears. "These young gentlemen have other things to be on their minds right now. Now, go." She pushed against George's broad chest to turn him toward the truck. "Be off with you, and be safe. Take no unnecessary risks, *mi amor*."

Seeing George and Claudine interact like this left a hollow place in Remy's stomach, just below his heart. Expelling a gentle sigh, he wondered if Trinny was all right. Was she hurt? Had she been alone, or had she had someone to ride the storm out with? At that moment, it was a very good thing that Remy had no clue Trinny was trapped beneath a blessedly sturdy shelf in the middle of a pile of rubble.

* * *

By the time George arrived at his parents' home, Ruth and her husband Dell, along with Miriam and their brother David, were already there. A tree had blown over and landed on the roof of the front porch, thankfully, sparing the side with his mother's beloved porch swing. Dell was up there with a chainsaw, chiseling away at the downed cottonwood to make it easier to remove, while David, with his own chainsaw, was having a go at a maple that had fallen on the chicken coop out back. Miriam and the children were busy tracking down and chasing the traumatized fowl that had escaped and taken shelter all over the property.

Using one of the branches from a downed tree as a shield, Miriam laughed as she and a couple of the children did their best to corral a persistently obstinate rooster. George watched them and smiled. Ever since the day he'd confronted his father, his oldest sister seemed . . . changed. Brighter. Lighter. She even looked a little younger. Now, she looked more like Ruth, who, hearing the truck pull up, had come from around back to see who the new arrivals were.

"George!" Ruth brightened when she saw her baby brother. She ran to open the truck door for him, then leaned in and hugged him before he could even get out. "Honestly, after the last time, I never thought to see you here again. Oh, you are the best, most wonderful . . ." She pulled him out where she could fully wrap her arms around him.

Then, turning to the back of the truck, Ruth gestured to her nephews to hop out and give their aunty an obligatory hug.

Pretty sure he was safe from the expression of feminine affection, Remy hopped out the back and lowered the tailgate so George could pull out whatever he thought they'd need while they were here.

"Hold on, there; don't be thinkin' you've escaped your turn, Mr. Dubois."

Hearing his name, Remy turned to find that he was now the target of sisterly affection. Ruth grabbed him into a hearty hug and thanked him for coming to help her parents.

"It's gratifyin' to know that after somethin' like this . . ." She covered her mouth with a loose fist as her lips quivered. "To know that there are people all around who care enough to . . ."

Remy quirked a small smile, embarrassed by the attention. "I hope you never doubted that I could be counted on."

Ruth looked at George, her nephews, and Remy. "No, I never doubted you. Any of you."

"Ruthie," George said, "is mama okay?"

"She's right as rain. Right now, she's in the kitchen supervisin' a handful of ladies from the aid society. They're makin' food to distribute to some of the rescue workers in town. George"—Ruth shook her head in dismay—"it's awful; it's just awful! The news that keeps comin' over the radio and the television, it's just, well, beyond awful."

"I know. If you don't mind, I'm gonna leave the boys here to help. As soon as I know we're good to go, Rem and I are gonna head closer to town, see where we can lend a hand. We're also gonna stop at A & D, hopefully catch Rem's pop there. I used my lunch break to head this way, but everyone else should still be at work. I'm hopin' the fact that the supply company is a couple miles outta town will have saved it a lot of damage. From what I hear, Oil City center is an absolute mess."

George looked to see where Remy had wandered off to so his friend wouldn't overhear what he said next. "I know Rem is tryin' to keep up a brave face, but Trinny works smack-dab in the heart of town, and I know he's a lot more worried about her than he's lettin' on."

"Oh no." Ruth exhaled as she laid a worried hand on her brother's arm. "I'll be prayin' for her. And I'll go in and make sure Mama and the others put Trinny on their prayer list as well."

"That'd be much appreciated," George said. Then before Ruth could get away, he asked, "Hey, Ruthie, uh, what about . . . Daddy? Where's he?"

Worry lines creased Ruth's brow, and she wrung her hands together. "Oh, George, no one seems to know. Since the last time you were here, he migrates as far away from home as often as he can. People say they've seen him wanderin' willy-nilly all over the place. In church, he just sits lookin' all blank and vacant. Like no one's home, you know?"

A momentary twinge of guilt registered on George's face, but he allowed the feeling to pass. He'd done nothing more than what he'd been prompted to do by the good Lord. He'd known it wouldn't be easy on his father, but the man needed to face the music of the tune he'd been playing for so long. If the result was that he now marched here and there alone, well, that wasn't George's fault.

* * *

"Rem!" Lynne Anne exclaimed when she saw her son walk through the A&D office door. She ran to him, threw her arms around his shoulders and sobbed joyfully.

Remy held his mother close as her tightly strung emotions quickly unwound. Pulling back, she asked, "Bits, is she okay? Where is she? What happened out your way? George!"

Lynne Anne released her son and went to George. Adrenaline had made her a bundle of nervous energy.

"George, is your family okay? How's your house? What about Orvalee? Oh, my goodness gracious, I can't seem to stop talkin' or huggin' everyone I see. I think that's why I came to the office, so I could be where I might here more news." She patted her heart, as if that could calm the jitters that had her flittering about like a piece of cotton-fluff on the wind.

Without needing to be asked, she answered the men's question. "Alexander's out there somewhere"—with a broad sweeping gesture, she indicated the entire warehouse and receiving yard beyond the office's big, second-story observation window—"lookin' over the damage and arranging to send out whatever big equipment we have that could be useful downtown for cleanup. George, dear, if you've been able to see to your family, I know Alexander could use you right now. You know this place better than anyone other than him."

"That's why I'm here." With a peaceful intonation, George added, "Don't you worry. My family's all squared away. My time is now his."

"Oh, bless you. We need all hands on deck right now. You know better than I where to look for him, so I'll let you get to it. And thank you again." Lynne Anne squeezed George's arm in appreciation.

With a backward glance at Remy, George grabbed a hardhat and headed out to do his job.

"Now, Rem, I've had a call from both Sienna and Janelle. They and their families are just fine. Thank heaven they weren't here for me to worry over too. I told 'em I'd give 'em a call as soon as I heard from you. But maybe it'd be more reassuring if you were the one to talk to 'em."

Lynne Anne went to the big desk and pointed to a couple of numbers written on a pad of paper. "Here's where they're at. Would you mind?"

"Course not Mama." Remy smiled and pulled the phone and pad across the desk. A&D was lucky the phone poles out their way had escaped being snapped in two, unlike so many others.

When Janelle heard her brother's voice, Remy was rewarded with a shrill cry of pleasure so loud, he had to move the receiver away from his ear.

"Praise the Lord!" Janelle's voice carried so far, even Lynne Anne heard every word. "Bits? Orvalee? Trinny? Everyone? How is *everyone*?"

"Janelle, if you can't dial it down a notch or two, you'll have done more damage to my hearing than the storm."

"Sorry, sorry." Janelle took a few deep breaths to calm herself. "Whew, okay, I think I'm better now. How's this?"

"Much better, thank you." It warmed Remy's heart to know just how concerned his sister had been. Not that he liked being the one to cause her pain or worry, but since becoming a father, he had grown enough to see his family's expressions of concern as coming from a place of love and care, rather than condescension.

Janelle said, "Mama filled me in on how she and Daddy weathered the storm, but how about you? What happened to you?"

He explained how he and George had been forced into isolation, away from their loved ones, and how that was the most difficult part of their ordeal. The house, the shop, and most of the trees had come through no worse for wear, though repairs would need to be done here or there.

"So, Bits and Orvalee were all alone? Oh, what that must have been like. If we'd been home and I'd been separated from Michael, I'd have probably felt as worthless as a bucket under a bull. I'm just . . ." Remy heard the emotion in her voice and could tell she was tearing up. "Remy, I just can't tell ya how relieved I am to hear from you. I'm so glad Mama had you call. Make sure to call Sienna; I know she's been in a dither over y'all too."

"I have her number right in front of me and will give her a jingle as soon as I say goodbye to you."

"Well, then, not that I want to shoo you off, but I'll say goodbye so you can get on to her. I'll make sure Michael and the kids know I was able to talk to ya. I love you, Remy."

"I love you too, J. You just finish out your vacation and don't worry about us."

When Remy dialed Sienna, he was rewarded with the same exuberant cry of joy. "Thank you, thank you, Lord! Oh, Rem, the reports we're hearin' on the news do not a pretty picture make. I'm so glad y'all are safe. Oh, Jiminy Cricket, my heart's poundin' a mile a minute. Wait, you did tell me Bits was safe, didn't you? Or am I just gettin' ahead of myself?"

"Bits is fine." Remy related the same information to Sienna that he had to Janelle.

"Not that I'm glad you were separated from your daughter through all that happened—heaven knows had it been me kept from Andy and Jeremy, I'd have gone ballistic—but I am glad Orvalee had someone to see her through. No one should go through somethin' like that all alone."

Remy hadn't thought of things from Orvalee's perspective, and he could see how having someone to comfort and care for may just have kept her safer than any of them knew. Had he been alone, what might have happened? Would he have allowed fateful imaginings to overrun common sense? Would he have tried to go out into the storm to "rescue" his daughter and paid a price beyond imagining? The thought made him shudder.

"Before I let you go, the only one ya haven't mentioned is Trinny. How's she? Do ya know yet?"

Remy swallowed hard, "Um, I'm not sure yet about Trinny." He had to stop and take a deep breath. His hands had suddenly gone clammy, and his heart wanted to leap out his throat.

At the mention of Trinny, Lynne Anne scrutinized her son's reaction and saw how he was nervously twisting the phone cord around his fingers. She moved in to take the receiver from him, but Remy waved her off. "George and Dad are seein' to what equipment we have that can help with cleanup and . . . possible rescues. Soon as I hang up with you, I'm gonna find out more. All I know right now is that downtown got hit bad, and that's where Trinny is."

With that said, Remy handed the phone to his mother and leaned on the back of a chair for support. Drawing in a deep breath, he headed out the door to find George and his father. The last thing he heard his mother say was, "Take care, my girl. Y'all just keep having fun, 'cause I *really* need to know there's still joy out there somewhere."

Chapter 24

Aftermath

The convoy of vehicles that headed out from A&D Oil Supply consisted of a diesel tow truck, two diesel flatbeds loaded with three forklifts and a Bobcat skid-steer loader, a skip loader, and eight pickups filled with jackhammers, wheelbarrows, pallets, shovels, barrels of water and men. Lots and lots of able-bodied men.

State troopers guarding the barricade into town signaled the convoy to a halt. From the passenger seat of the diesel tow truck, Alexander Dubois asked for directions to where the county police and fire rescue units had been set up.

"They're at the Breverton car dealership, sir. You can head on over there. They'll best know how to put all you good people to work."

Before Alexander was able to signal his driver to pull

forward, the officer added, "And thank you, sir, for bringin' all this equipment. It's gonna be put to good use today."

The A&D convoy stopped at what used to be the Breverton car dealership. Now, about half the cars were missing from the lot and could be seen scattered up and down the road. One lay on its side, wrapped around a shattered telephone pole. Some had been accordioned into one another as the extreme winds played shuffle board with them, shoving them into the concrete wall of the Billups gas station across the road.

The once-proud, thirty-foot-tall "Fill-Up with Billups" sign now lay atop one of the stray Breverton cars like a spatula on a pancake. The roof and front wall of the gas station lay in a crumbled heap.

Dumbfounded, the men from A&D could only stare at the devastation, which was beyond any they'd ever seen. Only those who had served in a war could have any sort of reference for the scene that spread itself before them.

From whatever vehicle they were in, each man's foot touched the ground with silent reverence, almost as if they were stepping onto a grave.

Remy could not believe his eyes. From where he stood, all he could see was sheared-off electrical poles and buildings missing pieces of themselves, if they were lucky enough to be standing at all. His breathing stopped. Trinny was out there, in the *somewhere* of what used to be discernible city blocks. His grief was dry and left him feeling as parched as a desert. Weakly, he swiped the back of his hand across stiff lips.

A large hand rested reassuringly on Remy's trembling shoulder, "She's okay. I know she's okay."

Remy gestured helplessly at the scene. "This looks like something from '*The Day the World Ended*'. I hated that movie." He shook his head. "But I hate this more. This can't be real. George . . . She just has to . . . I haven't said all the things I've been rehearsing. I haven't taken her on a real date, like you told me to. We've just sort of, been together, you know? At the house, on walks, with Bits . . . I was afraid, George. Afraid that if I asked her on a real date, she wouldn't want to be seen with me, 'cause I'm . . . Oh Lord, I wasted so much time bein' afraid. I want it back! I'll do better this time. I will." On the verge of losing himself to despair, Remy fell against the side of the truck and buried his face in his arm.

George dug deep into his own past and said kindly, "Rem, I *know* what you're feeling. I know what you're seein', and I know—"

"How can you possibly know what I'm feelin'? I mean, I understand you've seen . . . this." He waved a disgusted hand at the scene of devastation. "But Trinny is *in* that. Claudine was . . ."

George cut him off. "Claudine was in somethin' like that too."

Remy looked at George in disbelief.

A slow, broad, sad smile spread across George's face as he remembered. "It was in Le Portel that I first saw her. She was like an angel—an angel of ash and soot. And she was . . . She was so damned thin." It physically hurt George to think of the depravity Claudine and the others had suffered.

"Because of their position, the Allies used that poor town in a diversionary maneuver, tryin' to fool the Germans into thinkin' there might be a landing on the English Channel. Generals . . . Sometimes, I have to wonder what goes through their minds. Anyway, the town, of course, was bombed. Just about destroyed the entire thing. Over three hundred and seventy people were killed. Innocent people. I happened to be part of the liberating force, and that's where I saw her."

Remy stayed quiet while George paused. He didn't remember George ever telling him exactly how he and Claudine had met.

George went on. "She was sittin' on a pile of rubble that used to be the town's pharmacy. She'd worked there before it was destroyed, so she knew a little about doctorin' and medicines. Needless to say, the folks of that village had run short of damn near everything, so Claudine often sifted through the rubble of the town to see if something useful had been overlooked."

Remy could picture Claudine carefully scavenging through all the debris.

"She later told me that word had spread we were coming, and she wanted to be the first to see for herself if it was true. After what the Allies had done to 'em, she wasn't big on trust, and that pile of rubble offered her the best view of the road into town. I was probably just one of a hundred faces she saw that day, but the minute I laid eyes on her, saw her bright green eyes alive and flashing, I knew hers would be the only face I saw from that moment on."

George's shoulders rose and fell with a heavy sigh. "I don't need to go into detail on what it all looked, smelled, or felt like, 'cause all you've gotta do is look around. And no, I did not know Claudine at the time she went through hell, but based on my own version of it, when I found out what she'd been through, I felt it all the same. Now, you and Trinny have each experienced your own version of the same hell, and that can bond ya, if you don't lose yourself to the fear of it."

George stood. With a gentle hand under Remy's arm, he steadied his friend. "Trinny needs you to be whole right now. She needs you to be strong. The kind of strong that'll send itself through the layers of destruction straight to her heart so she'll know you're comin' for her. Undoubtedly, she is gonna need someone to lean on, and you want that someone to be you. Right?"

Remy's voice came out as a whisper. "Of course I do."

"Well, then, take a deep breath, focus, and let's get to it."

"George! Rem!" Alexander said, panting as he trotted over to them. "I've spoken to the fire chief, and he says that right now, we have to wait for the all clear before they'll allow civilian workers into the main part of downtown."

Before Remy could protest, his father said, "And yes, son, I know bein' patient at a time like this just makes your ass itch, but goin' off half-cocked'll only bring trouble. Plus"—he held up a finger to emphasize his next words—"I have arranged for *us* to be part of the first civilian group they let in."

Remy just about fainted with relief.

George beamed. "See, Rem, everything's under control. The good Lord'll keep her safe 'til you're by her side."

* * *

While the Army National Guard and trained emergency workers were making sure that all gas mains had been shut off and downed electrical wires were no longer live, those from A&D were put to work helping clear roads for rescue vehicles and fire trucks. They chopped up the damaged power poles and toppled trees, then took all the wood to an area set aside for recyclable materials. They shoveled debris, hauled tons of brick and concrete, and, surprisingly, enjoyed every minute of hard labor. Nothing bonds people like pulling together as a community.

Before long, Mary Dollis and her ladies' aid society caravanned into the approved perimeter parking area, set up tables and umbrellas for shade, and began handing out sandwiches, apple slices and glasses of sweet tea.

Local doctors and nurses came to check all rescue workers for signs of exhaustion, heat stress, carbon monoxide exposure, and to stitch up whatever needed stitching. From experience, they'd learned that nearly half of all tornado-related injuries would occur during rescue attempts, cleanup and other post-tornado activities. Nearly a third of the injuries they treated after tornadoes resulted from stepping on exposed nails.

Thankfully, all the men from A&D wore good, sturdy boots. They also had heavy leather gloves, wore long sleeved-shirts and were prepared with battery-powered lanterns and flashlights. After going through something like this, the last thing anyone wanted was to set off an accidental gas explosion with a candle.

Through the grapevine, Remy learned that three children had been killed at the roller rink when the roof collapsed. The elementary school had been leveled. He thought of Bits and the hundreds of other kids who might have been there today. Oil City could count its blessings that school was out for spring break.

Chapter 25

Discovered

Night had settled in by the time Alexander got
word that he, George, and Remy could go
further into town in the fire truck with the
chief. As they drove slowly through the maze of now-indiscernible buildings, Remy pressed his forehead to the side window
and mourned all that had been lost.

The slowly turning red light of the chief's truck cast an eerie
glow onto dust that still clung to the air. Little puffs and swirls
of it could be seen dancing in the rose glow as their passing
stirred it to life.

The odd way that a tornado could completely demolish one
building while leaving its neighbor intact had never ceased to
amaze Remy when he'd seen pictures in *National Geographic*.
Pictures were one thing—*this* was another.

Pictures may tell a good story, but unless it's *your* story, it's
just . . . well, incomplete.

He would never look at pictures the same way.

Remy didn't know that at George's request, his father had asked if they could be driven on a circuitous route to the Red Cross tent. The fire chief complied, and one of the buildings they drove past was the office of *The Ladies Home Companion*.

"Stop!" Remy commanded. "Please," he added.

The chief did.

"Rem," George asked, "what're you gonna do?"

Remy made to open the door. "I just, I just have to see it, you know? So, I'll know what you know when you look at Claudine."

Alexander and the fire chief weren't sure what Remy meant, but with an encouraging nod from George, the chief said, "I'll let ya get on out, but you *cannot* walk into the ruins. Everyone's been cleared from the building, so there's nothing for ya in there, son. Understand?"

At the word *ruins*, Remy swallowed hard, but said, "Yes, sir. May I touch the front of the building?"

"Why for?"

"I'm not exactly sure. I just . . . feel the need."

"Okay, but that's as close as you get, got it?"

"Yes, sir."

Alone, Remy exited the vehicle. Hand outstretched, like he was approaching a fawn in the forest, he tentatively inched his way toward the exterior wall. The big front window had been blown in; a lifeless power pole lay within its gaping maw, like something that hadn't been swallowed all the way.

Remy thought of the times he'd just "happened" to be passing the office building and looked through that same big window, hoping to catch a glimpse of Trinny coming or going. Of course, he never had, but the anticipation had been thrilling.

Hand met stone, and something in him heard screams. High-pitched sounds of terror that made him close his eyes.

"Oh, Trinny," was all he could say.

Stepping back, Remy craned his neck to look up to where

the rest of the three-story building should have been. It looked like a giant child had gotten frustrated with an ill-formed creation and simply snapped off the top.

Remy's heart ached at the sight. Turning, he saw that what had been a by-gone era town square, now looked like a scene that could well have been in *The Day the World Ended*. "She's okay," he said to himself. "She's at the aid station. I know she is. So get back in the truck and keep on goin'."

It took Remy a minute to gather enough strength to pull himself away from the grisly sight of the building, and the park, but when he finally managed to make his feet move toward the truck, he knew that when he found Trinny there would be no going back to the way things had been. He was irrevocably on a new path, one that stretched forward, with her.

Within a few minutes, the truck pulled to a slow stop in front of the Red Cross first aid station, where dozens and dozens of people wrapped in blankets had been settled wherever a comfortable spot could be made for them. Despite the blank, lifeless stares of some and the bandage-wrapped arms, legs, or heads of others, these were the lucky ones. Those who hadn't needed transport to one of the many surrounding hospitals that would no doubt be operating at full capacity tonight.

As they got out of the captain's truck, Remy, George and Alexander didn't know where to look first. There were so many people.

"I'm not the one in charge here," said the fire chief. "But if you'll step inside the tent there, Ms. Swensen'll either give ya a chore to help with or maybe know who it is you're lookin' for."

"Thank you, sir." Alexander shook his hand. "We sure appreciate you gettin' us here. We'll do our best to be of whatever help we can."

"Sir, you and your men have already been more help than you know," the chief assured. "Oil City is lucky to have you." With that, the chief slapped Alexander on the back, thanked George, and with a knowing tilt of the head, wished Remy luck.

Before the three men made it inside the tent, they heard a voice boom across the crowded parking lot behind them. "Mr. Dollis! George!"

Recognizing the voice, George pivoted quickly and saw Reverend Marrs headed toward them at a jog.

"Well, hello." George waved and smiled with genuine affection. Reverend Marrs was the best of men. "Shoulda known you'd be here."

"Of course, Brother George, I knew *you* would be." Reverend Marrs wrapped his hands around each of theirs in turn, and shook them like he was filling a bucket with a pump. "God is good, is he not? God is good." He just about choked on the last word and looked like he wanted to say more, but then, the good reverend teared up. He pulled George into a firm hug, clinging to him long enough that George began to wonder how the man was truly holding up under the pressure of tending to so many frazzled souls.

"George," Remy said, "Dad and I will just step on in the tent and, you know, ask about . . ."

"Yeah, I'll join ya directly."

Remy and Alexander ducked inside the makeshift headquarters while George and the reverend moved off toward the back of the parking lot, where food and water tables had been set up by the Red Cross.

"I know it's a stupid question, considerin' where we're standing," Remy said. "But I wonder what's got the reverend so upset. It seems . . . personal, you know?"

His father looked back over his shoulder. "Not sure. To a man of the cloth, I'm thinkin' a good many things can take on a more personal meanin' than they would for most of us."

An exhausted female voice drew their attention. "Can I help you?" Both men turned to see a woman in a Red Cross uniform. She studied their faces, then said, "You're lookin' for someone, right? Of course you are. Name. Description. Any determining features that'll help speed identification."

Despite her obvious fatigue, the woman's dogged efficiency was a little intimidating.

"Trinny Jenks. Uh, long, straight black hair. Medium height." Remy raised a hand to just an inch or so above his head. "Artist at *The Ladies Home Compani*—"

Alexander, who had been looking around while his son talked to the aid worker, suddenly tugged on Remy's sleeve and pointed to the opening of the tent. There stood a bedraggled Trinny, holding a tray of food she'd gotten for herself and Dorothea. The older woman had indeed broken her wrist, but she'd been attended to and was currently resting on a cot at the back of the large tent along with a number of others from their building.

Dorothea and Trinny had actually weathered the storm far better in their little cocoon than those who had sheltered in the break room, many of whom had been severely injured by falling debris when the upper stories were ripped off.

Remy turned and locked eyes with Trinny; the focus of his concern, anxiety, apprehension . . . and desire. The path that had drawn his feet away from the remnants of past longing, of looking through the window but not daring to venture across the street, now carried him right to her. To his mind, he was moving in slow motion. Like a movie close-up, Remy's focus zoomed in on Trinny, and the only two people in the world gravitated toward one another.

Trinny's eyes were wide, and glistened with tears.

Smiles filled with every possible emotion, from the pain and fear of having nearly lost everything, all the way to sheer joy, animated both of their faces. Remy had the presence of mind to take the tray from Trinny and place it in the uncomprehending hands of whoever it was to his right. Then, without embarrassment or hesitation, he placed a hand behind Trinny's head and drew her into a soul-searing kiss.

A hush fell over the tent, and then everyone erupted into a cacophony of cheers and wolf whistles. From sickbeds, the injured egged them on. Aid workers clapped, and Alexander beamed. After the day they'd all had, watching two people enjoy the outcome they hoped for themselves, was just the balm they needed.

Remy drew back and gazed at the first tears he had ever seen Trinny shed. They were the most beautiful manifestations of acceptance she could have offered him. As they stood there, holding one another, Remy felt the soft, warm colors of a sunset wrap around them. He pictured a golden sun dissolving over the horizon. It felt as if the world was going to sleep, where it would rest in a haze of beautiful dreams and gladness, to awaken to a bright, glorious new day.

* * *

Mary Dollis had just pulled in the driveway after a very long, arduous day. She was looking forward to putting her feet up and sitting with her prayer book and a glass of wine. With a heavy sigh, she looked at the unlit windows. The electricity out here should be on. Mont must not be home. She paused. Or, if he was, and he was sitting in his chair with the lights out . . .

Standing half in and half out of the car, Mary debated whether to go in the house or drive . . . somewhere. Mont did not deal well with trials, and right now, she was in no mood to take the necessary precautions in order to keep peace.

Her shoulders rose and fell with another bone-weary sigh as she decided to drive to George's and just park a bit away. It had been a Jonah day. She could simply sit in the car, look up at the stars and count her blessings.

Oncoming headlights caught her car in their glare, reflecting harshly in the rear-view mirror. She shielded her eyes. The car pulled to a stop, and the driver turned off the lights and cut the engine. For just a second, Mary's heart raced fearfully. She was all alone. She was too old to outrun an attacker. If she screamed, would anyone hear?

"Oh, sweet Jesus, not today. Please, I just can't handle any more," she prayed out loud.

Two doors opened simultaneously, and uniformed men emerged from each one.

Open-mouthed, Mary stared as the men approached. Closing the door on a possible retreat, she found her voice and stepped toward them.

"Evenin', officers. Is there somethin' I can help y'all with?"

The men took their hats off, and the one with the sergeant's stripes said, "We're sorry to be comin' up on ya like this, ma'am. I know it's quite late, but after the day we've all had, we thought you might want to know so you wouldn't be left wonderin' . . . umm, about—" The man sucked in a fortifying breath.

The other officer held out a familiar handkerchief bound with a rubber band. "Ma'am, I believe these belonged to your husband. His name was Mont." He pulled out his little note-book and checked the name he'd written down. "Yes, Mr. Mont Dollis."

Was? Belonged? Why were they speaking in the past tense? Mary took the handkerchief and removed the rubber band. The cloth fell away to reveal her husband's wedding band, billfold, and pocket-knife, as well as seventy-two cents.

The ground suddenly rocked beneath her feet, and she swayed. The two men quickly took her by the arms and led her to the porch, where they sat her on the newly reinforced swing.

"Ma'am?"

Mary bent forward, her mind giving her body all sorts of confusing signals. Cry? Wail? Vomit? Pass out? None of them felt right.

"What . . . what happened?" she finally asked.

In a soothing voice, the sergeant said, "After the tornado passed, some farmers were out scouring their fields, lookin' for runaway or . . ." He almost said *dead* animals but stopped himself. That wouldn't have been right. "Strays, you know, scared away by the storm. Well, a"—he checked his notes—"a Mr. Jones came across the b . . . He found your husband in his field. Not knowin' who the . . . your husband was, Mr. Jones was kind enough to transport him to the Red Cross first aid station in town. Here, by way of a National Labor Union card, we were able to identify him. A"—he checked his notes again—"Reverend Marrs was there, saw your husband, and was able to give us your name and address. He also asked that we deliver your husband's personal effects to you."

Mary did her best to take it all in. "Will I be required to . . . to identify—him?" She'd seen people do that on television and didn't relish the idea.

"No, ma'am," the other officer said quickly. "You won't need to be doin' that. The reverend gave us all the assurance needed." What he could not tell Mary was that her husband's body had been badly damaged by the storm. He must have taken a good hit to the head by flying debris because his skull had been cracked, and small bits of things were embedded in his torso. No wife should have to see something like that.

"Plus," the sergeant said, "another man, I believe he was your son . . ." Notes were again consulted. "Yes, a George Dollis. The reverend managed to find your son at the Red Cross station, and he too was able to add a positive ID."

Their least favorite job done, the officers' shoulders relaxed, and the sergeant asked, "Ma'am, you gonna be all right?"

"Where is he? My husband. What do I do now?"

"I believe your son said he'd take care of all the arrangements." The officer looked at the dark, quiet house. "Do you have somewhere you can go so you're not alone right now?"

"I . . . suppose I can . . ." Mary looked thoughtful. "No, thank you. I think I just want to sit alone with this for a while."

"Are you sure? I can go in and turn your lights on so the house won't be dark, at least."

Mary's eyes filled with gratitude, knowing that few white men would offer to do that for her. Doubting that she was the only recipient of this sort of news today, she could appreciate just how difficult *their* Jonah day must have been. "Thank you, but that's not necessary. Truly. You've both been more than kind. I know this can't have been easy, and I guess *my* Jonah day won't be endin' when my head hits the pillow, will it?"

Not knowing what to say to that, the officers bid Mary a good night and turned to go. In parting she walked to the edge of the porch and called, "'Scuse me."

Both men turned.

"Can each of you do somethin' for me?"

They nodded.

"I know today has most likely been one of the worst you've had in your lives, and I'm sorry for that. Truly, I am." Her voice choked with emotion. "But when you finally make it home, will you be sure to give your sweet families some lovin'? Hug and kiss 'em all, 'cause at the end of the day, they're really all we have, aren't they? Family is all we have."

Touched by her concern for them at such a time as this, the officers promised they would do as she asked.

Mary went back to sit on the porch swing and watched as the taillights turned from the drive and disappeared.

The swing's chain needed to be oiled.

It squeaked companionably as she swayed, not really knowing what to feel.

Chapter 26

Dazed and Rattled

Saturday, April 4, 1959

"There is nothing noble in being superior to
your fellowman. True nobility lies in being
superior to your former self."

—Ernest Hemingway (1899–1961),
American author and sportsman

Every able-bodied person for miles around converged on Oil City. Blankets, water, food, clothes and other possible necessities, right down to toothbrushes, had been gathered and loaded into a donated semi-trailer and sent to the ravaged city.

Throughout Louisiana, Texas, and Arkansas, where most of the storm's damage had been concentrated, constant news updates could be heard coming from open windows and car radios.

Remy had his own television on as he prepared lunch for Bits.

"This is Cabe Bramwell on location with Pastor Fullmer. He and his family were hard at work inside their Lady of Hope church when the storm hit. Thankfully for him and the other Vivian residents, it touched down south of their city. Though, being just a quarter mile from that spot, the Lady of Hope church sustained major damage and will need a great deal of work. Pastor Fullmer, can you please tell us what you experienced while inside the church?"

"Yes, thank you, Mr. Bramwell." Pastor Fullmer grabbed the microphone, nearly wrenching it from Cabe's grip as the man sought to milk his fifteen seconds of fame. "We, my family and I, heard a lot of debris *pelting* the building. From the large storage room we hid in, it sounded like we were being peppered with *buckshot*. Then, a great, rushing wind *howled* down on us, like I imagine banshees from hell might do. Then, we heard the stained-glass windows *exploding* in the chapel and could hear glass flying everywhere. I can tell you, we were sore afraid and huddled in family prayer. When we were finally able to emerge from our place of shelter and witness the damage, my prayer was that all was not as dire as it looked. 'Cause it sure looked to be something awful."

Cabe Bramwell had to pull the microphone back toward him. "Thank you, Pastor Fullmer, for your first-hand account."

"Oh," the other man interjected as he shoved his face in front of the reporter, "all donations to help pay for repairs to the church will be greatly appreciated."

"Yes," Cabe said as he skillfully angled his large shoulders away from the man, trying to edge him out of the shot. "Thank you. I believe the Lady of Hope is listed in the phone book."

Not quite out of camera range, Pastor Fullmer nodded a vigorous yes.

"Well, then, all donations may be directed through that number. Thank you, sir." Cabe took a couple of steps to the left to regain proprietorship of the frame. "I have also been asked to remind the public that you might not be able to return directly to your homes. It may take emergency crews a few more days to assess all areas for safety hazards or carry out needed rescue operations. Do not, I repeat, do not attempt to re-enter your neighborhoods until they have been declared safe."

A broad, devastating swath of damage had been cut by the massive storm that had spawned not only the EF4 tornado that destroyed Oil City but also two smaller tornadoes. Doors and windows all across the areas of Texas and Arkansas that bordered northern Louisiana had been cordoned off with yellow tape to indicate severe damage.

Signs instructing residents not to cut or walk past the caution tape were posted everywhere. Some structures bore color-coded signs. The news had instructed that before entering one of these buildings, one must first check with city officials for information about the sign's meaning.

Cabe Bramwell's pedantic tone solemnly related all the latest information. "Just a day after one of the worst tornadoes in over a decade, I have the responsibility of reporting what we know for sure. Fact: The unexpected tornado struck Oil City at lunchtime yesterday. Fact: Eighteen people trapped in their cars died. Fact: Three children at the Twist and Shout Roller-Rink were killed when part of the roof collapsed on them. Five others were found dead, having been ravaged by the storm's fury with no shelter close at hand. Fact: Ten buses parked at the Sandborn Transit Company depot were sucked up from the lot by the twister's winds and completely destroyed. One landed in the nearby yard of a Mr. and Mrs. Jackson Owens. All this reporter can say is, thank heaven it landed in the yard and not on the house, a mere twenty feet away, where the Owens family was huddled together."

The reporter's dialogue was interrupted by an emergency broadcast from the governor's office.

The governor looked haggard and began solemnly, "Yesterday's severe weather impacted multiple parishes in Louisiana, with reported small-scale tornadoes and large hail compounding the unspeakable and grand-scale damage done to Oil City. I am declaring this emergency in order to make sure the impacted parishes and any additional areas that may see further severe weather are able to get assistance from the state. The damage is devastating and a good reminder that everyone in Louisiana should stay weather aware. My heart goes out to all who are not only impacted by loss of property but through the loss of a loved one as well. Know that as your governor, I will do all in my power to offer the needed aid and support the good people of Louisiana deserve. I now send you back to your regularly scheduled programs."

Seeing the cue that their broadcast was once again live, Cabe Bramwell's voice grew gravelly as he struggled to keep emotion from filtering through his commentary. "Folks, I'm going to break away from the script because now is a time to come together from wherever we are, to join as a community. Just yesterday morning, we all woke to what we thought would be an ordinary day. Breakfasts were made, jobs gone to, and chores done. We were to have come home that evening to be with family. Perhaps some had weekend plans with friends and neighbors. Sadly, too many are now planning funerals, including my own sister-in-law . . . for my brother."

For those watching the news, seeing the handsome, robust, sandy-haired reporter wipe a tear from his cheek as he struggled to keep his voice even brought a tear or two to their own eye.

Then, Cabe lowered the microphone and bowed his head as he took a few steadying breaths. The viewing public held their collective breath with him, and prayed.

"I am reminded of a quote by someone I've recently come across, a man named Khalil Gibran. In a poem, Mr. Gibran said, 'When you love you should not say, "God is in our heart," but rather, "I am in the heart of God". And think not you can direct the course of love, for love, if it finds you worthy, directs your course.'"

Cabe swallowed hard. Gripping his microphone with both hands, he stared straight into the camera, almost daring the viewing public to disagree with him. "Loss is loss. I defy anyone to claim that spilled blood, no matter the source, does not run red. Doesn't seep between the fingers of the empty hands that will never again caress the face of the one they've lost. Let us follow the example of our Lord and mourn with those that mourn. Weep with those that weep. Let us be found worthy by the gift and light of love to, to be in the . . ."

The man could take no more. The microphone suddenly looked too heavy for him to hold, and his arms slowly lowered; his shoulders sagged. With a battle-hardened blankness, he turned and walked out of the frame.

Off camera, voices could be heard whispering, "Mr. Bramwell . . . Cabe, we still have two and a half minutes . . ." "Someone get out there." "Do we have a commercial ready?"

The experienced camera operator simply held the frame steady, waiting for someone to step in . . . or not.

To the viewers, the unexpected show of emotion from someone they felt they'd come to know and trust brought the message close to home. And the faceless airspace that still had nearly two minutes before a commercial break held them captive like no fill-in could have.

In silence, the camera operator began to slowly, painstakingly pan over the devastation. No narrator was needed to tell viewers what they were seeing, for they were being given a glimpse at the current state of their own hearts.

Chapter 27

Different Shades of Black
Saturday, April 11, 1959

"It is a brave act of valor to condemn death,
but where life is more terrible than death,
it is then the truest valor to dare to live."

*—Sir Thomas Browne (1605–1682),
English author and polymath*

"You about ready, Bits? Times a wastin', and we still have to pick up Trinny and Orvalee."

"Coming!" Bits called back. "Come on, you." She grimaced at the old French Market Coffee can under her bed. It had somehow been knocked deeper than she could reach, and the boot she'd gotten from her papa's closet to use as a hook, was not doing its anticipated job.

"Come on, just about . . ."

"Bits! What on God's green earth is ta—" Her papa's voice trailed off when he stopped in the doorway and caught sight of her, tail end praising the sky, as she reached deeper beneath the bed for her quarry.

"Land's sakes, gal-o'-mine, what *are* you doin'? We don't wanna be late for the funeral."

Bits sighed and backed out from beneath the bed. "I wanted to wear the bracelet Uncle George brought me from France, but it's in my treasure can, and the darned thing just doesn't want to be got."

"Here, let me get it while you straighten your pretty new hair ribbon and smooth your dress." Remy reached for the elusive coffee can and emerged with both it and his boot. "Dare I ask why this"—he held up the boot—"is beneath your bed."

"I was usin' it as a hook," she said matter-of-factly.

"A hook? Oh, never mind. Here's your can. Now, hurry and grab the bracelet and skedaddle on out to the car. We are late."

"Yes Papa." Bits hurriedly obeyed, and soon they were on their way, first to Orvalee's and then Trinny's.

"Papa, do you think Uncle George is really okay? Aline says he acts all right most of the time, but then he'll just stop what he's doin' and get a far away look." Bits lowered her voice to a whisper, like she was telling a secret. "Once, she even caught him cryin'."

"Yes, Bits, I believe Uncle George is doin' just fine, considering he just lost his pa. It doesn't matter how old you are when you lose a parent, it's still hard."

"Even when . . . uh . . ." Bits hesitated.

"Yeah? Go on."

When Bits still didn't reply, Remy looked in the rear-view mirror and caught her eye. "You know you can ask me anything ya like."

"Well, I know Uncle George and his pa weren't really . . . They didn't . . . George's daddy really didn't like him none, did he?"

"No, sweetheart, they were not what you'd call friendly."

"Bein' that they weren't friends, does that make it easier for Uncle George not to miss him so much?"

Remy thought about it. George had confided the state of his father's body after he'd been called upon by Reverend Marrs to identify the corpse. No matter his feelings toward the man, George would *never* have wished this ending for him.

They had just pulled up in front of Orvalee's. Normally, Remy would go to the door to fetch her, but this time, he just honked three times, then turned to face Bits over the seat.

"I think that maybe not bein' friendly with his pa might actually make it harder on him. See, there can be a lot of things left unsaid between two people that don't get along. Things that can weigh on a body when the other person isn't there to have the chance to make up to. Things that—"

Orvalee hopped in the back beside Li'l Bits, took one look at the pair, and said, "Land's sakes, but you two look serious. Do I need to give y'all a minute?"

"No," Remy said as he faced forward. "Bits was just askin' after how George is coping."

Orvalee reached over to give Li'l Bits's hand a comforting squeeze. "You're a sweet child. Heaven knows losin' a parent is never easy, but your uncle still has his wonderful mother and all those brothers, sisters, nieces and nephews to command his attention." Orvalee's face brightened. "And as an added bonus, he has us, right?"

Bits's face lit up. "He sure does. He'll *always* have me."

"Come here sweetheart." Orvalee scooted Bits onto her lap. "You are the best thing that happened to *all* of us."

When they pulled up to Trinny's, Remy got out and ran to the door. Trinny had seen them coming and was on her way out when the two collided. Remy grabbed onto Trinny to steady them both, and their eyes met. Though Trinny blushed, she didn't turn away or try to pull free of his grasp.

"You look lovely," Remy said, as he took her hand and led her to the car.

"Thank you. You look lovely too. I mean nice . . . I mean,

handsome." Trinny flushed and dodged in through the door Remy opened for her.

"Hello, Orvalee," Trinny said brightly. "Bits, you look lovely. Black suits you."

Li'l Bits loved being told that she looked nice and returned the compliment. "Trinny, you look divine. Your dress is all shiny and looks like it has some other colors in it."

Trinny was still getting used to accepting compliments and looked to Orvalee for support. Since the night Remy had kissed her, she and Orvalee had talked about the new road they were all on. Their little group dynamic was shifting, and it would take some getting used to. The older woman nodded.

"Thank you, Bits. My dress is silk, like the kimono I wore to your fifth birthday party. Do you remember that dress?"

"Oh, yes, I sure do. It was the most beautiful dress I ever saw. It was yellow and made you look like a garden."

"Wow." Trinny was impressed. "That's right."

"I remember wantin' a dress just like yours, only I wanted mine to be blue."

The rest of the drive to the church was taken up by talk of pretty dresses and what colors looked best on who. But color faded from the conversation as they pulled into the church parking lot, where every person walking in wore varying shades of black.

Black—the color of formality, sadness, secrets, and night. In the case of funerals, or rather, for half of the attendees of *this* funeral, black might also mean release. Bitter-sweet release. Bitter because losing someone that's always been part of your life is never an easy thing, but sweet because now the air-sucking presence that had commanded space in everyone's life was gone.

The church was hosting two funerals and was jam-packed with mourners. Alongside Mont's closed coffin at the front of the church lay the body of young Antione Sumner, who had been one of the eighteen killed while trapped in their vehicles. Mr. Sumner had been a delivery driver for the Coatsdale Brewery and, sadly, had not finished his route that day. Laying serenely in his polished wood coffin, he looked younger than his twenty-four years, while his devastated parents looked eighty.

Claudine had been on the lookout for Remy, Bits, Orvalee and Trinny. When she saw them sneak in the back of the church, she waved them forward to sit on the family pew. Orvalee indicated that they would just stand along the back wall, but Claudine would have none of that. She tugged on her husband's arm. He bent down, and she whispered into his ear. George looked back, then maneuvered past his family and out into the aisle, where his mammoth frame and beckoning arm could not be ignored.

Trinny, Orvalee, and Remy moved forward hesitantly, trying to be as unobtrusive as possible and highly doubting that a group like theirs had ever stepped foot in this church before. Li'l Bits, however, was completely unaware of the spectacle she was part of. All she saw was friends. She'd even come to know Ruth when the woman had come with Claudine to help clean up Orvalee's greenhouse and yard. Li'l Bits liked Ruth and was more than happy to receive a hug from her as everyone settled into a place on the long bench.

A few of the congregation that knew of the group's friendship with George, nodded a greeting at the visitors, while a great many inquisitive heads bobbed together, wondering why *these* people were here.

Before sliding in next to Remy, George scanned the assembly and casually adopted the imposing stance he'd mastered while in the army. A pose that let others know he'd stand for no nonsense on his watch. Then, with a quick tug on his coat lapel as if to straighten it, George nonverbally cut off any contrary comment before it could even be uttered. He had wanted his best friends here for support, and they had come.

Reverend Marrs stepped to the podium and silenced everyone by clearing his throat. "My brothers and sisters, though it is a solemn occasion we gather for today, I like to believe it can also be a joyous one. For we here, have come together to celebrate the lives of two souls that are now back in the arms of our everlasting Father in Heaven: Antione Sumner, who was at the beginnin' of life. He was full of thoughts of adventure and changin' the world, and he possessed one of the kindest hearts God saw fit to bless a man with. And Mr. Mont Dollis, father of seven bright, lively souls and husband to one of God's earth-angels."

Remy smiled at how the reverend had lightly sidestepped all Mont's faults by instead associating him with the wife he'd had the good sense to snag and the family he had created with her.

"Before we begin the celebration of life for these two good men"—Reverend Marrs fanned both hands out to indicate the caskets before them—"I want to remind all here how our departure to the cemetery will go. To commemorate the *twenty-six* souls that lost their lives last week, the governor of our fair state, in a gesture of *far-seein'* inclusion and to echo Mr. Cabe Bramwell's declaration that 'loss is loss,' has arranged and paid for plots in the Asbury City Cemetery for *all* the storm's victims."

Reverend Marrs had been quite overcome when he read the statement that had been sent to the clergy who would be conducting the funerals all over the parish. The governor had chosen a city cemetery because recent court rulings had upheld non-segregated burials in non-private cemeteries. He'd wanted no trouble, just the opportunity to alleviate a small portion of the overwhelming burden of loss. And those who had chosen to bury their loved ones alongside already deceased family members had been more than welcome to do so.

"A commemorative plaque bearing the names and ages of the tornado's victims has been placed near the burial site and will be unveiled after the lowering of the caskets. As our service here concludes, so too will services throughout the parish. As we file forth, please fill each vehicle as full as comfortably possible, for we will thence follow the hearses and converge at various points along the route to the cemetery with our fellow mourners."

Everyone had seen the news announcement about the cavalcade. Those attending the funerals were going to be brought together into one long procession routed through the heart of Oil City. Roads had been cleared through the devastation, and American flags had been erected to mark the route. People had been instructed that if they wished to hold up signs of condolence or well-wishes, they were welcome to do so. However, police had been posted along the route, and no "shenanigans" from wayward observers would be tolerated.

"Brothers and sisters, though our loss seems a load beyond bearing, let us not forget that the friends and families of twenty-four other victims are feelin' the same. And *eight* of those beautiful souls were children. Let us ask a special prayer of blessing for the families that will *never* get to see their little ones grow."

Claudine unconsciously reached out to lay an appreciative hand on Aline's arm and whisper a prayer of thanks for each of her children. George wrapped a protective arm around his wife and, with a knowing look, leaned close and kissed her temple. Remy and Trinny had simultaneously reached for Li'l Bits, who sat between them.

Observing her friends, Orvalee's heart melted with gratitude, and a little sadness too. She longed to reach for her son, the only one she had left, but beside her was empty air.

Reverend Marrs took a minute to compose himself. He leaned heavily on the podium, his head sagging, and he looked like he was bearing a great weight. But when he lifted his eyes to face the gathering, there was a fierceness to them that lit him from within.

"I hope y'all were blessed to see Mr. Cabe Bramwell's report last Saturday. He and his family are right where we are at this *very* moment. Mourning their own loss. Havin' to face tomorrow, and the day after, and *every* day after that without their loved one. *Just* as we are. Brothers and sisters, I looked up the Mr. Gibran he mentioned, and the words I found filled me with inspiration. I found something I wanted to share with y'all. Something I think adds to the message Mr. Bramwell was tryin', without sayin' as much, to get across."

Remy had seen that broadcast and had been touched by the message he felt the reporter was trying to send. Loss is loss. Whether colored or white, life had been tragically ripped away from unsuspecting people that day. Spilled blood, no matter the source, leaves an aching void in the hearts of those left behind to continue the job of living without them. What he heard Reverend Marrs saying let him know that this man had *felt* the same message, and he respected him all the more for it.

The reverend put his glasses on to read from his notes. "I quote, 'And though death may hide me, and the greater silence enfold me, yet again will I seek your understanding. And not in vain will I seek. If aught I have said is truth, that truth shall reveal itself in a clearer voice . . . I go with the wind . . . but not down into emptiness; And if this day is not a fulfillment of your needs and my love, then let it be a promise 'til another day.'"

The reverend took off his glasses and carefully laid them near the top of the podium. "Let us think on this a bit more, shall we? 'And if *this* day is *not* a fulfillment of your needs and *my love*,'"—with heartfelt emotion, he pounded a fist against his chest—"'then, let it be a promise 'til *another* day' . . . but *not* down into emptiness."

In subdued silence, many of the mourners allowed their heads to hang low as tears dripped freely. Some had indeed felt let down, betrayed by the God they believed in. How could so many be allowed to die? This question bled out of every heart.

"My brothers and sisters, none here are exempt from loss. Be it a family member, a job, or hope, when we lose somethin', it leaves an ache. *This day*"—he tapped the pulpit with a heavy index finger—"is a day of letting go. Of release. And as we allow our hearts to be open to the pain of loss and allow the silence of that void to *enfold* us, let us yet again turn our hearts, as they are ready, to the truth that will reveal itself with a clearer understanding. The understanding that it is a *sin* to take *today* for granted."

At this, heads bobbed in agreement, and hands covered hearts; who was not guilty of that?

"If, in *this day*, you are not given what you wanted or hoped for, then *do not* let it slip into tomorrow without offerin' sincere thanks for the lesson of *humility*, of *patience*, of knowin' it was not the right time. For there yet remains a promise for *another* day. And oh, the joy that will shine from our eyes when fulfillment of a prayer knocks unexpectedly on our door, and we answer."

Remy was feeling a kinship with all the reverend was saying. There had been so many nos in his life, both the ones that had been said to him, and those he'd said to himself. But with the little ray of sunshine that sat next to him had come a new hope, one he had chosen to believe in. One he had secretly nurtured. And when that hope had knocked on his door, it brought him his heart's ultimate desire, and *she* sat next to his little miss sunshine. Despite where he was, Remy had never felt more full of life than he did right now.

Chapter 28

A New Hope

> "I guess that's just part of loving people:
> You have to give things up. Sometimes
> you even have to give them up."
>
> —*Lauren Oliver (living), American author*

Flags gently flapped in the breeze as the cavalcade made its way along the route to the cemetery. Funereal faces followed the progress of the numbered, flower-bedecked hearses, many of which had been recruited from mortuaries outside the parish, so great was the number of dead.

A shattered community watched as car after car glided behind the silent police escort. Handmade signs of condolence were held aloft by people of all ages. Children sitting atop their fathers' shoulders waved small flags. Some had gathered flower petals, which they threw on the road as the cars passed.

An NLBC camera crew had set up in front of what had been the Twist and Shout Roller Rink, with Dan Devries filling in for Cabe Bramwell, who was in one of the passing cars.

"It is with deep sorrow that we stand here," the substitute reporter lamented. Those watching the procession from home could tell the new guy was nervous to be on camera. He had a comfortable, lived-in sort of face, but he lacked Cabe Bramwell's polish and charisma and made it obvious that he was reading from cue cards.

"Our hearts go out to the families and friends of those who were lost to the storm as we gather with them today in a show of communal solidarity." Dan did his best to keep his tone somber and respectful, but his naturally mild, nasal intonations were distracting.

"The scars of last week will remain for a great while as we learn to live with the outcome of what I'm sure has changed us all. With a grief so deep, it cannot find expression through simple tears, the mourners that have gathered along the funeral route today wear their hearts on their sleeves as they honor the dead. Tomorrow evening, NLBC will broadcast the taped unveiling of the plaque at Asbury Cemetery that will forever commemorate the names of our fallen. But for today, we honor the desired anonymity of the families."

Trinny, Orvalee, George, Claudine, and the kids were piled on top of one another in Remy's car. Driving in the slow procession gave them plenty of time to stare curiously at the remains of what had been a prospering downtown. It was the first time they'd been back to the city's center. When they passed the former *Ladies Home Companion* headquarters, Trinny shakily reached for Remy's hand.

Being the one sought to offer a gesture of comfort made Remy's heart race. But he did not like the solid tension he felt in her grip.

Claudine too was reliving a few of her own ghosts as they skirted the skeletal remains of buildings that had once held so much life. George pulled her close in a quick hug and whispered, "No worries, *ma belle*. Never again."

"I know, *mon Guerrier*. I know." Her throat tightened, and she allowed herself to be swallowed by his large, protective arm.

As the procession filed through the cemetery's arched, wrought-iron gates, each hearse was directed to the burial site with its corresponding number. The mourners had been told in which numbered plots their loved ones would be interred. They parked wherever they could and made their way to their designated spots.

Hugs were shared among the throng as they wove past one another on the way to their respective gravesites. Tears were shed, and handkerchiefs passed between mourners as freely as paper on the wind.

After the brief graveside services, everyone gathered around the memorial plaque for the unveiling. No one seemed to notice or care who they stood next to. Black or white, affluent or working class, the tragedy of their combined loss served to bond them, at least in this moment, and the diversity made the day more beautiful.

Cabe Bramwell, his face just as blotchy and tearstained as everyone else's, had been asked to perform the unveiling, so he took his place on the small dais that had been erected for the occasion. Whatever lay beneath the black velvet cover was much larger than any of them had expected. And none had anticipated the four benches placed in a square around the seven-foot-high black drape.

Cabe cleared his throat. "Friends, part of me is sorry that any of us have to be here today. But as I look out at everyone, I'm also grateful. Grateful that those we are here to honor have such a bounty of love—" The man's voice broke, and he had to stop. Sniffing, he took a deep breath and kept going.

"Of loved ones. As we work to rebuild our fair city, I have no doubt our efforts will be guided from above, for we now have our own network of angels looking out for us. I also have no doubt that many of us will seek refuge from sorrow by returning to this very spot, lounging on one of these very benches and gazing with fond memories at whatever lies beneath this covering. I say *fond* because I know that as I think of my brother, all I will remember is the laughter, the jokes, and the fun. All the good."

He swiped at his nose with a handkerchief. "I would like to invite my nieces, nephews, and all the other children to assist me in revealing whatever it is that will come to mean so much to us all."

He motioned the children forward, and the crowd parted to let them through. Li'l Bits moved forward, but Remy pulled her back. "No, darlin', this is for those who lost someone."

"Oh, okay." Li'l Bits looked at all the children who stepped in close to take part. There were so many.

"Papa." She tugged on Remy's hand. "Will you hold me so I can see better?"

"Sure thing, sweet pea." Remy swung her up.

From her higher vantage point, Bits could see the faces of the children. She could see the faces of their parents. She looked at George to see how he was doing; he was watching his children. Claudine's gaze darted between her children and her husband. Orvalee seemed to be taking everything in. Trinny's gaze was fastened on the black drape. Bits couldn't see her papa's face. With a hand on his cheek, she turned it so she could look into his eyes.

"Yeah?" he asked.

"Nothing, just . . . I love you. Thank you for lovin' me and for bein' here. Not where their papas are."

Remy just about lost it. He squeezed his eyes shut and hugged her tight, but Bits didn't complain.

Once everyone that wanted to participate was up front, there were enough children that Cabe had them fan out the base of the black fabric on the left side of the object so they could each gain a handful.

To make them feel like this was all for them, Cabe enthusiastically asked the children, "All right, are you ready?"

"Yes!" They all said, beginning to fidget with excitement.

Trinny whispered to Remy, "It's a wonderful idea to involve the children like this."

She had missed the touching exchange between him and Bits.

"Look at their little faces. I think being able to do this will help soften the loss for some of them."

Remy just said, "Mmhmm."

"One!" Cabe shouted.

"Two!" The children joined in.

The entire gathering added their voices on, "Three!"

The black velvet drape slipped off, and there was a collective gasp of appreciation. A four-foot-tall granite pedestal supported a delicately balanced, three-foot-tall bronze sculpture of a twisting tornado. The sculptor had captured the very essence of the moving winds. The open funneled top coiled up from the pinpoint base that seemed to magically connect with the granite.

Wanting to reach out and touch it, Claudine marveled aloud, "How does it not fall over?"

"By golly, I have no idea," George replied.

Many of the children did reach out to touch it. Each little finger found its way around the base to where the name of their family member had been engraved. Older children guided younger siblings to the name they were looking for. Adults teared up as they mutely watched little hands explore the textured surface of the intricately carved angel wings that topped each side of the base and gently curved down to embrace the names below.

Hoping to encourage those who viewed the sculpture not to focus on the tornado's destruction, but instead, on the love that can still exist even when things go wrong, just above each set of wings, the artist had included different Shakespearean quotes:

"Being deeply loved by someone gives you strength, while loving someone deeply gives you courage."

"Who could refrain, that had a heart to love, and in that heart Courage to make love known?"

"When you fear a foe, fear crushes your strength; and this weakness gives strength to your opponents."

"Love looks not with the eyes, but with the mind."

Orvalee watched as a little girl, about seven-years-old, pasted her hand across her father's name and began to cry. The girl's mother moved forward to kneel beside her and said, "See, sweetie, Papa's right here, and the angels are guardin' him."

Through sniffles, the girl said, "But the twister's on top, and that's what took him. I don't like it."

Inspired by the quotes on the monument, the mother said, "Aw, sweetie, that twister's not gonna take him anywhere, not anymore. What it is gonna do, is when we come back and talk to Papa, those winds'll carry our words straight up to him in heaven."

Still dubious, the little girl did calm down enough to reach up and try to touch the bronze tornado. Her mother lifted her so that she could get a good look. With a tentative hand, the child probed the curves and contours.

"I think I can feel it," she whispered.

"Feel what, darlin'?" her mother asked.

"The openin' to heaven, where Papa is."

Orvalee covered her mouth to stifle a sob. To her, the trusting innocence of children was always a marvel. This child's mother told her the twister had a dual purpose, and with unwavering faith, the child had found it to be true.

The mother's eyes filled with tears as she hugged her daughter close. "We can come every Sunday after church and have a picnic with Papa. How would that be?"

"Could we bring his favorite pickles from the cellar?"

As the duo walked off, Orvalee heard the mom say, "Of course; what a good idea. And you can . . ." They were swallowed by the crowd.

Orvalee sank back to the rear of the throng. "Avner," she

whispered. Just hearing his name somehow made her feel better. "You and the boys help all the newly departed find their way round heaven, okay? I'm sure a few of 'em would appreciate you pointin' the way to all the best fishin' spots." She chewed her lower lip.

Unable to take any more, Orvalee found Remy and told him that she would be waiting at the car.

He looked concerned. "You all right?"

"Perfectly fine. Just tired of standin'. Need to give my legs a rest." Saying nothing more, she walked away.

Remy watched her go. The past few months had seen a change come over Orvalee, and he didn't like it. She seemed to be fading, if you could call it that. He'd have to talk to Trinny, George, and Claudine to see if they had noticed anything. If they had, then some sort of intervention might be called for.

The drive back to the church to drop the Dollis family off at their car was more upbeat than when they'd headed to the funeral. It had helped George's children to be with their cousins and all the other children. None of them were alone in what they felt, and there was comfort in that. Plus, maybe especially for George's children, it had been extremely beneficial to see black and white mix together. All they usually got was an either-or situation, with them lost somewhere in the middle.

At the church, every head in the front seat swiveled around to say goodbye. Jeremy, Beau, and Aline all scooted out one side and ran to their car. George opened the back door to get out, but stopped.

"Rem, Trinny, Orvalee, Bits, I just wanted to thank y'all for bein' with us today. It made our family feel complete. Y'all didn't have to take up your day, but I'm mighty grateful you did."

"Hear, hear," Claudine said. "You are the best of people, and away from my home, you *are* my family."

Dress and all, Li'l Bits used her papa's arm as a step to climb over the back seat and right into her uncle's arms. "You can always count on me, Uncle George." Pulling Claudine into the hug, she said, "You too, Aunt Claudine. I am so, so lucky to have everyone I love around me all the time. I've never . . . I just . . ." Li'l Bits couldn't find the words to say what she wanted, so she buried her face in George's neck.

He stroked her hair. "You'll always have me too, sweet Bits. Whenever you need. You helped save me, and I owe you for that."

Pulling back, Bits had no idea what her uncle was talking about. "How could I save you? You're a hundred times bigger than me."

"One day li'l miss, I'll tell ya the story. And it'll be just like a fairy tale because it has such a happy ending. Now, get on back up front. Y'all have supper to get to."

"I'll just stay back here and have the *whole* seat to myself," Bits said as George and Claudine slid out. Sprawled out in their place, she said, "Mmm, this is nice."

George leaned in and kissed the top of Bits's head. "You're a real pip, kiddo."

Eyes closed, Bits smiled. "I know."

George shut the door, waved goodbye, and headed to his car, ready to spend some quality time with his family. He'd been given a week off to deal with the funeral, and he was going to enjoy every remaining minute.

Still thinking about the impression he'd gotten of Orvalee at the cemetery, Remy pulled out of the driveway and asked, "Orvalee, how'd you like to come over for some warmed up apple pie and ice cream? So we wouldn't have to cook after spendin' the day at a funeral, Mama made scalloped potatoes, baked ham with biscuits and the pie. We've got plenty."

"My, my, that is tempting, and thank you. But after the day we've all had, I think it'll suit me to just sit on my porch with a glass of tea. Feels like a sippin' day to me."

"Tea?" Incredulous, Li'l Bits popped up to a sitting position. "When you could have pie, ice cream *and* ham."

"I know, sweet heart, seems hard to imagine, but sometimes my digestive system likes to keep things simple."

"What's a sippin' day?"

"It's what I call the days when food sounds too heavy to eat."

"Heavy? A biscuit isn't heavy. Even I can carry one of those. Remember how I carried in the whole basket of 'em last Thanksgiving?"

"Yes, Bits, I remember. And you didn't drop one of 'em. However, I do seem to recall seein' a little hand dart beneath the cloth cover and come out with one."

Bits smiled sheepishly. "You saw that? Drat. I thought I was bein' pretty sneaky."

"I saw it. And how much somethin' weighs isn't really what I'm talkin' about, but I guess for reference, it'll do. I thank y'all for the offer, but I just need to keep things light today."

Bits stood on the seat and leaned forward. "All righty, I guess your stomach knows what's best for you. But mine can hardly wait for . . ." Pointing toward Orvalee's fast-approaching house, Bits asked, "Hey, who's that?"

Orvalee's head swiveled forward, and she let out a strangled breath.

"Orvalee! What's wrong? Who is it? Is it a bad guy? Should Papa take care of him?"

Heedless of the fact that the car was still moving, Orvalee opened the passenger door. Had Remy not immediately slammed on the brakes, she might have been terribly hurt.

Poor Bits, leaning against the seat as she was, was propelled forward and landed upside down in the front seat between her papa and Trinny.

In front of Orvalee's house, a young man stood by an old van that looked like it had seen more miles than the Michelin Tire Man. After a graceless exit from the car, Orvalee ran a few steps toward the figure, then halted.

Right side up now, Bits stared out the window. "Papa, who's that?"

Remy exhaled a powerfully slow breath. "Oh, sweet girl, I *hope* it's who I think it is."

Entranced, the car's three occupants watched as Orvalee hesitated, then tentatively moved forward again.

Hand outstretched, as if expecting who she saw to be nothing more than a hallucination, Orvalee jerked to a stop when the young man moved toward her.

"Hello, Mama."

"Ervyn?"

Chapter 29

What's in a Name?

Sunday, July 5, 1959

"Don't be satisfied with stories, how things have gone
with others. Unfold your own myth."

—*Rumi (1207–1273), Persian poet, scholar,
theologian and mystic*

Bits loved Sundays. They were days to sit back and rest from whatever had ailed you during the week. In her case, outside by her tree, today would be dedicated to contemplating everything that had happened since the big funeral.

Ervyn, Orvalee's youngest son, had come home. Uncle George, Papa and everyone else were calling him the Prodigal Son. When she hadn't understood why they were calling him that, Papa read her the Bible story.

When they got to Luke 15:13, where it says, "and took his journey into a far country, and there wasted his substance with riotous living," Bits had asked, "Is that like what I see sometimes about riots in the news, on the television? When they talk about how black and white people shouldn't be livin' together?

Did Ervyn do stuff like that? You know, that just makes me mad."

Remy had let out a long, heavy sigh. He was doing his best to protect his sweet girl from well, the only way he could describe it was shit-thinking. But shades of it crept in through unseen cracks every day. When they rode the bus, Remy hated having to think that if George and Claudine had been there too, Claudine could sit with them, but his daughter's beloved uncle would be relegated to somewhere in the back. Without doubt, Bits wouldn't give a second thought to joining him, and what a hullabaloo that would create.

Public restrooms, restaurants, drugstore soda counters, pretty much every aspect of day-to-day living was against two of the best people he knew. Thank heaven they'd been married in France, where there were no anti-miscegenation laws. Remy wasn't sure how George and Claudine held up so well under the scrutiny, but he did know of a surety that living in the community they did made all the difference.

As Remy had let go of the misconceptions of his father, he'd come to see the truth of not just what his father had built—A&D Oil Supply—but also *who* his father was. Alexander Dubois had helped a good number of people through some pretty rough times, and many of those people had, in turn, ended up doing very well for themselves. But every single one of them knew they owed what they had to one man, and they would not cross him. Alexander Dubois was a champion of George Dollis, and in Oil City, that was all that needed to be said on the matter.

"No, Bits. Thankfully, his was not the kind of riotous living we see on the news. However, just as the prodigal son in the Bible found that he had gotten lost doin' the sorts of things he thought would make him a man, Ervyn lost himself to doin' what he thought would help him run away from the pain of losin' his brothers and his pa."

"But he left Orvalee all alone. Didn't he know how bad

that would hurt her? I mean, I know he wrote letters and sent pictures, 'cause she showed 'em to me, but I always saw the tears in her eyes. The ones she wouldn't let fall when anyone was around."

Bits scrunched her face in anger and confusion as she tried to order things in her mind. "Sometimes . . ." She was unsure if she dared share her secret thought, but then she looked into her papa's warm eyes and let it spill. "Sometimes, when I could see those tears hidin' themselves deep behind her eyes, I really wanted to kick that boy of hers. I wanted to yell at him, loud, and let him know how much he was hurtin' the person who loved him most in all the world."

Bits ducked her head, fearing reproval for the admission. When none came, she looked up and could tell that just maybe, her papa had wanted to do the same thing.

"Papa, was it wrong? Was that a mean thought to have? Do you think Jesus is disappointed in me?" Bits's chin and lower lip quivered. She didn't want to have thoughts that might have led her to act like some of the people in the news. What they did was ugly, and she didn't want to be that kind of ugly.

Papa had pulled her onto his lap and smoothed back the hair from her temples. "No, my girl. I think Jesus understands plain enough how you feel. It's because you love Orvalee and want to protect her that you felt that way, right?"

"Yes."

"Well, if there's one thing Jesus understands, it's love. And just like in the prodigal son story, where his own pa forgave him for all the hurt and worry the boy had put him through, now that he's back, Orvalee is so full of love for Ervyn that's all she sees. The time he was gone has faded into nothin' but a bad dream. And you know what?"

"What?" Nothing distracted Bits like a mysterious question.

"Do you know what, or should I say *who*, Ervyn brought back with him?"

"Of course, I know that," Bits said indignantly. "Dierdre. She and Ervyn are gettin' married. Orvalee told me."

"That's right," Remy said. "But that's not the *who* I'm talkin' about."

"Well then, what *are* you talkin' about?"

"Orvalee has let me know, and told me to pass it right along to you, that we can all look forward to . . ." Remy drew out a long pause. By the time he finished the sentence, Bits was practically bouncing with anticipation. ". . . her first *grandchild*. Coming sometime in December."

Li'l Bits's eyes grew as wide as tea cup saucers. "A baby? Her son is gonna be a papa? That's . . ." Was that good? Bits had managed to act happy about the news, but if Orvalee had a grandchild to dote on, would she still have time for Bits? Would she still want to teach Bits how to make salves, tinctures, specialty teas, and all the other things they've worked on? Her whole life had been spent at Orvalee's side, either in the greenhouse or foraging for ingredients for their latest project.

Still pondering how to feel about *one* new baby entering the picture, to top it off, at the Fourth of July celebration yesterday, Aline let it slip that come sometime in November, she was going to be a big sister. Aline had been so excited that she'd prattled on and on about how she was going to help change diapers, and read to the new baby, and take it on walks, and . . . There were so many *and's* that Bits lost count.

Why hadn't her uncle been the one to tell her? Or her papa? Claudine, Orvalee, or Trinny? She'd been told about Ervyn's baby. It hurt to think that she'd been left out of this very important, very special news. Though, knowing this information, other things now made sense. Like how Trinny and Orvalee had been spending more time at Claudine's. How Uncle George always had a hand at Aunt Claudine's back, like she was going to fall over or something. And Aline's Granny Dollis and even some aunts had been coming over.

Once, when she'd been playing with Aline, she'd heard

Granny Dollis say to Claudine, "It's so nice to finally be able to do this. Thank you for not holdin' the past against me. I'd've come if I could."

Claudine had assured her all was well. There had been lots of hugging and tears. Orvalee was more apt to cry now too. Even Trinny had been seen swiping at a stray tear or two. Trinny! Crying? Li'l Bits had begun to think that the older women got, the more they cried.

Change. Maybe life was just getting so crazy that it had them wanting to throw up, sort of like she had wanted to do all morning. That's why she was out by her tree. Her ever-faithful, always constant, never-changing oak. Not even the storm that hit back when the tornado happened had been able to break her friend. Granted, it had lost a few large limbs, but as none had damaged the house, Papa hadn't cut it down out of frustration. It would break her heart if anything ever happened to this tree.

In this spot, nestled between two raised roots that formed armrests, she had always felt like she could pour out her heart and know that someone was listening. That someone cared. Bits began thinking about babies, mothers, fathers, and families.

She loved her papa so much, but she wanted a mother. Over a year ago, she'd written to Santa about it. She had wanted Trinny. But can you just choose your own mother like that?

Her papa had never made a secret of the fact that she had been given to him, like Moses from the Bible had been given to his mother. Nana had called this "divine providence." Could this same power bring her a mom?

Li'l Bits snuggled in closer to the tree, feeling its support, and for some reason, felt like she was being wrapped in arms that loved her so much, they didn't want to let her go. She closed her eyes, her breathing slowed, and she could hear the hint of a song. *Somewhere . . . somewhere* kept repeating over and over in her mind. *Somewhere . . .*

Bits jerked awake at the sound of someone calling her name. Well, it was her name, but not *her* name. It wasn't Bits, or Li'l Bits, darling, sweet pea, or any of the other endearments she'd been called. It was . . . an actual name. Closing her eyes, she could almost hear it.

So many things were changing, maybe now would be a good time to change something else, too. She would be eight in a couple of weeks, and Papa had said that with the new babies coming, she would be old enough to help babysit. Did that mean she would be old enough to make some of the choices that were running through her mind? Could she choose a new name, like she wanted to choose a mother?

Li'l Bits plucked a blade of grass and absentmindedly chewed on it. Not recalling the name from the dream, she thought about those she liked. Jesslyn was nice, but it was already taken. Now that she got to thinking about it, there were so many she liked, how could she choose just one?

Maybe she didn't have to. Could she pick two and put them together, like Amy Jo and Ellie June? She thrummed her fingers against the rough bark of the roots, her tree, her oak . . . Oak?

Oak was strong. Papa said that red oak was one of the easiest woods to work with for stairs, railings, and the posts that go at the end. The ones you don't want to hit your hind end on when sliding down the banister. Sadly, she knew that firsthand from an experience at her grandparents' house. She nearly rubbed her tailbone at the memory.

She liked the thought of oak and stairs, because stairs meant you could go up as high as there was another stair to take you. She liked being able to look down from Nana's staircase. To see the high gloss of polished wood in the entryway. To see . . . Bits's face lit with a smile that came from deep in her heart, and she folded both arms contentedly behind her head. She knew what she wanted her name to be.

Chapter 30

Li'l Bits's 8th Birthday Party

Sunday, July 19, 1959

"The afternoon knows what the
morning never suspected."

—Robert Frost (1874–1963),
Pulitzer Prize-winning American poet

After church, everyone gathered at Pine Hollow Grove for Li'l Bits's birthday picnic. This year, Trinny had helped make a pinecone-and-floral wreath to hang on a tree for decoration. You couldn't have a party without decorations.

Ribbons had been knotted and tied to small stakes that were spaced at intervals around the blankets on the ground. A couple of large sheets had been strategically attached to trees to help create shade for the picnickers, and some of Orvalee's special bug-repelling candles were wafting their protective aromas around the enclosure.

Even Mother Nature added to the festive atmosphere by gifting them with a gentle breeze that kept everyone cool and happy after being cooped up in church.

To help the kids burn off some energy, the adults let them scavenge for treasures that had been hidden beneath fallen branches, around rocks, and in the small stream that ran through the Grove.

"Damian Marcell!" Janelle yelled at her son, who gave her a blank look. Wagging a finger, she said, "Yes, you! I see what you're doin'. Don't you be teachin' those kids how to tell what scat belongs to what animal. We are gonna be eating shortly, and I do not want to be wonderin' what your hands have touched as I watch 'em go to your mouth." She saw his shoulders sag and knew that he would do as he was told.

"That's right, boy," she mumbled to herself as she sat down on a low cushion beside her mother, Trinny, and Claudine. "He knows that should he disobey, this mama will see him go to bed as hungry as a bear fresh from hibernation."

"You're almost as good a mother as I am," Lynne Anne teased.

"Mama, today I'll choose to take that as a compliment." Janelle fanned herself with a napkin. "That boy has been watchin' Westerns on the television. Now, he thinks he's Texas John Slaughter or one of Mackenzie's Raiders."

Lynne Anne patted her daughter's knee. "It's nice to see that you care enough to keep track of what he's watchin'. Just don't let him turn into one of those alien zombie creatures by lettin' him sit in front of the thing all day."

"That's not likely. I think he simply watches those programs to get ideas for all his outdoor shenanigans."

Sienna, Dierdre, and a beaming Orvalee came over to join them on the large patchwork quilt.

"Here you go." Lynne Anne solicitously passed a pillow to Dierdre. "This'll make sittin' a mite easier. How are you feelin' these days?"

Dierdre gratefully accepted the pillow and cautiously lowered herself to the ground beside her soon-to-be mother-in-law. "Much better, thank you. Now that I've been introduced to Orvalee's ginger tea, the nausea and throwing up are getting much better. But if I get overheated, I do find myself slipping back into the horrible middle ground of being queasy enough that I *want* to throw up but can't seem to. And today might be one of those in-between days." She fanned herself with a paper plate. "So, pardon me if I don't eat much. As delicious as I'm sure it all is, well . . ." She waggled a hand in a side-to-side motion.

All but Trinny nodded their heads in commiseration.

Claudine patted her own healthy baby bump. "I have been blessed most abundantly when pregnant. The nausea is not something that plagues me, simply fatigue. That, I am happy to deal with."

With a crooked finger, Claudine drew the women in close and said conspiratorially, "I also must admit to abusing my poor husband's kindness during these times. He is so concerned for my health that with a simple sigh or groan, I get out of doing more than I should."

Every woman laughed.

"As well you should, my dear," Orvalee said approvingly. "Men do it to *us* when they have nothin' more than a simple cold. I swear, they are the worst patients. My Avner, bless him, was a tremendous doctor with a healing heart of gold, but when it came to bein' sick himself, he was as worthless as gum on a boot heel."

While Trinny sat silently, listening to the women share stories of how pathetic their menfolk had been during times of illness, she was gratified to see how happy Orvalee was. Since her son's fortuitous return, Orvalee seemed revitalized. She was back to her old self. Actually, she was better than her old self, because now she could talk about her long-deceased husband. That had to be a good thing. Especially when she could laugh about the silly, happy times.

By the time all the women were done gossiping about their husbands, even Trinny was laughing.

"Well, my dears," Lynne Anne said as she stood up and shook her skirt out, "it's about time we set out the feed bag. I'm sure the men and children have all worked up a good appetite."

Sienna stood too. "That's for sure. Have you seen how the men are chasin' after the kids, pretendin' to help find the treasures?"

"That's what parties are for, Si," Janelle said as she stood up. "I think Michael has more fun than the kids at these things. He's talkin' about takin' a family vacation to that new Disneyland Park. The one in California. Said he's heard some really great things about it from the men at work."

Dierdre said, "I'd upchuck if I went on the rides now, but Ervyn and I went last year. It was great, and I think you'd have so much fun. They have this Autopia ride where even the kids can drive their own cars."

Janelle and Sienna each gave her an interested look.

"It's great. You're on an enclosed track, and though you do actually steer the cars, they have bumpers on them, so it's safe. And then there's the Jungle Cruise. You get on a riverboat and float through a jungle paradise. There are animatronic elephants, crocodiles, hippos, and all sorts of jungly creatures. It really makes you feel like you've traveled someplace exotic."

"Hmm," Janelle mused. "Maybe I will let Michael take us there. I've read about how the park is divided into different lands, like the Tomorrowland. It might be like takin' five or six vacations all in one."

When the call was made that vittles were ready, the men and children flocked to the food table like vultures. After all, dining alfresco tended to make one more comfortable eating with fingers or simply slurping melting things from the plate.

Carrots were tossed behind parents' backs like projectiles, and black olives covered every child's finger until they were slurped off one by one.

By the time the birthday cake was uncovered and the candles were lit, the different icing colors had begun to run together in a sort of abstract art pattern. But that didn't affect the flavor, and after an off-key rendition of "Happy Birthday," everyone dug into their piece with gusto.

Cleanup was made easy when they all pitched in to help. Gus, Andy, Jeremy, and Beau enthusiastically volunteered to climb the trees and loosen the ropes that had secured the sheet-shades. Ellie June's mother came to pick up Jesslyn, Amy Jo, and her daughter. So, with smiles and giggles, the three girls insincerely apologized for *having* to leave and promised to help cleanup next time.

"Hey! No fair," Bits said as she watched her friends climb into the pink-and-white 1957 Packard Clipper. Hands on hips, Bits stated, "I'll bet you guys planned this getaway."

"What can I say?" Ellie June shrugged. "My mom has really good timing."

Bits waved as they drove away. Each of her friends' laughing faces were pressed to a window as they waved back.

Dierdre, Claudine, and Trinny were standing by Remy's car when Bits, Aline, and Amanda carried Bits's unwrapped birthday bounty over. Before Bits and Aline could follow Amanda and scamper back to the others, Dierdre said, "Hey, girls."

The two turned to look at her. "Yeah?"

Dierdre hadn't known them long, but was aware of how much they meant to Orvalee, so she wanted to include them in her upcoming wedding. "I've already asked your parent's permission and they've said yes, so, if you want to, I'd really like the two of you to be flower girls at my wedding next week. Would you like that?" Dierdre looked hopeful.

"Would we!" The shocked duo exclaimed in unison.

"Yes!" Bits said enthusiastically.

"Of course!" Aline bounced excitedly.

Dierdre bent down to give them each a hug. "I'm sorry it's last minute. I've talked to your moms," she said before thinking and looked at Trinny, whose cheeks held a rosy glow. "I'll get your dresses squared with them. To keep everything simple,

I don't have a particular theme, so is there a certain color you would like to wear?"

Aline immediately said green, which was her all-time favorite. Lime, emerald, grass color, it didn't matter, as long as it was green.

"Green will be perfect," Dierdre assured.

"Woo-hoo!" Aline skipped off to gloat to the other children.

"Bits, do you have a favorite color?"

Li'l Bits could see herself marching down the aisle between white chairs as she daintily scattered rose petals on the ground for Dierdre to walk on. She was wearing the dress of her dreams—one of blue silk, just like Trinny's.

"Bits," Trinny encouraged.

Li'l Bits looked longingly at Trinny, and Trinny knew. "I think Bits would love to wear blue."

Chapter 31

Revelation

"It takes courage to grow up and become
who you really are."

—*E.E. Cummings (1894–1962), American poet,
essayist, painter, author and playwright*

L i'l Bits was quiet on the drive home. All she could think of was being a flower girl. What an honor! She'd always thought it must be wonderful to be part of something so special, and now she was going to find out for herself.

When they reached the house, she, her papa, and Trinny each grabbed things that needed to be taken inside. Bits could barely see over the pile of presents she was carrying and nearly tripped over the vase of flowers that sat right in front of the door. Her traditional birthday bouquet of daisies, carnations, and a single red rose had not been there when they left.

"Oh, Papa, thank you for my flowers. I always love them so much." Sidestepping the vase, Bits went inside, quickly deposited her birthday bounty on the sofa, and ran back for the flowers so they wouldn't get knocked over. Inhaling a deep whiff of their heady floral scent, she asked, "But why didn't you bring 'em to the party? They could have been a centerpiece on the cake table. And oh, there's a card too! There's never been a card before."

Remy hurriedly deposited his load on the kitchen table and turned, but before he could stop her, Bits pulled the small white card from the floral company's card holder and was reading. "'For the birthday girl. All my love.' Oh, Papa, thank you. I love how you made hearts for the *o's*." Then, she looked at the card again.

Remy swallowed hard. He knew what she was seeing as she looked from it to him and then back at the little card.

"But . . . wait." Bits's forehead creased in confusion, "I can read this real clear. Your handwritin' is so squiggly, I can't usually make head or tail of it. And I know it's not Trinny's writin'. Papa," she accused good-naturedly, "did you have someone else write this for you? You didn't have to do that. I would've been able to puzzle it through. But I do like the hearts."

The lump in Remy's throat made it feel like he was being swallowed by a boa constrictor from the inside out. Tarnation . . . the day had finally come. Looking to Trinny for a shot of confidence, Remy pulled at his shirt collar.

Clueless and just as curious as Li'l Bits, Trinny simply shrugged her shoulders and motioned for him to get on with it.

"Well, ladies." Remy sort of shuffle-stepped his way toward the door. "We still have a lot to bring in from the car, what say we—"

Trinny patiently cut him off. "I'll work on that. Right now, I think you should address your daughter's question." Remaining inside, she closed the door.

Both she and Bits stared at Remy.

The longer he took to answer, the more curious his two ladies became.

Oh, hell, he thought to himself. *Best get this done and over with.*

Pointing to the couch, he simply said, "Sit," then quickly added, "Please."

As he fetched the foldout step ladder from the back porch, Trinny and Li'l Bits sat down. Remy came back in and disappeared down the hall. From their position on the couch, Trinny and Bits heard grunting as he shifted things on the closet floor, then the click of the ladder as its safety latch snapped into place, thumping, a garbled muttering as something tumbled from a shelf, then his feet hitting the floor, and, after a pause, his footsteps in the hallway as he returned.

Remy carried a carved wooden box, about the size of a man's boot box. He turned the rocking chair to face the couch, then carefully sat across from them.

With a steady gaze, he held both pairs of curious eyes; then, he looked down and ran a careful finger over the daisies, carnations, and rose that he'd carved around a capital *B*.

Li'l Bits was on the verge of spoiling the mood by saying something, so she gripped Trinny's hand to help herself stay quiet.

When Remy finally looked up, he captured his daughter's gaze, again seeing the bright, corn-flower blue eyes that had first peeked up at him from the basket. Had it only been eight years ago?

"As you both know, I woke up one day to find a basket on my doorstep. A basket not filled with a grocery delivery or baked goods from Nana Lynne Anne, but filled with . . .?" He looked to Bits.

"Me!" She bounced up and down.

"Correct." He turned the box so Bits could see the lid.

"What letter is this?"

"It's the first letter of my name."

"Correct again. So, who do you think this box belongs to?"

"Me?"

"Again, you are right."

"But Papa, I've never seen it before. How can it be mine?"

"Because, my little snapdragon, I made it for you."

"For my birthday?" She bounced up and down again. "Does that mean I don't have to use the old coffee can for my treasures anymore?"

"No, sweetheart. I can make another box for that if you'd like. But this box *does* hold a treasure of sorts. A treasure that . . . that has to do with you . . . and where you came from."

Trinny did a quick intake of breath and covered her mouth with the hand not holding on to Bits.

"Where I come from?" Bits thought hard. "Like . . . do you mean . . .?" Her eyebrows rose and then furrowed as she worked her question into words. "The basket. Are you talkin' about who left the basket on the porch? Like, that sort of come-from?"

Remy exhaled a quick, relieved burst of air through his nose. "Yes, sweetheart. That's what I'm talkin' about. Inside that basket was you, three bottles of milk your mama had prepared, diapers, a rattle and a letter."

Li'l Bits sat straight, and her breathing increased. She had never heard the word *mama* paired with her before. It felt odd, but good.

When she didn't say anything, Remy continued. "Every year on your birthday, a vase of flowers has been left for you. I'm assuming they're from your mother. Each one has had a note that says the same thing. The same as what's on the card you're holding."

Both Li'l Bits and Trinny looked at the card in Bits's hand.

"I don't know why I took the note from the flowers before I set 'em out. Maybe now that I had you, some part of me wanted to keep you to myself. That may have been selfish, but I did hold onto all the cards, and they're here in the box." He tapped the wooden lid. "Safe and sound."

The card in Li'l Bits's hand shook as she raised the note to read it again, this time with new eyes, because now she knew that she was probably looking at her own mother's handwriting. The *o's* that had been turned into hearts took on a whole different meaning.

"Can I see the other cards?"

"Sure thing, sweet heart." Remy carefully passed the box to her.

Trinny helped her scoot farther back on the couch so she would have more of a lap to rest the box on.

Li'l Bits traced a finger over the carved rose. As always, her papa had done a remarkable job. The wooden flowers looked nearly as alive as the real ones in the vase on the floor next to her. For some reason, she was having a difficult time lifting the lid. It was almost like something bound her arms from behind so that she could only move them so far.

Seeing Bits's little hands quaking, Trinny leaned down and tenderly smoothed the hair back from her face. Tucking it behind the child's ear, like she always did, Trinny asked, "Would you like help?"

Wordlessly, Bits nodded yes.

Trinny lifted the child to her lap and snuggled her close. Remy moved to sit beside them, and together, the three of them opened the box. Right on top was a folded blanket. One side was a pink, silky fabric, and the other side was blue. With no way to know what sex her child would be, the mother had obviously prepared for both. Beneath that, side by side, lay the glass bottles and rubber nipples, the rattle, and the other flower cards tied together with string.

"Where's the letter you said was in here?" Bits asked, looking through it all again.

Remy unfolded the blanket to reveal the letter, safely tucked inside. "Do you want to see it?"

"Uh-huh." She nodded and extended a trembling hand.

Remy handed her the envelope.

Bits gently folded back the flap and carefully pulled the paper from inside. Right now, in this moment, her whole life was changing; she could feel it. She was no longer a motherless orphan who had been given away. The handwriting on the paper meant that she had come from a real place that had other real people.

"Papa, it's in cursive. I can't read that yet. Will you read it to me?"

Remy swallowed a hard lump that had worked its way up from his gut and was choking him.

"Bits," Trinny interjected softly, "would you mind if I ask to be the one to read it? I'm sure your papa already knows what it says, whereas you and I don't."

Remy looked gratefully at Trinny. He didn't need to look at the paper to know what it said; he had it memorized.

"Would that be okay Papa, if Trinny reads it instead?"

Remy nodded, then turned his head and coughed to dislodge the knot.

"All righty," Trinny said, taking the letter from Bits. "Let's see what we have here.

"'*Dear sir, I know what you must be thinking of me, and I can't blame you, because I feel the same. Know that if I had any other choice, I'd never leave my precious baby like this. My story doesn't matter. What does is the story I want her to be able to tell when she's grown.*'"

Trinny sniffed and hugged Bits tighter on her lap.

"'*I did not leave her to you without knowing a bit about you. One day, when I traveled into the city, I saw you and knew you were the one. Something told my heart that you could raise her up with the loving she deserves. I asked around about you. I know that even though you aren't as small as she is, you know better than anyone some of the things she's going to face as she grows. And I'm not saying that as a judgment, it's just what I saw. You hold yourself as proud as any full-sized man, and the one time I passed close enough to see your eyes, what I saw in them is what made me know you were the one.*'"

Trinny could appreciate that observation. And in the time

that had passed since Bits arrived, Remy had only grown more confident, more kind, more handsome.

"*'God led me to you because he heard my heart crying every night. I never gave my little one a name. I think part of me always knew I wouldn't get to be the one to raise her up. So I leave it to you to do the choosing. She was born last July on the nineteenth. All I have to leave with her is this rattle. It isn't much, but my granddad made it. Could you let her know? And if she ever asks, please tell her that her mama did, and always will, love her.'*"

At this, Trinny had to wipe away a tear. Li'l Bits wasn't officially hers, but heaven knew how her own heart would shatter if she ever had to give this child up.

"*'I don't want her thinking that she was just given away for no good reason. I'm so sorry. I'm so, so sorry. I hope that you and God will forgive me, because heaven knows, I may not be able to forgive myself.'*"

Trinny swiped at another tear, unable to fathom what must have happened to make an obviously loving mother make such a desperate choice.

"She loved me."

The words were so faint, neither Remy nor Trinny had understood them.

"What?" they asked together as they bent closer to Bits.

"She—loved me," Bits said louder. "Oh Papa, she loved me . . . But if she loved me . . ." Bits's large eyes filled with tears, and she blurted, "If she loved me, then why'd she leave me? I was a baby. I was hers. Oh, Papa," Bits jumped up from Trinny's lap and flung herself at her father, draping her arms around his strong neck. "Why did she leave me?"

Remy cradled Bits and slowly rubbed a gentle hand up and down her back as he cooed soothing words into the hair at her ear. "Shhh . . . It's okay, baby girl. Papa's gotcha. I'm right here . . . right here. Shhh . . ."

Trinny had to get up and go for some tissue. Ever since

the storm, she had uncharacteristically felt like a watering pot. Crying when she first saw Remy in the Red Cross tent. Crying with Orvalee afterward as she puzzled through her emotional awakening. Crying at the news of two new babies coming into the world. Now, she was crying again. She would have to buy a whole new supply of Kleenex the next time she went to the market. For heaven's sake, maybe she'd start crying over how beautifully the birds were singing and need to store some in her car, too.

When Trinny returned to the couch, Remy and Bits each grabbed a few tissues from the box she'd brought back and blew.

"How you feelin', sweetheart?" Remy dried his daughter's cheeks. "You okay? Do you have any questions you'd like to ask?"

Bits sniffed. "The only one I keep thinkin' of is why she left me."

"That, sweet girl, is not one I know the answer to. Maybe one day, you'll get to meet up with this woman and ask her yourself. 'Til then, all we can know is what this box of treasure tells us."

Li'l Bits reached in and took out one of the glass bottles. "Well, I guess she didn't want me goin' hungry. There's three bottles."

Trinny wrapped the old baby blanket around Bits's shoulders and gave her a snuggle. "We also know that she wanted you to be warm and cozy. This is a very nice blanket."

"We also know"—Remy took out the rattle—"that she wanted you to have a connection to your family, to your past. She said your great-granddad made this, and experience tells me this man was a very good craftsman."

"My *great*-granddad." Bits looked thoughtful as she took the rattle from her papa and ran her fingers over the smooth surface. Having watched her father work in his own shop, she tried to imagine a gray-haired man bending over a workbench, making this . . . for her. Papa said that each item he made took a little bit of love with it when it left his shop. She wondered if there was some of her great-grandfather's love left in this rattle.

"A great-granddad . . ." Bits's head whipped up. "Hey, I have a granddad *and* a paw. I have two!" she announced triumphantly.

In a motherly gesture, Trinny smoothed the hair back from Bits's face, cupped her cheeks, and placed a kiss on her forehead. "Two is as many as I have. No one can love a little girl quite like a grandfather."

"Two is more than I've ever had," Remy said. "I only had my mother's pa. Never knew the other one. From what I hear, it's not much of a loss. But I can tell you, sweet girl, you're going to have . . . no wait." Remy leapt from the couch. "Trinny, please excuse us a moment?"

Sweeping a surprised Bits into his arms and then onto his back, Remy left a stunned Trinny sitting on the couch as he jogged down the hall to his room, Bits clinging to him like a baby monkey.

Mouth slightly agape, Trinny just sat there, looking after them.

Soon, giggles and an excited squeal emanated from the back room, and Trinny itched to know what was going on. After what seemed like forever, the duo returned, looking pleased with themselves.

Without a word, Bits, wearing a sparkly cape from one of her Halloween costumes, dragged a TV tray from the kitchen and sat it up next to Trinny. Then, she climbed up to the kitchen table, where she took a crochet doily from beneath the vase of dying wild flowers, transferred it to the TV tray, and set the fresh vase of birthday flowers on top.

Meanwhile, Remy rummaged through a kitchen cupboard looking for his best crystal candle holder, the one his mother had given him two Christmases ago. Upon finding it, he got a new white candle from the pantry, which he lit and placed in the beautiful holder, setting it next to the vase of flowers on the tray.

Then, while Remy drew the curtains to block out as much daylight as possible, Bits sifted through the record collection until she found the right one. With a giggle of delight, Bits set it on the turntable. She was just about to start it when she noticed her papa wasn't quite ready.

"Papa," she hissed through clenched teeth. Grabbing at pretend lapels, she nodded toward his room.

Looking down, Remy said, "Oops, right," and dashed back down the hall. A second later he reappeared in his best Sunday jacket and a tie.

For the life of her, Trinny could not fathom how they'd gone from talking about grandfathers to . . . whatever all this was.

At Remy's signal, Bits set the needle to the record, and the words "My love must be a kind of blind love; I can't see anyone but you . . ." flowed through the room like warm honey.

Trinny knew this song—knew it well. "I Only Have Eyes for You," by the Flamingos had been her favorite song ever since she and Remy had become an unofficial couple. She'd felt like a complete sap listening to it over and over as she worked on projects at home. But the secret smiles the song had brought to her face were nothing compared to the one that was currently spreading from ear to ear.

Bits tried to mimic the moves she'd seen the singing groups do on television, and with every sha-bop-sha-bop, her sparkly cape caught the light of the candle.

Remy lip-synced, "Are the stars out tonight; I don't know if it's cloudy or bright," and on, "I only have eyes for you, dear," he pointed to himself and then at Trinny.

Trinny found herself giggling. She never giggled.

Her reaction spurred the two performers on to greater heights.

"The moon may be high, but I can't see a thing in the sky,"

Remy crooned and covered his eyes. On "I only have eyes for you," his hand lifted to reveal two misty eyes that were staring straight at Trinny.

Her heart melted.

When the sha-bop-sha-bopping and the lip-sync ended, Bits stopped the record while Remy laid two pillows on the floor at Trinny's feet. Together, father and daughter got down on one knee, each taking one of Trinny's hands.

"Oh my gosh," Trinny whispered excitedly. "Are you really . . .?"

The elation on Trinny's face left Remy with no doubt as to the outcome of what he was about to do. Had there been any, he would never have allowed his sweet daughter to be part of something that might break her heart.

Remy placed a gentle finger over Trinny's lips. "Shhh, we have something to say to you."

Bits bobbed her head. "Yes, we do. And *I* get to go first."

Trinny scooted forward to the edge of the couch so Bits could better grip her hand.

"Trinny," Bits said matter-of-factly, "I have been wantin' a mother *forever*. I even wrote to Santa about it, and I have been as patient as a nun in church."

Trinny's frame spasmed as she wanted to laugh but managed not to.

"I'd just about given up on the idea, and then we read the letter. I'd never thought of the fact that somewhere out there, I had an actual mama. Someone who must've loved me enough to find me the best home she could." Bits had to stop for a second. She closed her eyes and scrunched her nose as she thought of the words from the letter. The woman who had left her here had wanted her to be happy, and right now, Bits was nearly overpowered by that very emotion.

"Knowin' that, and havin' you right here made all my hopes come back. So, when Papa told me the plan that had just come to him, I knew my Christmas wish had *finally* come true, even though it's July. I didn't know Santa could work magic in the summertime, but I'm sure glad he can, 'cause Trinny, I love you." On these words, she did cry and Remy released Trinny's hand so that she could pull Bits into an embrace.

Scooting the TV tray aside so the candle wouldn't get knocked over, Remy handed some Kleenex to his women-folk. Based on how quickly they seemed to be going through these lately, he knew he'd have to keep a good supply of the little things on hand. They were so much more convenient than fabric handkerchiefs.

When Bits finally released Trinny, she knelt back down on her cushion, heaved a contented sigh, and said, "All right Papa; it's your turn now."

"Thank you li'l miss." Remy chucked his daughter's cheek. "You did a good job."

"I know. And you'll do just fine too. Now, go on."

"Your faith sustains me," Remy said. His voice conveyed the amused smile that Trinny saw in his eyes. Light amber eyes that intensified with longing as he looked at her. That look sent shivers of anticipation up and down her spine.

Remy was surprised that his hands did not shake as he held Trinny's. For a second, he gazed at their linked hands, marveling at how well hers looked in his. He'd never thought about how hands fit together. But, like a Chinese puzzle box, their fingers fit together perfectly.

"Trinny." Remy smoothed a thumb over the back of her hand as he again captured her gaze. "The love I have for you has come along over time. It's so entwined within all my . . . my heart, my mind, even my hands. Sometimes, when I've been workin' on a project, I'll look at it and wonder what you'd think. You're so gifted . . . so talented. I, I wanted you to be proud of me."

Looking into her eyes, Remy still found it difficult to believe that this beautiful, talented, wonderful woman could possibly want to be with him. He may not have George's height, but his heart was just as big, and everything it held was focused on these two women: the young one by his side, and the one gazing back at him with as much love as he was pouring into her.

"I've never been one for sayin' much. Heaven knows we've both had our issues with words."

Trinny squeezed his hand and grinned, knowing they had both grown so much because of Bits.

"But I'll promise that as we go through life, I'll do my best to always say I love you. To apologize when I make mistakes. Which we all know I will."

Bits covered her mouth and giggled at this.

"I promise to do my best to give you the life you deserve. A life filled with laughter. With companionship and love. Most of all, love. We've been the best of friends for a long time, and I'd like that friendship to come along with us as we grow in all the ways a couple can. So, to that end . . ." Remy reached into his jacket pocket and pulled out a small, round, maroon velvet box.

"Trinny Jenks." He flipped open the top. "Would you do me"—he looked down at his daughter and amended his question—"do *us* the honor of accepting our proposal? We would be honored if you would join our family."

Bits sucked in an anticipatory breath while Remy held his own.

Trinny had never been so happy. With an exuberant "Yes!" the deal was done.

Now, Remy's hands *were* shaking. Fumbling with the ring, he took a couple of steadying breaths before he managed to slip it on the correct finger.

Trinny held her hand up to get her first look at the single piece of jewelry that would be with her the rest of her life. The gold was a soft white. A squared center was divided into fours, and each section held a platinum heart dotted with a small diamond, angled as if to guard the larger center diamond.

Trinny could hardly wait to see the wedding band nestled next to it.

Li'l Bits jumped up and wrapped her arms around Trinny's neck. "I'm so excited. I'm so excited! Let me see."

She grabbed Trinny's hand and softly said, "Papa, you did good."

"Yes, he did," Trinny agreed, tears shining in her eyes. "It's absolutely perfect."

Remy stood and pulled Trinny up along with him. "Bits, if you don't mind, I'd like to kiss my future wife right about now."

Trinny blushed from ear to ear, guessing that she'd have to get used to being kissed in front of little eyes.

"You go right ahead." Bits held up a hand and made a face as if the thought of kissing repulsed her. "Now that the good part's over, I'll just go to my room, 'cause I don't need to be seein' that."

"You'd better get used to it!" Remy called to her retreating form. "Because there's gonna be a *lot* of it from here on in."

"Is there?" Trinny asked shyly.

"Is there what?" Remy turned back to her.

"Is there really going to be a lot of kissing from now on?"

"Darlin'"—the word came out with a possessive edge to it and Remy pulled her in close—"there is gonna be *so* much huggin' and kissin' that one day, you may feel the need to run from me. I've got a lot of years to make up for."

Trinny placed a playful kiss on the end of Remy's nose.

"You missed. Here, I'll show you how it's done, then let you take another practice shot."

"Oh no, you don't." Trinny said. "You're not the only one who has a lot of years to make up for."

"Mmm," Remy said right back. "I think I'm gonna like bein' married to you."

Emboldened by the ring on her finger, Trinny planted her lips on Remy's.

In one swift motion, he swept a hand up her back to the nape of her neck while the other nestled at the crook of her slim waist, holding her close.

Trinny tentatively allowed her hands to explore. One combed through the back of his wavy curls, and she was glad he didn't pomade his hair like most men did. Her other hand caressed his cheek, moved down his neck, and then wrapped around his shoulder.

When they finally broke apart, each breathing heavily, Trinny sighed. "I think, Mr. Dubois, I will like being married to you too. But can I ask one thing before we continue?"

Remy quirked a questioning eyebrow. "Ask away."

"Before you ran off with Bits, we were talking about grandfathers. How did we jump from that to what happened next?"

Remy chortled. "Sorry. I was about to tell Bits that she'd be able to add your dad and grandfather to her list when I realized I hadn't officially offered for your hand. Thought I'd better do that before I promised her two more grandfathers."

"Thank you. And for the record, I love how it all came about. I love that you kept her treasures and that you made a special box for them. I *love* that you safeguard the hearts of those you love."

"Trinny, your heart will always be safe with me."

"I know it will." She kissed him lightly. "And yours will *forever* be safe with me."

Chapter 32

Happy Day

Saturday, August 1, 1959

"The deeper that sorrow carves itself into your
being, the more joy you can contain."

—*Khalil Gibran (1883-1931), Lebanese-American
writer, poet and visual artist*

From the day after Li'l Bits's birthday party, everyone had been in a flurry of activity getting ready
for Ervyn and Dierdre's wedding. Still feeling guilty
for dropping in out of nowhere with the bombshell announcement of both a wedding *and* a baby, the couple had wanted to
keep things simple. But Orvalee wasn't going to let her only
remaining child tie the knot in anything other than the best
possible style she could provide.

But in the extended family she belonged to, that meant
whatever they could *all* provide.

Remy's parents had volunteered their back yard for the
festivities, so that became command central. After a full day
of work had been put in, both Remy and Trinny had pulled
together to create a stunning crescent-moon backdrop.

Remy cut the crescent so that the lower curve hid a small bench for the couple to sit on between greeting guests. Dierdre had mentioned that being pregnant, she tired easily, and Remy didn't want her pooping out before her own party was over.

Behind the moon was a solid piece of plywood that Trinny, through her artistic magic, and access to promethium paint from work, had turned into a glowing night sky. A soft light hidden at the base, behind the crescent moon, cast a soft upward glow that caught in Trinny's stars and shaded clouds. She had given the moon itself a smiling face that would gaze lovingly upon the couple seated on the bench.

As a finishing touch, Remy had loosely draped twinkle lights around the upper curve of the crescent. Working together on the project had gotten Remy and Trinny thinking about what they might want for their own wedding. They hadn't decided on the particulars yet, but they did know that they wanted it to be in December so they could take advantage of Christmas break to go on a honeymoon.

Bits didn't get the blue silk dress of her dreams, but she did get a gorgeous sky-blue cotton dress with an overlay of lace that matched Dierdre's off-white wedding gown. Aline's mint-green frock complimented her eyes perfectly and made her feel like a princess. Each girl would also get to carry a small basket of flower petals with a colored ribbon that matched her dress.

Between making the girl's dresses and preparing flower arrangements, boutonnieres and corsages, Orvalee and Claudine had practically worked their fingers to the bone.

Lynne Anne, Sienna and Janelle had been tasked with the wedding cake, refreshments, and helping with flowers and decorations. Remembering how good Orvalee's flower essence-infused frosting had been at Li'l Bits's seventh birthday party, Lynne Anne had Orvalee dig up the recipes. After much trial and error, the lemon-rose-vanilla infusion won out, pairing nicely with the milk chocolate cake.

To make the heat more bearable, the wedding wasn't scheduled to begin until seven thirty pm. Fans were going in every room of the house, and—fingers crossed—by the time the wedding began, an evening breeze might aid the big electric fans Alexander and George had brought from the warehouse and positioned around the perimeter of the yard. With the moving air and Orvalee's special wedding-scented bug candles, being outdoors wasn't going to be uncomfortable.

The morning of the big day arrived, and Orvalee gathered her troops in the backyard for a pep talk. But seeing George and his whole family, Remy and his family, Trinny, and her precious Li'l Bits . . . she came near to tears.

Trying to conceal her emotions, she charged in. "All right, y'all, we have a lot to do this mornin' before it gets too hot, then we'll take a breather. Ervyn and his groomsmen will come in about an hour. If anyone needs to ask Dierdre anything, she's tryin' to keep cool in the upstairs guest room. And, well, I can't thank everyone enough for all you've done so far. I never . . ."

Until she'd seen Ervyn just after the tornado hit, she had lost all hope that a day like this would ever come. And right now, she was happier than she'd been since before the war, and that was a *long* time ago.

"I honestly can't believe that we're finally here. And I cannot think of better people to share this day with. Y'all've been such a wonderful family to me, and I know that Ervyn, Dierdre, and my new grandbaby are gonna to be just as blessed by y'all as I have been."

"Hear, hear!" George agreed.

"Well, I don't really know why I'm tryin' to tell ya what to do, because you've been doin' a marvelous job so far, so let's get to it. I have a family to grow!"

The men and boys toted tables, table cloths, and other supplies from the wedding supply and catering trucks out to the backyard, setting them up as Orvalee instructed, with the moon backdrop as the centerpiece.

At the big dining room table in the house, all the women

and girls began filling small paper cups with assorted colors of butter mints and a variety of nuts. The cups were put on big silver trays to be taken out to guests as needed. The caterer was providing finger sandwiches on pastel-colored bread, small chocolate eclairs, cream puffs, relish trays, and gallons of vanilla ice cream that would be scooped into each cup of sparkling punch.

The women gathered in the kitchen—to go over the list of whatever might be left to do, watch Janelle put the finishing touches on the wedding cake, and chat. Mostly chat.

"Janelle," Trinny said in wonder, "this cake looks incredible. I didn't know you were a decorator."

Pleased, Janelle flushed. "I'm not. Other than birthday cakes and school cupcakes for my own kids, this is the first big thing I've done. But I did prepare by takin' a couple of classes over at the bakery. And I must say, I really like it."

"You have quite a natural talent." Claudine said, as she scooped a teaspoon through the frosting bowl and then licked some off, sighing with pleasure. "And this!" She took another lick. "This is as good as anything I have ever had. Chefs back home would salivate over it."

Lynne Anne and her daughters beamed.

"You can thank Orvalee for the frosting," Lynne Anne said. "Let's see, you weren't at Bits's seventh birthday party, were you, Claudine?"

"Sadly, no."

Lynne Anne also swiped a taste of frosting. Wiping some from the corner of her mouth, she said, "That's right. George left just after that to go fetch ya back home."

"That he did." Claudine tenderly rubbed her growing belly. "'Twas a long wait, but I am so, so happy he did."

Sienna asked, "How on earth did you manage bein' away from him for so long? I'm not sure I woulda had the patience."

"One day at a time. Plus many words of encouragement from *ma mere* and many more prayers."

Lynne Anne scooped Claudine into a hug. "I'm very glad you have such a wonderful mother. I wish I could say the same for Dierdre."

All the women stopped what they were doing to stare at her.

"What do you mean?" Sienna asked.

Lynne Anne let out a heavy sigh. "Last night, Orvalee called to tell me that Dierdre's parents finally let her know they would *not* be coming to the wedding today. I can only surmise they waited until the last moment to let her know, just to twist the knife a *little* deeper."

Every woman let out a dismayed gasp of surprise.

"Why on earth aren't they coming?" Trinny asked.

Claudine was aghast. "Not attend your own daughter's wedding?"

"I know." Lynne Anne could only wag her head in uncomprehending dismay. "For the life of me, I don't understand it, but apparently, they made it *abundantly* clear that they are . . . to put it kindly, *not happy* with the fact their daughter is pregnant before the wedding. They are also not pleased with her choice of husband, him bein' a 'vagabond' and all. Orvalee wouldn't tell me all they said because she was still fuming. I think she ended up calling because she needed someone to vent to. And I think last night's conversation is the main reason Dierdre has sequestered herself upstairs until the ceremony tonight."

"*Och, mon dieu!*" Claudine clasped a hand over her heart. "That poor child. We *must* make this the best day of her life."

"I agree," Lynne Anne said. "I also think that Orvalee is gonna need some extra lovin'. What they said about Ervyn cut her to the bone."

On that note, the women set out to do everything they could to make this the best, most memorable day of the Benson family's life.

By seven o'clock that evening, the DuBois backyard had been transformed into an enchanted garden. Luminaries hung from branches and shepherd's hooks around the yard's perimeter. Small spotlights were angled to cast a soft glow up along tree trunks, and once the sun went down, the crescent moon backdrop would become the celestial body overseeing the magic.

Anxious to see his lovely bride, Ervyn was already milling about with the childhood friends that had agreed to be his groomsmen, near the makeshift altar in front of the moon where the minister would stand.

Looking dapper, Ervyn had paired a traditional tux jacket and pants with a a soft brown-and-orange, sunset-style plaid vest, bowtie, and matching pocket handkerchief. His longish, dark-brown hair had been cut short on the sides and styled into a somewhat messy, mop-top greaser cut. The look complemented his playful attire.

Remy, George, and the other men sported their Sunday best. After all the work they'd done, they were anxious to get on with it. Bring on the dancing and food—mainly just the food.

The women were all upstairs, putting on their finishing touches and clucking around Dierdre, who *seemed* to be in high spirits. "I took a peek at the backyard a little bit ago," she said, "and really, I can't thank everyone enough. It looks *incredible.*"

"Nothing you don't deserve, sweetheart." Orvalee whispered close to Dierdre's ear as she fitted the off-white, beaded tulle veil to the base of her updo.

Fluffing out the veil so that it cascaded down to Dierdre's shoulder blades, Orvalee stood back and looked admiringly at the soon-to-be mother of her first grandchild. "I hope my grandson has your beautiful cheekbones, my nose, and his daddy's eyes, 'cause those eyes were his daddy's, and I'd like to see those passed on."

Dierdre laughed and touched her rounding belly. "You think it's a boy, do you?"

Orvalee scanned Dierdre from head to toe with a long, appraising look. "No, I don't think. I *know*."

Dubiously, Dierdre asked, "How can you know something like *that*?"

"Ah, *la petite amie*," Claudine scolded. "New to our little family you are, but learn this you will; when Orvalee says that she *knows* something, she knows. She has said *I* carry a girl. Another *belle fille*, and my heart soars. I have said nothing to George, but I know when he sees his new daughter, his already large heart will grow yet more." Claudine's eyes misted over, and she pulled out her handkerchief. Just thinking about another sweet baby being cradled by his large, strong hands had her crying.

"So sorry. I seem to weep all too easily these days," Claudine dabbed at the mascara beneath her eyes.

"Hey!" Trinny said. "No more of this or we'll *all* have to redo our makeup, and I don't think the men will stand for any delays. Have you seen them prowling around the food tables?"

"Yes," Sienna said. "They shoo the children away and then sneak a little somethin' for themselves. There may not be anything left by the time we get down there."

"As long as they leave my cake alone until the photo of you cuttin' it has been taken, they'll survive," Janelle stated forcefully.

Lynne Anne entered the room. "Ladies, it's time. The minister just got here and has taken his place. Poor Ervyn keeps lookin' at the back door. I think he's tryin' to will you down the backstairs and into his arms," she teased Dierdre.

"Are the girls ready?" Orvalee asked.

"Are you kidding? They've been ready as long as the men have. They've each practiced throwin' flower petals, then run to gather 'em back up again. It's so cute." Lynne Anne chuckled.

"Well, then." Orvalee gazed lovingly at the women in the room. "I guess it's time."

Following the others out the door and down the back stairs, Orvalee walked Dierdre to the kitchen, where Alexander took over escort duties so that Orvalee could watch her son's face as Dierdre made her way down the aisle.

With the first notes of music, Aline and Bits walked side by side, just as they had practiced.

The gathering drew in a collective breath when they saw Dierdre come into view. Dressed in a tea-length, strapless, off-white satin sheath with a scoop-neck lace overdress, Dierdre beamed brighter than the sun when she saw the look in Ervyn's eyes.

That look dissipated any trace of the sorrow and guilt she'd felt over her parent's harsh words. The slow march down the flower-petal strewn aisle allowed her to soak in the smiles of Ervyn's childhood friends and neighbors, and the love of Orvalee's extended family. With all these kind people sharing the best moment of her life, what did it matter who was *not* there?

Focusing on the growing life within her, Dierdre chose to place both her attention and her heart on the family she was creating right now. And that was enough.

I do's were said.

The cake was cut and playfully smashed against resisting lips.

Hands were shaken; hugs given.

Chairs and tables were cleared to make room for dancing and revelry.

Everyone wanted a photo taken on the crescent arch of the glowing moon.

The bride and groom ran to their car amid a cascade of rice thrown by exuberant well-wishers.

And just like that . . . it was over.

The wedding supply truck would arrive first thing in the morning, so men shrugged off jackets and rolled up sleeves.

Women kicked off shoes and donned aprons.

And Orvalee, exhausted but happy, took a moment to sit on the moon's bench and relive each wonderful moment.

Had it been only four months ago that terrible storm had rolled through? No—it was a lifetime ago. A life she no longer cared to remember, because *that* life held nothing of the joy her current one did. She had come so close, so close to doing the unthinkable. Had Bits not come along when she did . . . honestly, Orvalee wasn't sure she would have made it to this day. To this beautiful, wonderful, magical day.

Perspective is . . . It's everything.

"You okay?" asked a small, tired voice.

Orvalee looked down to see a concerned look in Li'l Bits's eyes.

"Why do you ask that, sweet thing?"

Bits stepped closer and took Orvalee's hand. "You were wipin' tears from your face."

"Was I? I didn't realize."

"You okay?"

"Yes, darlin'. Actually, I'm more than okay. Come on up here." Orvalee lifted Bits to her lap. "You and Aline looked lovely walkin' down the aisle. And you threw the petals perfectly."

"We practiced so not too many would land all in one place. We wanted it to look even. Did it look even?"

"It certainly did. Why, I remember thinking that very thing, how they looked so evenly distributed."

"Whew—that's good, because we worked hard at that."

Orvalee hugged her close and pointed to a bit of frosting on the neck of her dress. "I also see that you worked hard at making sure you got your share of the eclairs."

Bits crossed her eyes as she tried to see where Orvalee had pointed. "Drat, I tried to stay clean. Papa's not gonna be happy."

"Sweet thing, I think your papa will have other things on his mind. And besides, I think it's completely reasonable to get a *little* somethin' on your dress when there's not only eclairs but chocolate cake as well. Don't you?"

"Yep. Now, you can be the one to make sure papa knows that too. I think he'll understand it better if *you* tell him."

"Oh, child, how I love you." Orvalee gave Bits a huge squishy hug and kissed her forehead.

"So." Bits hesitated. "Now that Ervyn's back and you're gonna be a gran, you're not gonna forget me, are ya?"

"No, sweetheart, I could never, not in a million, not in a hundred million years, ever forget about you. You are my saving angel."

Orvalee rested her lips on top of Bits's head and whispered, "I'd have nothin' if it weren't for you. Nothing."

"What do you mean?" Bits looked up and could see more tears in her beloved friend's eyes.

"I mean, sweetheart, that you are and always will be one of the most precious people in my life. Don't you *ever* worry about that. I will always be here for you."

Bits sighed and sank into the comfort of Orvalee's arms.

Amid the laughing, joking, and yawns as the others continued to clean up, Orvalee and Bits sat, just the two of them, being together.

Chapter 33

Color Me Wonderful
December, 1959

"I think of a hero as someone who understands
the degree of responsibility that comes
with his freedom."

—*Bob Dylan (living) American singer-songwriter,
musician and poet*

1959 had been a whirlwind year. Spring had roared in like a lion, bringing with it one of the worst tornadoes in decades along with Li'l Bits's first taste of loss. Through the death of George's father and all the others killed by the storm, she had watched her uncle, his family and the community work their way through grief and become all the stronger for it.

A prodigal son had returned, bringing with him a wealth of love and renewed life to her beloved mentor, who would be a grandmother any day now.

Bits had turned eight, attended her first wedding, *and* been a flower girl.

A few weeks ago, on the twenty-first, Aunt Claudine had given birth to a daughter. Uncle George had been over the moon to have another girl, and Aline could talk of nothing else. Baby Emilie Catherine Dollis was the apple of her entire family's eye.

But the best had been saved for last, because by the end of the week, she would be out of school for Christmas break, and on Saturday, the wish she'd made two years ago was finally going to come true. Trinny would become her mother.

"Bits," Jesslyn whispered none too quietly. "Bits . . ."

Li'l Bits felt something hit the back of her head, and she looked to see what on earth Jesslyn was about. Her friend was pointing to the front of the class, where their teacher, Mr. Doutré, was patiently waiting for Bits to answer the question he had just asked her.

Sheepishly, Li'l Bits looked around her teacher at the blackboard for some clue as to what the question had been. *September 21, 1897* was written next to *Francis Pharcellus Church*, and Bits remembered something about a famous response being given to a girl named Virginia.

"Uh . . . yes?" Bits crossed her fingers, hoping that was the right answer.

With a slight upward turn at the corner of his mouth, Mr. Doutré countered, "Yes, what?"

Bits's eyes darted to Ellie June. Her friend made some sort of motion with her fingers that looked a *little* like reindeer prancing. Behind her hand, Bits mouthed the word, and Ellie June smacked her forehead with the palm of her hand.

The other kids in the class laughed.

Okay, reindeer wasn't the answer.

Bits looked back at Mr. Doutré, who was still waiting, arms patiently folded across his chest. Crooking a single eyebrow, the man encouraged Li'l Bits to answer.

Sucking in a fortifying breath, Bits said, "Yes, I think it was a good idea for Virginia to write that letter."

Mr. Doutré's shoulders rose and fell with a silent chuckle. The week before Christmas break always found more than one child being caught off guard as their minds wandered to whatever magical thing they were envisioning.

"Good recovery, Miss Dubois, but no." Mr. Doutré turned back to the board and underlined Francis Pharcellus Church.

Bits leaned heavily against the back of her wooden chair. Embarrassed, she did not allow her mind to wander during the rest of class.

The week passed quickly, and before Bits knew it, she was racing out the school doors on Friday with all the other excited children, each one guarding some treasure or other they had made in class to take home as a Christmas gift for their parents.

Bits was closely guarding the eight-inch-high, papier-mâché Christmas tree that had been her class's project. She really liked the pictures she had chosen to cut out of the magazines Mr. Doutré had collected for them to use. Around the base, she'd pasted the smiling faces of families. Then came small Norman Rockwell images, because she remembered that Trinny really liked his art. Then, there were pictures of handcrafted wood items for Papa. At the top, near the yellow origami star, was the image of a little girl, hands clasped in prayer. Next to this image, she had written the name she'd chosen for herself just before her eighth birthday. This little girl was her because her prayers were finally being answered.

This beautiful tree was not going to be a Christmas present; rather, it was a wedding gift for her parents. She liked being able to think that way now. She was going to be part of a family—not that she and papa hadn't been a family, but now, they were going to be . . . well, a *different* kind of family. One that was all her own. She didn't have to share it with friends or cousins. She was going to be a musketeer, like in the book Trinny had been reading to her. One of the *Three* Musketeers.

As she neared her aunt's car, she heard Janelle say, "Hey there, my sweet things."

Bits climbed onto the running board and into the car with her cousins.

Wearing a green and red striped elf hat with a bell dangling from the end, Janelle cheerfully asked, "Y'all ready for two weeks of holiday fun?"

All the kids whooped and cheered an exuberant, "Yes."

"Aunt Janelle." Bits had to raise her voice to be heard over the din of excitement in the car.

"Yes, Bits?"

Janelle kept her eyes on the pedestrian-filled road as they slowly pulled away from the school.

"When we get to your house, do you think you could help me wrap this?" Bits lifted her tree so her aunt could view it in the rear-view mirror. "I don't want Papa or Trinny to see it until tomorrow. It's a wedding present."

"Of course, we can wrap it." With a gasp of surprise, Janelle almost cursed out loud when a group of exuberant children darted right in front of her and she had to slam on the brakes.

With so many kids in the backseat, Bits managed not to fly forward with the momentum, and only one cousin lightly smacked her precious tree. Bits inspected it for damage and heaved a sigh of relief when none was found.

"Is everyone okay?" Janelle looked over the backseat to check the children, then stated, "I do not want any of you doing somethin' so foolhardy as those kids just did, you hear me? Why, my poor heart's thumpin' a mile a minute. What have I told y'all about crossin' busy roads?"

All the children recited, "Look left, then right, then left again, lest you sign your death warrant with the Grim Reaper's pen."

"That's right! And none of you better forget it."

"No, ma'am," they droned.

By the time her papa came to pick her up that evening after work, Bits had the tree securely padded and wrapped in a box. Glad they had been able to find one to fit, Bits was happy with how the present was disguised. Her papa and Trinny would never be able to guess what it was.

"Hey, there, my little snapdragon," Remy said as she thrust the wrapped box onto the front seat before her and then climbed onto the running board and into the car. "How was school? You excited for Christmas break? When will you be seein' Amy Jo, Ellie June and Jesslyn again, I wonder?"

The wink he gave her as they pulled away from the curb did not go unnoticed.

"Papa, you know darn well it's not gonna be just any 'ole Christmas break, and I'll be seein' my friends *tomorrow*, at the *wedding*."

For just a second, Remy's voice took on a deep, dreamy tone. "Ah, yes, the wedding." His voice returned to normal. "Are you ready for tomorrow my girl? I mean, are you *really* ready? For so long, it's been just the two of us, and after tomorrow . . ."

"I know," Bits piped in. "It's gonna be different, but it's gonna be, well, it feels like . . . *more*. You know?"

"Yes, sweet thing, I know exactly what you mean. And it's a very good kind of *more*, isn't it?"

"It's the *best* kind of more! It's like extra whipping cream on your hot chocolate."

"That is somethin' special," Remy agreed. "I just wanted to make sure that . . . with everything that's been goin' on, I . . ."

Li'l Bits laid a hand on her father's thigh. "I know Papa. But all of this is my wish comin' true. So, I'm happy. Plus, I got an extra part that I didn't even know would come along with it."

Curious, Remy asked, "What's that?"

Li'l Bits snuggled into his side. "You light up now. Even when Trinny isn't around, you still have a *twinkle* in your eye that wasn't there before. I remember seein' it spark up a few times after Rudy hit me with the rock, and Trinny was comin' over to help take care of me. But ever since the tornado, it's like you don't try to hide it anymore, and I like that."

Remy shook his head. "I've always said you're too observant and too smart for your own good or, should I say, for *my* own good. Sometimes it's hard to believe you're only eight years old."

Remy got quiet for a minute, then said, "You know, sweet thing, the day you showed up on my doorstep was the best day of my life."

He sniffed and swiped at a tear that leaked from the corner of his eye. "I know I've said this before, but the good Lord sure does move in mysterious ways, and that day was one of the most mysterious. Without knowin' what on earth I was doin', I became a father. And now, because of you and all you've taught me, I get to learn how to be a husband, and *that,* my darlin', is not somethin' I ever thought I'd get to be."

"Why not?" Bits asked innocently.

Remy thought of all the obstacles he'd placed in his own way. The obstacles he had learned to overcome by having this sweet child in his life. Being a father hadn't allowed him the time to wallow in nonexistent problems, and as a result, he'd left them behind. Now, looking back, he was ashamed to think that he'd allowed trivialities to take on such mammoth proportions. Before Bits had come, he'd been as sour as a lemon, and couldn't believe how much he must have put his poor family through—what he'd put his own father through.

But now, he was truly a *man.* A title, he realized, one does not automatically get to assume based on age. Being a man is a role one must *grow* into. The responsibilities of being a man no longer frightened him . . . Well, strike that; they were still a little scary. But the fright was now paired with exhilaration, surprise, and yes, even fulfillment.

"You know what?" Remy said. "From where I stand now, I have a hard time recollectin' all the things I thought would go wrong in my life. It's funny how that works. When you *expect* bad things to happen, they just do. It's like we open a door to all the monsters we're afraid of and then say, 'See, I told you so' when the beasts wander through the dang door."

"But now?"

"Now, sweet thing, I know with all my heart that life is what we make of it. It's like a beautiful blank canvas, and we get to use whatever colors we want to make it come alive. I see now that what I thought were dark, shadowy places where the monsters hid were nothin' more than shady places beneath a tree, or the mouth of a cave that I got to explore. Every life needs both the sunshine and the rain clouds. Remember that, okay? Sunshine warms the earth and makes things grow, but if there's no rain, then that warm earth gets too dang dry and chokes the livin' right out of things."

Li'l Bits was quiet the rest of the way home. As they pulled into the driveway, she said, "Papa, Trinny is gonna add more colors to our painting, isn't she?"

Remy swiveled in the seat. "Yes, Bits, she will. And with her bein' an artist, who knows what beautiful things she's gonna come up with to show us. You ready for an adventure?" Palm down, he put his hand out.

Bits slapped her hand on top of his. "You know I am!"

Chapter 34

A Wish Fulfilled
Saturday, December 19, 1959

"A joyful life is made up of joyful moments
gracefully strung together."

—*Brene Brown (living), American professor,
author, lecturer, and podcast host*

The non-denominational church's hall had been readied for the reception, and once again, the crescent moon backdrop from Ervyn's wedding would preside over the festivities. The actual ceremony would be a unique combination of Christian and Shinto and was taking place in front of the twenty-foot-high stained-glass window of the church's chapel. After his conversation last night with Bits, Remy appreciated the symbolism of the colored light that would frame his vows. And though they had rehearsed the 'ceremony of the *tamagushi*', he was still nervous he would forget everything.

Remy fidgeted from one foot to the other as he and his groomsmen—George, Michael, Oliver, and Trinny's brother, Tomi—stood at the front of the chapel. Some late guests straggled in and slipped silently into the back row, grateful they had made it in time to see the bride walk down the aisle.

"Rem," George bent low to his friend's ear and whispered, "I hope you visited the outhouse before you walked in here, because you've got so many ants in your pants, it looks like you could use another trip."

Remy exhaled a nervous laugh. "George, I'm excited and happy, yet I sort of feel like I want to throw up. Is that normal?"

In his usual gesture of comfort, George laid a warm hand on Remy's shoulder. "Yes, believe it or not, it is. But just wait, when you get your first look at her, you'll calm right down. Promise."

Remy took a deep breath and caught his mother's eye. The woman was already tearing up, and no one had said a word. She fluttered her handkerchief at him, wiped her nose, and clung to her husband's hand. Alexander looked at his wife and tenderly patted her arm, then beamed a radiant smile upon his son.

Nervously, Remy smiled back and saw that Trinny's mom, Rose, was an emotional carbon copy of his own. He needed to stop looking at the women.

George's shoulders moved with a silent chuckle. "Rem, just focus on the aisle. Look at the flowers, the ribbons, anything but the people."

"Right," Remy agreed. "The flowers."

Focus on the flowers, focus on the flowers . . . They really are pretty.

The organ burst to life, startling Remy and he jumped. George smiled, and the gathering turned to face the back of the church.

When no one immediately appeared, for one horrific moment, Remy was afraid Trinny had thought better of marrying him and bolted. But then, from the right, Bits rounded into view and made her way down the aisle, an enormous smile plastered across her face.

This time, she *was* wearing the dress of her dreams: an ice-blue silk kimono embroidered with contrasting flowers and birds. Trinny's mother had had it made in California as a wedding gift, and it couldn't have been more perfect.

She also had her own fan and *hakoseko*—a little purse—which she held close to her body. Her hair had been done in a Japanese style and was adorned with white flowers. She wore the traditional tabi, and the split-toed socks matched the white zori she was trying to clench her toes around to keep from flipping off as she walked. But she managed herself with a grace that left her papa as proud as a strutting cockerel.

Behind Bits came Trinny's sister, Louelle, and then Sierra and Janelle. Each wore a slim, ice-blue, Japanese-style silk dress and had their hair pulled up and adorned with flowers that matched Bits. Each was also carrying a fan and a hakoseko.

Remy exhaled a long, slow breath, knowing that Trinny would be next.

The organ changed from the slow timbre of introduction to the dramatic prelude of the wedding march.

Trinny and her father entered from the right side at the back of the chapel. Remy's view of his bride was blocked by her father's larger, uniformed body.

Daniel Jenks had chosen to wear his army dress uniform and the medals he had won in combat. His back was ramrod straight as he escorted his youngest daughter to the man that had been lucky enough to win her heart.

As impressive a sight as his father-in-law was, when they rounded the back pews, Remy only had eyes for Trinny. The first thing he noticed was the white floral crown atop her upswept hair. Delicate, elongated crystal prisms dangled from the front of it, like those on the most expensive chandeliers. Captured light from the church sconces danced within the prisms, illuminating Trinny's glowing face.

Dressed in a traditional bridal *shiromuku,* the all-white kimono made Trinny look like an angel as she floated toward him. Rose had performed a miracle by finding one they could rent and have shipped.

Thunderstruck by the vision of beauty walking toward him, Remy more than appreciated all the trouble and fretting. It had been worth it.

When they reached Remy, Daniel shook hands with his son-in-law, then handed his daughter into Remy's keeping. Before letting go of their hands, Daniel gripped them both tightly and then, with a tear in his eye, went to sit next to his wife.

Bride and groom turned to face the Shinto priest that had traveled all the way from the West Coast to perform the ceremony. The white-haired, ebullient-faced man motioned them closer and began.

New to all of this, the Louisiana guests sat in rapt attention as they soaked in the beauty and meaning of the Shinto ceremony. The priest had decided against the sacred dance performed by the *miko*, as Japanese maids were scarce in this part of the country, but the *tamagushi* ceremony was not something Trinny had wanted to leave out.

In lieu of traditional sakaki leaves, the priest held up the cedar boughs that had been fashioned into a small, mat-like form. To this was attached the *shide*, and small pieces of red-and-white cloth were tied to it with *asa*.

In a voice as loud as he could project, the priest explained, "The *tamagushi* represents our *sincere* hearts and spirits, which we offer to *Kamisama*, or God. It is made from evergreen boughs that represent the eternal nature of our spirits and hearts—our connection to nature, or the natural world and the physical world."

The man angled the *tamagushi* so the guests could better see the sacred piece. "The *shide*, as you see here, is made from white rice paper cut into two lightning-bolt strips that drape down either side of the *tamagushi*. The *shide* represents energy and the spiritual side of our world. We shape it like lightning to symbolize our energy connection to *Kamisama*. To show that we are divine sparks connected to the world of spirit. The paper's whiteness represents purity."

Unsure if very many could see the *asa* and bits of red-and-white cloth, the priest pointed them out, explaining, "Red and white pieces of sacred fabric are tied to it with *asa*, or hemp fiber. These represent the formal dressing of our hearts and spirits to be offered on the physical plane to *Kamisama*. Why is cloth sacred, you may ask?"

Fascinated, most everyone nodded at this question.

"Cloth is sacred, for it is gained by uniting the resources of both heaven and earth. From heaven, the combined powers of the sun, rain, and moon nourish plants and animals we create fabrics from. The earth is the womb from which all life nourished by the heavens can grow."

The priest touched the *tamagushi* to his forehead in a sign of reverence, then again held it aloft. "Physical and spiritual together."

The priest turned to Remy and Trinny, gesturing for them to hold out their left hands. He placed the *tamagushi* on their open palms, telling them to pinch the stems with their right hand. As he guided them to the *hassouku*, a special offering table, Remy miraculously remembered everything he was supposed to do.

As one, he and Trinny bowed forward and raised the *tamagushi* to their foreheads. Upright again, they turned the stems toward their hearts and the leaves up, toward *Kamisama*. Then, with two distinct quarter-turns to the left, the stems now faced *Kamisama*, and the leaves, their own hearts. This was the symbolic action of drawing God's energy to them and then focusing their energy toward God. Next, they placed the *tamagushi* on the *hassouku* and loudly clapped once to draw *Kamisama's* attention to the energy of their offering. Bowing deeply, they again faced the priest.

With great pleasure, the man asked, "Do you have rings you wish to exchange?"

Most of the guests took a deep breath, enjoying the familiarity of the words; this part they knew.

Remy turned to George, and Trinny motioned Bits closer. George passed Remy a ring, and Bits carefully opened her *hakoseko* and pulled out the ring for Trinny.

Tokens in hand, the newly-weds exchanged their symbols of dedication and commitment. Then, upon pronouncing they were now husband and wife, to everyone's great delight, Remy swept Trinny into a dip and kissed the stuffing right out of her.

Whoops, cheers and whistles egged him on.

Bits jumped up and down excitedly.

Rose Jenks and Lynne Anne Dubois were each held by their husbands' supportive arms as they openly wept.

When Remy finally allowed Trinny up for air, she was crimson from the tips of her ears to the tip of her nose, but the smile she wore had never, ever been wider.

Securing his bride's hand in his, luminous with joy, Remy led her back down the aisle, through the double doors on the left side at the back of the chapel, and into the activity hall that housed the smiling moon.

Li'l Bits, the matrons of honor, the groomsmen, and the parents followed close upon their heels. Behind them came everyone else. Filtering into the hall, the guests chatted and laughed, still caught up in the exuberance of Remy's declarative kiss.

Unwilling to release Trinny's hand for even a second, Remy gave a one-armed hug to all the well-wishers who greeted him and slapped him on the back. Likewise, Trinny held to her groom as she graciously accepted hugs and congratulations.

Alexander DuBois stepped to the hall's microphone and when he touched it, the blasted thing whined like a human dog whistle. Everyone reached to cover their ears. Tapping it, like the action would calm the temperamental thing down, Alexander tentatively put his mouth to it. "Sorry," he said quickly and then took two steps back.

When no more whining static threatened to deafen them all, he tried again. "Well, I made a hash of that, didn't I? Sorry; I hope y'all still have some hearin' left."

Everyone chuckled.

"If you'd please find a seat, we'll have the bride and groom move on up to the head table with their parents. The tables flanking the head table at an angle are reserved for the families. Beyond that, just let your keisters land where they will."

Orvalee—minus Ervyn and Dierdre, who were home awaiting the imminent arrival of their new little-one—along with George and his family, were guided to the reserved tables alongside the Jenks and Dubois clans.

After everyone had found a place, Alexander again stepped to the microphone and crossed himself, as if praying for its cooperation. Everyone covered their ears just in case.

When touching it elicited no ear-piercing whines, Alexander took the thing securely in hand. "Friends, before we put on the feedbag, I know that George, Mr. Jenks, and I, each have a few words we'd like to say."

From somewhere near the back of the room, someone shouted, "Keep it short, Zander! I know you, and I'm hungry!"

Alexander shielded his eyes from the glare of the hall's lighting and looked to where the admonishment had come from. "Cut the gas, Smitty! I shoulda known you'd be the first to whine. You've been complaining about somethin' or other since we worked the rigs together."

To one of the waitstaff, he said, "Get that man a plate so his mouth'll be occupied while the grown-ups talk."

Everyone laughed.

"George, you're up first."

George took his place behind the microphone, but the stand was too short for his frame. As he wiggled it free, the danged thing whined again, and every head drew down like turtles into their shells.

"Daggonit." George had to shake his own head to clear it.

"Y'all may have to stuff bread in your ears to make it through, which'll suit me fine, 'cause I'm not used to makin' speeches. But for my best friend, I'm makin' an exception."

George turned to look at Remy and Trinny, and paused. Hand to heart, the big man swallowed hard as he spoke around the emotional lump in his throat. "Rem, you're the best friend a fellow could ever have. We've been through some ups and downs together but have come out all right."

Remy solemnly nodded agreement.

George sniffed. "I'll keep my part brief and use the words of someone who describes love in a way I never could but that I wholeheartedly agree with." George reached into his interior jacket pocket and retrieved a piece of paper. "In sonnet one hundred and sixteen, Shakespeare said it best:

> "Let me not to the marriage of true minds
> Admit impediment. Love is not love
> Which alters when it alteration finds,
> Or bends with the remover to remove.
> O no! it is an ever-fixed mark
> That looks on tempests and is never shaken;
> It is the star to every wand'ring bark,
> Whose worth's unknown, although his height be
>   taken.
> Love's not Time's fool, though rosy lips and cheeks
> Within his bending sickle's compass come;
> Love alters not with his brief hours and weeks,
> But bears it out even to the edge of doom.
> If this be error and upon me prov'd,
> I never writ, nor no man ever lov'd."

The room had grown quiet as the listeners became absorbed in the heartfelt rendition of the bard's beautiful words.

"My amazing wife gifted me with an understanding of the power, the true power, that love can hold when honor is held sacred within a marriage. When, despite bein' pushed and tested to all mortal limits . . ." George's lower lip began to tremble violently, and he had to stop.

Claudine had to ask for an extra handkerchief to blow her nose, and those who knew all that the Dollises had been through just shook their heads as they too, dabbed at their eyes.

"When . . . when love literally travels to the edge of doom and does not alter . . . Well, that's somethin' worth living and fightin' for. I am proud to say that I have that. And my friend, with all my heart, I believe that you and Trinny have the same."

Li'l Bits understood some of the poem her uncle read. But when he started to get all emotional and almost cry, she knew that something important, something that pertained to her, was being said. The looks that passed between her papa and Trinny, her grandparents, George and Claudine—these looks were unmistakable. She may not have known the right words to describe them, but she knew how they made her feel, and there *were* no words to describe that.

Chapter 35

A Temporary Parting

Once the new couple had cut the cake, hugged every last person and danced their last dance, it was time for them to change into traveling clothes. Four days in wintery New York awaited. Remy planned to take Trinny ice skating at Rockefeller Plaza, see the famous Christmas tree, browse through FAO Schwarz, walk through the Central Park Zoo, and attend every museum Trinny could drag him to.

But, before any of that, it was time for some private Three Musketeer time.

Alone in the bride's dressing room, the newly minted Dubois family enjoyed the quiet pleasure of being away from the crush of wedding guests that continued to party in the church hall.

While Remy was behind the privacy screen changing, Li'l Bits asked, "Papa, would it be okay if I gave you and Trinny . . ." Bits looked at the woman she had known all her life, suddenly not knowing what to call her.

"Trinny, what do I call you now?"

Motioning Bits to her, Trinny sat down and began helping her out of the kimono. "What would you like to call me? Or rather, what would you feel *comfortable* calling me?"

Bits thought about this as she was gently unwound from the garment's bindings.

"Well, I know you're my ma now, but I think your real name will always be the first thing that comes to mind when I make to holler atcha. Not that I'm gonna be mean or anything. I didn't mean that kind of holler."

Trinny kissed the top of the child's head. "I know, Bits. Throughout your life, I have seen you ornery, frustrated, inquisitive, and contemplative, but I have never seen you be mean."

"Contempta . . . What's that you said?"

"Con-temp-la-tive."

"Yeah, what does that mean? Is it good?"

"It's good. It means that you can become lost in your thoughts. That you're a good thinker." Trinny lifted the kimono over Bits's head and gave her a dress to put on.

"I think I'm just gonna stick with Trinny, if you don't mind. But I might slip a 'ma' in here or there, just to see if you're listening."

Remy came out from behind the screen doing up his last button. "As long as I'm still Papa, that's all that matters to me."

"You'll always be my best and only papa." Bits gave him a big squeeze.

"That, my little snapdragon, makes me the happiest papa in the world." He sat on a cushioned ottoman and pulled her onto his lap while Trinny took her turn behind the screen.

Remy asked, "Do you remember talkin' about the adventure that today was gonna start us on?"

Bits nodded.

"Well, that adventure is startin' off with you and me bein' apart for the very first time. I know we've talked about it, but are you feelin' prepared for spendin' the next few days at Nana and Paw's house?"

"Yes, sir," Bits answered heartily. "Nana told me all the things she has planned for us. Plus, all the cousins'll be in and out all the time too. We're gonna go sledding, make snowmen and snow angels, make cookies and hot chocolate, cut out paper snowflakes, make paper Christmas chains, string popcorn and cranberries, and . . ."

"My, my," Remy teased. "Why, Mrs. Dubois," Remy said loud enough for Trinny to hear, "I don't think our Li'l Bits is gonna miss us at all."

"Oh, Papa." Bits slapped his arm. "I know right well you're teasing, because I know that you know that even though I am gonna do my best to enjoy everything Nana has planned, 'cause I won't disappoint her, I'll miss you every night you're not home to tuck me in." Saying the words made the separation real, and she sniffed.

"Oh, my girl." Remy hugged her tight, locking the feel of her in his arms. This temporary parting was going to be as hard on him as it would be on her. If only long-distance phone calls weren't so expensive, he'd be checking in every night just to hear about her day and tell her a bedtime story. "I will miss you."

"Papa, I made something to give you, to both of you," she said loud enough so that Trinny could hear. "Maybe it'll help you not miss me so much."

"Shouldn't we wait to open Christmas presents until next week? I know you're anxious, but with all the fun in between—"

"No!" Bits interjected sharply. "It's not for Christmas. I made you a wedding present."

"You made . . . Thank you, sweetheart." His child was making it hard to think of leaving, but then, Trinny stepped from behind the screen. A glimmer of light caught in the diamond of her wedding ring, and his heart did a happy dance.

Fingering the one he now wore, Remy let out a contented sigh. What more could a man want?

"Trinny." Bits practically bounced out of her papa's lap. "Come sit by Papa, and I'll get the present I made."

Bits ran to the corner where all the coats had been heaped on a chair. Layer by layer, she peeled garments aside until she could finally reach beneath the chair. With a small tug, she wrenched her box free and proudly carried it to her parents.

"Aunt Janelle helped me wrap it. Do you like the bow and curly ribbons?"

"You did a marvelous job," Trinny said admiringly. "I never expected a wedding present. This is so kind of you."

"When we were makin' Christmas presents in school, I asked Mr. Doutré if mine could be for today. I made it special, just for us."

Remy automatically made to comb an affectionate hand through his daughter's curls but stopped just in time to avoid ruining her pretty wedding hairdo. "Just for us. I like the sound of that. How about you, Trinny?"

"I rather like being part of an 'us'." She squeezed her new husband's hand. "Should we just rip at the paper or unwrap it carefully?"

Remy quirked her a mischievous smile and said smoothly, "I'm all for gettin' down to business."

Trinny felt an unaccustomed blush blossom from head to toe as her body responded to the suggestion. Soon, she and Remy would be on the road to Shreveport, where they would stay for the night before leaving in the morning for New York City. A couple of days ago, her mother had attempted to have "the talk" with her, and it hadn't gone well. More because her poor mother had stammered, hemmed and hawed, turned ten shades of red, and finally let out a sigh of relief when Trinny had assured her that she already knew how things worked.

Rose had wanted to ask her daughter how she'd come by

the information, but as that would have meant forming coherent sentences, she hadn't been able to press any further.

Sensing her mother's distress about the acquired knowledge, Trinny had explained. "Mom, I am an artist, you know. In art school and college, what are some things I *may* have drawn? How do you think I came to learn the human form so well?"

Trinny had waited as the blank look on her mother's face morphed from childlike innocence to that of wide-eyed knowing.

"Greek and Roman sculpture . . . come to life?" her mother had squeaked timidly.

"Yes, mom. That's . . . fairly accurate. Plus, I did just turn thirty-three."

Grateful she had not simply had to rely on her mother's ability to adequately inform her of the goings-on within a marriage, Trinny had let her squirming mother off the hook by changing the topic to the innocuous subject of china patterns.

Impatient for the unveiling, Bits pulled Trinny's mind back to the present by saying, "Well, get to it. Get down to business and take the wrappin' off."

Remy snorted at his daughter's choice of words, and Trinny covered her face with her hands as she laughed too.

"Come on." Bits sighed. "I don't have all night. Nana'll come get me soon."

"You're right, baby girl," Remy said as he placed a finger at one of the present's corners. "It's time to *strip* the wrapping off my gift. Can't wait to see the treasure that's been hidden."

Trinny folded over, looking like she needed a paper bag to breathe into. Remy rubbed her back soothingly and feigned innocence.

"You okay? Has the excitement of the day finally caught up to you?"

Taking a couple of deep breaths, still slumped over, Trinny muttered, "I know something will catch up with me real soon.

When it does, I hope I have the energy to . . ." Trinny couldn't finish. She just shook her head, propped her elbows on her knees, and rested her face in her hands.

"Bits," Remy said, "Trinny's a bit out of sorts. Could you grab her a glass of water?"

"I'm fine," Trinny squeaked. Taking a deep breath, she sat up. "I'm fine, see?" She used both hands to point to the big smile on her face. "I am sorry, Bits. I didn't mean to be such a goof."

"That's okay. I know you're probably tired and just want to go to bed."

Despite the provocation, the two adults were able to rein themselves in and finally open the present. When they pulled out the decoupaged tree, they gave it their full attention.

"See what I did?" Bits pointed to the smiling, familial faces all around the tree's base. "Because we're a family now, I chose pictures showin' all the different things we're gonna be doin' too. Like here, they're ridin' in a car, because I know we're gonna have fun on trips. In this one, they're havin' a picnic, like we did on my birthday. In this one, they have a dog, 'cause, you know, Papa, I *might* like one."

Remy closely examined all the pictures. "Any other hints in here that you're tryin' to drop on my head?"

Bits clasped her hands behind her back, cocked her head and looked as innocent as she could. "Maybe . . ."

"Thought so," he said with satisfaction. "I know you."

Trinny asked, "Are these Norman Rockwell images for me?" Tracing a finger around the tree's perimeter, she also saw small paintings of flowers, cutouts of miniature magazine covers, and the image of an art set.

"Yep, all the art stuff is about you. And then, here is all the stuff for Papa. See the rockin' chair, the toys here, and the big wood bed." Bits pointed to each picture excitedly. "Papa has made all this stuff in his shop."

Remy zoned in on the praying child at the top. "Is this you?"

"Yep," Bits said with deep satisfaction. "Because today, my wish came true, and I'm thanking Jesus."

Trinny noticed the handwritten word next to the praying girl. "Is this what you named the girl?"

"Nnno . . ." Bits drew the short word out and looked at the floor. Sucking in a breath of courage, she said, "It's what I want to name *me*."

"Name you?" Remy asked.

"Yes, sir." Bits looked her papa square in the eyes. "I've been thinking, a lot, and . . . and I . . . I'm eight now, and I'd like a name. A *real* name."

Remy crooked a tender finger beneath her chin and angled her face up to his. "And this is the name *you've* chosen?"

"Yes, sir."

"Oaklynne," Trinny read. "I like it. You know, when a person is lucky enough to choose their own name, that name says a lot about them. What prompted you to choose this one?"

Seeing no reprisal for her choice, Bits explained. "Before my birthday, I got to thinkin' about all the changes that were happening, what with Ervyn comin' back and the two new babies and all. I was . . . I don't know, just thinkin'. I was by my tree and thought of how I always feel something special right there. Somethin' I don't feel anyplace else."

Remy drew his daughter into the circle of his arms as she continued.

"I got to thinkin' about how you talk about oak and all it's good for. That got me thinkin' about Nana Lynne Anne and how much I love her. How I feel when I'm at her and Paw's house. I always feel so . . . loved. And, well, I thought if I put the names of things that make me feel loved together, it'd be like . . ."

Bits mulled over how to say what she wanted. "It would be

like always havin' that love with me, wherever I am. It might even help me feel better when I don't feel like bein' happy."

Trinny placed a gentle kiss on her cheek. "I think that's beautiful, and it makes me like the name even more."

Li'l Bits looked to her father for approval.

This child left him in awe. Placing a kiss on her other cheek, he crooned, "I love it!"

Bits brightened. "I was hoping that could be my Christmas present to Nana. Do you think she'll like it?"

"Like it?" Remy said. "She'll be over the moon. It's a great honor to have someone *want* to take on your name." He looked pointedly at Trinny. "A great honor."

"So, do you like my wedding present?"

Remy teared up, "Sweet pea, this tree—I'm gonna call it our family's tree of life—and the ring on my finger"—he twisted the gold band—"have made this day the most absolutely *wonderful* day of my life."

Trinny pulled them into a family huddle. "I love you both so much." Her voice broke, and she paused before continuing. "Thank you for making me part of your family."

Remy kissed her on the temple. "Darlin', from here on, it only gets better."

Standing, Remy carefully placed the wedding tree back in the padded box. "Let's take this out to Nana and Paw and let them know it will need some extra lookin' after until we can put it on the mantel at home. It'll be there, watchin' over us for our very first Christmas as a family."

"And it will be there every Christmas after that, too," Trinny added.

"Trinny," Remy said, taking Li'l Bits by the hand, "before we leave, what do ya say we go out and introduce everyone to *our* daughter, Oaklynne? Oaklynne Dubois."

Chapter 36

Epilogue
May, 1973

"No one ever made a difference by
being like everyone else."

—Jenny Bicks and Bill Condon (living),
The Greatest Showman

The college's auditorium thrummed with the steady, excited chatter of hundreds of voices. From her seat on the stage, Oaklynne Dubois watched as people continued to trickle in and find available seats. Her parents and brothers were already there, front and center, having arrived a good hour before the graduation ceremony was slated to begin. With so many seats to save, they had needed to stake out a good bit of territory.

Each of her parents had claimed an aisle seat, while her brothers, Alex and Daniel, guarded all those in between. This had been a strategic maneuver on the part of her parents, because at twelve and ten, her brothers had had the entire row to rough house in while they passed the time.

With fifteen minutes to go, Oaklynne gazed at her family adoringly.

Where had the time gone? It seemed like only yesterday that Daniel had been born, followed nearly two years later by Alex. Each of her grandfathers had been so excited to have a namesake.

Oaklynne smiled and returned waves as Orvalee, Uncle George, and Aunt Claudine were the first to slide past her papa. Pleased as punch, her papa slapped Uncle George on the back and pointed at the podium to where *his* girl would give the salutatorian speech for the graduating class in environmental science.

From this unaccustomed vantage point, for the first time in years, Oaklynne was able to look down on the head of her beloved uncle and was shocked to see how much gray streaked through his black hair. At least he still had hair. Claudine, too, bore the passing signs of time, but not to the same degree as her husband.

At nearly seventy-four years old, with five grandchildren who ran her joyfully ragged, Orvalee still retained some color that peppered her silver hair. And Oaklynne had never really taken notice of the fact that her father also sported a little gray. Her mama, however, still had a mane of sleek, jet-black hair.

Before taking his place on the teaching staff row, her favorite professor, Dr. Albert Hunter, climbed the steps to the stage and shook Oaklynne's hand, congratulating her and reminding her not to forget their meeting in his office tomorrow.

"No, sir," Oaklynne assured him. "I will most definitely not forget. And thank you, sir, for choosing me to fill the apprentice slot. My whole family is so excited."

"As well they should be, my dear," the professor said kindly. "Brazil is an incredible place, and I know you'll love it as much as I do. So much land to work with. Though, I hope the year away won't be too taxing."

"Oh, no, sir. I've already been practicin' my Portuguese, though I'm far more fluent in French."

"Well, a fair number there do speak French as well, so between that and what Portuguese you can learn before we leave, I'm sure you'll get along just fine. And girlie, I'm anxious to hear what you have to say at that podium. Not many thought you would make it, but you've proved them wrong."

Oaklynne blushed. "I may be the one givin' the speech, but if it weren't for you and Professor Anderson, I might not have graduated at all."

"Nonsense!" Professor Hunter said a little too loudly. Covering his mouth sheepishly, he looked to see if he had drawn attention, then continued more softly, "Nonsense, my girl. You simply needed a little wind to fill the sail you already had up and trimmed. And as you well know, I can be a bit blustery."

"And I say nonsense back to you," Oaklynne stated with an endearing smile. If there was a kinder teacher at this school, she didn't know them. "You are far from blustery, and I know of no one who has called you that. But I will agree that you have been a propelling force in my choice of career. Growin' up with the mentor I had, agronomy was a natural choice, and I'm lookin' forward to learning what you can teach me in the farming fields of Brazil."

In a gesture of appreciation, Professor Hunter patted her hand. "I'd better sit down now. There's only a few minutes left until it's time for you to shine. Make me proud."

"I'll do my best, sir."

Professor Hunter took his seat, and when Oaklynne looked back at her family row, she saw that it was filling in. Grandparents, aunts, uncles, and much-loved friends jostled one another amid hugs, waves directed at the stage, and being told where to sit by her brothers, who had taken it upon themselves to act as ushers.

Her mom's parents were here from Utah, and her Uncle

Tomi had come from Hollywood, where he'd made his dream come true by making a living in the film industry.

Jesslyn and Ellie June waved enthusiastically when they saw that she had seen them. Oaklynne waved back and blew them each a kiss.

Following in her father's footsteps, Jesslyn had gone into business and finance. Her graduation ceremony had been yesterday, and she already had a job lined up at her father's bank. He was making her start at an entry-level position so that she could learn the business from the ground up, just like he had.

To no one's surprise, Ellie June would be graduating tomorrow with a degree in home economics and hoped to teach at their former high school. Their old home economics teacher, Ms. Beese, had put in a good word for her. So, odds were, she was a shoo-in for the job.

To *everyone's* surprise, Amy Jo had been the first of their foursome to get married and have a baby. She, her military husband, and their one-year-old daughter, Savannah, were living in Germany. Even though she hadn't been able to make it back for her friends' graduations, Amy Jo had sent them each a beautiful card and a special ornament from a Christmas market she'd gone to in Frankfurt. Each year when they hung their ornaments, they were to think of her and how much she loved and missed them.

Oaklynne fingered the star pendant her parents had given her last night.

"*My* girl," her father had said, pride beaming from his eyes like a lighthouse beacon, "you are gonna shine as bright as a comet shootin' through a night sky. Your light always was the brightest thing in a room."

From behind his back, he had produced a long, red, velvet box wrapped with a gold bow. "While you're away, we hope this will help ya always remember to let your light shine."

When she had opened the beautiful case and seen the even more splendid pendant, she'd nearly cried.

Her mama had taken up the exquisite white-gold chain and secured it around her neck. The pendant was also made of white gold, and its light-yellow undertone brought the star to life. Five small diamonds created its cosmic tail, indicating flight.

"You know," her papa had said, "some say that a shootin' star means good luck. Others think that seein' one means you'll achieve your destiny. But as far as I know, everyone agrees that a shootin' star is a positive thing and my girl, if there's *one* thing you have always been, it's positive."

"Oh, Papa!" She had flung herself at him and been engulfed by the strong arms that had always been her anchor. There were no words to describe how much she was going to miss those arms while she was away in Brazil. And Trinny, the incredible woman who had seamlessly joined their family and become her mother.

Oaklynne didn't remember when the transition from calling her Trinny to Mama had happened, but it had, and that's what Trinny was.

Oaklynne rested a hand over the pocket in her skirt, where a piece of paper crackled as she pressed it close. Even through her graduation robe, she felt the exhilaration and comfort of its message. Today, graduation would not be the only thing changing her life.

Oaklynne took a deep breath and patted the folder on her lap that held her speech.

Just then, Dr. Jackson, the dean of her department, stepped up to the microphone to ask that everyone take their seats. It was time to begin.

Holy cripes! Oaklynne almost said out loud. *As soon as he's done, I'm up.*

Though Dean Jackson was a good *speaker*, he was not very entertaining. Watching heads throughout the auditorium sag backward, or incline toward the person next to them in quiet conversation, Oaklynne hoped she would be able to hold peo-ple's attention better than he was doing.

"And now, I give you this year's salutatorian, Ms. Oak-lynne Dubois," she heard him say as he stepped away from the podium and slid the steps that had been borrowed from the theater department, into place behind it.

Steeling herself, Oaklynne slid from her chair to the stool and then the floor, wishing that she could quiet the sound her heels made as she clip-clopped across the hardwood stage. Sheepishly looking across the sea of faces before her, she tried not to home in on any particular one. Instead, she focused on climbing the steps and not tripping on her robe.

Alone at the podium, it felt like she could hear every whisper of breath. She accidentally caught the look in someone's eyes and had to quickly look down at her folder. Shock and perhaps some judgment had been in those eyes. She'd seen that look a thousand . . . no, more like a million times throughout her life. But as Professor Hunter said, she had wiped that look off her naysayers' faces by proving them all wrong.

You've got this, she said to herself. *You've done it before. You can do it again.*

Despite her pounding heart, she organized her notes, gave a genuine smile to the crowd, and began.

"'True, I am young, but for souls nobly born valor doesn't await the passing of years.' Pierre Corneille. I love this quote and will forever be grateful to Professor Anderson for intro-ducin' it to me in philosophy class. This and many other exam-ples pay tribute to the education I have received at this great institution."

As the words flowed, Oaklynne became more confident. Doing her best to soak in the glory of the moment while at the same time remaining on point was easier than she'd thought it would be. A bubble of "rightness" shimmered protectively around her and she basked in it.

Before she knew it, she was turning to the last page of her

notes. The last words she would utter within the hallowed walls of a place she had come to love.

"And so, just as I prepare to embark upon a quest that will lead me to unknown places, to unknown people, and to as-of-yet unknown joy, I know that each of you here are settin' off on a similar but separate journey. So, I say to us all by quoting Corra Mae Harris, 'The bravest thing you can do when you are not brave is to profess courage and act accordingly.' I'm not sure about y'all, but I know *my* actin' skills have never been put to a test like this. However, I have no doubt when I say I am one-hundred-percent positive Professor Hunter will provide plenty of opportunities for me to work on 'em."

Oaklynne cast a quick glance over her shoulder to where the smiling man sat. He gave her a double thumbs up, and the crowd chuckled.

"May the shell that encased our understanding when we walked through the doors of this university four years ago now be fully broken open. Let *us* be open to our new and ever-changing world so that *we* can be the vehicles that move thought, that innovate industry, and that create a commonality open to one and all. *We*, the class of 1973, are the new hope. We are the new horizon. And beyond these walls, as long as we continue reachin' out to embrace all that lay beyond, the world *will* reach back, and we will *each* have all we ever dreamed of."

Oaklynne took a deep breath, closed her folder, and the crowd erupted into applause.

Her papa and Uncle George were the loudest of all. Fingers to mouths, they whistled loud enough to beat the band. Her brothers were jumping up and down; her mama was crying; Orvalee and Claudine stood arm in arm, as proud as mother-hens; Jesslyn and Ellie June were clapping so hard, Oaklynne thought their palms might blister; her aunts, uncles, and grandparents were all either crying or clapping and whistling. She had the loudest, craziest, most amazingly dedicated family in the world.

Oaklynne clip-clopped back to her chair, the clapping subsided, and the graduation program followed through to its conclusion.

Once she and the other graduates had walked across the stage to receive their long-awaited diplomas, they were free of the auditorium and headed outside to various school landmarks to take photos.

One of Oaklynne's favorite places had been outside the library's large, curved, stained-glass façade depicting the history of creation. She had spent many an evening sitting on the benches there as the library's interior lights illuminated the series of ten by twenty-foot panels.

In the first panel, vivid reds, oranges, and yellows had been used for the fiery and turbulent volcanic creation of the earth's crust. The second had rich shades of purple, cobalt blue, violet, and honey browns that created mountains overshadowing verdant flower-bedecked fields and flowing blue water.

At this point, the panels wrapped around the building. The last one depicted high-rise offices, factories, and automobiles that took over where horse drawn vehicles and traditional dwellings had begun to fade out.

Sometimes, when she'd been here at night sorting through some trouble or imagining her future, she would mentally draft what might be depicted in a next panel of creation, if it was hers to create.

"Okay, everyone," Remy instructed. "Tall people stand behind the benches; grandparents can sit down. Children, y'all sit or stand wherever you fit. Oaklynne"—he motioned his daughter to the center—"I think if you stand on the edge of the bench, just there"—he pointed right in front of her Uncle George—"that'll put you smack in the middle of everyone."

While they all jostled into position, Remy set up his tripod and staged the shot. "Daniel, you move between Nana and Paw. Okay . . . Claudine, turn yourself a skootch to the right . . . All righty, smile now, okay . . . Perfect!" He held up a hand, indicating everyone should freeze right where they were. "When the timer is set, it'll take three pictures three seconds apart. So, no one move! Got it?"

"Yes," the entire group said.

Remy set the timer and ran from the tripod to the place Trinny had saved for him. Through clenched, smiling teeth, he said, "Say cheese."

In something that sounded like a groan, everyone droned, "Cheeeese . . ." for as long as it took the flash to go off three times. With the third click, a communal exhale was heard, and their happy chatter resumed.

"Oaklynne," Remy said, "is there anywhere else you'd like to take a picture?"

From her perch on the bench, Oaklynne scanned the campus as she tried to decide. Her gaze became fixed on a pair of eyes that were staring right at her. She knew those eyes . . . didn't she? Though the ones she remembered were much harder and belonged to a very different face on a much smaller body . . . yes, she knew those eyes.

The eyes blinked rapidly as they darted between her and the large group surrounding her. The chest below, sucked in air like a great bellows as the eyes closed momentarily in resignation, then opened, filled with sorrow-laden determination. The large body that didn't fit with the one she remembered moved tentatively forward.

Never breaking eye contact, Oaklynne mouthed, "Rudy."

The young man moved forward, hat in hand, and stepped bravely into what must have been akin to the lion's den. Hand extended in greeting, he said one word: "Bits."

Despite all the chatter that had been going on, hearing the long-unused name brought the conversation of those closest to a standstill. A few heads turned to see who had moved into their midst. The genial smiles that had been on Jesslyn and Ellie June's faces were immediately replaced by fierce scowls. Though Rudy had never thrown a rock at them, each young woman had endured their own forms of torment at his hands when they were younger, so they moved defensively to stand on either side of Oaklynne.

Recognizing them, Rudy swallowed hard but stood his ground, hand still outstretched. "I, uh . . . I'm here for my cousin's graduation." He pointed vaguely over his shoulder. "I saw you and I . . . I knew I . . ."

With Remy's attention focused elsewhere, the warrior in George took over when he saw the protective stance assumed by Jesslyn and Ellie June. Stepping to them, he said, "Ladies, will you introduce me to your . . . friend?"

Both Ellie June and Jesslyn started to say that Rudy was no friend when Oaklynne cut them off. "Uncle George," Oaklynne started, then looked at Rudy as if to ask, *"Are you sure you want to do this?"* Rudy gave a slight bob of his head, so she kept going, "I would like to introduce you to Rudy Galbraith. We knew him back in primary school."

George silently mouthed the name. Rudy felt cold pricks of dread as he saw signs of recognition slowly cross the imposing man's face.

"Uncle George, Jesslyn, Ellie June," Oaklynne said serenely, "wasn't it nice of Rudy to come over to say hello?"

This time, Remy heard the name. A name he'd been more than content to relegate to the past. His head whipped around in alarm, catching everyone else's attention. The entire gathering fell silent.

Rudy looked around with growing panic. The only eyes that held any kind of peace were the ones Oaklynne kept trained on him; everyone else had steel in their gaze. Realizing his hand was still extended, hanging in the air like a broken signpost, Rudy slowly lowered it and wondered if he should have come over in the first place.

Oaklynne's family slowly circled the wagons, silently and defensively gathering around their girl. The similarity of what was going on right now was not lost on Rudy, Oaklynne or

Ellie June, the only three original participants to the drama their current situation was re-enacting. Only, this time, it was Rudy who was outnumbered and in danger.

George and Remy instinctively stood between Oaklynne and the invader.

"Um, *excuse* me," Oaklynne protested loudly from behind the hulking form of her uncle. "I have a guest that has come to say something, and if you two louts'll get outta our way, he may be able to congratulate me, as I'm sure he intended to do."

With harrumphs of wary displeasure, Remy and George moved aside so that Rudy was once again face-to-face with Oaklynne.

Rudy's Adam's apple looked like a racecar. It made so many trips up and down his throat, Oaklynne was sure it was trying to burst out and get away.

It was obvious to everyone but the two watchdogs that it was taking all the courage this young man had just to remain upright. Claudine and Trinny moved to their husbands' sides, linking elbows in a form of restraint stronger than any chain could provide.

Oaklynne had not taken her eyes off her former nemesis, and now, for the most part, it was just the two of them.

"Rudy," Oaklynne said softly, "I hope your cousin is havin' as lovely a day as I am."

Rudy's tortured hat, if you could call it that anymore, received another twist as he tried to calm himself enough to reply. "Yes," he squeaked, wishing he had a glass of water. "Yes, he is. Thank you. And I'm glad you're havin' a nice day too. I just . . . when I saw you, I knew I . . ."

As large as he'd grown, Oaklynne could see a glossy sheen in his eyes. In memory, she could still plainly see the eyes of his seven-year-old self, and those eyes did not match the ones that now plead for understanding.

"Rudy, I really appreciate that you took time away from

your cousin to come on over and say hello. Do you remember Jesslyn and Ellie June?"

"Yes. Yes I do. Nice to see ya'll again." He nodded a weak greeting.

At Oaklynne's prodding, the two young women responded with a simultaneous, and unenthusiastic, "You too."

"Bits, I just wanted to . . ." Rudy sucked in a fortifying breath. "I wanted to apologize for what I did. But I also wanted to thank you."

Puzzled, Oaklynne asked, "What on earth are you thankin' me for? I've done nothin' for you."

"You've done more than you know," Rudy replied quickly. If he was going to survive this, he just needed to plow on through. So, he unleashed the story. A story that filled in quite a few gaps for everyone listening.

"That day, the one where my folks had to go meet with Principal Judson and Mrs. Sanders—I know you were there too, sir." He nodded at Remy.

"When my pa came home, he was none too happy. He got, well . . . He punished me for what I'd done, and my arm ended up broken."

Oaklynne inhaled sharply, as if feeling the pain of it herself. Ellie June and Jesslyn both blanched.

"My pa wouldn't let me go to the after-school garbage cleanup I was supposed to do with Principal Judson, so the principal came to my house to check on things. For a couple of days, my ma wouldn't let him see me, sayin' I was sick. But when Principal Judson threatened to bring the police with him the next day, my ma let him in. When the man saw my arm, saw that it was broke and that I hadn't been taken to the doctor, his face grew a shade of red I'd never seen. Ain't ever seen it since, either."

Rudy let out a nervous little chuckle. His mild acceptance of what he'd been through went a long way to softening everyone's heart.

"Principal Judson told my ma that she could come along if she wanted, but regardless, he was takin' me to the hospital. When my pa came home from work that night and saw the cast on my arm, he was . . . he was not happy. Got to callin' my ma . . . names for throwin' good money after bad. She showed him the warning Principal Judson had the doctor and nurse sign, sayin' they were reportin' what had happened to the police. Next day, the police came. Went through our house. Guess they even went to my pa's work."

A small, nearly imperceptible grin lifted the corner of Rudy's mouth at the memory.

"Knowin' that now he was really bein' watched, rather than come home after drinkin' away his paycheck, my pa took to stayin' later at the bars. Guess that gave him more time to get in trouble of his own."

Rudy was no longer simply relaying the story; he was reliving it. Oaklynne could see it in his face. Every bite of his lower lip, every frown that tangled his brow, every eye twitch spoke of vivid remembrance.

"Ya know, no matter how big and mean ya think you are, there's always someone meaner, if not bigger. Late one night, my pa got to mouthin' off to someone like this and got the livin' tar beat out of him. Couldn't even make it home on his own. A drinkin' buddy brought him. My pa got beat bad. Bad enough my ma kept him propped up on the livin' room sofa so blood from his broken nose wouldn't drain down his throat. His eyes were swollen, his . . ."

Rudy looked at Oaklynne and hauled in a steadying breath. A few tears dripped quickly down his cheek, but he didn't reach up to wipe them away. "I thought of you and what I'd done. I'd heard you needed stitches, a good many of 'em. That you'd been outta school for weeks, and I knew I'd done that to you. Just like someone meaner than my pa had laid him up. Turns out, my pa had some sort of brain damage. Doctors sent him home to die. He died right there on the sofa. I watched him.

Watched him breathe his last and I . . . I couldn't feel sorry 'cause I kept thinkin' of you. My feelings of weak and strong got all jumbled, and . . ."

When Rudy didn't seem to be able to continue, Oaklynne gently prodded, "Rudy, what happened then?"

Like someone dragging themselves from an all-encompassing fog, Rudy's eyes slowly focused on Oaklynne, and a slow but sincere smile lit his face. "Then? Then life got better. My ma sold our house and we moved away. Went to her parents'. She went to school, got a job in an office, and was able to support us on her own."

As Rudy's tale began to lighten, so did the mood of everyone listening. His explanation had been short but intense, even more so for those who had played a part in the original drama. Even George, who had promised to kill the person responsible for injuring Bits, finally released an anger he hadn't known was still smoldering.

Rudy's face held genuine pride now. "I was able to graduate high school and got a job with my uncle, who's a plumber. I've done well enough that I have my *own* truck, and in a year, I'll have enough saved to get my contractor's license."

Meaning every word, Oaklynne said, "Rudy! That's wonderful. I bet you'll be the best contractor around."

Rudy shook his head disbelievingly. "Bits, I don't know how you do it. I never did understand how you could always be so danged positive. Lookin' back, I think that's one reason I . . . I felt the need to stop you. The world, at least my world, was anything but sunny, and you, little miss ray of sunshine"— Rudy's lips played with a smile—"you were always just . . . you. I think I was jealous, and that confused me."

"And now?" Oaklynne asked.

With a genuine smile, Rudy said, "Now, I've had a taste of sunshine myself, and I think I understand you a bit better. That's the reason, when I saw you standin' here, I wanted to come over. I *needed* to tell you how sorry I was. That it was never you; it was *me*. Those things I said . . ."

"Rudy, please feel free to lay those words down and leave 'em behind. They have no place where you're goin' now, do they?"

Rudy shook his head no.

"I don't hold 'em against you. And honestly, because of that day, I got two of the best friends I've ever had. Amy Jo and Ellie June have never left my side." Smiling, Oaklynne added, "And besides, we *both* know that if Jesslyn hadn't been sick that day, she'd have kicked your behind into next week."

Jesslyn puffed with pride at the compliment. She had always blamed herself for what happened that day, and for the first time since, she felt that she could lay that burden down too.

"Well," Rudy said with a slight bow, as if thanking a queen for an audience, "thank you for lettin' me say my piece. It meant a lot."

"Rudy," Oaklynne said, extending her hand, "thank you for being as brave as you are and comin' over to say hello. It's meant a *lot* to me too. And just so you know, I chose a new name a long time ago. My name is Oaklynne."

"Oaklynne," Rudy said as he shook her outstretched hand. "It fits you. I wish you all the best. Truly, thank you." Rudy backed out of the circle, turned, and walked away to find where his cousin and family had moved on to.

"Well, tie my tongue to a wagon wheel," Orvalee said in awe.

Remy watched Rudy go until he was swallowed up by the milling crowd.

Releasing her hold on Remy, Trinny turned to Oaklynne and wrapped her arms around her daughter. "I'm so proud of you," she gushed. "Facing him like that took courage."

Jesslyn and Ellie June joined the hug.

"Oh, my holy Aunt Hannah!" Ellie June exclaimed, still shaking a little from the encounter. "You were cool as a cucumber. I never could've done that. It was hard just watchin' you." She patted her hand over her heart.

"You were magnificent!" Jesslyn added. "Do you realize what just happened?"

"What happened," George said, "is that we all witnessed a full-blown miracle."

Still under the spell of calm that had sheltered her during the encounter, Oaklynne said, almost to herself, "I'm really happy for him." Only then did a few tears fall from her own eyes.

Not fully understanding why this encounter had been so momentous, Daniel, Rose, and Tomi listened to Lynne Anne recount the basics of what had happened all those years ago.

"No wonder that poor boy acted out like he did," Rose said when Lynne Anne was through. "It's a wonder he turned out as well as he has."

"Sometimes," Daniel said with a faraway look, "the hardest things end up being the greatest blessings. 'The price of anything is the amount of life you exchange for it.'"

"Thoreau, right Daniel?" Rose asked.

"Yes. Life was given to that boy. A life that can never be taken away. Priceless." He stepped toward his granddaughter. "You are a treasure beyond price. As much as we will miss you, the people of Brazil are going to be blessed to have you."

"You know," Alexander said, "I don't think I can wait a whole year to see our girl again. Lynne Anne, I think we should start plannin' a trip abroad. One that includes a *lengthy* stay in Brazil."

His wife clapped her hands together and let out a gleeful squeal.

Remy asked, "Can you afford that much time away from the company?"

"Of course, I can. Why do you think I stepped down as CEO and put George here in charge?" Alexander slapped George on the back. "You can cover all the business stuff, right?"

"That I can," George agreed. "As long as you bring me back a souvenir, there should be no trouble at all."

Janelle and Sienna looked at one another and then at their husbands. With hand gestures, they silently telegraphed their intent to work on their men to ensure their parents' trip to Brazil turned into a family affair. Their children were all grown and living on their own; why shouldn't they have a little vacation fun too?

"You know," Alexander said as he stroked his chin thoughtfully, "George, if you came along, we could write the trip off as a business expense. I've been lookin' into the Brazilian oil industry, and I think there's a niche there we could fill. What do you say? Claudine could come along too." Alexander winked at her.

Claudine looked pleadingly into her husband's eyes.

George smiled, "With an incentive like that, I don't see how I can refuse."

Giddy, Claudine bounced up and down and wrapped her arms around her husband. "I am sure Emilie could stay with either Jeremy or Beau. They are always wanting her to help with their children."

"Rem," Alexander said, "by the look in your sisters' eyes, they already have plans to ensure they get in on this little getaway. How about you and Trinny? Think you could take time away from your fancy-schmancy design store to tag along?"

Ten years ago, with Trinny's art and design skills, Remy had taken a chance on expanding his furniture business. It was a risk that had paid off, big. Together, they had come up with designs that rivaled Alvar Aalto, Eileen Gray and Le Corbusier. Trinny, however, tended to favor more colorful patterns for the fabrics and finishes, which were finding favor within the new decorating trends.

With a glint of mischief in his eyes, Remy looked at his wife. "Well?"

Their sons were jumping up and down, begging not to be left out.

Trinny laughed. "All right, all right," she told the boys. "Calm down, and I'll *think* about allowing you two trouble-makers to tag along." She ruffled each of their dark heads. "But you will both need to be *very* mindful of your chores, and no back-talking. Understand."

Hands steepled beneath their chins, both Daniel and Alex promised, on their word of honor, that they would be the most angelic boys ever to walk the earth.

"Hmm." Remy harrumphed doubtfully. "I guess we'll see how long sugar-fluff promises actually last."

"No, really Papa." Alex burrowed beneath Remy's arm. "I promise, I extra promise to be so good, you'll think I'm not even me anymore."

At this honest assessment of his usual self, a peal of laughter rang from every adult.

"Well," Orvalee said, "sounds like we all have some serious planning to do."

"You know," Oaklynne stated, "if y'all come to Brazil and expect me to be able to spend any time with you, Professor Hunter is gonna put you to work. And *I* will be your supervisor, which means that each and every one of you"—she pointed—"will have to do *my* bidding."

"Isn't that what we've been doin' since you first came along?" Remy said none too quietly.

Oaklynne laughed. "I guess it is."

Lynne Anne called the group to order. "All righty. Before we all go off half-cocked, let's finish out the day we're in, shall we?" She encouraged them all forward. "Oaklynne, sweetheart, did you mention another place you'd like some pictures?"

Oaklynne had been about to say that she would like one in front of the twelve-foot-tall sculpture of the school's pelican mascot when Rudy had come over. Still standing on the bench, she looked that way again to see if another group had already gotten there. Oaklynne's breath caught. Instinctively, her hand went to the piece of paper in her skirt pocket.

As if in a trance, Oaklynne seemed to be affixing a landmark for reference. "Uncle George, please help me down." Smoothing her robe, she said, "Mama, Papa, everyone, would y'all mind waitin' a minute? I see someone I need to say hello to."

Without waiting for a response, Oaklynne moved forward, her feet carrying her toward another momentous change.

Remy stared after his daughter. Following her line of sight, he focused on an older blonde woman, forty-five, maybe fifty. Beside that woman stood a younger one, mid-to-late twenties, and a young man in his late teens or early twenties.

A group of people moved between them, and Remy made to follow his daughter, but a light touch stopped him.

"Rem," Trinny said. "She needs to do this alone. She'll bring them over when she's ready."

"What's going on?" Oliver asked.

With a silent plea, Remy looked at Trinny. As much as he wanted his daughter to do this, he still struggled with feeling protective. This woman had abandoned Oaklynne once; what was to say she wouldn't do it again?

Trinny motioned everyone to gather round. George, Claudine, and Orvalee were already aware of what was going on, but the rest were clueless.

While Remy kept a wary eye on his daughter, Trinny explained. "With graduation coming and her apprenticeship abroad, Oaklynne got it into her head that she wanted to 'wrap up loose ends' so that she could fully look to her future. A few months back, she took out an ad in the personals. Ever since she was eight-years-old, she's wanted to meet the woman who wrote the letter. A month after she placed the ad, she received a reply . . . with a return address."

Rose covered her mouth in astonishment.

"For two months, Oaklynne has been exchanging letters with Melva Danielson. She's read every one of them to us, and

I must say, the woman seems like a lovely person. She already had a daughter before she gave birth to Oaklynne. Her name is Pamela. Oaklynne has taken to calling her Pammy. I assume that's the young woman you can see Oaklynne talking to right now."

Every head swiveled to look where Remy had continued to stare.

"A few years after she gave Oaklynne up, Melva had a son named Dennis. Again, I would assume that's the young man with them."

Seeing a story in every scenario, like a true thespian, Tomi said thoughtfully, "You know, this would make a terrific movie. I wonder if there would be a part in it for me?"

"So, Mama," Daniel piped in, "if the woman Oaklynne is talking to is the one who left her in the basket, that makes her Oaklynne's real ma. Then, does that make Dennis and Pammy, Oaklynne's brother and sister?"

"Yes, sweetheart." Trinny smoothed her son's hair. "Though I am her mother too, Melva is the one who gave birth to Oaklynne, so that makes Dennis and Pamela her siblings, just like you two are her siblings."

Alex joined his brother and asked, "Well, if those two are Oaklynne's brother and sister, and we are her brothers, does that make them our brother and sister?"

Trinny didn't know how to answer that one.

Alexander squatted down to be eye level with his grandsons. "Boys, in our family, it's not necessarily blood that joins us; it's love. Love can form stronger bonds than blood any day. So, as we get to know Oaklynne's new family, *if* they want to get to know us, and we get to lovin' one another, then I'd say there's a good chance you may come to look on Pamela and Dennis as your kin. Just like George, Claudine and Orvalee are our kin."

"Oh," they said in unison. Since they fully accepted George and Claudine as an aunt and uncle, and Orvalee as a grandmother, the boys understood how this process could work.

With one more puzzle piece to fit into place, Alex asked his grandfather, "Will that make Melva our aunt or a grand-mother?"

Lynne Anne tussled the boy's hair. "I think that since I see your sister leading them over here, we should save that question for later. Will that be okay?"

Shrugging noncommittally, Alex let it go.

As Oaklynne led the three newcomers over to her family, the soft lawn sucked one of her heels into the ground, causing her to trip. Dennis quickly reached out a steadying hand. When he saw the entire group appraising him, he reddened and removed his hand.

Always a good judge of character, George appreciated the boy's automatic response, immediately assessing a protective nature and kind heart. He crossed his strongly corded arms and uttered a grunt of approval.

When the foursome stood before the close-knit family group, Remy reached for his wife's steadying hand, nervous to meet the woman that had forever changed his life.

"Papa, Mama," Oaklynne said, taking her birth mother by the hand and pulling her forward, "I would like to introduce Melva, Pamela, and Dennis Danielson. Melva is the one who loved me enough to give me to y'all. Pammy and Dennis are my brother and sister."

Maybe meeting this many of her clan all at once had been asking too much of her three new family members, but Oak-lynne watched as the Danielsons bravely offered shy smiles and nervously bobbed their heads in greeting.

Oaklynne's family offered genial waves, nods of approval and murmured hellos.

"Danielson family, I would like to introduce Remington and Trinny Dubois, my parents." Remy gamely shook each of their hands, while they received a welcoming hug from Trinny.

"And *this*"—Oaklynne proudly fanned a hand in a broad arc to include everyone else—"is my family."

Author's Note

As all good stories go, this one has a happy middle; I will leave the end to your imagination. In parting, I leave you with a final quote:

> "Sometimes, what we fear needs to be loved
> so that it, too, may ascend."
>
> —*Donna J. Wray (living), author, massage therapist,
> mother, and grandmother*